Three-times Golden Heart® finalist **Tina Beckett** learned to pack her suitcases almost before she learned to read. Born to a military family, she has lived in the United States, Puerto Rico, Portugal and Brazil. In addition to travelling, Tina loves to cuddle with her pug, Alex, spend time with her family, and hit the trails on her horse. Learn more about Tina from her website, or 'friend' her on Facebook.

Susan Carlisle's love affair with books began when she made a bad grade in mathematics. Not allowed to watch TV until the grade had improved, she filled her time with books. Turning her love of reading into a love for writing romance, she pens hot Medicals. She loves castles, travelling, afternoon tea, reading voraciously and hearing from her readers. Join her newsletter at SusanCarlisle.com.

D1589665

Also by Tina Beckett

The Surgeon's Surprise Baby
A Family to Heal His Heart
A Christmas Kiss with Her Ex-Army Doc
Miracle Baby for the Midwife
One Hot Night with Dr Cardoza
Risking It All for the Children's Doc

Also by Susan Carlisle

Nurse to Forever Mum
The Sheikh Doc's Marriage Bargain
Highland Doc's Christmas Rescue
Firefighter's Unexpected Fling
The Neonatal Doc's Baby Surprise
Pacific Paradise, Second Chance

Discover more at millsandboon.co.uk.

IT STARTED WITH A WINTER KISS

TINA BECKETT

THE SINGLE DAD'S HOLIDAY WISH

SUSAN CARLISLE

MILLS & BOON

All rights reserved including the right of reproduction
in whole or in part in any form. This edition is published
by arrangement with Harlequin Books S.A.

This is a work of fiction. Names, characters, places, locations
and incidents are purely fictional and bear no relationship to
any real life individuals, living or dead, or to any actual places,
business establishments, locations, events or incidents.
Any resemblance is entirely coincidental.

This book is sold subject to the condition that it shall not,
by way of trade or otherwise, be lent, resold, hired out
or otherwise circulated without the prior consent of the publisher
in any form of binding or cover other than that in which it is published
and without a similar condition including this condition
being imposed on the subsequent purchaser.

® and TM are trademarks owned and used by the trademark owner
and/or its licensee. Trademarks marked with ® are registered with the
United Kingdom Patent Office and/or the Office for Harmonisation
in the Internal Market and in other countries.

First Published in Great Britain 2020
by Mills & Boon, an imprint of HarperCollins*Publishers*
1 London Bridge Street, London, SE1 9GF

It Started with a Winter Kiss © 2020 by Tina Beckett

The Single Dad's Holiday Wish © 2020 by Susan Carlisle

ISBN: 978-0-263-27987-0

MIX
Paper from
responsible sources
FSC™ C007454

This book is produced from independently certified FSC™ paper
to ensure responsible forest management.
For more information visit www.harpercollins.co.uk/green.

Printed and bound in Spain
by CPI, Barcelona

IT STARTED WITH
A WINTER KISS

TINA BECKETT

MILLS & BOON

To my family: for helping me follow my dreams.

PROLOGUE

Fifteen years earlier

PINK-PLUS. OH, GOD.

Maura picked up the pregnancy test and brought it closer, thinking maybe she wasn't seeing it correctly. Then she closed her eyes, a wave of hope crashing through her heart as she struggled to process what had just happened. Fearing the news and yet welcoming it all the same. She was going to have a baby.

A baby!

Maybe this was the Hail Mary shot she needed to salvage her relationship with Dex and set it back on the right track. The track they had started on in high school. Until tragedy had rocked his world. And hers along with it.

He'd never been the same. Maura had waited around, hoping against hope that once he'd had a chance to work through his grief, he would come back to her emotionally. But so far nothing had worked. He was distant. Unreachable.

Even when they made love.

And as far as grief went, he'd been strangely stoic.

Even at the funeral, he'd never broken down and cried. At least not in front of her.

He needed those tears. *She* needed those tears. Just to know that he was still capable of feeling. Of loving.

And if he wasn't?

A trill of terror swept through her, and she pressed her hands to her abdomen.

Maybe she should feel him out before telling him about the baby. Or at least take a breath or two before rushing in with the news. The last thing she needed was to have him agree to stay with her for the wrong reasons.

A lifetime of living with this same unreachability? No. She couldn't do it.

She set the pregnancy test on the bathroom counter and stared at it. If he could no longer love her the way he used to, would he be able to love their child? Was she willing to risk this child growing up with a father who could not show affection?

There was only one way to find out. She needed to call and meet him to discuss things. Ask him where they stood and where he saw their relationship going.

And if he didn't give her the answer she desperately needed to hear?

Then she would have no choice but to break things off with him, give herself a few weeks to center herself and think things through. Then and only then would she figure out how to tell him he was going to be a father.

Fingering the toothbrush in a cup that sat next to hers, the one that hadn't been used since the day this baby had been conceived, she sent up a prayer that today would be the day. The day when the Dexter she knew and loved would come back to her.

God, she hoped that was possible, with every fiber of her being.

Walking from the bathroom, she found her phone on the bedside table and sank down onto her mattress. She scrolled through the list of contacts and found Dex's name among all the others. Only unlike all those other names, this one had a red heart icon next to it. He was her heart and had been from the day she'd first laid eyes on him.

And now it was up to him whether that heart remained intact or whether it splintered into a thousand pieces.

Swallowing hard, she drummed up enough courage to push the button that would either set the wheels in motion to continue their relationship or freeze them in their tracks forever.

Please, Dex, give me the answer I need.

She splayed her hand over her lower abdomen once again.

Give me the answer we both need.

CHAPTER ONE

SNOW. GREAT. HIS least favorite thing.

It came down even harder as Dexter Chamblisse exited his truck and trudged through the parking lot. He could hear the snowplow in another section of the medical center, struggling to keep the area clear enough for cars and emergency vehicles alike.

The hospital's entrance was a mere fifty feet away, but as a big flake clung to his forehead, he shoved it away with irritation. Although it never stuck around long in this part of Montana, the snow always managed to wreak havoc somewhere…for someone. About this time every year, he wondered why he stayed in this damned state. The short days and icy cold winters were always a reminder of what could happen. Of what *had* happened.

But his mom still lived here, and he felt a responsibility to her since he was her only surviving child. And she refused to move away. He understood her reasons, but it didn't mean that Dex shared them.

Shrugging his collar up to protect the back of his neck from the fierce wind, the heel of his boot skidded on a patch of ice for a second before he righted himself. "Dammit!"

His throat tightened. All it took was a split second…

Shadowy memories slid from beneath a locked door in his brain and threatened to materialize as they'd done hundreds of times before. But not today. Not when he had a full roster of patients waiting for his help. He needed to concentrate on the living and leave the rest for another day. Preferably a day far in the future.

Stepping onto the sidewalk outside the emergency room doors, he spotted an ambulance parked in the bay with the EMTs slamming the vehicle's doors shut. He gave the one in the driver's seat a quick wave, getting a smile in return.

He wondered if *she* was on duty today and, even more, wondered why he kept entering through these doors. Maybe because he'd been doing it forever. Just because an old flame had started working at the hospital a couple of years ago didn't mean he should change his habits. Besides, it would look pretty obvious if he suddenly started using another entrance.

And it had worked out fine. As if by some unwritten agreement, he and Maura rarely ran into each other in the hospital. Even here, in the department where she worked. He had a knack for sensing when she was present, the hair at the back of his neck going up. When that happened, he moved quickly down the corridor and away, usually before he actually saw her. And when he did see her, they studiously avoided chitchat, settling for the wave of a hand as he passed through her territory.

The plan was to do the same today.

Except, once inside the ER, he found chaos.

"I don't care how many phone calls you have to make, just find me one! Now!"

He glanced to the side and saw the flash of an all-too-familiar face as she ran behind a stretcher, a tiny spatter of blood staining one of her cheeks. No more wondering if she was working today. She obviously was.

It was then that he realized his cell phone was buzzing in his pocket. A dark sense of déjà-vu slid through him, and he quickened his pace, catching up to her in a flash. Maura Findley, his ex—well, long-ago ex—had a glove-covered hand pressing on someone's chest. A boy—teenager, actually.

"What have you got?"

Her head turned, and she fixed him with a glare that spoke volumes. "Where the hell have you been, Dex? We've been trying to get ahold of you, or anyone, for that matter, for the last ten minutes."

The EMS vehicle had been carrying this patient.

Maura's tone should have taken him aback, but she'd never been one to mince words. Which was why when she'd asked him where they stood all those years ago—and he hadn't been able to give her a straight answer—she'd broken things off between them once and for all. And she'd gone on to marry someone else a year later. Hell, it had taken her almost no time to move on, something that had always bothered him. Because he'd had a damned hard time moving on with his own life.

"I just got here. Traffic slowdown because of the snow. Sorry." He tossed the word out, hoping it didn't sound like he was apologizing for their past.

He wasn't. Having that relationship end was the best thing that could have happened to him.

And her, if he was honest with himself.

He hadn't been a good catch then. And he definitely wasn't one now. Although it didn't seem like she'd made out too well with her next relationship, either. He'd heard she'd gotten divorced.

A sense of regret speared through him. One which he immediately rejected.

"We've got a penetrating chest wound with a pneumothorax—object is still embedded…traffic accident caused by the slick conditions. More are on the way."

"Holy hell!" The growled words came out before he could stop them, and she gave him a sharp look before it softened slightly. Dammit! He didn't want her sympathy, he never had.

He and Maura had been a thing in high school—voted most likely to marry, actually. He'd agreed with them at the time. He'd even looked at rings. Planned how he would pop the question. And then the unthinkable happened and his world came apart. Their relationship continued for a while in college. But he could never get his head on straight.

Turning his attention to the kid on the stretcher, he spotted a twelve-inch piece of what looked like a galvanized pipe sticking out of the right upper quadrant of his chest. Dozens of options sped through his head. A pneumothorax was a life-threatening event if not treated quickly, and compounded by a chest wound…

"Good thing the EMTs didn't try to remove it. Let's get him into a room." He needed to be stabilized before they took him into surgery to remove the pipe.

Once in the exam room, Maura grabbed a dressing and waited for the patient to exhale before affixing the tape around the pipe to prevent more air from seeping into the patient's chest cavity.

Her hands were sure and steady, her decision to seal around the foreign body straight out of the medical books. Maura hadn't changed a bit. She was still the same mouthy, decisive girl he'd once known and loved. He gritted his teeth and sent that thought packing.

"Where are your chest tubes?"

"Third drawer on the right." She didn't even glance up as she threw the words at him, her dark ponytail falling over one shoulder as she kept working.

He used to love the natural reddish streaks in that silky hair. Loved to slide them between his thumb and index finger and...

One of the nurses came in and started getting vitals just as he found the tubing kit right where she'd said it would be. He grabbed a pair of gloves from the dispenser on the wall. "How many other victims?"

"Five or six. I'm not positive." This time she did look up. "At least one other chest wound. The weather is affecting the EMS's travel times, too."

That damned snow and ice. He couldn't think of one good thing about winter. He would rather be traipsing across places that were closer to the equator this time of the year. Places where Christmas was spent in flip-flops and colorful shirts. Maybe a trip to Brazil would be put on his agenda next year. He'd saved up enough vacation time to spend a month there. Maybe more, if he added in his personal days. Or he could volunteer with Doctors Without Borders and aim for regions in South America or Africa.

And vacation while doing that? Not very likely. But

he would be able to do some good for someone other than just himself. And avoid the icy winter months and the memories that went along with them.

"His pressure is low. Blood ox in the low eighties."

Swabbing the area between the fourth and fifth ribs and placing a drape over the area, he numbed the spot with a local even though their patient was unconscious. Maura helped him elevate the head of the bed and readied a large-bore needle. "Ready?"

"Go ahead," he said.

She carefully inserted the needle into the plural space and was rewarded almost immediately with a steady hiss of air that had been trapped in his chest cavity.

"Good job."

She glanced up at him, dark eyes on his. A hint of a smile played on her lips. "I have done this a time or two, you know."

"I know. I've just never seen you in action."

Not this kind of action, anyway. And right now, he didn't need to be thinking about any other kind.

"No. You haven't." Her smile faded. Or maybe it hadn't been there in the first place. He'd been known to see only what he wanted to see. Including the fact that she'd wanted more from their relationship right at a time when he was numb to everything but the pain inside of him.

And now that the pain was more chronic than acute?

He still wanted nothing. It was easier that way. Besides, she was over him. Her marriage had proved that, even if it hadn't lasted. He shook his thoughts away from the past once and for all.

"Let's go ahead with the chest tube."

The tube would help ensure the lung stayed inflated, draining away any remaining air from the wound, as well as fluid and blood. Maura waited as he placed the tubing in the correct position and then helped him secure it.

"That looks about as good as it's going to get," she said. "And I need to prepare for the other casualties coming in, so he's all yours."

"I'll move him into the OR to remove the pipe and assess for internal injuries." He glanced at her, the urge to brush away a tendril of hair that had fallen over her forehead coming and then going. "Call me if you need me."

Her eyes jerked toward him, and then she nodded as if realizing what he meant.

What had she thought he was referring to?

Oh, hell. They'd often said goodbye on that note after kissing each other until they couldn't breathe and then giggling over the double meaning behind the whole "if you need me" phrasing. A new sense of regret washed over him. She'd said she had something she wanted to tell him back then. Right before their relationship ended on angry words with no real sense of closure.

But there was no way to go back and fix things.

Or was there?

No. Not now when a patient's life was on the line. He'd better just accept that they'd gotten as much closure as they were ever likely to get. To try now would just rip open ugly wounds that neither of them needed to revisit.

So he gave the nurse some instructions on getting the patient to the third-floor OR and gave Maura a quick wave. The same wave he used whenever they happened to accidentally catch sight of each other. "See you later."

"Goodbye, Dex."

Goodbye.

His heart chilled. And there it was. No "see you later," or "talk to you soon." She may not have meant it to sound that way, but her meaning came through loud and clear: she had no desire to interact with him again. Now, or anytime in the near future. And he was fine with that. So, brushing her words away, he headed off to make arrangements for his patient's surgery.

Maura watched the door swing shut behind Dex, her muscles going completely limp. If not for the nurse who was still present in the room, she might have oozed into the nearest chair in order to slow her racing heart. And it wasn't just due to the burst of adrenaline from treating their patient.

God, why did she allow him to affect her like that? She'd gotten used to ducking away whenever she saw his lithe form strolling up the sidewalk toward her department as he came on duty. She wasn't sure why he insisted on coming though the ER, but it certainly wasn't because of her.

Not that she wanted it to be. Not anymore. At one point in her life, the sight of him would have made her woozy for a completely different reason. But now it was the kind of queasy awkwardness that made her cringe.

Sure, Maura, keep telling yourself that.

She was very glad her ex-husband didn't work at this hospital. Their divorce had been in part because she didn't want to move to Idaho, where he'd been offered a primo position. When she'd asked him not to go, he'd refused and walked away from their marriage instead. Looking back, it was telling that she wasn't willing to go and he wasn't willing to stay. It seemed like she had a knack for attracting men who had no desire to hang in there and stick out the tough times.

Although to be fair to Dex, he'd suffered a horrible loss during their time together. The problem wasn't that. It had come when he couldn't see past the tragedy to envision a future that honored his family's memory while continuing to live his life—making room in his heart for happiness. For starting their own little family.

Thank God she'd never needed to tell him about the baby.

Damn. She had more patients coming in, and now was not the time to dwell on things she couldn't—nor did she want to—change.

Even as she thought it, the doors to the ER swung open as the next EMS vehicle discharged a new accident victim—a girl of about ten with an obvious break to her leg, judging from the odd angle of the area below her knee.

"Let's take her back to exam room six." She glanced at Matt Foster, an EMT who was a very familiar face around these parts. "Are the rest of the victims coming to New Billings Memorial?"

He walked with the gurney, keeping his hand on the girl's arm as if to reassure her. He was wonderful with his patients, having many nurses and doctors alike asking him if he didn't want to change his career to nursing or even a doctor. But he said he loved his job. And obviously his job loved him.

This was the type of man she should be attracted to. Kind, caring and in touch with his feelings. But, unfortunately, all she felt for Matt was friendship, even though there were hints that he might like to ask her out.

"I think there's one more en route. But some of the others have been diverted to Our Lady of Mercy, since it's a little closer to where the accident happened."

So the other chest trauma case was probably going to the other hospital. A little ping of something bounced around her stomach. It wasn't disappointment. The last thing she wanted to do was see Dex again this afternoon.

Right?

Absolutely. She just needed to keep reminding herself of that fact before her brain began to put two and two together and came up with some kind of astronomical number as an answer.

She waved goodbye to Matt, who gave her a wink and a smile. "See ya later, Maura."

Turning her attention back to her patient, she said, "So what's your name?"

"Marabel Campbell." The girl sniffed, and the paleness of her features and glazed look to her eyes made Maura realize shock was setting in. It was the only reason for the child not to be screaming in pain. Hell, Maura would probably be shrieking the walls down if she'd had that kind of an injury.

"Well, Marabel, we're going to try to fix you up so you'll feel better. Is that okay?"

"Yes." She blinked a couple of times. "My mom and dad. Are they okay?"

Her heart sloshed around in her stomach before resurfacing. She hadn't thought to ask Matt about any relatives. "Let me get you settled, and then I'll ask someone."

She caught a nurse's eye. "Can you check on her parents? No one came in with her, so I don't know if…"

"I was with my aunt. My mom's at home."

"Do you know your mom's phone number?"

"My phone is in my pocket." The girl was still eerily aware of what was transpiring. Maura was shocked that Marabel, only ten years old, had a phone.

"Does your leg not hurt, Marabel?"

"My leg…" Her eyes traveled down her limbs and stopped. "No. Why is it like that?"

Torn nerves or shock could all make what should be an excruciating injury fade into the background. She had a feeling more was going on here than met the eye, though.

Just then the girl looked into her eyes. "I—I have a disease that makes me not feel things."

Not feel…

That explained a lot.

"Do you know if it's called CIP?" Congenital Insensitivity to Pain was rare, but she'd seen at least one other case during her time as an ER doctor. A man had come in complaining of nausea and sweating, only for them to discover that he was having a heart attack and hadn't been aware of any kind of pain.

"I don't know. It's a long name. But all it means is I can't feel it when something hurts. Even when it's something like burning my hand on the stove." She turned her palm over to reveal a thick ropy scar that had probably come from a burn wound. "Can you straighten the leg out?"

The girl said it in clinical tones as if her leg weren't a part of who she was as a person. Detached.

Just like Dex and his emotions.

If anything, Maura was even more worried than she'd been before. What if the injury was worse than it looked? "We're going to do our best to make sure it's as good as new."

She took the girl's phone and pushed the icon on it that read "Mom." When a woman answered, she quickly relayed what had happened and where her daughter was.

"What? Oh, my God, I had no idea. Is Marabel okay? And my sister?"

A nurse held up a piece of paper with the name of the hospital. "She's headed to Our Lady of Mercy hospital. I'll get you that number."

"I'm on my way to where you are. Oh! And Maribel has congenital insensitivity to pain. She can't tell if something hurts."

"Yes, she did relay that to us. It looks like she has a break to her right leg. We're getting ready to send her to X-Ray if you can give us verbal consent."

"Of course. Do whatever you need to. I'm at work, but will be there in about fifteen minutes."

"Perfect."

"Can I talk to her?"

"Yes, she's right here." She passed the phone to Marabel, who immediately burst into tears.

"My leg… What if I can't walk again, Mom? What if I can't swim?"

She wasn't sure what the woman said to her daughter, but she soon had her giggling. "Okay, I love you. I'll see you soon."

Maura already had a call in to the hospital's orthopedist, and she had the nurse contact Radiology.

Getting her young patient into an exam room, she noted her vitals, which all looked good. Maybe in part because she couldn't feel the damage to her leg. Normally blood pressure went up in reaction to stress or pain, so it was weird for her instruments not to be registering anything out of the ordinary.

Maybe Maura should have wished her own heart were a little more pain-proof and maybe she wouldn't have made some of the mistakes she had in her life.

Including not telling Dex the truth? And marrying Gabe a year later?

Probably. But pain served a very real purpose. It steered you clear of danger and taught you ways to avoid being hurt again. Like the whole stove burner thing.

So, although she might wish for a way to avoid being hurt, she needed those early-warning systems. Or she'd repeat the same mistakes of the past. And that was the last thing she wanted to do.

She immersed herself in Marabel's treatment, making sure she got what she needed, even while she gathered her own pain around her like a cloak and hoped to hell it kept everything at bay.

Like what? Dex?

Maybe. He was the only one around who could make her act stupid. Take stupid chances. She needed to be on guard and make sure that she was well protected.

No matter how many layers of fabric she had to wrap around her heart to cushion it against future breaks. Because this time, she wasn't sure she'd be able to gather the pieces and glue them back together again.

CHAPTER TWO

Dex left the hospital eight hours later, moving across the freshly plowed parking lot. He was dead tired, but at least the snow had stopped. He passed someone bundled in a red wool coat with a matching knit cap pulled down over her ears. The person kicked her back tire, swearing in a loud voice as she did. The tire was flat. Completely flat.

He smiled even as a spear of sympathy went through him. "Need some help?"

"I'm just waiting on a tow truck. My spare's no good, either. What are the chances?"

She turned around.

Oh, damn. What were the chances, indeed?

She pulled the hat even lower as if she could hide her identity. Too late. He'd recognize that upturned nose and smattering of freckles anywhere.

He swallowed. "Maura? I thought that was you."

"Yep, although right now I'm wishing I was someone else. Anyone else."

The words hit him like a punch to the gut, which surprised him. He'd taught himself to keep most of his reactions under wraps.

His mom had often lectured him about how apathetic he seemed to be about what had happened. And she was right. But it didn't change anything. If Dex hadn't been sick enough to stay home that night… His dad had offered to wait for another night to see the movie. But they already had tickets and Dex had urged them to go without him. His mom had opted to stay at home with him while the rest of his family headed out. And look what had happened.

As if realizing how her words might have sounded, Maura cut into his thoughts. "I'm talking about the flat tire."

He relaxed slightly. "I can help you get that off and take it someplace."

"I couldn't ask—"

"You didn't. I offered." There was no way he was going to walk away and leave her here to wait in the cold. Plus, even in Montana, there were dangers such as human trafficking, and he didn't want to be responsible for abandoning her.

Sure, Dex, keep telling yourself that's the reason.

The reality was, as much as he hated it, his heart rate had shot up the second she had turned around, revealing her identity. And although he would have helped anyone—man or woman—in the same situation, this was different. It always had been. Just because his head understood that there was no longer anything between them didn't mean his body wanted to listen to reason. Or his heart.

But she sure looked cute as hell in her matching coat and hat, the big fluffy pompom on top bobbing with every sharp breeze that rolled across the parking lot.

Her dark hair streamed from beneath the cap in wavy lines, and her earlobes—where tiny hoops dangled—peeked from beneath it.

"If you're sure you don't mind. How's our patient, by the way?"

"The pneumothorax? We got the pipe out without any problems. Amazingly enough, it didn't hit anything vital."

"Wow, that's great."

"It is. He was extremely lucky." If Dex didn't know better he'd think she was stalling. "Where's your jack?"

She glanced at her trunk and grimaced. "Well, it's kind of…in there. Wait here, and I'll get it for you."

There was a tenseness to the words that put him on edge as she pushed a button on her key fob. Something released and her trunk popped open. Disregarding her words to stay where he was, he rounded the end of the car and looked down to see her trunk piled high with clear plastic packages filled with what looked like bedding. Or something. It was the same kind of knitted stuff as her hat.

Now he understood her hesitation. "What is all this?"

Her half shrug seemed irritated. "Just some things I was going to take down to a local shelter."

He fingered one of the packages, which contained a pink and blue blanket. Something tugged at him. "Did you make these?" As far as he knew, she hadn't knitted when they were together, although how would he really know? And that made something squirm inside of him. How much of their time together had been about him and his own needs?

"It's just something I do in my spare time."

Since her divorce? He didn't want to picture her sitting alone at night on her couch, making blankets for women who were even lonelier than she was. Or maybe she wasn't lonely at all. Maybe she went out with a different man every night. Or had one special someone...

Somehow that thought was even worse, so he blanked it out. "We could drop them off on the way to getting the tire fixed, since we'll have to take them out of the trunk anyway to get to the jack. Let me get my car and pull it around."

"You don't have to. Really."

"I'm off for the rest of the afternoon so it's not a big deal. I'll just be a minute."

Without giving her a chance to argue, he headed a few rows over to his car. Starting it up, he came back around to where she was parked. He opened the door to the back seat, went over and scooped up an armload of the blankets, and loaded them into his car.

She watched him for a minute, hesitating as if unsure of what she wanted to do, and then she finally started helping. "I'm sure this is the last thing you want to do with your time off."

She was wrong about it being the last thing, but it certainly wasn't the smartest thing to be doing. "I didn't have any plans so it's fine."

Not that he normally made many plans outside of work.

A few minutes later everything was unloaded, and he raised the cover in her car's trunk to find the spare. It was just a metal rim, with no tire on it at all. She was right when she said it was no good. But at least her jack and lug nut wrench were right where they should be.

In short order, he had the bolts removed and gave a tug on the wheel removing it. He loaded it in his own trunk and slammed the lid. "Ready?"

She nodded. "Thank you, again."

Opening the passenger door for her, he waited for Maura to slide inside. "Not a problem."

At least he hoped it wouldn't be. The last time he'd been in a car with her was…

On the day they broke up. He wasn't sure what had precipitated that last showdown, but she hadn't given him any wiggle room at all. He'd known for a while she was tired of waiting for him, but all thoughts of rings and popping the question had died along with his family. And when he'd finally admitted that he didn't know what their future looked like, her eyes had watered, and she'd said they were done.

As far as he knew, she'd walked away without ever looking back at that decision. It was better if he didn't revisit that day, either. It would change nothing.

Soon they were off hospital grounds and he turned on Central Avenue heading into the heart of the city. He'd programmed the GPS for the address she'd given him. It wasn't far. Less than five miles.

"When did you start making those?" He inclined his head toward the back seat.

"Around three years ago. A friend mentioned the center, and it just seemed like something I wanted to get involved in after my…"

Her voice dropped away after that word, and she shot him a glance without saying any more. She'd only been divorced for a year, so if she'd started making the blankets three years ago, it wasn't because of that.

"I take it the ones in the car were made more recently."

"About four months. I can get two done a week under most conditions."

"That's a lot of knitting."

She glanced over at him with a smile. "Crocheting, actually."

"There's a difference?" He couldn't stop his own lips from curving. It felt good. He couldn't think of many things that made him smile anymore.

"Knitting needles are used in pairs and are straight. A crochet needle has a hook."

"Like a bone hook?"

This time she laughed. "I guess you could compare it to that, although I've never tried crocheting with one of those." She glanced out the window. "It's just a few blocks up on your right. The Nadia Ram Crisis Center for Mothers."

"Is Nadia Ram the founder?"

There was a second of hesitation. "No. Her family founded the center in her honor."

She didn't offer more than that, and a dark foreboding set up shop in his gut. Was Nadia a casualty of domestic violence? Oh, hell... Was Maura?

Pressure built in his head when he thought of someone hurting her. Physically or mentally. If that were the case, he might have to track the man down and give him a little taste of his own medicine.

"Your husband didn't... He wasn't..." He couldn't force himself to finish the sentence.

"It's *ex*-husband. And, no, he didn't." She hesitated. "I had a miscarriage years ago. It was a hard time, and I never really got over it. My friend suggested helping out at the center where there were babies and children in trouble. Nothing more than that."

She'd had a miscarriage. When? Had it been what ended her marriage? There was a depth of meaning in her last sentence that told him her involvement in the center was a lot more than "nothing." But the tension in her voice told him that further discussion on the matter wasn't welcome.

Fortunately, the GPS warned him that they were about to arrive at their destination. And sure enough, a plain brick building came into view on the right. There was no signage other than an abstract rendition of a mother holding a baby. He could understand why they wouldn't want to announce their presence, although he was pretty sure most locals would know exactly what the building was used for.

"There's a parking lot and entrance around back. That's where I normally drop off things."

"Okay." Swinging into a narrow lane that led to the rear of the building, he was surprised to see two long banks of windows and a brick patio area with chairs and picnic tables. There was also a glassed-in porch, where a young woman in jeans sat in a rocker, leaning over a wrapped object. When she lifted her head, even from this distance, he could make out two butterfly bandages on her left cheek. And one of her arms was in a navy blue sling. He swallowed hard, averting his eyes to give her privacy.

What had he expected to see? Happy faces and ladies drinking tea in fancy cups?

Maura didn't seem as taken aback, however. She waved, and as soon as the car came to a stop, she grabbed a plastic-wrapped packet from the back seat and leaped out of the vehicle. Leaving him in the car, she headed for the woman, who slid her baby into a nearby crib and opened the door for Maura. The two hugged, and Maura opened the package and held out the blanket. The woman used her good arm to shake the creation open, looking at it for a second before holding it tight to her chest. Then she hugged Maura again for a long moment. The ER doc leaned back and looked in the other woman's face, saying something. They both went over to the crib, and Maura smiled at the infant.

Her mention of a miscarriage came back to him. He hadn't heard anything about that, and normally the hospital grapevine was a wealth of information, even when the last thing he wanted to do was hear about who was dating whom.

A lot had happened since he and Maura had called it quits. At least in her life. She'd married, lost a baby, gotten a divorce and who knew what else. And she was now an ER physician. He wasn't surprised at that. They'd both talked about becoming doctors when they were dating. But in terms of anything in his own private life, things were pretty stagnant.

Stagnant. That probably wasn't the best word to describe where he was. But even if it was, that's what he'd wanted. What he still wanted. At least he hadn't given Maura or himself the additional heartache of a divorce and a lost baby.

As if hearing his thoughts, she turned to glance at him and said something to the woman. Then she opened the screen door and came back down the sidewalk toward the car. He powered down the window.

"Sorry about that. She's waiting for her parents to get here to take her and the baby home to Kalispell. I was afraid with my tire problem I'd missed saying goodbye to her."

Located in northwestern Montana, Kalispell was a good four hundred miles from Billings. A long way to travel unless this move was to be a permanent one.

"I'm glad you made it, then."

"Thanks to you." She gave him a look that he couldn't read, and then said, "Let me go in and get a cart so I can take the blankets in and we can be on our way."

"Do you want to wait with your friend until her parents get here?"

"I just wanted to make sure she was okay and that they really were coming. The relationship has been strained over the last couple of years because of her husband. Obviously, their instincts about the man turned out to be right."

Meaning the woman's husband really had been abusive. "Damn. I hope he got what was coming to him."

"He won't. Not this time. She's not pressing charges. She just wanted out of the relationship."

So the man was free to do the same thing to another woman. The thought made more acid churn to life in his stomach. "Can't the authorities do something?"

"Not when she claims she fell off a bicycle. They went and talked to him, but you probably know how much good that does."

He'd dealt with a few broken bones caused by domestic violence and had seen exactly what Maura was talking about. It still made him angry. But he did understand the desire just to get away and never have to face that person again, which if charges were pressed they almost certainly would.

"I've had a case here and there where I've seen the same thing." He glanced again at where the woman had gone back to holding her baby. "Did the baby have to suffer any—?"

"No, thank God. That's part of the reason for this place. It's where women can come with no pressure and no judgments. The important thing is that they left their abuser, so the emphasis is on getting them patched up both mentally and physically. Making sure they're strong enough to move forward in life."

He nodded, realizing she was still standing in the cold. Getting out of the car, he said, "Between the two of us, we should be able to carry those blankets inside. That is, if it's okay for me to go in."

Some shelters were protective about who came on the premises—with good reason—since some of these women probably suffered from PTSD symptoms.

"Thanks. It should be okay. They try to keep the residents out of the main lobby, where anyone off the streets can come in. There are separate social areas inside the facility."

Smart.

They carried the remainder of the blankets in through a back door. The person behind the desk greeted them with a smile. "Hi, Maura. Did you get to see Celia?"

"I just did. I'm glad her parents are almost here."

"So are we." The young blonde woman behind the desk shifted her gaze to him.

"Oh, sorry," said Maura. "This is Dexter Chamblisse.

He's a doctor at the hospital where I work. I had a flat tire, and he offered to help drop off the afghans."

Her description of him could have been about any doctor at their hospital.

Because that's what you are, Dex. Just another doctor that she works with.

And damn if that didn't bother him on a level he'd rather not examine.

"Nice to meet you, Dr. Chamblisse." She shook his hand. "I'm Corbin."

"Call me Dex." He sent her a smile even as his peripheral vision kept careful track of Maura's movements. But she stood still, not twitching so much as a muscle.

"Thanks, I will." She glanced at the bundle in his arms. "Just set those on the desk."

They both placed the blankets on the wooden surface as Corbin oohed and aahed over several of them. "I've had people, from when you first started bringing them, contact us asking for your name. Why you won't let them send you thank-you cards is beyond me."

"Because it's not about me. It's about them. It always has been. I'm glad they seem to enjoy them, though."

"They do. Especially the baby afghans."

She made some of these for infants like the one in that closed-in patio. He remembered her saying it was because of her miscarriage. So many questions came to mind. How far along had she been? Had the child she'd carried been a boy or a girl? Why had she opted not to have another baby afterward? She'd made it clear she didn't want to talk about it, though, and he was going to respect the unspoken request.

But Dex could remember the days when he'd dreamed of having children with her. That had never happened. Nor would it.

Corbin gathered several of the blankets and slid them into what looked like a hotel laundry collection cart.

"Are there other people who make things like these, as well?" he asked.

"We have some folks who make rag quilts or stuffed animals or even kid's pillowcases. Our rooms are pretty Spartan by necessity, so it's a touch of home that can make things seem *hopeful* rather than hopeless. And it's something they can take with them as they start a new—and hopefully better—life."

"I can see how those things would be treasured." The image of the woman clutching Maura's blanket to her chest as if it were a lifeline was burned into Dex's head. It would be a long time before he forgot that.

What was he doing for anyone outside of his job as a surgeon? Nothing. At least nothing like this. Maybe he really should start thinking about ways to give back. Like donating his services to a medical relief organization, as he'd thought about earlier.

But maybe it was time to do more than just toy with that idea. Maybe it was time to throw his hat into the ring and do what he hadn't thought to do in the past: help those who were unable to help themselves.

Dex was quiet on the way to the big-box store to see about fixing her tire. Was he regretting helping her? Or maybe the side trip to the crisis center for moms made him uncomfortable. She wouldn't blame him. It wasn't an easy thing to see a woman with a cheek that had been split open by someone who supposedly loved her. But the cuts and bruises that were inside of Celia Davis were so much worse than the wounds visible on the outside. At least her baby would be spared from witnessing her mom being beaten.

Was that what was bothering Dex?

As horrible as it sounded, she hoped that was it. Because if it wasn't...

Surely he couldn't have guessed the truth. She wasn't even sure why she had mentioned her reasons for crocheting those blankets. It had just slipped out, the way it did when anyone asked about her reasons for helping with the crisis center. She had stopped the actual words from coming out when he first asked, only to reveal it a little while later. But she hadn't explained everything, and if she could help it, she wouldn't. Not ever.

She'd been devastated when she had lost her baby, although what she should have felt was relief. But it was as if her last connection with Dex had been severed—the last reminder of what they'd once had. She'd cried for weeks, only sharing with her family and closest friends what had happened. No one at New Billings knew about her loss. There was no reason to bring it up. Not with them, and certainly not with Dex.

And there was no reason to. He hadn't asked whose baby it was. At this point, she hoped he assumed it was her ex's.

And if he didn't?

Well, she couldn't go back and change things now, and Dex had given her little choice when they were together. Maybe deep down he'd known something was up and hadn't wanted to face it...or deal with it. Maybe that's why he'd been so ambivalent about taking their relationship to the next level. And she definitely hadn't wanted him to commit for reasons other than love. But he didn't even offer.

She'd only just found out about the pregnancy herself, so there was no way he could have guessed what was up back then. And after losing his dad and siblings, something inside of him had changed. He'd made love to her a day after the accident with an intensity that had shocked her. But afterward, he'd become increasingly moody and detached, and who could blame him? As time went on, it had only gotten worse. Instead of moving back to his normal loving self, he'd become a stranger she no longer recognized.

Even after all this time, she sensed the same detached attitude in him. Having lived through it once, she wanted no part of who Dex was now.

She would just keep her secret to herself. To reveal it now wouldn't bring anything good, and it wouldn't undo what had happened.

And if she hadn't miscarried?

She would have told him about the baby. Right?

Yes. She would have. Even after their breakup, she'd formulated plans and scratched them out again. Then she'd lost the baby and there'd been no reason to.

"Everything okay?" His voice knocked her out of her musings, and she realized they had arrived at the big-box store.

"If you want to drop me and the tire off, I can call someone to come get me when it's ready."

"I don't mind waiting, unless there's a reason you'd rather I didn't."

There was one. But if she didn't kick these melancholy memories away, he was going to start asking questions she'd rather not answer and bring back memories she'd rather not face.

"Nope, I just don't want to keep you from whatever you have going on."

"Like I said earlier, I don't have any special plans, so it's not a problem."

How sad was it that neither of them seemed to have much of a social life anymore?

Well, hers was of her own choosing. She'd failed at two relationships so far and didn't relish attempting a third one. Or repeating an old one. There was a part of her that realized her marriage to Gabe had been an attempt to cover up the gaping hole left by her miscarriage and her breakup with Dex. She'd been wrong to get involved with him when she was still trying to come to terms with her own grief.

Matt Foster, the EMT, had sent little hints that she pretended not to pick up on. She didn't want to ruin their friendship by going out with him when she knew her heart wasn't in it. And using a relationship to cover up yet another hole in her life would be repeating the same mistakes. She needed to break the cycle before it became even more destructive.

They dropped off the tire and were told it would be about an hour before it was ready.

An hour. Lord, she'd hoped it would be a quick fix and that she'd be on her way in fifteen minutes. Evidently, it was not to be.

So here she was sitting in a nearby restaurant with him, trying not to look at him through the young, dewy eyes she'd had when they first met in high school. He'd been on the baseball team, and she'd sat in the stands and gawked at him game after game. And when he asked her to the prom, she'd been over the moon. He'd been so sure of himself. So sure of what he wanted. And what he'd wanted back then had been her.

She hadn't been able to get enough of him. Separating that man from the one who now sat in front of her was hard. Which was why the avoidance game at work had become so critical to being able to work at the same hospital as him.

The man was still a looker. In fact, he'd just grown more attractive over the years. With his bronzed skin and sharply cut cheekbones, he hadn't grown flabby with age. The same traits that had made her swoon back in high school were still there. As were those pale green eyes that had made her want to fall into their depths. Those eyes had been warmer back then—not the chilly pools they were today. The hardened edges of the Dex that sat across from her had crinkles radiating from the corners of those eyes, although she'd rarely seen him smile. There was also a frown line deeply etched between his brows.

It made him look forbidding. And cold.

And it also awoke a little part of her that said she could fix him. Heal him from whatever seemed to be tormenting him. But she hadn't been able to do that fifteen years ago after that tragic car accident. And she knew enough from life experience to understand that she couldn't fix him now. Dex had to heal himself.

If he even needed healing.

Maybe he was happy with the way he was, and it

was her psyche that was dredging up the torment from the past. The pain she'd seen in him after the accident that had claimed everyone in his family except him and his mom.

How he'd hated the snow after that. Had avoided driving in it, if at all possible.

Did he still hate it?

She knew he drove in it, since it was pretty hard to avoid that reality in Montana.

Heavens. She was staring at him. But when she glanced quickly at his eyes, she saw he was looking out the window, not even paying attention. Probably ruing the fact that he'd offered to help her out. It had turned out to be quite a time suck for him.

"I'm really sorry this is ending up taking so long."

His attention snapped back to her. "Not a problem. I need to eat anyway, and so do you if your day was as busy as mine was."

"We were pretty hectic. Besides that big traffic accident, there were several other fender benders because of the weather this morning."

"No fatalities?"

"None that I heard of."

He nodded, his face grave. "Good."

Was he thinking about his family? She was pretty sure that was something you never got over. Maybe if she'd given him some more time…

Somehow she doubted it.

The waitress had already taken their orders, which would hopefully be here any minute. She was feeling more awkward by the minute.

"I'm sorry about your miscarriage."

His words came out of nowhere, his eyes focused on her with an expression she couldn't decipher.

Oh, God.

A rush of tears welled up in her throat before she could stop them, and for a minute she couldn't make her voice work. She blinked, willing the flood to recede before it overflowed the levy banks she'd erected many years ago. Taking a slow, careful breath, she tried to keep her expression neutral. "It… It was a long time ago."

"But it still hurts."

"Yes." What else was there to say? There were times she could barely breathe it hurt so bad. She'd wanted that baby desperately, despite the breakup, despite the fact that she might very well have had to raise the child all by herself. What she'd done by herself, however, was face the loss of that same child. She'd lain on her bathroom floor the morning it happened and sobbed until she'd had no strength left. It had been too much. She'd lost Dex and her baby almost back-to-back.

And while those things might have happened a lifetime ago, it didn't mean the raw emotion from those events didn't rear its ugly head at times. Nor did it mean she didn't wonder what might have happened if things had been different. If Dex had been able to love her and be there for her when it happened.

But things weren't different. And they never would be.

If she was smart, she would keep that thought at the forefront of her mind. That Dex had been lost forever to her the day she'd broken it off with him. Actually it had happened before that, when his father and siblings had died in the terrible crash. The process of pulling away had been steady and inexorable, and nothing she'd done to combat it had had any effect.

There was no going back and undoing the past. For any of them. And trying would only bring more hurt and more heartache. For her. And probably for Dex, too.

CHAPTER THREE

TWO DAYS AFTER his outing with Maura, Dex awoke still feeling hungover and out of sorts.

Except he hadn't been drinking. Planting his palms on the bathroom counter, he tried to get the image of that woman—what was her name… Celia?—out of his head. He tried to imagine the fear and horror that would come from realizing the person you loved wasn't who you thought they were. Or that they'd changed over the course of a year…two years.

Which was why Maura had broken things off with him. She had suddenly realized he wasn't heading toward marriage anytime soon. Maybe never. She'd been right. But it hadn't always been that way. In his younger days—before the accident—he'd been moving steadily toward making her his partner for life. In fact he hadn't been able to imagine a universe in which they weren't together.

Somehow hearing about her miscarriage had brought it all back to him. If things had been different, that might have been *his* child she'd carried…and lost. He'd been sitting there thinking about that exact thing when they'd been in the restaurant. Even though it wasn't, it was like there was a grain of sand under his skin that just kept chafing at him. It refused to go away, no matter what he tried.

He'd just have to let it run its course. He rubbed a palm over the stubble on his face before picking up a razor and getting to work removing it. His shift started in a little over an hour. But for the first time in quite a while, he found himself sluggish and out of sorts. He'd succeeded in going almost two years, with little interaction with Maura other than a random sighting as he moved around the hospital. And that's the way he preferred it.

Yesterday had changed that—and hell if he hadn't been the one who'd initiated the contact and opted to extend it. Not a smart move. Because it was making him see things he'd been blind to at the time of their breakup. Like the fact that in trying to protect himself, he'd probably hurt her terribly.

At the time, he'd made himself believe he was sparing her from being with someone who no longer knew how to feel. Who no longer *wanted* to feel. Because the guilt of being a survivor when he should have died along with the rest of his father and siblings had eaten at him until there'd been little left.

How could he eat, drink and be merry? How could he get married and have children knowing that he'd been spared because he'd had a sniffle and had whined that he didn't feel like going to see the movie? He'd wanted to call Maura, instead, and have a nice long chatty conversation about what they were going to do over the next couple of days.

All the while his dad and sisters had been on a collision course with death.

He hadn't been able to face it or let Maura in on that truth, so he'd blocked it out and let her walk away. He still blocked it out whenever he could.

If the universe was lining up the stars in hopes that they would force him and Maura back together, they were going to be disappointed. Neither of them wanted to travel down that road again. He dropped the razor back into his toothbrush holder and sluiced his face with warm water, washing away the last of the shaving cream.

There. He felt a little more human now.

He dried his face, slinging the towel around the back of his neck and walking back into the bedroom, where his clothes for the day were laid out on the bed.

The bed that was only rumpled on one side.

Dammit! Whether he shared his bed for a night—or not—didn't matter. What did was that he was the one who decided when and where any of those encounters occurred. And how long they lasted.

Which was almost never longer than a week or two. The women knew that up front and most seemed happy with the arrangement. At least he'd never heard any complaints. Had never been asked what his intentions were.

Maura had been the only one who'd actually stood in front of him and demanded he tell her where he saw the relationship going.

Then again, she was the only one he'd ever had an actual relationship with. And he'd destroyed it.

Not purposely, but in the end, it had been the right thing to do. The only thing he could do.

Still, no more offering to run her places. Next time he'd wait with her until the tow truck arrived and then be on his way. No more little forays into the past. Or into the present. And definitely not into the future.

With that thought in mind, he got dressed, glancing again at his bed with a frown before straightening the covers and erasing the evidence that he'd slept alone.

Slept? Not much. But that was going to change. He'd faced the problem and dealt with it. His conscience was clear when it came to Maura and their breakup, and it would stay that way.

Even as he thought it, a little voice in his head warned him to not be too sure, because he hadn't yet seen what the day had to bring.

The day brought chaos with a capital C.

He got to the hospital and found a host of television cameras stationed outside the entrance to the Emergency Room. And news vans were parked every which way in the lot behind it. What the hell?

Swinging into one of the physician's parking places, he decided he was going to use a different entrance today to avoid whatever was going on. Then he spotted a red bobbing pompom. It was making a beeline for that mob of reporters. Great. He knew that hat. And that quick, confident walk.

Why was she heading straight into the fray?

Because Maura had never backed away from anything in her life. Except for him.

And there was probably an emergency case in there

she was needed for. He had to make sure she made it inside without incident.

Before he could talk himself out of it, he exited his car and slammed the door—a little harder than necessary—moving with long strides toward her.

If he was smart, he'd just veer away and avoid whatever was going on, like he'd planned. It wasn't like the reporters were going to knock her to the ground, so he wasn't sure what he hoped to accomplish by going over to her. But all that rational thinking did nothing, because he just kept on walking.

He caught up with her within a minute.

"What's going on?"

She glanced up at him in surprise. "You haven't heard the reports?"

"What reports?"

"There was a shooting down by the moms' crisis center."

The place where they'd taken the blankets? "*By* the center? Or *at* the center?"

"At. I was about a mile out when it came across the news. I couldn't get here fast…" Her strides faltered and she cleared her throat. "I'm not sure how bad it is, but one of the center's residents was hit as she was coming out to go to work."

"Only her?"

"Yes. They suspect the husband, but he fled the scene before anyone knew what happened."

They reached the group of reporters, who waved microphones in their faces and launched a bevy of questions at them.

When someone jostled Maura, he put an arm around

her waist and drew her close, forcing his way through the group. A security guard immediately came out of the door and briskly waved the reporters away from the door. He came back in with an apologetic grimace. "Sorry about that, Maura. The police are en route from the scene. Hopefully, they'll clear out those reporters."

The hospital was private property, but it was hard for one guard to force them away. "Thanks for the help."

"Where is she?" Maura glanced at the man.

The guard didn't ask who they were talking about. "Room four. They're trying to stabilize her before rushing her up to surgery. She took two bullets to the chest."

Dex felt Maura flinch against him. Room four was one of the trauma rooms.

"Who's the surgeon, do you know?"

"Dr. Hodges, I believe."

Realizing his arm had tightened around her and that she was actively leaning against him, he eased away before anyone got any ideas—especially the reporters outside, whose eyes he could feel on them. As if coming to the same conclusion, Maura jerked sideways. The guard's head tilted, but he didn't say anything.

Perfect, he'd probably made it look even worse by doing that.

"Dr. Hodges is a good trauma surgeon."

She glanced at her phone. "I know. I'm going to run back and see how she is."

Dex nodded again at the security guard. "Thanks again for your help."

"Not a problem."

Moving away from the man, he asked, "I'll come with you in case they need an extra set of hands."

"Thank you."

Just then two nurses rushed by them, one of them shoving a crash cart in front of her.

Dammit. He knew exactly where they were going. Room four.

They entered the large room, finding mass confusion and a floor littered with bloody gauze. Dr. Hodges was already inside yelling out orders to those around him. He spotted Dex. "Get in here, I need your hands."

Moving over to his colleague, he saw immediately what was wrong. An abdominal wound pulsed blood in steady, rhythmic gushes. "There's a nicked artery in here somewhere. I need to get it clamped and move her to surgery or we're going to lose her. Pressure's falling."

While Hodges worked on finding that artery, widening the hole with a scalpel, Dex worked on getting her pressure up so she didn't completely crash. Maura was against the wall somewhere, although he didn't take the time to look up. There was only room for so many doctors at a time. If he hadn't been here, he was sure Maura would be the one beside Hodges. And by how shaky her voice had been for a few moments when they'd entered the hospital, it was probably a good thing she wasn't.

Not an easy situation for anyone, but especially when it was someone you either knew or had an interest in.

"Got it. I need a clamp." A nurse passed one over and the trauma doctor sealed the vessel. "Let's get her to the OR right now. Can you scrub in?" He shot Dex a look.

"Yes. I'm right behind you."

Together they got the patient's bed moving, slamming through the doors at the end of the emergency department. He spotted Maura. "I'll let you know as soon as we know something."

The words were tossed across in a way that was totally impersonal, but it was the best he could do at the moment. He couldn't make her any promises. Something he seemed to repeat when it came to Maura. No promises. No firm commitments. But this time it was more a case of *can't* rather than *won't*. Because right now, he wasn't sure the patient was even going to make it to surgery.

Maura let one of the nurses know where she'd be and asked her to call if she was needed. She had gotten to the hospital a half hour before her shift started, just as she always did. Most of the time it gave her an opportunity to get up to speed on what was going on and gauge the feel of the ER. If there was frenetic activity, she would join in to help immediately. But on a quiet day, she'd take the time to have a coffee and get her mind where it needed to be.

She didn't recognize the shooting victim from the center, but she was young. So very young. And to have someone do this to her almost before her life had begun was unfathomable.

She hoped they caught the bastard who'd shot her. Even more than that, she prayed the girl would live to see another day. Although the center tried to stay low-key, with most of their clients finding out about them by word of mouth it wouldn't be hard for an abusive partner to discover where they'd run to.

And that was another thing. Most of the women who arrived had a child in tow or were pregnant. The center even offered childcare for those women who were working and didn't have day care arrangements.

Was there a baby or toddler at the center wondering when her mom was going to come back?

Or if she would?

The pressure that had been steadily building in her chest grew tighter, and she struggled to breathe past the constriction. She used the time to call the moms' crisis center, only to have it go straight to voice mail. They were probably dealing with the same problem with the press that the hospital was. She left her name and phone number and asked if there was anything she could do to help. She was sure they had already notified next of kin, which was strange since no one had arrived that looked like family. Maybe they were from out of town like Celia Davis's family was. One thing controlling people liked to do was isolate their partner so that they were almost completely dependent on the abuser for necessities like money, companionship and medical care. Having no place to turn to and no money even for bus fare made it that much harder to leave when things became unbearable.

Or maybe this woman's family was as dysfunctional as the rest of her life was.

Maura wrapped her arms around her waist and stared over the banks of chairs in the waiting room. It was still early enough in the morning that the surgical ward was not yet in full swing.

Just sit down. Dex said he'd let you know.

She wandered over to the nearest chair and slumped into it. It had only been about twenty minutes. If they'd lost her, surely he would have already come out to tell her. That had to be a good sign then, right?

She swallowed. The feel of his arm around her waist had been solid and comforting, like old times. Times when they'd laughed as they slipped away to a little-known creek that had been their favorite hangout spot. A place where they'd talk. Where they'd made love. Where she'd felt a sense of belonging.

Only she didn't belong. Not anymore. And once she'd realized she was relishing his closeness a little too much as they'd walked toward the hospital, she'd been horrified, especially when he tried to extricate himself, probably wondering why she was suddenly snuggled up against him.

She hadn't been. But she had been leaning against him. Needing his strength like she had back when they were together.

It had been the shock of the situation.

Her phone buzzed and she tensed, glancing at the screen. Not Dex. Although why she thought it would be, she had no idea.

It was the women's center.

"Hello? This is Maura Findley."

"Dr. Findley, this is Colleen Winters, director at the women's center. Are you at the hospital?"

"I am."

There was a pause. "Any news on Sylvia? I would have called the hospital's main number but…"

"I understand." She had to be careful how much information she gave out. "Did Sylvia make the center one of her emergency contacts?"

"Yes, I faxed it to the hospital this morning. It's one

of the first things we do so that the abusive party doesn't step in and try to make medical or financial decisions for these women. It takes away a chunk of their power."

"Good. I'm relieved to hear it." She'd wondered if the man would come here, even though the police were looking for him. "Did they catch him?"

"Yes. About a block and a half away from the center." There was a long pause. "Unfortunately, he turned the gun on himself before he could be apprehended."

"He's dead?"

"Yes."

Damn. She hated that he wouldn't face justice. If she lived, that was. "Sylvia is in surgery. So far no news, but it was touch and go in the OR. Does she have family nearby?"

"No. She grew up in the foster care system until she graduated from high school."

"Wow." Somehow that made it even worse. There was nowhere for her to turn except for the shelter.

"I know. The system does the best it can, but I'm sure you know how difficult it can be to place a teenager in a permanent home."

She didn't know from experience but could imagine it would be hard.

Just then Dex came out of the back, looking wrung out and tired. And his day had only just begun. Just like hers.

"Can you hold for just a minute? I see one of the surgeons." She hit the mute button on her phone. She studied his face but couldn't read anything in it.

Just like that last day they'd been together, when his expression had revealed nothing. No frown. No tears.

No surprise. Even as she was breaking off their relationship. Down by their little creek. Only that creek wasn't theirs any longer.

She waited until he reached her. "Did she make it?"

"It was touch and go, but so far she's hanging in there. We won't know for a couple of days if the severe blood loss affected her brain or other organs."

"Oh, no!"

She got back on the phone. "Does Sylvia have a child at the shelter?"

"Yes, a three-year-old boy."

Who might wind up in the foster care system, just like his mom, if she didn't survive.

"She made it through surgery, but nothing's certain right now. What will happen to her son while she recovers?"

"He'll have to go into the system, but we do have a couple of staff members who are certified as foster mothers, so it may be that he can stay here for a bit."

Dex's head tilted. He had to be wondering who she was talking to. She covered the mouthpiece. "It's the crisis center."

She finished up her call with Colleen, who said they would send someone over to be with Sylvia as soon as they had enough help to cover what needed to be covered.

Until then Sylvia was alone. In more ways than one.

Her heart ached for the young woman who had received such a rough start in life and for whom things had gotten no better once she was out on her own. But if she survived, hopefully, this would be a turning point for her.

"Is she in ICU?"

"Yes. She's on a ventilator in a medically induced coma at the moment. Her body needs time to heal. We had to give her six units during the surgery to repair the artery."

"She has a three-year-old son."

Dex frowned. "Hell. Hopefully, he's not in the care of whoever did this to her."

"No, he's not. And the shooter turned the gun on himself before he could be arrested."

He took a step closer before stopping where he was. "Did you know her?"

"No. So many of them come and go in a short period of time. I've really only interacted with a few of them. But the center has asked me to teach a first-aid course over there. I'm seriously thinking of saying yes."

"Do you think that's wise, Maura?"

She frowned at him. "Sorry? Why would there be anything wrong with educating them on—"

"There's nothing wrong with that." He held up his hands. "I meant for you. These are women who have been in unstable relationships. Violent relationships that sometimes end up with them fighting for their lives."

She still wasn't sure what he meant. "I don't follow."

"That could have been you." He took another step forward and touched her hand. The briefest brush of fingers against fingers. "What if you'd been delivering blankets today, or teaching that class?"

A shaft of something went through her. That same feeling of belonging that she'd had earlier. She shoved it aside. "It could have been anyone, including the people who work there or another resident."

"I know but…" He dragged a hand through his hair. "Hell, I need a coffee. You?"

She hesitated, but something in his demeanor told her to go with him. Maybe she wasn't the only one who'd been affected by what had happened. "That sounds wonderful. But I can't take long. I'm due in the ER."

"I'm due on rounds as well, but they'll call us if they need us."

"Okay."

They got onto the elevator around the corner and Dex stared at the ground, not saying anything. What was going on? First his concern and the touch of hands that had sent a shiver through her, and now this brooding silence.

"What are you thinking?" It was a stupid question, and one she really didn't want an answer for. But there was no taking it back now.

He was silent for a moment longer before making eye contact. "When would you teach this class?"

She blinked, then realized he was talking about the first-aid class she'd mentioned a few minutes ago. "I'm not sure. I haven't said yes yet—although I think I will—so nothing is carved in stone. Probably in the late afternoon after my shift normally gets over and when most of them would be home."

"Well, let me know. Maybe we could team teach it."

A tinge of shock made her speechless for a second. "Team teach? I don't understand."

"If you're talking late afternoon, you'd probably still be there after dark, yes?"

"Probably, why?"

"I just think it would be safer to have more than one person there."

It hit her. He was worried about her.

A rush of warmth went through her, pulsing through her veins despite all her efforts to stanch the flow. She lifted her chin, praying he wouldn't see the truth mirrored in her eyes. Forcing her voice to stay cool and even, she said, "I've been doing things on my own for a very long time now."

Since before her divorce, even, as she and Gabe had seemed to be on different pages for most of their marriage. It had held together a lot longer than she'd expected it to.

And maybe some of that had been due to laziness on both of their parts. But once he'd been offered the position in Idaho, it had forced both of them to take a good, hard look at their relationship before deciding neither of them had the energy or the desire to fight for their marriage. It had been the right decision. For both of them. Maybe the true reason for that was now standing in front of her.

God, she hoped not. Her divorce had come after she'd started working at the hospital and realized that Dex also worked there. Had that played a subconscious role in her decision not to go with Gabe?

The thought horrified her. What if it was true?

Well, at least she knew her ex-husband wasn't going to come back to track her down and try to kill her in a fit of jealous rage. Not that there was anything to be jealous of. Dex had made his thoughts about her clear fifteen years ago.

She did understand where he was coming from in

not wanting her to go to the center by herself, though. And she appreciated his concern—more than she would admit. Even if it was unfounded. "Look, if you want to come and help me teach the class, that's great. But do it because you want to, not because you feel like you have to."

"I'll tell you what. Let me have a couple of days to think something through before you give the director your answer, okay? Maybe we can offer to do a series of hospital-sanctioned seminars in different areas, like finances. Self-defense. Prenatal care. First aid. Postpartum depression. I want to ask if we have a budget for community outreach."

She hadn't thought of that. "Thank you. That sounds like a great idea. And it would be a great help to those women."

"So you'll wait?" They stepped off the elevator and headed down the hallway to the cafeteria.

"I will. It'll give me a chance to think of what I'd like to cover if I teach the class." She hesitated. "Do you think the reporters are still out front?"

"I don't know. It depends on whether they got what they wanted or whether they were run off by the police."

The coffee shop was busy, but no signs of anyone with cameras or microphones. Not that there would be. She was pretty sure the security guard would have ushered them out of the hospital corridors if he'd had his say.

"Grab a seat, and I'll get the coffee."

She glanced around and spotted a table. "Okay, thanks."

"What do you want?"

"Skinny vanilla latte. Two sweetener packets, please."

"I'll be right back."

She studied him as he waited in line. A head taller than the other folks who were there, Dex had always stood out from the crowd, and it wasn't just due to his height. It was his presence. There was just something about him.

He'd been worried about her. She could have sworn that was why he was suddenly interested in helping at the center.

And she liked it.

So very much. She leaned back in her chair. Of course she'd liked him "so very much" once upon a time, too. It's why their breakup had ripped her heart from her chest. And the fact that her baby might very well have grown up without a daddy. When she finally got up the courage to tell him about the pregnancy, she'd started cramping. And then her heart broke all over again when she realized she was losing the baby.

Sigh. So many of her decisions back then had been a result of what had happened between her and Dex.

Looking back, she could see that Gabe might have been a rebound boyfriend. She'd been so blinded by grief from everything that she might have jumped into that relationship before she'd gotten over any of it.

And she'd paid a steep price for that mistake.

Well, she wasn't going to pay the price for a second one. She needed to be very, very careful how she behaved around him. Heaven only knew she was still just as taken by his looks as she'd been back then. And by even the most casual of touches. So she needed to tread with care, or she was going to wind up being hurt all over again.

And this time that hurt might be harder to get over than it had been last time.

Ha! Last time? She wasn't sure she'd ever completely gotten over it.

But if not, she needed to do whatever it took to keep those embers from bursting back to life.

She was going to douse them with water every time a spark appeared. Again and again, for as long as it took for them to believe the truth: that she and Dex had been over—for a very long time.

CHAPTER FOUR

THE HOSPITAL APPROVED the funding for the women's crisis center project a week later. A week in which Dex had had the chance to examine the whys of his suggestion with eyes that were a bit clearer than they'd been. Now he was wondering what the hell he'd gotten himself into. Especially since the hospital administrator had suggested he and Maura head it up and hold a Christmas party for the moms and kids in the hospital's name, buying presents and funding a big meal.

What if the center was already planning a party? he'd asked. The response had been: Well, then they'd add to it—make it something extra special.

He doubted the crisis center had the funds to host a big celebration. But the hospital had some donors with deep pockets, and they were all for it. Especially since this would be great publicity. The center, which had seen such tragedy, would have its spirits revived by the hospital that had saved one of their own.

As much as he hated his cynicism, he could see the hospital's point, except now he was having to help the hospital use that tragedy for its own benefit. What was worse was that the hospital had said it would be great if fate gave them snow on that day.

Even better? Not for him.

He'd yet to break the news to Maura yet. She'd probably be thrilled by the prospect.

Dex and his big mouth.

On a good note, the gunshot victim was slowly recovering. Her EEG readings were promising, as was her ability to speak and reason, although she was still slurring her words a bit.

He folded the papers with the funding amounts and shoved it in his pocket. The patient had been moved from ICU to a regular room this morning, and he wanted to check on her and see how she was doing.

Giving a sigh, he made his way down the hallway to room 205, giving a quick knock on the door before pushing through it. "Hi, Sylvia, how are you feeling today?"

Just then, he noticed the chair pulled up beside the bed and the person in it, holding a squirming child. "Maura?"

She glanced at him with a smile that made his mouth go dry as she shifted the child back onto her lap. "You can't sit on Mommy right now. She has some boo-boos that need to heal."

Ah, this was Sylvia's child. Just then the dark-haired boy broke free and darted toward the bed. Dex intercepted him, scooping him into his arms. "Where do you think you're going, young man?"

The boy looked up at him with a surprised expression, and Dex willed the child not to cry. He didn't. Instead, he giggled. "Do again."

He blinked unsure of what the boy meant, then he got it. He lifted the child, swooping him into the air and pivoting on his heel. Just in time to catch the openmouthed shock on Maura's face. He propped the child on his hip and pretended it was no big deal, even though it was. He wasn't sure what had prompted him to play "airplane" with a complete stranger's child. Especially since he'd never felt particularly comfortable around children.

"What's his name?"

Sylvia spoke slowly, carefully enunciating each syllable separately. "Wes…ton."

He pretended not to notice the difficulty she had in saying the name. "Weston, huh? How old are you, kiddo?"

The child held up three fingers one at a time. "I free."

"Free" for three?

"Well, a big boy like you can sit in a chair for a minute. How about if I give you some paper to color on?"

"Color!"

He felt his pockets and drew out the papers from the administrator, turning them over and thinking, *To hell with it.* If the hospital wanted a party for kids, this was part and parcel of that.

He found a pen and laid it on top of the pages.

Weston started scribbling on the back of the page, while Dex took Sylvia's vitals and discreetly checked the bandages covering her wounds. Everything looked good. "Your pain levels are okay?"

Part of the slurred speech could be the result of the heavy painkillers they were using to help alleviate her discomfort. Fortunately, the woman didn't have a history of drug use, which would have made the situation more complicated. According to the rest of the staff, she hadn't asked about her ex. Maybe the things that had happened that day were still blurry. Or maybe she'd blocked them out. He couldn't blame her if that was the case.

He glanced at Maura, wondering what they'd talked about before he got there, and how she'd managed to bring Weston to visit. She'd obviously been over to the center, which made a little pinpoint of discomfort stir in his gut.

She's a grown woman, Dex. She doesn't need your permission or anyone else's.

Besides, that's how he'd gotten into this mess of a Christmas party.

So he asked a completely unrelated question. "How is Weston getting home?"

She looked at him. "I'm taking him back in a few minutes. Sylvia had asked if he was allowed to see her. Her doctors said yes." She tossed a smile at Sylvia. "And I thought it would be good for her."

Hmm… Dex was one of Sylvia's doctors, and Maura hadn't asked him. Maybe she wanted as little to do with him as possible, which didn't bode well for them working together.

"I wanted…to make…sure…he was…okay." Sylvia's eyes filled with tears that spilled over.

So she did remember what had happened. If she'd been carrying the child out of the center the day she'd been shot… Hell, he didn't even want to think about the fact that they might have had two patients. Or maybe her ex had planned it to be a murder/suicide all along.

"He's just fine, as you can see. The staff is taking great care of him."

He wondered if someone from the center was staying with the boy in their assigned room. Maura had mentioned that a couple of staff members were approved foster parents. If so, he was glad the child's world wasn't going to be upended more than it already was. Another good thing was that Weston was too young to really remember much about his father. Hopefully, the abuse hadn't extended to the child.

"I'm off duty, so I'll go with you to take him back to the women's center. I have something I want to talk to you about, anyway."

Her glance shot his way, the dismay in her eyes unmistakable. "You do?"

"It's nothing major."

Ha! It was pretty major, actually. But he wasn't going to say anything in front of Sylvia, especially since he wasn't sure how Maura was going to take the news. What had started off as a simple class in first aid had morphed into a full-blown hospital-funded publicity event. Hell, he wasn't sure how he felt about it, himself. It seemed like recently he'd been sticking his nose where it didn't belong and getting it singed in the process.

Well, it stopped after this. They had three weeks before Christmas, and then it would be over. As would everything else they did together. Except for maybe teaching a class or two together.

As much as it pained him to admit it, though, in all the dismay over this, there was an element of anticipation. Hadn't he been thinking about how he could give back? Maybe this was the beginning of that. He still planned to apply to Doctors Without Borders, but instead of dwelling on how much he hated winter, he could keep himself busy and do some good in the process.

Sylvia had zoned out and looked like she was falling asleep. He glanced at Maura to see that she'd noticed as well. She stood and laid a hand on the other woman's arm. "Hey, we're going to take Weston back. You need your rest."

"When can I go...?" Sylvia tried to lift herself off the pillow, but failed and fell back, drawing a deep breath. "When can I go back and be with him?"

It would be weeks before she was well enough to get out of the hospital. She had no idea how close she'd come to dying. If they hadn't been able to clamp off that artery when they had...

Her organs were going to need time to recover from the shock. And so was her mind.

"You don't worry about that," Maura said. "You concentrate on getting stronger. You can only do that if you rest."

"Okay." She reached out a hand to Weston.

Dex picked the boy up and carried him over to his mother. She held his hand in hers. "I love you, Wes."

The boy wriggled a little, trying to get to her, but Dex held him tight. The last thing she needed was for him to bounce on her wounds. "We'll bring him back soon."

When he turned around, Maura had the paper Weston had colored on and was looking at the other side of it, her brows puckered. "What's this?"

"Uh…yeah, that's what I wanted to talk to you about. Ready?"

She stared at him for a second before taking Weston's hand and waving it at his mom. "Say bye, honey."

"Bye, baby. See you soon."

Then they were out of the door and heading down the hallway. "I need to get my coat and hat," she said. "And I'm serious. What is this?"

As she got her winter gear on, he explained as best he could.

"Remember me asking you to hold off on giving the center an answer, that the hospital might want to contribute to the educational effort? Well, they do. Only they want to do more. They feel like having a Christmas party will help build goodwill between the hospital and the community, especially after what happened to Sylvia."

"What happened wasn't the hospital's fault." She tucked a strand of hair behind her ear so that it stayed toward the back of her knit cap.

"I know that and you know that, but they think if they use the whole turn-a-tragedy-into-something-good plan, it might turn the hospital into a kind of hero." He shrugged. "And the center might get something good out of it, as well. Like an increase in donations or volunteers. Or maybe job offers for the residents who need them."

She still looked dubious, but at least she didn't look angry. And *dubious* suited her. Her eyebrows were puckered in a way that drew attention to those dark eyes. Eyes that shimmered with compassion and a little something else.

"So you're going to do what? Play jolly old Saint Nick, while passing out presents?"

"Me? No. I'll leave that for someone who believes a little more in the season."

They went outside, and he started toward his car only to have her stop him. "I'll drive. I already have Weston's car seat buckled in." She grinned. "It took quite a while to figure it out. I even had to ask Mr. Google for his help. I'd rather not have to go through that all over again—unless you know how to install it in your car?"

Maura's smile had never failed to take his breath away back when they were dating. It still did. Those pink curving lips pointed at the delicate bones in her cheeks, hollowing them out underneath. In fact, she was a little more slender than she'd been back then. Maybe it was the stress of her divorce, since it had only been a year ago. He was surprised she'd never had children with her husband. Maybe her miscarriage had done something that made that impossible.

Something jabbed his midsection at that thought.

Before most of his family had died in that accident, he'd pictured Maura and himself married with three or four children. Of course that had all changed in an instant and left him wanting no ties at all. Not to a wife. Not to children.

Even his relationship with his mom had been strained over the years, despite him staying in Montana in case she needed something, especially as she hadn't remarried. She'd gathered her friends around her as she'd grieved. Those friends had helped her more than Dex had, which just added to his guilt. He knew he'd been distant and apathetic, but he hadn't been sure how to be anything else back then. That apathy had become a habit that he'd had a hard time tossing aside. And he wasn't sure he wanted to, at this point.

Seeing Sylvia almost lose her own life had just brought home all the reasons for his apathy. If she'd died, her son's life would have changed forever.

Just like Dex's had.

No, it was better when he only had himself to worry about.

Why had he been so insistent on helping Maura hold classes at the women's center?

Because he'd been uneasy with her being there alone—at night. Although he couldn't afford to have her in his life, there was still a part of him that needed to know she shared the same world he did. That he only needed to walk through her department to catch sight of her. Or pick up a phone to hear her voice.

Not that he would call her—it was just the assurance that she was still here. That her heart was still beating in her chest. That she could sigh and smile...and *live.*

It was the whole reason he hadn't gone after her the day of their breakup.

"Okay, your car it is."

They reached it, a little red compact that fit her to a tee. "You sure like the color red, don't you?"

She had a red coat. A red hat. And now a red car.

"I never really thought about it." She glanced down at her coat. "I guess maybe I do."

She opened the door and pulled his seat forward to be able to get Weston into his car seat in back. It was a little more complicated with a two-door, but they managed. When Dex went to slide into the passenger seat, his knees pressed into the dashboard.

She laughed. "Sorry. I don't normally have anyone riding in that seat. I pulled it way forward because of Weston. The handle is on the side."

Tugging on the lever, he pushed the seat back a couple of inches, careful not to crush Weston's legs. He was beginning to think maybe they should have wrestled the boy's car seat into his BMW after all.

"I bet you get great gas mileage in this thing."

One thing he was doing his best not to think about was how this vehicle might crumple if she ever hit anything. Or if anything hit her.

Something in his throat tightened.

"As a matter of fact I do." She tossed her hair, buckling her seat belt. "I'm all about efficiency in every area of my life."

Was that why she'd dumped him all those years ago—because he messed with her sense of efficiency? No, she'd dumped him because he wouldn't—couldn't—give her what she wanted: the security of knowing she was The One for him. She'd done the right thing when he'd hemmed and hawed over an answer.

They dropped Weston off at the center, and Maura gave the director an update in quick, concise phrases. And although her words matched her whole "efficiency" line, there was an undertone of compassion that didn't seem to fit into her self-described box. He liked the juxtaposition of soft crocheted blankets and her cramped fuel-efficient car. It was a complicated mixture. As was everything about Maura.

It was one of the things that had attracted him to her

in the first place. And he was finding it still attracted him. She'd been all about academics in high school, and yet she had this laugh that came straight from her belly and poured over him. A laugh that could still make his body tighten, even today.

She'd challenged him to be a better student back then. She'd taught him some study techniques after class. And seeing the dark hair slide over her cheek as she explained shortcuts that worked for her had made his teenage hormones ramp into overdrive. No other girl had done that for him.

Then or now.

Their first kiss had happened standing beside their creek as the snow drifted down around them. Her lips had been warm and soft, her breath sliding in gentle gusts over his chilled skin. He'd had a hard time pulling away and walking her home.

Hell. The best and worst moments of his life had happened in the snow.

They got back into the car a few minutes later. "So tell me about those papers Weston was drawing on. I thought you were asking for help with classes like the first aid one."

"I was. The hospital wanted that and more, like I told you earlier."

"Well, I could use a coffee…or a drink. So if you can stand being confined to my car for a few more minutes, we can go back to my place and you can tell me exactly what the hospital wants. And I'll tell you whether or not I'm willing to go along with it. If not, I'm still going to do a first-aid class they asked me to do. New Billings Memorial can fire me, if they want, but they can't stop me."

Great, this wasn't quite how he'd envisioned this going, although he hadn't been all that thrilled, either, when he'd walked out of the administrator's office with the paperwork. Paperwork they would both need to sign if this was to happen. And really, without Maura—who the center already knew and trusted—he couldn't see the director letting a bunch of strangers in there, Christmas party or no Christmas party. He couldn't blame them. Especially not after what had happened to Sylvia.

"Coffee sounds good." Actually, a stiff drink sounded better, but he'd take what he could get at this point.

Fifteen minutes later, while Maura made coffee, Dex wandered around her living room. The space was sparse, almost cold, with furniture that looked like it came straight out of one of those nail-it-together-yourself stores. Mostly white and beige, there were no pops of color. No framed artwork on the walls. No books littering the end tables. It all seemed strange to him. Despite being a straight-A student, the Maura he'd once dated had been warm and welcoming…messy and carefree. This new Maura had a place for everything. Maybe she'd always been this way, and he just hadn't recognized it back then. She'd certainly needed to find exactly where she fit in his life. And when he wouldn't help her do that…

Back to the same old tired arguments he'd had after his dad and siblings died. Coming here was probably a mistake on his part. He'd been fine working at the same hospital when their paths rarely crossed. But all of a sudden here they were—having coffee and getting ready to discuss working together on a much deeper level than they did at the hospital. The fact that this was a project neither of them really wanted didn't help matters.

She came into the room carrying a white tray and an equally white coffee carafe. Each new thing made him a little more uneasy. Was this colorless space the place she'd lived with her ex-husband? Had her marriage fit into this same boring mold?

Because there'd been nothing boring about what Dex had shared with her. That fact made him take stock, as well. Surely their breakup had not caused that big a change.

Maybe her husband hadn't been a fan of color. Maybe she'd adapted to make him happy.

Except her crocheted blankets were filled with all kinds of different hues. He hadn't seen a beige or white one in the bunch. And then there was that red coat and hat. Which was the real Maura? The one she gathered around her in the privacy of her home? Or the one he'd once known?

Setting the tray down, she poured their brew into mugs and set one in front of him. "I wasn't sure what you took in yours, so there's sugar and cream."

"Black is fine." He accepted the proffered mug and took a sip. "Thanks."

"So, you want me to ask the director if the hospital can throw a Christmas party?"

He looked at her over the cup and paused as he thought through his answer. "I think it has to come from you. The center trusts you. So do the clients and the administration. Look at Celia and Sylvia. And even Weston."

"So if I say no, the hospital won't ask about throwing one?"

"I don't think they will. And I'm pretty sure the center isn't going to let a bunch of strangers go in there and take over."

She balanced her mug on her knee. "And what do you think of all this? Do you think we should give the hospital what they want?"

"I think we should do what's best for the residents of that center and their children."

"That's what I was afraid you were going to say." She sighed and closed her eyes for a minute. When she opened them, they were warm and met his with a sincerity that took his breath away. A sincerity that made him want to cup her face in his hands and get lost in those dark brown irises. "I think we should have this party, Dex. Not because of the hospital, but because those women and kids deserve it."

Before he could stop himself, he said. "I think they do, too."

"I wish I could take their pain away and make every one of them feel safe and loved."

That was the problem. Sometimes you couldn't, no matter how much you wanted to. "No one can do that for anyone. The best you can hope for is to show you care and point toward resources that can help them cope."

Except how many times had people tried to send him to grief counseling groups only to have him refuse to go, to shrug things off as if they were no big deal?

"I know. I just want to do more."

"Making those blankets is more. Taking Weston to the hospital to visit his mom is more." He smiled. "Having this Christmas party is more."

She tilted her head and regarded him. "I never thought about it like that."

"You've been a good influence on me, believe it or not. And not just when I was a dumb kid. Taking those blankets to the center that day made me take stock of my own life and how little I give back to the world around me." It was true. His thoughts about Doctors Without Borders had crystallized over the past week. He'd even contacted the organization yesterday about getting paperwork to start the process.

After taking one last sip of his coffee, he set down the cup. "So we'll have the party, and it will make me feel like I've given back, if only in a minuscule way."

"It won't be minuscule to those women." She paused for a few seconds. "Or to me."

Or to me.

The words made him look at her. Really look.

Her eyes shone with a warmth and hope that made the breath hiss from his lungs.

Damn, she was the most gorgeous thing he'd ever seen. In this pale room, she was the only thing that was vibrant. Colorful.

Alive.

Her dark hair shimmered against the cream-colored sofa, and her lips were soft and pink and would be so very...

Warm. Just like at the creek all those years ago.

A tingling started in regions best left alone. "I should go."

"Okay." She gave a visible swallow. "If you think you should."

The way she said that…

Hell, he didn't only *think* he should, he *knew* he should. "Unless you think we should do a little more planning."

Maura gripped her coffee mug. "Planning. Yes."

Planning was the last thing on his mind. A thousand memories from long ago sailed through his head, getting caught up in the stormy recesses. Some sweet, some incredibly hot and sexy. They kept spinning through his mind until he could no longer separate one from the other.

Or yesterday from today. It was all twined together in a cacophony that was impossible to mute. And he didn't want to. Maura was part of the fabric that made him who he was today, despite them being no longer together.

He resisted the urge to reach for her, even as he struggled with the need to tell her the truth—that he was headed down a dangerous path, one he couldn't seem to veer away from. Honesty won.

"Maura, I don't want to plan the party."

"You don't?"

"Hell, I know we should. I know that's what I came here for. But I can't stop thinking about…you."

Her cup went onto the tray, and she inched closer, her fingers going to his cheek and trailing down the side of his face. Her eyes closed as if trying to capture the feel and post it to memory, just as he had. "That's funny, because I was just thinking about you."

He leaned forward and pressed his forehead to hers. "You were supposed to make me listen to reason."

She laughed. "Right now, I can't think of a single reasonable thing to say."

His hand slid beneath her hair and cupped her nape, and he leaned back to look at her. And yep, the feeling was still there, getting stronger by the second. So he took one long, deep breath before plunging beneath the water and putting his lips to hers.

CHAPTER FIVE

How had this happened?

One minute they were talking about helping the women and kids at the crisis center and the next he was kissing her.

And not just any kiss. It was hot and deep and rivaled anything they'd done in the past. And some of those meetings of the lips had made her go weak in the knees at the time.

She was finding out they still did.

To be honest, she'd wanted this since he'd stopped and helped her the day she'd had the flat tire, and when he'd gone with her to deliver the afghans. She'd seen something in his face that said he understood what she was trying to do for those women. The knowledge had made a familiar yearning come roaring back down the road, heading straight toward her. She'd avoided him for so long, and maybe it had been the wrong thing to do. Maybe this kiss was part of that elusive thing called closure.

His lips moved, dragging her attention back to the luscious things he was doing to her mouth. To hell with closure. She could worry about that later. Right now, all she wanted was…this.

Her tongue edged forward, nudging at the entrance to his mouth, and he opened and captured it with a suddenness that took her breath away, using gentle suction to pull her inside.

He was hot, with an intensity that was chipping away at the edges of her self-control, making her want a whole lot more than what he was giving. She twisted sideways in an attempt to get closer, her hands sliding over his shoulders and gripping tight.

Don't stop, Dex. Please, God, don't stop.

He didn't.

Half-dragging her over his lap, he set her so she was straddling him, and the quick change from a kiss that was anything but chaste to full-on contact sent her mind spinning. "God, Dex…"

His fingers tunneled into her hair as he held her against his lips. "I love hearing you say that."

One hand went to her butt, hauling her against him until she felt exactly what she was doing to him…what he was doing to her. She wanted him. Wanted to rip off his clothes and feel him thrust home, like he'd done so many times before.

This position had always been one of their favorites. How could she have forgotten?

In his car. By the creek. In his bed. He loved her on top of him, loved gripping her hips and guiding her as she rode him to completion. Then the aftermath of those times had been…

So sweet. So…them. Their own secret world where nothing else intruded.

She needed that again. Wanted it.

In a split second, she made a decision. She nipped his lip before reaching down and grabbing the hem of his polo shirt, hauling it up and over his head. There was no hesitation as he helped her. He leaned back and watched her unbutton her own shirt, taking it from her and tossing it to the side.

Warm hands skated up her belly, making her muscles ripple as they went before cupping her breasts, his thumbs finding her nipples under the fabric of her bra with laser accuracy.

It was just like before. Just like she knew it would be.

"Are you sure, Maura? Tell me now, if not."

"Ahh…yes. I'm sure." She let her body answer any other questions as she arched into him, relishing it when one hand reached behind her back for the clasp and undid it. It soon joined the other pieces of discarded clothing. Then, with one palm against her bare back, he drew her forward until his mouth found her, suckling and nipping at her sensitized flesh. A flame of need shot straight to her center, and she pressed tighter against him in an effort to keep it at bay. It didn't work. And the pressure inside of her was beginning to build in a familiar way.

No, not yet. Please not yet.

"Hell, Maura. I need to get those pants off you. But I don't. Want. You. To. Move." Each word was punctuated with another pull on her nipple.

Leaning her face against his neck, she gave a pained laugh. "I don't want to move either, especially when you're doing that. But here goes."

She hauled herself off his lap and, with hands that

shook, she shed her slacks, hesitating at her underwear before shoving them down her legs. He was busy doing the same, retrieving something from the pocket of his khakis as he went.

A condom.

The shot of regret came out of nowhere, piercing her heart and causing a burst of pain before she beat it back. It wouldn't happen again. It couldn't. He was making sure of it.

The fact that she hadn't given a thought to protection, even after what had happened in the past, was a testament to how much this man disrupted her thought processes.

But right now, she needed him. Needed to forget the horror that had happened at the women's center with Sylvia. Tragedy could strike anyone anywhere. So why not live in this moment and just let herself feel. Experience. *Live.*

When Dex held his arms out to her, she went willingly—gladly—settling back on his lap and closing her eyes at the utter ecstasy that came with feeling him again, skin to skin. "I'd almost forgotten…"

She couldn't finish the sentence, but it was true. She'd forgotten so much, and yet the second she was with him, it all came rushing back.

"I know."

Those two words were profound, and she knew he wasn't saying that he knew she'd forgotten, but that he too had just experienced the very same thing.

Her first time with Gabe hadn't been like this…an overwhelming connection of one person to another. She'd assumed it was because there were no "firsts" like that "first" first. She was wrong. Being with Dex, after so many years had passed, made it happen all over again. And she remembered every second of her first time with him.

They stayed like that for a minute or two before Dex's lips gently touched hers, and soon it was washing over her again. The need. The longing. The craving for a release that only he could give.

She wanted him inside. Now.

Taking the packet from beside his thigh, she ripped it open and slid back far enough to expose him, to slide the condom down him with a slow, smooth stroke that had him groaning.

Her lips curved. Dex had always been a vocal lover, holding nothing back. And she'd loved it. Had missed it.

Not letting go of him, she raised her hips and lowered herself onto him. His flesh was hot, stretching her in ways that made her weak. Her breath exited with a hum that changed to something that defied words. Or logic. Something that wiped away thoughts of the women's center, the hospital…and even their own past.

The only thing that mattered was what was right in front of her.

His fingers wrapped around her hips as she found a rhythm and an angle that was so very perfect. Her body remembered. Sought out what she knew was there.

Each time she lowered onto him, it sent shock waves through her. Those waves grew with each thrust, the intensity making her cup his face and kiss him.

Tongues tangled. Teeth found hidden nerve endings. Need ratcheted everything to a new level of ecstasy.

He urged her to move faster, take him deeper, which

had her matching him thrust for thrust until her whole world shifted with a suddenness that took her breath away. Something ignited deep inside of her, the spark becoming a flame that devoured everything in its path.

It grew hotter. Brighter. Then exploded in a fury of want and need that swallowed her whole. He joined her almost immediately, muttering words against her skin that her brain couldn't process—didn't want to process.

Then it was over. She lowered herself onto him one last time as the final tiny spasms worked their way out of her system. Breathing heavily, she closed her eyes and leaned against him, waiting for her senses to return. For the sweet aftermath to take over, like it had in the past.

And all too soon, it did. But it wasn't the same, wasn't as sweet as she remembered. Because *they* weren't the same. They were no longer that carefree couple who could love each other without reserve.

They were…strangers.

She swallowed as cold reality of that word washed over her. She'd just had sex with a man she had once loved. A man who hadn't been able to commit to her—who hadn't *wanted* to commit to her. Who'd left her brokenhearted, carrying a child she hadn't been able to tell him about. All because she didn't want him staying for any reasons other than love.

Why? Why now?

Maybe it was muscle memory. Maybe an old neural pathway she hadn't been able to entirely obliterate.

Whatever it was, it wasn't happening again.

Climbing off his lap as gracefully as she could manage, she began gathering her clothes, yanking them on with a fury that was aimed squarely at herself.

A hand wrapped around her wrist, stopping her just as she'd shrugged into her bra. "Hey. Stop for a minute. Are you okay?"

"Just peachy, Dex. Can't you tell?" Realizing the words were said with a bitterness she hadn't been able to disguise, she glanced over at him. "This was a mistake, and you know it."

"Yes. And I'm sorry. I don't know what got into me."

It was unfair of her to let him take the brunt of her anger. "Hell, it wasn't you. It was me, you…both of us."

She searched around for something more to say. "It just can't happen again. I've had two failed relationships now, and this—" she motioned at the rest of their clothes "—is something I just can't handle right now."

"I understand." He turned her toward him, tipping up her chin. "And it won't happen again. I promise."

The solemnity of those words made tears prick behind her eyes. What had she been hoping for? That he would say he'd been wrong all those years ago? That he'd never stopped loving her?

She had no idea. But as great as the sex was, there was an ache gnawing at her insides that hadn't been touched by what they'd just done.

The tears grew when his hands went behind her and gently redid the clasp on her bra. "What can I do to make this right?"

She shrugged, not meeting his eyes. "There's nothing to make right, because what just happened means nothing. Changes nothing. And I don't want it to. I just want us to go back to whatever professional relationship we had before this, and to pretend it never happened."

"Pretend." He said the word in a musing tone as if trying to figure out what it meant.

And she was right. It would all be pretend. Because as much as she might wish otherwise, nothing was going to change what had happened in this room. Every time she sat on her sofa, she would picture him under her, moving inside of her. Every. Damn. Time.

She didn't know what she was going to do about that, but she'd better figure it out. And soon. Because the last thing Maura needed was to let a man who'd once wrought devastation in her heart slide past her defenses all over again.

She was going to do exactly what she'd said she was going to do: pretend. And hope to hell that if she did it often enough and for long enough, her heart would eventually believe it to be true.

Dex leaned over his sink and gave himself a long, hard look. He'd been selfish and careless…and wrong.

Two days later he was still beating himself up over what had happened at Maura's place. He never should have gone to her house to discuss the Christmas party. They should have done it at the hospital. In a coffee shop. At the zoo. Anyplace but somewhere private. Because he knew himself well enough to know that as much as he might deny it, he'd never gotten over Maura. Yesterday had proved that beyond a shadow of a doubt.

He also knew that he wasn't in a place for that to change anything. He was still the same miserable, empty guy he had been the day Maura had broken things off.

He should tell the administration that he couldn't do the Christmas party, to find someone else. But wouldn't that be just as selfish as sleeping with her? He was an adult. He could work with her. She'd said as much, that she wanted to go back to their professional relationship and forget what had happened.

No, she hadn't used the word *forget*. She'd used the word *pretend*. There was a huge difference between the two. He just wasn't sure why that difference mattered so much.

Maybe because he didn't want to forget. Oh, he could pretend along with the best of them. But forget? That was in a different category entirely.

It would have been so much easier if Maura was still married.

Really? Somehow, he doubted that. Oh, he might have managed not to have sex with her two days ago, but then again, he probably wouldn't have wound up in her house, like an idiot.

He knew absolutely that Maura wouldn't have made that offer if she wasn't damned sure it was safe. He'd known better, and he'd gone anyway. But there'd been that knife edge of adrenaline urging him on, telling him he could resist his own urges. Like those worst-ideas-in-the-world videos, it had backfired spectacularly.

And he'd ended up hurting her. Again.

She'd never said it outright, but it had been there in her eyes. In the frantic way she'd grabbed her clothes. In the way she'd said, *I can't do this again*.

Everything pointed to the fact that he was the only one who'd exited that room unscathed.

Really? He wouldn't quite characterize it that way.

And today they had a meeting with Colleen Winters from the Nadia Ram Crisis Center for Mothers about what the hospital was offering to do in a little under three weeks.

Worse, Sylvia was due to be discharged today, and when he'd spoken to the director on the phone, he'd offered to drive her back, since the center was short staffed today.

So were his brain cells, which were barely capable of putting two and two together without coming up with some outrageous number combinations.

He turned away from the mirror and finished getting dressed. He hadn't talked to Maura except in passing since that day at her place. But the hospital's administrative director said he'd spoken with her, and she'd freed up her schedule to go with him to talk to the center's director. But she hadn't called or texted to let him know she was on board. Maybe she was leaving it up to him.

Which meant he needed to do so—and quick, since the meeting with Colleen was today.

Wrapping a towel around his waist, he retrieved his cell phone and punched her number into it.

He could do this.

He waited through two, three, four rings and then her voice mail picked up. Great. She didn't want to talk to him. "Just checking in about our meeting today…"

Even as he was trying to lay out his explanation, his phone started buzzing in his hand. She was calling him back. He took a quick breath before clicking to accept the call, then put the phone to his ear. "Sorry, I was just leaving you a message."

"It's okay, I was getting ready for work."

He glanced down at himself. Was she in the same state of undress that he was? An image shot through his brain before he could stop it. He blinked it away. It didn't matter, and he certainly wasn't going to ask.

"I was checking on our meeting at the center?"

"Oh. Yes."

Was she going to tell him that she wasn't going to participate, not even to teach the first aid class? A pool of acid formed in his stomach and churned up his esophagus. If that was the case, he was going to withdraw so that she could carry on without him. It wasn't right for her to have to sit out on something that meant so much to her.

"You're still interested in being a part, aren't you?"

"Of course, why wouldn't I be?" Her words were stilted—overly formal.

We can just pretend it never happened.

She was taking those words and making them true. Well, two could play that game. "No reason. I thought we could ride over together, since we're supposed to take Sylvia back to the center."

"I can drive, if you'd like."

The image of her tiny vehicle with its cramped quarters came back to mind. He'd be close to her. Way too close. "How about if we take my car this time, since we took yours the last time?"

A slight pause ensued. "Of course. When would you like to meet?"

He hated how impersonal those words were, even

though he knew he was the cause of it. "How about if I check to see what time Sylvia is going to be discharged this afternoon and let you know?"

"Three o'clock."

"Sorry?"

"I've already checked with the hospital and they said her discharge time is three."

So had she decided to go over without him? Maybe his call had tossed a monkey wrench into her plans. "Would you rather I not be there today, Maura?"

A noise he thought might be a sigh came through the line. "I'm sorry, Dex. This is just a little awkward. But it'll be okay. I think Sylvia would like you to be a part, since you had a hand in saving her life."

"Not really."

"Um… You held her artery in your hand. Literally. So please don't say that to her. She sees you as an example of what a man should be like. Don't take that away from her. She's grateful—let her show it in whatever way she can."

It was ironic that a victim of domestic violence would think he was a good example of what a man should be. Especially since he was struggling with his image of himself this morning.

"Okay, we'll meet in Sylvia's room at around three, then? Or should we meet a half hour before that to plan our approach for the center?" Maura said.

"That works for me, since you know them a lot better than I do. How about in the waiting room?" A part of him was relieved that she was still okay with working with him on the Christmas party, even though it probably wasn't very smart of him. Well, he could just suck it up and deal with it. It was not quite three weeks of his life. Surely he could manage that.

Hadn't he already given himself this same lecture once before? It hadn't done him much good last time. What made him think this time would be any different?

Because he now knew what could happen if he was caught off guard, and he intended to make sure that never happened again.

From now on, he would be on high alert and spot trouble before it headed his way.

Easier said than done since, to his psyche, Maura was the epitome of trouble.

"Okay, see you there."

What he did over the next couple of weeks would say a lot about whether or not Sylvia's view of him was true. Or whether she was completely off base. If that was the case, the best thing he could do was pretend to be something he couldn't be in real life.

Two thirty came a lot quicker than he'd thought it would. And by the time he got to the waiting room, Maura was already there.

"Hey."

"Hi."

His teeth ground against themselves. Not because of the awkwardness, but because his mind was replaying every second they'd spent on that sofa. And that was not acceptable.

Lowering himself onto the seat across from hers, he unfolded the paperwork from the hospital, Weston's scribbling staring up at him. Okay. This was why he was here. To talk about Weston, Sylvia and the women at that shelter.

"So…thoughts? Do you think they'll go for letting the hospital take part in the Christmas celebration?"

"I think so. I made a quick call to Colleen and asked if she'd be open to funding or help to give the residents a good Christmas. She seemed relieved. Said that she had actually been worried about it this year. It seems with the fires in California this year, most people's thoughts are on that—and rightly so—but funding sources have dried up."

He hadn't thought about that, although the reports had been all over the news. "Maybe the hospital's offer came at a good time, then."

"I think maybe it did. I think we should make this something fun. Not formal like a gala or prom with fancy dresses."

He smiled. "No turquoise dresses?"

"Don't remind me." She laughed. "That dress was a disaster."

So she did remember. "At the time I was pretty happy that it was a bit long. You kept tripping and I had to keep catching you."

"I didn't make a very good impression."

Yes, she had. She'd made the best one possible. Only going down these old pathways probably wasn't going to help either one of them. "It actually helped settle my nerves."

"Nerves? You were always so sure of yourself."

Not when it came to her. Not then, and certainly not now.

"Believe me, I get nervous. I'm a little on edge about this meeting, actually."

"Don't be. Colleen is great."

The subject turned back to the matter at hand, and if anything, Maura's tone held a hint of excitement as she gave some insight into the center and the director who headed it up. "If she agrees, then I can guarantee the residents will, as well. They all love and respect her."

"So you said you wanted the party to be fun. Any ideas on that?"

"I do, but let's feel her out before jumping into that part. Especially since it might be a little outside of the normal Christmas box."

He thought about her monochromatic living room and how her current life seemed to be about keeping everything inside of the box. "Christmas boxes are meant to be opened, though, aren't they?"

"You could be on to something there."

He was definitely curious now. What did outside of the box look like to this new Maura? "Sure you can't give me a hint?"

Her grin made her nose crinkle in an old, familiar way. He forced himself to glance away before it affected him in ways that were just as familiar.

"Let's wait and see how the meeting goes before we start doing any real planning."

Start doing any real planning. So she was actually thinking of this as being a team effort. One that included him.

The little sliver of anticipation he'd had when he'd reached the waiting room ramped up to something a whole lot more. Something that he should be running away from as fast as his legs could carry him. Instead, he leaned forward. "I can't wait to hear all about it."

* * *

It had been right to use Dex's car. It had a lot more space for Sylvia, who at a little over a week out of surgery was still sore and weak. But she was anxious to get back to her son. They helped her out of the wheelchair and into the back seat of the car. Thankfully, the reporters had cleared out the day after the shooting had happened. For that Maura was grateful. The last thing Sylvia needed was to face them or have someone stick a microphone in her face.

"Are you okay?" she asked, knowing immediately that it was a stupid question. Sylvia had not only left an abusive husband, that same husband she'd once loved had then shot and almost killed her before turning the gun on himself. Nothing would erase that.

Maura's problems with Dex seemed ludicrous compared to what the other woman had gone through. And during their impromptu meeting at the hospital, she realized she'd probably been too hard on both of them after they'd had sex. But the aftermath of being intimate with him again had hit her with such force that panic had overwhelmed her and she'd taken that panic out on him.

Unfairly.

"I'm okay. I'll be glad to see Weston."

"You need to make sure you don't do too much too soon. You're still healing. He can't jump on you."

"I know. The lady from the center who's been taking care of him will still help with him. It's the only way the hospital would let me go without sending me to a skilled nursing facility."

It might not have been a bad idea for her to have gone

to one for a few weeks, but Sylvia had been adamant about going back to the shelter. And who could blame her? Christmas was rapidly approaching, and she had a young child to think about.

Maura paused before closing the door. "What's Weston's favorite animal?"

Sylvia chuckled before giving a quick grimace of pain. "A giraffe of all things. His room back..." Her voice fell to a whisper. "His room in the house we lived at was decorated with them. He had to leave his favorite one behind when we left."

Maura's heart ached for both of them. "Will you go back there?"

"No. The house was already in foreclosure. Things got a whole lot worse once Clyde got the papers in the mail."

Time to turn Sylvia's thoughts toward the future. "Well, that's all behind you now. You can finally finish that nursing degree you started."

"Yes, that's what I want to do. I want to make a better life for my boy."

"For yourself, as well. And you already are." Maura shut the door and moved around to the front seat. She'd tried to get Sylvia to sit there, but she'd refused, and Dex thought maybe sitting sideways would help take some of the pressure off her healing wounds. He'd been right.

At least about that.

She slid into the passenger seat and glanced over at Dex, who nodded at her. "I bet the hospital has some educational grant programs we can look into."

The words were meant for Sylvia, but they warmed Maura's heart. He was a good man. So many times she'd looked at the past and wished things had been different. That his dad and siblings were still alive and life had gone the way they'd planned. She had no idea what it was like losing a twin, let alone losing that twin along with a younger sister and a father, but Dex had changed after that.

Would their baby have looked like him?

She'd argued with herself repeatedly that losing the child had been for the best. But she never quite believed it. She was pretty sure Sylvia was glad she'd had Weston, despite the circumstances. That he was the one bright spot in a tragic situation. Maura's baby could have been that bright spot. The one good thing that would have come out of their failed relationship.

Except Dex would have known. And what had been a sad moment in her life would have become a sad—and complicated—moment that would have linked the two of them for the rest of her life.

No, better that it ended the way it did.

And sex with him?

Just a speed bump in the road that made up her life. A warning not to let herself race ahead when she needed to slow down and take stock of where she was.

Unfortunately, she'd hit that bump at full speed and had become airborne for several exhilarating minutes. Still, what goes up must come down, and the shock of that landing was still reverberating through her She was pretty sure she might have left a piece or two of herself behind in the process.

But she wasn't about to go back and look for them.

Like Sylvia, she needed to look to the future, and

that future did not include a certain hunky trauma surgeon no matter how much she might wish otherwise.

And she didn't wish it. She had a full, satisfying life with her job and crocheting blankets for the center.

She blinked. Wow, when she put it like that, it made her sound kind of sad and lonely, like she had no social life at all.

She didn't. Not really. Not since her divorce, which had left her wary of dating…and relationships in general. She'd invited two men into her life, neither of which had been willing to stick around for her. One of those men was in this car.

"Penny for your thoughts."

"Ha! They're not worth that much." Even if Sylvia wasn't in the car, there was no way she was going to admit she'd been thinking about him.

"I doubt that, but I won't press."

She glanced at him, and despite just having "known" him quite thoroughly, the sight of him still stirred up waters that were best left undisturbed. She doubted that would ever change. She was attracted to him. Probably always would be.

There she went again, letting her thoughts wander all over him.

That doesn't have sexual overtones at all, Maura.

She looked away from him, rolling her eyes and forcing them to stay on the road in front of them.

And there was the center. Just in time.

A woman stood at the front window holding a child. Probably Weston, although she couldn't tell with the glare of the sun. Dex pulled around back and quickly found a parking place.

He glanced back at Sylvia. "Do they have a wheel-chair inside?"

"I can walk. I might just be a little slower than most folks."

"You can take all the time you need."

Maura hoped he was including her in that sentence. Because right now she was a little slower than most folks, too. Only hers had nothing to do with her physical health and everything to do with her emotional health.

They managed to get out of the car and, with Sylvia in between them, they slowly made their way up the front walk. By the time they reached the door the woman was out of breath.

"Are you sure you're up to this?"

"Yes. I'll be fine. I can't heal if I'm worried about my son."

She had a point. Maybe Weston would be the healing tonic Sylvia needed—the hope for that future Maura had mentioned.

"I'll get the door." Maura stepped forward and pulled it open so they could go through. She heard the squeal of a child behind her.

"Mommy! Mommy!" She turned in time to see the woman who was holding Weston let him lean forward to hug Sylvia around the neck.

"Easy," the helper said. "Remember, Mommy has some ouchies."

"Ouchie, Mommy?" Weston seemed to look his mother over, searching for these mysterious boo-boos.

"Yes, Mommy has a couple of ouchies." She wrapped her fingers around her son's chin and drew him closer so she could give him a kiss.

He held out a crumpled paper. "For you."

"Thank you, baby." She glanced at the paper. "What did you draw?"

He pointed at one of the scribbled blobs and then the other. "Daddy and Mommy."

Sylvia's hand immediately covered her mouth and tears filled her eyes. "Oh, God, what have I done?"

Maura moved close to her and touched her hand. "What you have done is the right thing for your son. And you."

"Are you sure?" Her unsteady voice was a testament to the pain going through her.

"Absolutely. It was the only thing you could have done. *He* chose this. Not you. Remember that."

Sylvia took a deep breath and nodded, looking back at her son. "Thank you. I love the picture."

The woman holding Weston said, "Let's go back to your room and get you settled. I'll stay there for a while, and then I'll take Weston somewhere to play."

"Thank you."

With that the trio were gone, leaving Maura with Dex. She racked her brain for something to say that wouldn't seem flip after what had just happened and came up empty.

Just then Colleen Winters came out to save the day. "Hi." She shook Dex's hand and gave Maura a quick hug. "I'm so glad you've agreed to teach the first aid class, and I'm really excited to hear what the hospital has planned for our moms."

And just like that, the subject moved to things that had nothing to do with broken hearts or failed relationships. If Maura was very lucky, it would stay that way.

CHAPTER SIX

MAURA WAS TALKING to Matt Foster, the same paramedic he'd seen hanging around the ER several times. Okay… hanging around was probably not the right word for it, since it was normally in conjunction with bringing patients in. And EMTs, by virtue of their profession, often got to know the emergency room crews at the hospitals they normally went to.

This wasn't the first time he'd seen the man conversing with Maura, although that meant nothing. But there was a glimpse of something in the guy's eyes that he recognized. Because he'd once had that very same look when he talked to Maura.

Well, she deserved to be happy. And if Matt did that for her…

She had sex with you, Dex.

Sex they'd both agreed meant nothing. Nothing at all.

If anything, he should be glad, because it meant she wasn't placing her hopes on something that had meant… nothing. And hell if he wasn't suddenly throwing that word around as if he could convince himself of that very thing.

He didn't have to convince himself. It was true.

He took a few steps closer and cleared his throat. Matt looked up first and immediately stopped leaning against the nurse's desk, giving Dex a friendly smile.

But not nearly as friendly as the one he'd given Maura a minute or two ago.

Her head came up a second later, albeit with what seemed like a lot more reluctance.

She'd known it was him and wasn't nearly as glad to see him as she'd been to see the EMT. Damn.

Her smile disappeared, and she suddenly seemed unsure of herself. He hated that. Hated that his presence took away the happy demeanor she'd had a moment ago and replaced it with a wariness that was for him alone. "Hi, Dex. Did we have another meeting planned for today?"

"No, but I thought I'd come down and see if you were free." He didn't say what he'd hoped she was free to do, and as if Matt suddenly realized what was going on, he gave a quick wave. "See you later, Maura?"

"Of course." She flashed him a smile that wasn't real this time, waiting until he left before turning her attention back to Dex.

"What's going on?"

"Just thought I'd check in about the party and what your thoughts were now that we've gotten the center's approval."

"My thoughts about…?"

Okay, so he'd just been headed in to work and hadn't really come here to look for her. Matt's presence had changed his mind.

And that made him angry. At himself.

"About gifts and decorations. You told me you had

some ideas but wanted to wait until after the meeting with Colleen to tell me about them."

"Oh, okay. *Those* thoughts." Her muscles seemed to relax. "Well, as you heard, Weston like giraffes. I'd like to see what each of the kids like and get them something geared toward that. Plus a couple of extra things for kids that might arrive over the holidays. And as far as decorations, maybe just the standard. The center puts up a tree, and they normally have a modest party where they sing Christmas carols and have refreshments. What I was thinking was that a traditional party could turn maudlin if we're not careful. I'd like to shift it over a bit so they can forget their problems, if only for a night."

She glanced up at him. "I know this might sound corny, but what if we turned Christmas into a Christmas Hoedown, complete with square dancing and the like. The women could dance with their kids or with each other."

"You know how to square-dance?"

"Well, not so much square dancing, but I've line danced before. How hard could it be?"

How hard, indeed. But he liked the sound of it. It would be hard to dwell on whatever hard situation you were facing if you were kept too busy to think about it. He could imagine a lot of laughter as people tried to navigate the directions given by the guy calling out dance instructions.

"I like it. I think I know where we can get some bales of straw, though I have no idea who to contact about arranging a square dance."

Like magic, Maura produced a pamphlet from a deep pocket in her sweater and held it out to him.

"Square Dancers R Us." He looked up with a laugh. "Are you kidding me?"

"Nope. Everything you ever wanted to know about square dancing. And a few things you didn't."

"So you really did have an idea up your sleeve. The hospital administration put the right person in charge of this, I'll give them that."

Up went her brows. "I thought *you* were in charge."

And just like that, the mood between them switched from the heavy cloudiness of the last week to a much brighter, sunnier day.

"Of a hoedown? Not my forte."

"Mine, either, but it'll be fun, don't you think? And this way the ladies won't just sit around sharing war stories, not that I think the center's parties were anything less than warm and caring. But sometimes that can get cloying, if overdone. Can bring back memories that are best left in the past."

Like memories of them? Together?

Not the time, Dex.

"You're right. I think a hoedown is perfect, and with a place like this—" he waved the pamphlet "—what could go wrong?"

"My thoughts exactly. I told them I'd need to talk to you first, but they actually offered to come talk to us. Together."

"Here at the hospital?" He hoped so. Or at the center. Or anywhere else except her house. Because he knew if they went there it would happen again, despite his repeated lectures to himself. One look at that sofa and the memories would doom him to a Groundhog Day–type scenario that repeated again and again and again.

And while having sex with her over and over and over might seem like a dream come true, with it came the bad stuff. Consequences that weren't nearly as fun as what led up to them.

"Yes. I asked the hospital administrator if we could use one of the conference rooms, and he said yes."

About a hundred muscles relaxed at once. "Great. When is this meeting?"

"I told them I'd need to check with you about your schedule. Any idea when you'll be free?"

He thought for a minute. "I have surgery every day except for weekends and evenings. How about you?"

"I have this Saturday free, but that doesn't give us much time to pull it all together."

"How about this? If the company doesn't have a date before Christmas free, we can still decorate with straw bales and do a country-and-western-themed event."

"Can you be our caller?"

"Um…no. My knowledge of square dancing is *Swing your partner and promenade*. Beyond that I'm pretty much clueless."

"Oh, really?" She grinned and flipped a strand of hair backward. Before he could stop it, the image of those dark wavy locks tumbling across her naked back came screaming through his head. His mouth went dry as the events of that night swirled around him. His body took that as an invitation to start preparations. In quick order.

Dammit. He needed to knock this off before she realized exactly what his brain was working on. And it had nothing to do with Christmas parties or square dances. "So Saturday? Will they meet with us on a weekend?"

"Let me check and see—while the ER is quiet."

She held her hand out. It took a second to realize that she wasn't asking him to hold her hand. She just wanted the pamphlet. He gave it to her.

Glancing at the front of it, she took her phone out of her pocket and dialed. She waited for a second, then started talking. "So the other member of the committee can meet on Saturday. Would that work?"

Of course she didn't ask him if he had plans for this Saturday, but since he hadn't prefaced his days off with any activities, she couldn't be blamed for assuming.

"Eight o'clock?" She glanced at him, seeking his thought. When he nodded, she told whoever was on the other end of the line that that would work. "The conference room is on the third floor at the very end of the hallway. It's conference room one."

She paused and then said, "Great, see you then." Then she ended the call.

"Are you sure that time is okay with you?"

"Yep, or I would have said something."

She bit her lip. "Well, okay. Thanks then."

He couldn't stand it any longer. "Hey, thanks for doing this with me. I'm sure it's awkward after…that night. But thanks for not backing out. I think your idea will be a lot of fun and will mean a lot to the residents."

"I hope so. And I could say the same thing about you. I know this can't be easy. But it was a fluke. A remnant of the past that caught up with us." She tilted her head. "I've thought a lot about what happened. I don't think either of us got the closure we might have needed. I know I didn't. So maybe that's what part of it was all about. Getting closure."

Closure. That had an air of finality he didn't like. But what could he say? *Screw the closure and let's go into conference room one where we can have a meeting of our own? Just the two of us?*

Not hardly. And he did his best not to revisit the past any more than he had to. That led only to pain, whether the past was related to his family or to Maura. It helped nothing. And it made life harder.

He'd proved that on her couch.

"Maybe you're right," he said. "The past is the past. Sometimes you just have to make sure it stays there."

Her head snapped back, and she blinked a couple of times before responding. "Yes. You're right. It's up to us to make sure that happens. If you're worried about me, don't be. I have no intention of sliding back there for another visit. What's done is done. Thank you for reminding me of that."

Hell, he hadn't been trying to remind *her* of anything. He'd been trying to remind himself. He seemed to have screwed that up somehow, and he didn't know how to right it or if he even should.

So he did the one thing he seemed to be good at. He finished off the conversation as quickly as he could and said goodbye, strolling down the hallway without a single glance behind him. Once inside the safety of the elevator, he looked at the ceiling and shook his head.

"Way to go, Dex. Yet another witty rejoinder tumbles off the cliff."

All he knew was that this was the last time he was going to chase a man away from Maura Findley. And that's what it had been. He'd seen Matt talking to her and had barged over there like some jealous husband.

What had it gotten him? A scheduled meeting and being told by that same woman that sex with him was her way of slamming the book shut on him.

The only problem was that he wasn't sure he liked it being closed.

They ended up changing the meeting place. After talking to the Square Dancers R Us people, it dawned on Maura that she was leaving the most important people out of this particular conversation: the women at the shelter. They, more than anyone, deserved to have a say in what kind of party they wanted. So an hour before the square dance people were supposed to come, Maura and Dex were in the cafeteria area of the center, meeting with the thirteen women who were housed there, along with their kids, who played in a corner or were held on their mothers' laps. Dex had asked her to take the lead, so she stood in front of them, laid out what they had done so far and asked for the consensus.

"I really like it." Sylvia spoke up. "I've never square-danced before, but it would be fun to learn. Although I might not be as agile as I normally would be."

Her throat tightened. Sylvia was still healing from her ordeal.

"It's not about being agile or perfect. It's about being able to laugh and have fun with people who have been in similar circumstances."

Was that what she and Dex were? People who had shared similar circumstances?

It wasn't quite the same thing. And not everything about her and Dex's relationship had been bad. Some of it had been sweet and good…and perfect. Even their time on her couch?

Well, that didn't count, because they weren't in a relationship anymore.

Several more women spoke up, and all of them were in favor of the hoedown. "The kids would like it, too. I wonder what those fake bulls cost? The kind that twist and turn and you fall off. I bet the kids would love that."

"That's a great idea." Maura scribbled the idea in the notebook she'd brought with her. The hospital had pretty much given them carte blanche as far as costs went, so a bucking bull probably wouldn't break the bank. She glanced around the room. It wasn't huge, but put some tables up front with a Christmas meal, which would be served buffet style, and line the walls with straw bales for people to sit on and eat or watch the square dancers in the middle, and it would be fairly simple to transform this place into something out of the ordinary. Especially with a fake rodeo bull for the kids to climb on and try to ride.

Dex was sitting two rows back on the end, watching her. There was something in his eye that made her go warm all over. Hopefully, her face wasn't beet red in response. But this was turning out to be a lot of fun. If someone had told her a year ago, she'd be planning a square dance with her high school sweetheart she'd have said they were crazy. And maybe she was the crazy one for letting herself get roped into this. Still, it didn't feel crazy. At least not right now.

She'd thought that sex with him was a bad thing, that it had shown her to be weak. But maybe not. Maybe this could be a whole new start for them. Not as boyfriend and girlfriend, instead as friends. The place they'd been many, many years ago, before their first kiss in the snow.

She liked that. Liked the idea that they didn't have to be mortal enemies or avoid speaking to each other. Maybe there was a happy medium.

"Dex, do you have any thoughts you want to share?"

He leaned back in his seat. "That I want to share? I don't think anyone wants to hear those." He glanced at his watch. "I think the event planners are due here in a few minutes. Maybe we can break for refreshments."

They'd set up some cookies and juice. Maura was relieved that they hadn't rolled their eyes at the thought of a hoedown. Instead, she'd caught glimpses of excitement in their eyes. And for a group of women who didn't have a lot to get excited about, she was thrilled that the hospital was providing this for them.

While the women took their kids to the table to get snacks, Dex came over to her and bumped her shoulder. "Good job."

"I think they're happy about it, don't you?"

"I do." He gave her a smile. "The only thing I'm worried about is finding a mechanical bull."

She laughed. "I know, right? But I really want to find something, if possible."

"How about if I work on that?"

"Seriously?" She laughed. "Are you going to try them out to find the best one?"

"Can you see me on a bull?" His widening grin made her shiver. It had been so long since they'd been able to joke back and forth like this. It felt good. A little too good.

"I'm picturing it right now, but I'd need to see a video to be sure."

"That will never happen."

"You know what they say about never, don't you?" She tilted her head to look at him. This was one man who was easy on the eye, which was probably why she found herself staring at him more than she liked.

"I'm probably better off not knowing."

"Well, I'll take you up on finding the bull, if you're serious about looking for one."

"I'll do it."

Sylvia came over, holding Weston's hand, and said to Maura, "I just wanted to say thanks again for all you did for me." She glanced around the room. "And for all of us."

"It's really the hospital that's doing it."

She gave Maura a look. "None of this would have happened without you."

"Well, Dex is the one who presented a proposal for something, and the hospital offered to fund a party. So none of it would have happened without him."

"Well, thanks to both of you. This is going to mean so much to our kids. And us." She put a hand on her son's head. "It's been really hard with everything that's happened. I feel so terrible. If someone other than me would have walked out of the center at that exact time, he could have hurt or killed someone else."

"That's not on you, Sylvia. It's on him. Have you talked to someone about it?" Survivor's guilt was a very real thing.

"We have a counselor here, so yes. We've talked. And it's helped a lot."

She saw a sudden flash of fear appear in Sylvia's eyes, and she drew Weston close to her side. Maura looked out the window in time to see two men getting out of a white van, which had a company logo emblazoned on the back doors.

She touched the other woman's hand. "It's just the men from the square dancing place."

"Oh, okay." She looked embarrassed, although it was a natural reaction. "I'll go get Weston another snack before we get started."

Maura's heart ached. Sylvia's life was forever changed. And each of the women in this room probably had a similar story, each manifesting their trauma in different ways.

And Dex's trauma. How had it manifested? Oh, she'd been an eyewitness to the changes his loss had wrought, and they hadn't been pretty. And his hadn't been the only life that had been changed. Hers had, too.

She sat while the men from Square Dancers R Us presented their ideas for the party. This time Maura was able to sit and observe reactions among those in the room and, like Dex had said, there were nodding heads and smiles. One of the women raised her hand. "What if I have two left feet?"

There was laughter at that remark, and a couple of other women voiced similar concerns.

"It's not a matter of knowing how to move when, but enjoying the process."

Maura liked that explanation. Maybe that's what she and Dex needed to do. Enjoy the process of becoming friends again.

Unless that wasn't what he wanted. Although she got the feeling he was at least open to it.

The meeting ended on a good note and they agreed on a date. December 23, which was on a Wednesday evening. With a little less than two weeks to go, it was cutting it a bit close, but the event planner was handling the dancing itself and would provide all the speakers and microphones.

And there would even be costumes!

Maura had been thrilled to hear that they were going to bring a wardrobe of all kinds of fun things from neck scarves to the bouffant skirts worn by square dancers. They could wear as much or as little of it as they wanted.

Riding back with Dex, she leaned her head on the leather headrest, letting the darkness outside of the vehicle wash over her. His scent surrounded her, clung to her, slid inside of her with each and every breath.

Right now there was no place she'd rather be.

She'd better not let herself get too comfortable, though, because every time she let her guard down with this man, something happened. Sometimes good. Sometimes sad. And one time it had been horrible, like when she'd lost his baby and felt like the very last part of Dex had slipped away from her forever.

Her grief had been paralyzing even though the pregnancy was early, still in her first trimester. To have gone from the heights of joy when she learned she was carrying his baby to what she thought was the lowest of lows when she realized he didn't want to move forward with their relationship. Then she'd discovered there was something even worse than that. Worse than anything she'd experienced thus far in her life.

Gabe hadn't wanted children at all. For some reason, she'd been just fine with that, convincing herself that she didn't want them, either, that she'd dodged a bullet with the other pregnancy. But it was all a lie. Being with Dex again had made her realize that. She did want a child. Even if she had to do it on her own. Once this Christmas party was over, she was going to start the year with a brand-new resolution. She was going to be a mom, whether that meant having a biological child or adopting one. She'd been in a holding pattern for a long, long time, maybe even since before her marriage. Maybe that was ultimately what had done it in. But no more. She was going to move forward with her life once and for all. And to her, that meant having a child of her own.

"Are you asleep over there?"

She blinked her thoughts away and turned her head toward him. "Nope. Just happy with how the night went."

"Me, too. And I was just thinking about something." He glanced over at her. "How tired are you?"

"Not very, why?"

One of his brows went up, and he gave her a slow smile. One that made heat pool in the center of her belly and brought up visions of the last time they were together.

"Are you up for some excitement?" he murmured.

She licked her lips. "Haven't you had enough, um, excitement for one night?"

"Not quite. I told myself I'd do this on my own, but some things are more fun when done as a pair."

"As a pair?"

"Yes. I think I have the perfect thing to close out tonight, Maura." He reached over and twirled a strand of her hair, tugging it and sending shivers up and down her spine. "But only if you're ready to take a wild ride. One of the wildest you've ever had."

CHAPTER SEVEN

A BAR. HE'D brought her to a bar.

He pulled to a stop and aimed that stinkin' cute grin at her.

She laughed. Oh, hell, she'd thought he was talking about doing something a little naughtier than buying drinks. She'd been taking stock of what undergarments she had on, just in case.

She should be relieved. Very relieved that he'd chosen something completely innocuous.

"So what are we doing here?"

"Research." He swung out of the car and came around to her side before she could get her seat belt off, opening the door for her.

Was he kidding her? "Research?"

Climbing out of her car, she waited for him to close the door.

"It will all become clear in a minute."

She'd never been to this particular bar before, not that she had ever been a big bar hopper, even in her younger, wilder days. Back in high school, she'd had Dex, and that had been the only high she'd needed. The only thing she'd wanted.

And thinking about that did no good at all.

Dex reached the door to the bar and waited for her to catch up before saying, "Ready?"

"I think so, but at this point I'm not positive." She really had no idea what he had in mind.

He swung the door open and what greeted her was noise. And flashing lights. And someone being tossed around by a…bull.

Not a real bull. A mechanical bull.

"Oh, my God! Really?" She laughed, struggling to catch her breath. "A wild ride, huh? I should have known."

He gave her a sideways look, his own smile completely guileless. "What did you think I was talking about?"

That fake innocence gave him away. "Well, I knew you weren't talking about *that*. Because *wild* isn't the term I would use for…well…you know. In fact, that was pretty darn—"

"Don't even go there, Maura. My pride can only take so much." But his own laugh made her relax.

There was no way she was going to tell him that he really was the wildest she'd ever had. And the best. It made her feel bad for Gabe, but Dex truly had set the bar pretty damn high.

"Well, let's go see what this bull has to offer. Maybe they can at least tell us where we can rent one."

Dex somehow located a table in the crowded space and then ordered two beers, bringing them to her. She took one and lifted her glass to take a big sip as she watched the main attraction: the bull, which was evidently between rounds.

"Who's next?" someone called over the loudspeaker. "Two minutes on Bubba gets you a free beer. Which you're gonna need after taking this big boy on." Laughter filled the room, and someone stood and swaggered over to the big bull, which was complete with his own set of horns. Maura hoped those things weren't as real as they looked. A nasty gore would be something even a free beer couldn't fix. She made a note to make sure whatever bull they rented was sans horns, or at least had them made out of foam.

The guy climbed on, and someone motioned for him to hold on to what looked like a strap of some kind. There was cushioned material all around the perimeter for obvious reasons.

"Ready?"

The man gave a thumbs-up and the bull started up. Nice and slow. An easy back-and-forth motion was followed by a leisurely quarter turn, which the guy rode with ease.

"Well, that doesn't look too hard."

The gentle movements continued for another thirty seconds or so. At this rate, the guy was going to win a beer for sure. As if on a timer, though, a raucous country song started blasting through the speakers and the bull suddenly lurched forward while making another quarter turn. The crowd had evidently been waiting for this moment, whooping it up with catcalls and yelling for him to ride it out. The motions became jerkier and without a defined direction, one time doing a 180-degree turn. The man was actually doing an admirable job clinging to the machine. Another fast turn and a leap into the air was followed by twist to the left, and that did it. The guy went sailing into the cushioned wall, before leaping to his feet and pumping his fist into the air.

"One minute thirty seconds. Almost made it, folks. Give him a round of applause. And we're ready for a new victim…er… I mean contender."

She turned to Dex. "How did you even know this place existed?" It didn't exactly look like the kind of place he would hang out in. Then again, it had been a long time and maybe he'd changed.

He held up his phone. "I did a quick Google search when a mechanical bull was mentioned at our meeting. I thought it might be good to see one in action before we decide it's right for the party."

"Good idea. It looks like they can control how fast it goes. The kids would definitely like it, if we can get one that is made for fun. Not sure how many of the moms would ride it."

"Well, our patient definitely shouldn't try it, even with a little more healing time under her belt."

The next person climbed on the bull and had the same result, only he didn't make it quite as long.

"I used to ride horses when I was younger, but they definitely don't move like that. At least not the ones I rode," she said.

A spotlight spun around the room and found a third participant who wasn't quite as eager to go up but, with a little coaxing from the crowd, finally did. This person, a young man in a suit, of all things, got the kid-glove treatment. The person controlling the thing kept things light and easy until around the minute and forty-five-second mark when, without warning, the person seemed to simply slide down the side of the bull and drop to the ground. "Okay, well I think even I could have ridden that one."

As if someone in the audience had heard her, the spotlight suddenly picked her out of the crowd and held on. Horror swept over her, and she tried to shake her head even as the crowd started chanting. "Ride that bull, ride that bull…"

"Did you tell them to choose me?"

Dex leaned back, placing his hand over his heart. "I swear, I had nothing to do with it. But if you want a real test…"

"I am going to kill you." Maybe it was the beer, although she hadn't even ingested half of it. Maybe it was having Dex look at her in that expectant, challenging way, but she did something she never could have seen herself doing a year or two ago. She got up from her chair and walked toward the center of the room, where the bull waited. It was bigger than she expected, and the floor was more bouncy than padded. Kind of like a trampoline. Someone came up to her and showed her a raised padded platform that she could use to hop onto the bull's back.

What in the world was she thinking? But she climbed up and waited as the man showed her how to hold on. What she'd thought was a strap was actually a thick piece of rope with a wooden bead on it. "Hold here. Try to go with the movements of the bull as much as possible, using your other hand for balance. When you're ready to go, hold your hand up."

When she was ready? Well, that would be never. Taking a deep breath and glancing at the table where Dex had been, she was disappointed to see it was empty. He couldn't even be bothered to stay and watch her? Maybe an emergency call had come in and he'd had to go.

Well, it didn't matter, and she might as well get this over with. Raising her hand in the air, she gave the signal. The bull started with slow, gentle motions, just like with everyone else.

Okay, it really wasn't too bad. She did half a twist and saw Dex right there beside the ring, watching her. Then he was gone as the bull moved in another direction. The action picked up a bit, but it still wasn't too hard. Until a quick turn almost unseated her. She regained her balance, but the movements were becoming too unpredictable and it was all she could do to stay on. *Go with the movements.* Way easier said than done.

Hadn't she already passed the two-minute mark? It felt like she'd been going forever. The bull shimmied, then spun. And that was the end. She felt herself falling before she even realized what was happening, and then bouncing on the springy floor.

She laughed. It actually was fun.

"One minute thirty-five seconds for the lady. Good job!"

"Yes. Good job." A hand came down to help her to her feet. She grabbed it, thinking it was the helper who'd instructed her when she got on, but it was Dex. When her eyes met his, they shimmered with something that could have been admiration.

She took a step and then tumbled against him. "Whew, I'm a little bit dizzy. Or maybe a little tipsy."

He held her in place, hands on her hips. Something

went very warm inside of her. Especially when he seemed in no hurry to let go.

"It's probably the surface, it's hard to walk on." Then he moved, his arm curving around her waist to help her walk away from the area. "I can't believe you did it."

Once she got to the regular floor, it was easier going, but she still had a slight sense of vertigo.

"I can't believe I did, either. I looked over and thought you'd left."

"I was going to try to give you moral support, but they didn't have you facing my way very often."

She laughed. "I saw you. Right before they flipped me the other way."

"So, what's the verdict? Yes, for the party? Or no?"

"I say yes. The older kids will have a lot of fun with it and the younger ones…well, maybe there's a way to help them stay on."

"Most rental places send someone with the bull to operate it. I'm sure."

She put a hand to her ear and kind of yanked it away again, as she shook her head. "Wow, that really did a number on the otoconia crystals in my ear."

"I bet. Did you fix it?"

Maura peered around. "Yes, that's better." Otoconia crystals, which helped with balance could cause vertigo when displaced. Her mom had had problems with them, and she'd learned techniques on how to reposition them so they no longer interfered with balance. But she'd never had to use it on herself.

She took another sip of her beer and watched as the next lucky contestant got on the bull. "Sure you don't want to try it?"

"Believe me, I was right up there with you. Right until you crashed to the ground. Unlike you, I didn't ride anything that wasn't motorized as a kid, other than a bike. I think I would have been off on that first turn. But I'll admit to liking the way you rode him."

Something about the last sentence made her flush, because all she could think about was the way she'd ridden something that was a lot more cooperative than that bull.

Dex finished off his beer. "That's it for me, since I need to drive, but I'll get you another if you want."

"Nope, I'm good. I've always been a lightweight."

"Yes, you have." He chuckled. "We did some pretty stupid stuff back then."

"We did. I remember going down to that creek behind my house and using a flashlight to hunt for crawdads at night."

He ran a finger along the line of her jaw. "Hunting for crawdads wasn't all we did."

No, it wasn't. Dex had been her first, and she'd always believed he'd be her last.

But she wasn't going to ruin a nice night out by dwelling on that. "We had some fun times."

"Yes, we did."

He threw a couple bills on the table and stood. "Ready?"

"I am."

Dex started the car and backed out of the space. He couldn't believe she'd gotten on that bull. The Maura he'd known as a kid would have been one of the first to raise her hand and volunteer. This Maura, the fully grown adult woman, had changed in some undecipherable ways. There were times she seemed a little more unsure of herself than she used to be. Was that because of her marriage? Because of him?

"How's your ear?"

"All better. But I probably won't repeat that anytime soon. One time on a bull was enough for me. I'll leave that for the rodeo stars and the bar warriors." She laughed. "I should have realized something was going on when I looked at the bar's name. Just The Bull. Catchy."

"No catchier than Square Dancers R Us."

"Touché."

She leaned her head against the headrest. "Thanks for tonight. I think I needed a night out."

"It's been a while for me, too." It had been. Being involved with the women's center and this party were just what he needed. And Maura?

No. That had been settled a long time ago. He wouldn't go back and undo it, even if he could. They would have ended up in a divorce court the same way she and her husband had. He'd been a mess back then. He still was in a lot of ways. He told himself every winter that once his mom was gone, he was moving to Florida. Or South Texas, or anywhere that had no snowfall.

But while he'd recovered from what had happened—for the most part—his mom had not. She'd struggled for a long time before finally receiving a diagnosis and treatment for clinical depression. Dex had not been able to help her through any of it, because he'd been too busy just trying to keep his own head above water. Looking back, he hadn't done a very good job of that, either. He'd called and visited plenty of times since the accident, but maybe it was time to call her and have a hard talk about what had happened and what they each hoped from the future.

If he'd done that with Maura, would they still be where they were now? It was too late for recriminations now. She'd moved on, and maybe he could finally do the same.

As if the universe had overheard his thoughts and decided to test his resolve, a big flake of snow landed on the windshield, then another and another. Soon the snowfall increased. Not bad, but enough that his hands gripped the steering wheel, eyes searching for any irregularities in the vehicles around him.

He shouldn't have had that beer.

No, that was ridiculous. He was well under the legal limit and that single drink had been spaced out over the course of an hour, so much of it was already metabolized.

A hand touched his arm. "Hey, want me to drive?"

She knew. When he glanced at his knuckles, he saw why. They were white. He forced his fingers to loosen their grip.

Everything in him wanted to take her up on her offer, but his pride said no way. "I'm fine. Traffic is pretty light right now."

He drove to work in the snow every damn winter, so why couldn't he get over this? Maybe for the same reason his mom still struggled. Another reason to call her.

"Are you sure? I don't mind. I know this used to be hard for you."

It still was. And back then, he actually had let Maura

take over on occasion, but it had always rankled that he just couldn't seem to get his act together. On anything, including his relationship with her. With his mom.

"We're almost there, anyway. Just another five minutes." He cast around for something to say that would divert her attention to something else. "Do you and your ex keep in touch?"

"Gabe?" Her head swiveled toward him. "No. Why do you ask?"

"No reason. I was just curious." He wasn't about to tell her the real reason for the change in topic, but he'd obviously chosen the wrong one.

"There's not really anything to tie us together anymore. We don't have kids."

So maybe her miscarriage was like his aversion to snow? A trauma that had led her to avoid trying to have more?

He reached the hospital parking garage and she told him where her car was parked. "I'm sorry about that. You were really good with Sylvia's little boy."

"Thanks. I've been thinking lately that I might want kids."

A shaft of pain went through him at the thought of her having babies with someone else, but he forced himself to nod as if he understood. "I'm sure getting over your miscarriage was hard."

"You have no idea."

Dex found her car and pulled in beside it. "How long had you been married when it happened?"

There was a huge pause. Maura picked at a spot on her slacks before finally replying.

"Gabe and I weren't together when it happened."

His brain stuttered and stopped. Had there been someone in between the time he and Maura broke up and when she got together with her husband? It had only been a year, and it had almost killed him when he'd heard she was getting married. He'd almost stormed the church and been the single dissenting voice. But he hadn't. Because he had no right. He couldn't tell her that he wanted to slow things down and then expect she would just be fine with it. He'd subconsciously known she wouldn't, which was why he'd done what he did.

"I didn't realize you dated someone else after we broke up."

She shifted in her seat to look at him, her lips tightening. "Who said I dated someone else?"

"Well…" Maybe that beer really had affected him, because what she was saying made no sense at all.

"That baby…the one I lost…" Her chin tilted in defiance. "It was yours."

"Mine?" His paralyzed brain lurched forward, unseating him just like that mechanical bull had done with its victims less than an hour ago. He was missing something. Something big. He struggled to make it out, his mind going back over what had happened on the last day they were together.

One thing he was very sure of—she'd never mentioned being pregnant when she'd talked to him. "The baby was mine?"

She nodded but didn't say anything.

His mind slid down an ugly path. He paused before putting to words the question that pounded inside of him. "Did you know about it before you broke things off with me?"

"Does it matter? It doesn't change anything."

It did matter. A lot. He just wasn't sure why. He'd dealt with so much loss that last year, and to find out after all this time that he'd lost a child, as well…

A baby. *His* baby.

Raw pain boiled through his system, searing places he hadn't realized existed.

No. She wouldn't have kept something like that from him. She must have found out about the pregnancy after they broke up.

What if she hadn't lost it? Would she have gone through with carrying the baby to term and never told him the child was his? Or worse, let Gabe raise the child as his?

His jaw clenched as he worked to contain his emotions. "You didn't think I had a right to know I was going to be a father?"

"Believe me, Dex. I absolutely thought you did. But the night I came over to talk to you about it was the night you told me you weren't ready for a commitment." She touched his hand. "If you weren't ready to make a commitment to our relationship, then you definitely weren't ready to hear the news that I was pregnant. And you were still dealing with…so much back then."

Yes, he had been. But that didn't excuse the fact that he would have wanted to know the truth. He'd deserved to know. "Hell, Maura. If you'd told me up front, before demanding to know where you stood, things might have been different."

"Really? You seriously believe that?" She shook her head. "Even if that were the case, I didn't want you under those conditions. Didn't want that for our child.

So when I realized you were probably never going to be ready, were never going to be able to get past what happened to your family, I broke it off. And from where I'm sitting, it looks like you never did."

Was she talking about the fact that he was still a nervous wreck when driving in the snow? Or was she referring to the fact that he'd never gotten married?

He could be flip and say he'd never met the right woman. But that would be a lie. Because he had. He just hadn't been able to give her what she wanted back then. And honestly, he didn't think if she'd asked him to commit two years later or ten years later, it would have made any difference. He'd liked his life the way it was. When he'd only needed to worry about himself, not anyone else.

And if he'd known about the baby? Would that have forced him to think about something other than his own sad circumstances?

He didn't know because he hadn't had the chance to decide that.

As angry as that made him, he could still see her point. She hadn't wanted a marriage proposal based on the pregnancy. If she had, she certainly could have played that card and gotten what she wanted. But he knew Maura well enough to realize it was all or nothing. She would not settle for half measures. And she shouldn't have had to. He took a couple of deep breaths and said the one thing he absolutely knew was true.

"I'm sorry you went through all of that alone."

One of her shoulders lifted. "It's over. And losing the baby was probably for the best."

For the best.

Goddammit. How could she even think that? He closed his eyes for a few seconds. He'd done a number on her. Had hurt her in ways that were unimaginable. She probably did think it was for the best. If he'd been in her shoes, he probably would have done the same. He might have even ended the pregnancy.

He was glad she hadn't, even though she'd lost the baby anyway.

They were wild and crazy back when they were together, had done some sexy, risky things, but they'd always used protection. Every single time. Evidently something had gone wrong during one of their lovemaking sessions, and she'd gotten pregnant.

The word stuck in his brain like a claw. She'd been carrying his child, and he'd never had a chance to celebrate that fact…or grieve its loss.

He reached over and captured her hand. "I'm so sorry, Maura. So very sorry." He wasn't sure how to express himself without insulting her. "I hope you know I would have tried to do the right thing. Would have wanted to be in the baby's life, if he or she had survived. I wouldn't have left you to do everything on your own."

He thought of Sylvia and how she would be raising Weston on her own because of her husband's selfishness.

"I just didn't know what to do back then. I was hurt and sad, and the last thing I wanted to do was burden you with something else. All I wanted to do was get away." She squeezed his hand. "But I think after I'd had time to sift through my feelings, I would have done the right thing, too, and told you that you were going to be a father."

Well, they were a mess. Even now. Dex wasn't sure how to compartmentalize the sudden revelation or if he even could. His whole reason for breaking up with her had been because he couldn't deal with any more losses and the realization that there was no way to guarantee something wouldn't eventually happen to Maura, as well. It had all been too much.

No wonder she'd steered away from the topic back then. She probably figured it wouldn't change anything for him to know, so she'd simply kept the information to herself.

She said if she hadn't lost the baby she probably would have eventually told him. He needed to try to be content with that. "Thank you for telling me now."

"I wasn't going to, you know. Not after all this time. I'm not even sure why I did."

"Well, I'm glad you did." He took a deep breath, before giving her hand one last squeeze and releasing it. "You're going to make a great mom."

But it wouldn't be to his baby. And that thought made something shift in his chest.

She unlatched her seat belt and popped open her door. "I hope so. When the time is right."

And then she got out of the car and into her own. He stayed where he was as she started the vehicle and pulled out of the space, giving a quick wave as she drove away.

And still he sat there, his emotions and thoughts in absolute turmoil.

Maura had been expecting his child, and he'd had absolutely no idea.

CHAPTER EIGHT

MUCH OF THEIR dealings in the time leading up to the Christmas party had been via text message.

Maura hadn't wanted to tell him about the pregnancy, especially after all this time, but having him assume she'd had a boyfriend right on the heels of their breakup had made her angry.

He had no idea what she'd gone through back then. The devastation and overwhelming pain that had come from knowing he hadn't wanted her. And then when she'd told him the baby wasn't Gabe's—for him to have thought she could just jump into another man's arms and gotten pregnant by that person...

Well, it had sent her over the edge and the words had come pouring out. She'd wanted them to slice into him, the way his veiled accusation had cut into her.

After the anger, though, came hurt.

But once she'd worked through all that, his reaction to the news had surprised her. Although he'd obviously been upset that she hadn't told him about it back then, he'd also seemed relieved in some indefinable way, although it was the opposite of what she would have expected. If she'd been him, she would have hoped the baby *was* the product of a fling or her marriage, rather than discovering the child was his.

She'd tried to call him a couple of days after their trip to the bar, but then had disconnected when she realized there was really nothing to say. She couldn't go back and undo her decisions, and he couldn't undo his. And as she'd said about the pregnancy, it was for the best.

So how was she going to face him tonight?

The same way she'd faced him any other time. The news didn't change anything between them. Well, maybe it had put paid to the chance to be friends with him. From what she'd seen of his succinct messages that had come over her phone, he wanted as little interaction with her as possible.

Fortunately, the square dancing group had offered to do the decorating, once she'd told them what she wanted. And Colleen Winters used the food budget from the hospital to take care of the meal. That left getting the bull, and Dex had secured one of those, according to one of those text messages.

Some part of her grieved in a way that she hadn't during the loss of her child. She hadn't expected to get back together with Dex, but had hoped for a little more than what they were left with: quick glimpses of him as he traveled through her department.

But it was what it was. She should be used to it by now.

So she got dressed in a pair of dark-washed jeans and a white button-down shirt. Not exactly square dance material, but it was as close to Western wear as she could get. And even though she wasn't in a party mood, she was going to go with an attitude that this wasn't about her—it was about those women. Because it was true. No matter what was going on in her personal life, she wanted those moms and kids to have fun. They deserved a little hope…a glimpse of what life could still be like.

And after her talk with Dex, she had cemented her decision to have a child. It was going to happen. Relationships with men might not have worked out, but she could give a child a good and loving home. And that's all that mattered, in the end.

Brushing her hair and pulling it into a high ponytail, slicking on a bit of lip gloss and a touch of mascara, she looked in the mirror.

Well, that was about as good as it was going to get. Today, anyway. She needed to go and try to have a good time. Or at least paste on a smile and pretend. Ha! The same word she'd tossed at Dex after they'd made love. Gathering up the bags of gifts she'd bought for the kids based on the information the mothers had given them, she headed out the door and into the world.

She got to the center fifteen minutes early and spotted Dex's car already there, along with a box truck with the Square Dancers R Us logo on the side. There was another truck that had probably brought in the bull. Lord, she hoped all that had fit in the center's cafeteria.

But at least there was no snow in sight, for Dex's sake.

Her nerves gave a threatening twinge, taunting her to get back in her car and head down the road. But she'd given her word and that meant more than any discomfort this one night could bring, so she rang the buzzer and waited for someone to answer.

It was Colleen, who gave her a big hug. "I can't believe what they've done to the place. It's magical. And fun."

"Dex did a lot of the legwork." Like taking her to a bar so she could see a mechanical bull in action.

She'd been so hopeful that night.

Well, it wasn't all doom and gloom. Maybe they could get past this, too. Once the shock wore off, maybe Dex would forgive her for keeping her secret. He'd taken it a lot better than she'd expected, but not well enough to call or try to stop in the ER to talk to her.

"I know he did," said the director. "He's helping with the bull now."

"He is?"

"Yep, come on in and see what the hospital's generosity has done for us."

She went in and had to stop and blink at the change in the room. It was just as she'd imagined. No. Even better. Bales of straw lined the perimeter of the room, the way she'd pictured it, but each of those bales had a red ribbon draped from end to end. The bull was set up in a corner, with what looked like a big inflatable pool underneath it. The walls on either side of the bull were padded and the creature's fake horns each had silver tinsel wrapped around them. Kids surrounded the pit, touching and examining the bull, and Dex was holding Weston on the animal's back. The boy even had a tiny cowboy hat perched on his head.

She pressed a palm to her mouth to stop its trembling. Oh, Lord, she was not going to cry. She couldn't.

Long tables were laid out with two big centerpieces and what looked like a whole bevy of slow cookers and food offerings.

Colleen saw her glance and said, "The women decided they were going to cook, so they each made a dish or two."

"What a wonderful idea." It was so important for these women to have a sense of ownership, and their contributions made that happen.

She glanced back at the bull and found Dex's eyes on her. She gave a quick wave, with a smile that felt like it stretched her face to the limit. But what else could she do?

The center of the room had been totally cleared out, and the event company had actually laid out a wooden dance floor in a big octagon. Some of the kids were rolling and playing on it, but when she looked at the people who were still setting up equipment, no one seemed bothered.

So good. This was going to be so very good.

Her muscles relaxed, and she watched Colleen move over to the dessert section of the buffet table, talking to one of the residents about something.

It was now or never. She walked over to the bull. Dex had already lifted Weston down and was helping another kid perch on it. "Hey. Can you believe all this?"

"I can't. The decorations are great. Did you come over and help with them?"

She shook her head. "No, the event company did everything, and it's absolutely amazing. I hope the hospital is okay with giving them a generous tip."

"Already in the works. I made sure of it."

"Great." She glanced around. "I saw Weston, but I haven't seen Sylvia. Is she okay?"

"She was here a few minute ago. She's getting around much better. Her stitches are out, and her wounds are healing well. I saw her last week at the hospital."

And he hadn't called her to let her know. Why would he? She'd had almost no part in the case.

"I'm really glad. How are they going to work the bull?"

"They're going to use the lowest settings. Supposedly even a kid can make it through it. I imagine some of them might fall off on purpose, just for the chance to bounce on the inflatable tubes, though."

Looking closer, she realized that what she'd thought was a pool was actually a network of tubes that hooked into the raised edges, which were the same configuration.

She smiled. "Are you going to ride it this time, since they've ramped it down?"

He gave her a grin. "You never know. Although I imagine the kids are going to be fighting each other to get on it."

Just then the caller took a microphone off the stand and tested it, before giving the greeting. "Welcome to our first annual Christmas Hoedown! We've got some fun things planned and it looks like we've got a couple of wild animals in attendance, as well. And that doesn't include the bull."

Everyone laughed as more and more of the residents came into the room. "If you have any questions, feel free to ask any of us—we'll be scattered around the room. There's a costume rack behind me so feel free to come on over and choose something to wear for the festivities. After all, this is a hoedown. We need to dress the part."

She glanced at Dex and saw that he had on black jeans and a black shirt. The combination suited him. There was no scarf around his powerful neck, but he'd done a pretty good job at fitting into his surroundings.

The caller continued. "I'd like Drs. Dex Chamblisse and Maura Findley to come up here, if they will."

She glanced up at Dex, wondering if he was behind this. He just shrugged. She followed him up to the front and stood beside the man with the microphone, hands clasped tightly in front of her.

"I'd like to thank these two for calling us and giving us the opportunity to come and serve you. It's the opportunity of a lifetime. Most of you don't know this, but…" He paused before reaching up to pinch the top of his nose for several long seconds, as if trying to compose himself. Then he straightened his cowboy hat and looked up. "My daughter was in a position that many of you face right now. She got out and is safe, thanks to an organization very much like this one. She's remarried—to a good man, this time—and is happier than she's ever been. And that's what we all want, isn't it? The chance to be happy?" He cued someone who sat at a nearby sound table, and the sound of a banjo came over the loudspeaker, its bright tones filling the space. "So once we can get these two off the stage, we're going to get ready for some dancing. So go pick your costumes. Dex and Maura, you lead the way and show them how it's done."

The man patted Dex on the shoulder and waved them away.

Great. She hadn't really expected to wear anything other than what she had on.

"Are you going over there?" she asked Dex as he went down the steps.

"Well, unless you want to be a—you know—party pooper."

He infused the words with a hint of challenge. One she was going to accept. "Party pooper? Oh, believe me, I can party with the best of them. I think I proved that at the bar."

Her heart took off, feeling lighter than it had in ages. And it was all because of Dex.

"So you did." He glanced at the racks of clothes and the curtains that cordoned off the dressing area behind it. "Okay, give me fifteen minutes and I'll meet you back out here."

More of the residents were joining them, sorting through the offerings and holding them up for each other to see. The sound of giggles and laughter were all around her.

Maura found a beige cowboy hat and tried it on for size and found a matching neckerchief. Well, that did it for her. She wasn't planning on doing a ton of dancing, so she would leave the rest of the clothes for the residents. It was their party, after all.

She moved over to the food and popped a strawberry into her mouth, glancing back over at the costume area. Dex still hadn't come out. Adjusting the hat on her head and feeling a little ridiculous, she ate another strawberry. She was hungry. Her stomach had been in knots all day at the thought of seeing him tonight and her appetite had fled for most of the day.

But it wasn't as awkward as she'd feared. In fact, Dex had seemed almost like a different person. So her belly was now sorting through the sights and scents of the food and trying to decide what she wanted to try first.

Just then Dex came out, and she stopped chewing and stared. He still had on his black jeans, but he'd exchanged his black shirt for a different one. This one, while still black, had a black-and-white floral yoke with the same detailing on the cuffs. Man, if anyone could pull that ensemble off, this man could—and did. His black cowboy hat gave him a bit of a bad-boy look and the black belt with its wide silver buckle made him look the epitome of a rodeo star.

He was gorgeous. Breathtaking. And she realized her jaws had locked themselves in place.

Chew, Maura, chew. The last thing she needed to do was choke on a strawberry.

She made her way over to him and circled him as if examining his outfit. She was, but she was also checking out the entire package.

"How'd I do?" he asked.

"I'd say you make a pretty passable cowboy. That shirt fits you surprisingly well." She reached up and adjusted the shoulders, not because they were crooked, but because she needed an excuse to touch him.

"So does yours."

She smiled. "That's because it's mine."

"I know."

The weirdness that had been between them after they'd left the bar—and after her subsequent revelation—seemed to be gone, but she couldn't help but address it.

"Listen, I'm sorry about what happened. I shouldn't have said anything about the pregnancy."

"Yes, you should have. It just took me by surprise."

"I know, and I never meant you to learn about it like that."

"It's over and done, so let's just enjoy the night."

Before she went and ruined it? She hoped that wasn't what he was saying. But there was nothing in his face to indicate he was mad or upset. She was going to do as he suggested and try to have a good time.

He fingered the brim of her hat. "Nice touch."

"Ha! You look pretty at home in yours."

"Hmm… I've never owned a cowboy hat in my life."

Her head tilted. "You should. Your patients would probably have remarkable recoveries."

"Yeah…no. I'm not much of a rancher."

Honestly, Dex would probably look at home in almost any outfit he wore. Surfer dude? Check. Fisherman? Check. Surgeon? Already checked that box a couple of times.

"Well, you are now. For one night, anyway."

The caller was telling everyone who wasn't dancing to please clear the floor. "Dex and Maura? I'm going to need your assistance one more time, please."

Oh, no. What now?

She joined Dex on the dance floor. He gave her a look as if asking her what was going on. She didn't have a clue.

"I know a lot of you said you'd never square-danced before. Dex and Maura, have you done any?"

They both answered that they hadn't.

The caller smiled. "Well, that's perfect, because I'm

going to prove that anyone can do it. Dex, stand over here while Maura and I demonstrate." He waited for a second, then held out his hand for Maura. She took it, a little disappointed that it wasn't Dex, before she tossed that thought aside.

"Ready?" he asked.

"I guess we'll find out." She forced a smile.

He adjusted the hands-free microphone at his ear. "I'm going to go through four of the major dance moves and then I'm going to let Dex take over."

Her heart began to pound and she wasn't sure why. Hadn't she just wished he'd been her partner? Yes, but that was only when she'd thought there was no chance of that happening.

"Okay...do-si-do is done like this." Holding hands with her, he then asked her to face him as they both circled each other and came back to their original positions. "Let's try it again."

They repeated the move. Okay, that wasn't so hard. But when she glanced over at Dex, she saw he was standing to the side, arms crossed, a forbidding line between his brows. Because of the dance itself? Or because he was going to have to be paired up with her in a minute?

She realized she'd missed something the caller had said. "Sorry?"

"Things are going to be moving fast, once we really get going."

Was it her imagination or had he sent a sly smile Dex's way? Had he noticed how unhappy the surgeon was, as well? If so, he didn't seem to care.

They went through three other moves before calling a halt. "See there? You survived just fine, Maura. Now let's see what happens once we get Dex in here."

"I don't think—" Dex started, only to have the other man interrupt him.

"You'll have to try it sometime. Might as well show these ladies how it's done."

He came up beside her, seeming none too happy about being made to dance with her. "Sorry," she whispered.

Glancing at her, his expression softened. "It's okay."

"At least I'm not wearing a turquoise dress tonight," she said, playing on their earlier conversation.

"No, you're not."

The caller cleared his throat. "Let's start with do-si-do."

Instead of circling, though, they both stepped to the same side by mistake, only stopping when they were face-to-face. And far too close for comfort.

Her heart pounded all over again. "Looks like you don't need the dress."

She laughed. "You went the wrong way, not me."

A voice came over the loudspeaker. "If you two love-birds are done chirping sweet nothings at each other, some of these ladies might want to dance tonight."

Laughter sounded from around the room, and Maura's face flamed to life. She could only imagine how it sounded with Dex saying she didn't need a dress.

"Let's try do-si-do again."

This time they managed to circle each other without incident, Dex sending her a slow smile as he stopped in front of her once again. This time on purpose.

"Very good." The caller smiled. "Now, Dex, hold her hands…"

Maura heard nothing beyond that because, when Dex did as the man asked, they ended up standing looking at each other, their hands clasped.

If their lives had been different, they might have stood just like this in front of a minister. As it was, they were standing in front of a paid event planner and this was all pretend.

Pretend. Just like she'd said to Dex after they'd made love.

Thankfully, the caller soon had them moving again, doing something different; otherwise, there was every chance Dex might have noticed something in her eyes. Something she really didn't want him to see.

But even though they were running through dance steps, she was very, very aware of him. Everything about him. His scent. The touch of his fingertips against hers. The reassuring squeeze of his hand when she almost ran into him once again.

"Okay, you guys, thanks for showing us that maybe not everyone is cut out for square dancing." He laughed, as did the residents. "But, seriously, you guys can see how easy it is. And we'll stick to these moves. For now. I'm sure Dex and Maura won't mind showing us some more steps once we've gotten these down." He gave them a wink that held far too much meaning. Did he think they were together?

Great. It wasn't like she could set him straight in front of everyone. Nor did she need to. It wasn't like they were ever going to see him again after tonight.

The caller told everyone to grab a partner and get

ready to have fun. "We have room for two squares, each
one with four couples. Let's see what you've got. We'll
take it easy on you. For now."

Women paired up with each other and with kids.
Maura started to leave the floor only to be called back.

"We need one more couple in the second square."

Under her breath she muttered, "Oh, Lord."

"Surely dancing with me wasn't that repugnant."
There was a stiffness to the words that made her glance
up at him. "You didn't seem to mind dancing with him."
He nodded in the caller's direction.

It wasn't repugnant at all. That was the problem. "He
knew what he was doing."

The frown was back as he reached for her hand and
tugged her toward him until they were in position. "I
told you, I know nothing about square dancing."

"That's fine, that's fine," said the caller, obviously
overhearing Dex's comment. "We're going to do the
same steps we just went over. Has anyone here done
any square dancing?"

Someone in their group raised her hand, and a couple
of others did, as well.

"That's great. Okay, so your job is to help keep the
rest of us straight."

She liked the way the man included himself in that.
He was warm and encouraging, and knew how to in-
struct without being overbearing. Although Dex didn't
seem to have warmed to him as much.

The music started and there was no more time to
think as the caller started in with a singsong voice that
reminded her of an auctioneer.

"Circle to the left and when you get home, do-si-do your own…"

Maura struggled to keep up with the calls. It was one thing to go through them slowly, one at a time. Putting the steps to music with one move following the other at a dizzying pace was a completely different story.

She careened hard into Dex. They stood staring at each other for a second before his face suddenly cleared and he laughed. He simply took her hand and promenaded like they were supposed to be doing.

She continued to struggle while Dex seemed to catch on with a grace and ease that reminded her of the Dex of old times. And she had to admit that he still had the power to make her breathless, just like he'd had when they were together.

She relaxed, finally letting herself enjoy what was happening. There was a lot of laughter, and no one was getting the moves perfect. Periodically, the caller would reset the squares so they could clear their heads and start all over. But every time Dex took her hands to promenade, a little butterfly whisked around her belly in time with the music. Those wings began to beat faster and faster until she was worried someone was going to figure out that she was enjoying this a little too much.

Thirty minutes later, the squares were supposed to form again to let those who hadn't gotten to dance a chance to join in. She took that as her chance to slide out of there.

Dex was stuck, however, since they needed one more person. She stood on the sidelines and watched him dance.

His long legs carried him around the square, and he

smiled at whoever he was partnered with, the corners of his eyes crinkling in a way that made her catch her breath.

A way that terrified her and made her realize she was letting him slide past her defenses all over again.

Don't go down this path. It didn't work the first time. It won't end any better a second time.

Did she really believe that?

How could she not? And even if she didn't, the man hadn't contacted her once over the last week other than to type those impersonal messages about the party.

Which from what she could see was a wild success. She glanced over at the bull, which was going in a very slow circle. One of the moms was sitting on it along with her young child whose smile lit up her insides, making her forget about what she should and shouldn't be feeling today.

It was okay to just stop and enjoy herself. She could worry about the rest tomorrow.

The second dance ended, and Dex came out to join her, lifting his hat and running his hand over his hair, before settling it back in place. He reminded her of a country and western crooner who sang of heartbreak and hope. Of sunshine and pain. All she wanted today, though, was the sunshine, with none of the pain.

"That was harder than it looked," he said.

"You made it look easy, actually. Sorry for crashing into you that one time."

He grinned. "You can crash into me any time you'd like, even without the prom dress."

Yep. Sunshine. Not a cloud in sight. At least not right now.

He said something else that she missed entirely. "Sorry. What?"

"I asked what time the gifts are going to be handed out?"

"Around seven or so." She glanced at her watch and saw it was six thirty. The time was flying by far too quickly.

There were people sitting on the straw bales eating. She'd forgotten she was hungry. "Do you want to grab a bite to eat?"

"That sounds good."

They loaded up a couple of plates and found a spot to sit. Dex set his cup down next to him on the straw. "I'd say this was a success, wouldn't you?"

"Yes. I'm glad to see Sylvia out there." She spotted the woman across the way, sending her a wave. She was gratified to see her smile. "And I'm really glad the square dance leader said what he did. I had no idea."

"About his daughter?"

"Yes. I think it gives them hope that life isn't over just because someone abused their trust and hurt them. They can still be happy. With or without a partner."

"It certainly gave them something to think about."

Did he disagree with the man? Surely Dex had had his share of happiness over the years. Although her marriage had failed, it hadn't completely soured her on the idea that she could still find joy in the things of life.

"It's better than being paralyzed and stuck in the same place year after year, don't you think?"

He shot her a look, but didn't answer.

Did he think that's what she was? Paralyzed and stuck? She'd admit that after her divorce she had been for a while. But now that she'd made some decisions about her future, she was finally ready to move forward again.

Dex scraped at a piece of pasta on his plate. "I think everyone has their own timetable. It's not always as cut-and-dried as people like to think."

Okay, so it didn't sound like he'd been thinking about her, after all. Maybe it was a generalized statement.

Or maybe it was about him. She remembered his white-knuckled grip on the steering wheel when it had started snowing.

Maybe he thought she was judging him. "Hey, I wasn't talking about you. I was referring to the women here. I took what the guy said as a message of hope and encouragement. I think it took a lot of courage for him to share about his daughter. It made me glad we chose that particular company."

"You may not have been talking about me, but it hit home. About me. About my mom. She's never gotten over the accident. She's been under the care of a psychiatrist for years. And I—"

Sylvia and her son came over and interrupted whatever he'd been about to say. "Weston is asking for you to try Bully."

"Bully?" Dex asked.

"The bull."

"Ah... I don't—"

Maura spoke up. "You saw how slow it was going earlier. I'm sure they'll take it easy on you. Besides it knocked something loose in me, remember? Maybe it'll do the same for you."

"It knocked you off balance, if I remember right."

Sending her a look that promised revenge, he got to his feet and handed her his plate. "Save that for me, would you? Hopefully, I'll be well enough to eat it when I come back."

Sylvia laughed, her smile big and beautiful. "See, Wes? Dr. Chamblisse is going to try it."

She watched Dex walk away with the mother and son, his back ramrod straight, his steps sure and steady.

His voice said one thing, but his movements said another. This was one man who didn't show fear.

Except when it snowed.

That didn't make him weak in her eyes. It made him real and like every other human being on the planet, affected by the things that life tossed at you.

He was the sexiest man she'd ever known. And she doubted that would ever change. She might have moved on, but it didn't mean Dex had magically changed. It meant she had. Just like back then, she wasn't willing to settle for a man who held back the most important things in his life. Like trust. And sharing of burdens.

And love.

He got on the bull and held on, glancing over at her just before the operator turned the machine on. It started off in a circle, slow with up-and-down ripples of movement. Dex had no trouble staying on. Weston stood on the outside of the protective tubes and jumped up and down. She could have sworn she heard the boy yell, "Bully!"

Two minutes went by and then three, the bull getting a little more energetic with each pass, but nothing as crazy as the one at the bar. And then the ride slowed and came to a stop. He'd managed to stay on the entire time.

After getting off, he bent down to say something to Weston, and her throat grew tight. Two weeks ago, he had said that she would make a great mother. Well, he would have made a wonderful dad, despite his past.

Committing to a person because you wanted to spend the rest of your life with them was one thing. Dex hadn't been willing to do that. But having a child, and the blood connection that brought, was another thing. She was pretty sure Dex would have taken on that challenge even when he'd been unwilling—or unable—to promise her any kind of forever.

But maybe forever was overrated. Look at her and Gabe. They'd stood before a minister and promised to stay together come what may. That promise had been broken. So why make it at all?

Maybe taking things one day at a time—one night at a time—was a better way. Kind of like what they did the night they slept together. If they hadn't both made it weird, maybe it wouldn't have been.

Dex made his way back to her, and she handed him back his plate. "See? You didn't fall off at all."

"I couldn't let the little guy down."

"And you didn't. He looked pretty happy from where I'm sitting."

A slight frown marred his brow. "You're looking mighty pleased with yourself about something."

"I've just been thinking about how complicated people make life, when maybe it doesn't need to be that way. When maybe we're just meant to grab whatever happiness we can and hold on for as long as it lasts. Until life grows too frenetic, like that bull. And when that happens, we simply let go and fall away. No regrets. No saying we didn't enjoy the ride."

"This coming from the girl who'd once needed relationships to last forever."

"At the time, that's what I thought was important. I think I'm changing my mind." She caught his eyes. "Maybe one night is all I need, Dex."

His brows went up. "One night?"

"Yes. One night."

CHAPTER NINE

HE WAS ALMOST certain Maura had issued an invitation.

One he wasn't about to turn down, since he'd been thinking along the same lines for the last two weeks. Which was why he'd avoided calling her. Hearing her voice would have made it impossible not to ask to see her.

And he knew what would happen if he did.

Sitting through that gift exchange at the end of the party had seemed to take forever, and they hadn't been able to leave because Maura was in charge of handing out the presents. Weston's face, when he saw his giraffe, had been priceless. Good thing it was a toy, because if the child had squeezed a real giraffe that way, he was pretty sure the animal would have passed out from lack of oxygen.

But then it was over. And as they pulled out of the parking lot just after nine o'clock, he still wasn't certain where things stood with them. Until she put a hand on his thigh.

Okay, the invitation hadn't been in his imagination. It had been very, very real.

They'd both agreed the last time had been a mistake. So what had changed her mind?

Hell, did it even matter?

His body was telling him it definitely did not. He would take what he could get. And, like she said, they could just walk away at any time. Although the word she'd used had been "fall," which didn't sound nearly as easy.

But holding on could be even harder when things got too crazy. A little whisper went through his head that he brushed away. Of course he would choose to let go of the rope and hobble away. It's what Dex did. It's what he knew.

"We're going back to my place."

"Fine." She threw the word out with a nonchalance that wasn't like her, but it didn't make him change direction and take her home.

Could he really settle for one night?

Definitely. Because it was better than no nights at all.

They made it to his two-story home on the outskirts of the city. The house was bigger than he needed since it was just him, but he'd gotten the place for a steal. An elderly couple had wanted to downsize just as Dex was starting to look for something more permanent than a rental house. He'd snapped it up and had lived here for the last five years.

Unlike Maura's whites and creams, his place was all about dark wood and heavy, immovable furniture. Maybe because that's what his life had felt like. Or maybe it was like Maura had said: he was paralyzed and unable to move on. The big weighty pieces kept him anchored in place figuratively and literally.

Maura's hand was still on his thigh. Picking it up, he carried her palm to his mouth and pressed his lips against it. The smile she gave him clogged his senses. He wasn't positive this was really happening. But she sure looked real. Felt real.

They were back in their regular clothes, having left the cowboy hats and the "yeehaws" with the owner of Square Dancers R Us. They were no longer in the pretend world of the party.

He didn't want her to be disappointed by what she found inside. Or didn't find. "I don't have any Christmas decorations up."

It was two days before Christmas, and it seemed kind of a shame to let the date go by unnoticed, but wasn't this a much better present than a tree or lights?

It was for him. He wasn't sure about her.

"I don't care about the decorations, Dex. I'll be unwrapping the only present I want to see in just a few minutes. You." She leaned over and toyed with the skin where his shirt collar opened.

He swallowed. How was it that this woman knew exactly what to say to turn him inside out? Made him want her more than any other woman alive?

Sliding his hand in her hair, he tugged her close enough to kiss her. And the second his lips met hers, he was lost. So much for reality. She turned his world into a dream that he never wanted to wake up from, never wanted to leave.

"Inside. Now."

She laughed, but it was a little shaky. "I agree. But what kind of inside are we talking about? Inside? Or…*inside*."

He leaned forward and kissed her again. "Do I actually have to choose one or the other?"

"No. I just wanted to see which you wanted first."

With that, he snapped the door open and got out. "Don't tempt me. I'm pretty sure the neighbor to my left has a camera on his property. I don't think you want to be an internet sensation."

"Yikes! Probably not."

He opened her door and held his hand out. When she accepted it, he squeezed his fingers around it. He'd always loved holding her hand. Loved the way it felt to tow her behind him and know for sure that she was right there.

He hadn't realized how much he'd missed it until just this minute.

Or maybe he had. But he'd known there was no hope. Especially once he'd heard about her marriage.

He got her through the front door and slammed it behind her. Pressed her back against it. "There. Now, we're inside."

"Not quite. But you will be."

His chuckle came from a molten place within him. He moved close, pressing against her, his hands on either side of her head. "You're killing me here, Maura. I want this to last. Want you here all night."

"Don't you have someplace to be in the morning?"

"Mmm. I do. Yes." His hands slid to her butt and lifted her against him. Her legs wrapped around his hips as he carried her through the living room, past the kitchen and down the hallway to where his master suite was. After entering it, he bypassed his bed and went into the adjoining bathroom. He set her on the countertop, keeping his body between her legs, his swollen flesh already tight behind his zipper.

When her fingers went to her blouse, he shook his head. "No. My turn."

He made quick work of unbuttoning her white shirt, guiding it down her arms but leaving it over her wrists. Her white lacy bra pushed her breasts up, the soft skin beckoning to him.

He leaned over and kissed one of the soft mounds, his lips sliding up her neck.

Her breath hissed as he nipped the sensitive area just below her ear.

Then he found the snap on her jeans and undid it, slowly easing her zipper down. "Lift up."

She did as he asked and he tugged the garment off, letting it fall to the floor along with her black pumps.

Sitting on his counter in his bathroom, in just her bra and matching panties, she looked like a goddess. All feminine and sweet, yet with a raw edge of sexiness that drove him to madness. "You are gorgeous."

He reached behind her and raked his fingers through her hair, loving the way it was like silk across her skin. She was irresistible.

And tonight he wasn't even going to try.

He quickly divested himself of his clothes and sheathed himself before moving back to her, kissing her deeply.

His fingers slipped beneath the elastic on her panties and dipped lower, until he found what he was looking for. She was warm and wet, and that satiny skin would feel like heaven around him.

Maura moaned, her head tipping back, eyes fluttering shut as she gave herself over to what he was doing. He'd said he wanted it to last, but he was no longer sure he would be able to fulfill that promise as his body was demanding more and more and cursing when he offered it nothing.

Keeping one hand where it was, he used his other to pull her to the very edge of the counter.

"Oh, Dex…"

Hell. The way she said his name…

He made his strokes firmer, her hips beginning to move in time with each touch, lifting and falling in a way that mimicked what he wanted. What he needed.

And the sounds she made. Low. Throaty.

He was home. Back beside the creek. Making love in the shallows as the water gurgled around their bodies.

Sliding two fingers inside, he crooked them, continuing to stroke her with his thumb as he added slight pressure to the spot he knew she liked. He needed her to come. Wanted to know he still had the power to make her as mad for him as he was for her.

Come on, baby. Give it to me.

He quickened his pace, nipping at her lips, her jawline, her neck, before leaning back to watch her.

Her lips parted and she grabbed several quick breaths, hips lifting…reaching…

Her eyes flashed open and focused on him for a split second before she yanked her hands from the sleeves of her shirt and grabbed his shoulders.

He pulled aside the crotch of her panties and plunged home. She wrapped her legs around him the way she had when he'd carried her in here as he rode her, her movements every bit as sinuous as they'd been when she was riding that bull the night at the bar. Watching her had been a turn-on then, but it was nothing compared to having her here in his arms, acting like she couldn't get enough of him.

It was the same for him. He couldn't get enough of this women. Never had, never would, no matter how many times they had sex together.

It was earthy and raw and exactly the way he liked it. The way he liked her.

He thrust harder even as she nibbled at his lips, whispering against them. And when he could hold back no longer, he entered deep and went rigid as he spasmed, pouring everything he had into her.

When it was over, his legs went weak. Mind numbed to everything except the memory of what had just happened.

Keeping the connection for as long as possible, he carried her back into the bedroom and laid her gently on the bed, shuddering as he slid free.

Her hair was wild and free across his pillow. His side of the bed.

Accident? Or had he meant to put her there?

Right now he didn't know. There were too many tangled emotions trying to surface. He just kept pushing them back under. He didn't want to think. Didn't want to do anything except lie beside her and relish the feel of her next to him.

Except he wanted her naked. Completely naked.

He leaned over and slid her undergarment down her legs and undid her bra. She yawned up at him, her beautiful face shining up at him. She looked just like the Maura from many years ago. The Maura he'd slept with…the Maura he'd loved.

"Tired?" he asked, running the tip of his finger down her nose.

"Mmm…no. Happy."

The words the square dance caller had used came back to him, sending a slow shiver down his spine. *That's what we all want, isn't it? The chance to be happy?*

She'd been happy with him once before. Until he'd destroyed everything by telling her he couldn't be what she needed him to be.

He couldn't be then…and he couldn't be now, if he were honest with himself.

Why? The question thumped in the background, getting louder and louder until it demanded an answer.

An answer he didn't have, except that he came with too much baggage, feared loss far too much to try to hold on to anything. Certainly not something as elusive as happiness.

Hell, he'd even lost a baby without knowing about it. What if she'd told him about the miscarriage back then?

Another thought struck him. What if she'd died during it? Or during childbirth?

He suddenly couldn't look at her without an abrupt sense of panic stabbing through him. His heart pounded, and his mouth went dry.

What if she'd died? Just like most of his family had.

He needed to get out of this room. Now.

Heading toward the door, he stopped when she called out to him. "Where are you going?"

She was half-sitting up in bed, a strange expression on her face.

He cast around for something to say and grabbed the first thing that came to mind. "Just to bring us something to drink. I'll be right back."

The tension in her face eased, and she lay back down, not bothering to cover her breasts. "Okay, then. Don't be long."

"I won't."

He moved through the doorway, stopping just outside the room to lean a shoulder against the wall. What the hell was wrong with him?

Why were these old feelings slamming into him again? The fear he'd had all those years ago that Maura would die, too, and he'd be left totally alone.

He'd had sex with women since he and Maura had ended things. But he couldn't remember feeling this unsettled—this *afraid*—with any of them. He'd had the same sensation two weeks ago, before finally deciding he'd imagined it.

It was obvious he hadn't. Because right now the sweaty palms, the jittery sense of doom, was all very real. It was the exact same sensation he got when...

When it snowed.

When there were reports of black ice.

When he heard the sound of an ambulance screaming its way down the highway.

His hands fisted against his sides, another wave of horror washing through him and threatening to bring him to his knees. His eyes burned as a wall of water built up behind them.

God. Not now. Not when she might come out and see him.

Forcing himself to move, he tried to power his way through the maze his mind had constructed. But it was hopeless. He was lost. Just as he'd been for the last fifteen years.

He went into the kitchen and got two glasses for water. He put a couple of ice cubes in each one before stopping and studying the contents of the cabinet.

To hell with water. He needed something else. Getting down a third glass, he moved over to the bar. Picking up a bottle, he poured a finger of whiskey into the tumbler and bolted the contents down in one swift motion. The liquid seared his esophagus and hit his stomach with a jolt, the warmth spreading throughout his body. The only place it didn't touch was the iciness of his heart. But at least his mouth wasn't as parched.

It was the only thing that wasn't.

He planted his hand on the bar, holding himself up as he sloshed another measure into the tumbler. He squeezed his eyes shut.

"Dammit. What the hell am I doing here?"

He opened his eyes and gazed into the steady amber liquid as if it might have all the answers. But of course it didn't. He'd just put the rim to his lips when he stopped, his glance meeting Maura's. She was standing in the doorway, wrapped in a sheet, staring at him. Her expression was…stricken.

He'd seen that expression before. Had seen it in his dreams many times over the years.

It was the same expression she'd had fifteen years ago after she'd stood in front of him and asked him where he saw their relationship going. When he'd told her he didn't know.

He tipped the glass and swallowed the drink. Put the tumbler down.

She didn't say anything for a long minute before finally breaking the silence. "That bad, huh?"

"I don't know what you mean." The lie came out quickly. Easily.

She turned and nodded at the tall glasses on the counter. The ice in them was melting. "You said you were coming out to get us drinks. I just didn't realize you needed something a whole lot stronger than water to face coming back to the bedroom."

"It's not that."

"Really? Then why don't you tell me what it is."

He had no idea. He'd been standing here trying to figure it out, only to come up blank. "I really don't know."

"It's okay. I think I do." She licked her lips and drew the sheet tighter. She probably didn't realize it, but her silhouette was highlighted by the light in the hallway, every slender curve visible to him. He wanted it. He wanted it all. Wanted the happiness that old square dancer had talked about.

But dammit, he couldn't have it. Because the stuff sloshing behind his need of her was corrosive, eating away at his gut and leaving him a hollowed-out shell. The same shell that had been left after the accident.

He didn't deserve to be happy, no matter what anyone said.

His brain knew that wasn't true. But his emotions?

They sabotaged him each time he reached out to grasp at it.

To grasp at her.

She tossed her hair behind her shoulder. "I'm going to go, Dex. I've already called a cab. This was a mistake. Somehow I always knew it was, but I'd… It doesn't matter. You won't have to worry about it anymore. Or about me." Tears shimmered in her eyes, and she swiped at them with an angry stroke of her hand. "I hope someday you find what you need. I only hope it isn't too late when you do."

With that, she turned on her heel and disappeared down the hallway. To get dressed probably.

He made no move to follow her.

Because he'd already found what he needed. Except, she was right. It was too late. At least for him. He poured another drink, moved into his living room and sat on his sofa. This time he didn't gulp it. He sipped it, biding his time as he listened to every sound she made back in his bedroom.

He should go to her. Talk to her. Take her back to bed and make everything okay.

But he didn't, because there was no way anything would ever be okay. He'd only be delaying the inevitable. Or, worse, hurt her all over again.

So he sat there as he heard her pull his bedroom door shut with a soft click. As the sound of her footsteps came down his hallway. As she edged past the back of the sofa where he sat. As the front door opened and then closed.

And then she was gone.

Dex shut his eyes and leaned his head against the

back of the sofa. Some men might have considered this a win—evading the cuddles and pillow talk that came after getting what they wanted.

But it wasn't a win. He would never see this as anything other than a big fat loss. A loss of what could have been. Of what had been. A loss he would never get over be it fifteen years or seventy years.

And Dex had no idea how to make it anything other than what it was.

CHAPTER TEN

IT WAS CHRISTMAS.

But it sure didn't feel like it.

Maura hadn't heard from Dex since she'd left the house two days ago. Then again, she hadn't tried to call him either. And she wouldn't. She was really and truly done. When she'd seen him chug that drink like it was water and then pour himself another, she knew. He was having a panic attack. One that being with her had caused. And that just about killed her.

It would just happen again and again, and she was not willing to cause him even more pain and suffering than she already had.

To stay and watch him go through it had been too hard, so she'd let go and fallen away. Just like she'd told Dex she would.

She'd decided to take some personal time, which she'd saved up over the last couple of years, to try to decide what to do from here. The first thing she was going to do, though, was some award-winning pretending—something she'd suggested Dex do after they'd slept together that first time. She was going to act like it was Christmas and pretend it was a time of celebration.

She was going to do for herself what she'd helped do for the women at the center with that party the hospital had thrown: keep herself so busy that she had no time to stop and think about how much pain she was in.

Because it was deep. And seemed endless. And she was pretty sure she wasn't strong enough to climb out of the pit she found herself in. At least not today.

She would, though, just like she'd done once before.

So she'd gone to the big-box store in the center of town, where a few straggly trees sat looking almost as lonely as she was. She'd been half-surprised the store was open today, and she was glad it was. Because the more she moved, the less she thought.

She glanced at her car with its minuscule roof, trying to decide if she could at least strap the smallest of the trees to the top of it. Surely that four-foot one over there would be okay. She went over and stood beside it before paying the clerk, who was shivering in temperatures that had suddenly dropped well below freezing.

"Sorry about this," she said. "I just didn't plan things very well."

Ha! She hadn't planned them at all. And she certainly hadn't planned what had happened with Dex.

"It's okay. I have to be out here anyway. At least for another hour." He put the tree through a machine that bound the branches to the trunk and encased it in some kind of netting. Then he helped her set it on top of her car and ratcheted it tight with the straps she'd brought.

At least she'd planned for that. She wasn't entirely hopeless.

"Thanks." She waved to him and tossed the bag of lights and ornaments she'd bought to go on the tree into the car. She got in, giving an exasperated laugh when she saw the tree trunk hanging over the front of her car. The chuckle faded when the memory of Dex all scrunched up in her passenger seat came back to her. He'd almost been too big for her car. Just like the tree that now sat on top of it.

It was okay. She'd just go slow.

Like she'd done with Dex?

She rolled her eyes and pulled out of the lot, creeping along as the wind tugged at her vehicle. The streets were pretty much deserted, thank God. Everyone else was smart. They were all in their nice warm homes, celebrating with their families.

Well, Maura had already gone to her folks' house and tried to smile her way through brunch, exchanging the presents they'd gotten one another. She was glad she'd been able to get out of there before her mom sensed something was wrong and asked her about it. They'd had no idea that Dex had wandered back into her life, if only for a short time. Or that he was right back out of it again.

This time it was for good. She would make sure of that. When a sharp gust pulled at the vehicle, it wobbled a bit before righting itself. The tree had made the car a little more top-heavy than normal. Maybe getting it had been a bad idea.

No. This was step one of getting back to normal. She was going to celebrate Christmas, dammit, if it killed her.

She rounded a sharp downhill corner in the road, easing off the gas as she did. If she remembered right, there was a stoplight just ahead.

There. She saw it.

Her peripheral vision caught sight of something shimmering on the black asphalt in front of her. She looked and realized too late that it was a patch of ice that had developed from the rain earlier today.

The light. Oh, God. It was red!

Her muscles went rigid, and she tried to tap her brakes, but the momentum of the corner and the downhill slope sent her car into a sideways skid that picked up speed as she went. It dragged her right through the red light, barely missing another car as she struggled to regain control of the car. It was no use. She was going to crash. A light post loomed on her left and she hit it with enough force to slam her head against the driver's side window. Stunned, she sat there for a minute or two, her vision spinning around and around. She blinked, trying to clear it. She lifted a hand to feel for blood and winced as a sharp pain went through her wrist.

The world still slowly spun, and about every third rotation she spotted the tree trunk of her Christmas tree, lying in the exact spot it had been strapped.

Well, at least something had come through unscathed. In the distance she heard the eerie sound of her car horn blaring. She put her uninjured hand to her ear and tried to do the shake that had cleared those damned crystals last time, but it didn't work. Okay, she needed to at least call for help. Except her phone was nowhere to be seen.

She really hadn't meant the whole thing about celebrating Christmas if it killed her.

She needed to get out of the car.

Just then the passenger's side door opened and a

woman peered in at her. "Are you okay? You slid past me through the intersection."

"Was that you?" Her thoughts were fuzzy and it took a lot of effort to continue. "Can you help me get out?"

"I called 911. They told me not to move you."

"Oh, that's right." She was a doctor. She should know that. "Okay. Is—is my tree okay?"

The woman cocked her head and looked at her like she was crazy. "Your tree is fine. You should be more worried about you."

"I'm okay. Just a bump on the head and a sprained wrist." Except her wrist was hurting more and more. Maybe she'd broken it. Great. That was all she needed. How was she going to string lights with a broken wrist?

She took a deep breath as an urge to laugh appeared out of nowhere. Maybe the woman was right. Why was she worried about a tree?

The wail of a siren, joined by another one, sounded off in the distance. "At least the door opened."

"I'm sorry?"

"I won't need the jaws of life." This time the laughter couldn't be contained, though it sounded weird. Like it was coming from someone else. Okay, maybe she had a concussion in addition to her bum wrist.

Another head poked in the door next to the woman. She recognized him—he was a paramedic from the hospital. The laughter dried up.

"Ugh. I'm sorry you had to come out on Christmas night for my little fender bender. Why are you on that side of the car?"

"Have you seen the door on your side?"

"No. Is it bad?"

"Yep. We're going to have to get you out this side. Are you injured?"

"I sprained my wrist."

She heard the woman behind her. "She's been kind of out of it, talking about the Jaws of Life and worried about her Christmas tree. And I saw her rub her head."

She heard him speaking in hushed tones to someone else asking them to call ahead to the hospital. Then he popped his head back in. "You probably know the routine. We're going to stabilize your head and neck and slide you out of the car."

"Are you kidding me? I can scoot over if you'll help me."

"Do I look like I'm kidding?" The man's face was stern, without even a hint of humor.

"I guess not."

Five minutes later they had a backboard and neck brace in place, but when they went to slide her free of the car, someone's hand pressed on her left side and a moan slid out before she could stop it.

"What?"

"I—I just have a little something going on with my side." This was ridiculous. She'd been driving at practically a snail's pace. "I was going slow because of the tree. I shouldn't be hurt at all."

He looked her in the eye. "That tree probably saved your life. The salt trucks are doing their best, but the roads are icing up fast, and they're forecasting an inch or two of snow tonight."

Snow. Dex hated the snow. She remembered his white-knuckle grip on the steering wheel, and suddenly she was crying without really knowing why.

She was still crying when they got her out and lifted her onto the stretcher.

She tried to wave him off, giving a soggy hiccup as she did. "Can someone just run me home? I'm okay. Really." She was horrified that she might break down completely and that someone might guess the reason. Or, worse, that she might see Dex at the hospital and he might ask why she was so distraught over a tiny little accident.

It was normal to be upset, right? No matter how inconsequential her injuries.

Except this was how his dad and sisters had died. She didn't want to see his face when it all came back to him. It would be the same face he'd had as he threw back drink after drink at his house.

It was the same face that had caused her to walk out all over again.

"Sorry, no can do. Your hand is already swelling, and you've got some pain in your left quadrant, which means you probably have a broken rib or two from the side impact."

She was suddenly too tired to argue. "Okay, if you really think it's necessary, I'll go. What about my car?"

"I have your purse and your keys. It'll have to be towed."

So much for putting up a tree. Looked like she wouldn't even get to do that. She bit back another spurt of emotion. She must have a concussion. She was never this weepy.

Even after leaving Dex's house, she hadn't sobbed. Maybe this was all part of the grief process.

They arrived at the hospital fifteen minutes later.

Maura's world had finally stopped spinning in circles, although her head still hurt. They ran her through the ER, and she found herself having to refrain from issuing orders or pronouncing her own diagnosis to the attending physician.

It was weird being the one lying on the gurney rather than standing over it. A thought came to her, and she grabbed the hand of one of the nurses. "Dr. Chamblisse isn't here, is he?"

The woman blinked at her, but if she thought the question odd, she didn't react. "I think I saw him leave about thirty minutes ago. Do you want me to call him?"

"No! I mean no. We just had a patient in common and I wanted to…"

She wanted to what? Discuss it. There was no way the nurse would buy that. She glued her lips together so she couldn't say anything else stupid.

At least that meant she wouldn't be running into him. It was exactly why she'd decided to take some time off. To figure out if she could even face seeing him day in and day out. If her fear of him being at the hospital was any indicator, the answer to that was no.

She had no idea what she was going to do if that was the case.

"We're going to run you up to X-Ray and see what's going on with that hand and wrist—your ribs, too. I also think you have a mild concussion."

Maura leaned back against the pillow. "I see why he hates winter so much."

"Sorry?"

"Nothing. Just talking to myself."

While she was waiting for her turn in Radiology, a

nurse came with a pill and a cup of water. "The doctor thought you might appreciate a little something to take the edge off."

She was right. The pain had been steadily building, especially when she moved her left side. She swallowed the meds down. "Thanks. I'm sure I'll be better by tomorrow."

Really? Was she sure about that? Now that she'd had time to think, the clawing pain that had assailed her ever since she'd left Dex's house was back. She'd been able to ignore it over the last two days by filling her time up to the max, buying presents for her family, catching up on housework and a bunch of other trivial stuff. But now that she was lying on a gurney with nothing to do but think, the pain was back. And it was the kind of ache that no amount of medicine would take away.

They were finally ready for her, and although it hurt to slide from the gurney onto the X-ray table, the pill the nurse had given her was starting to kick in. They were done with her pretty quickly and she glanced at the tech. "See anything?"

He gave her a knowing smile. "I'll let the doc get with you about that."

"I'll bet you say that to all your patients."

His smile widened. "All the ones who dare to ask."

She came out of X-Ray, and they put her in a room down the hall. Surely they weren't keeping her overnight.

Except how would she even get home? She had no car.

The thought of lying in the hospital with nothing to do but dwell on what had happened at Dex's house terrified her. Because as he'd gotten up to go into the kitchen, she realized that she still loved him. Which meant that all her flippant remarks about only wanting sex from him were a smoke screen, an attempt to hide the truth: that she desperately hoped she might be wrong about him. That he might still care for her. Might be able to finally commit to being with her forever.

Then she'd caught him chugging down liquor like he couldn't erase the image of her fast enough.

God, how could she have been so very stupid. She wasn't a kid anymore. She was a grown-up who should be better able to make rational decisions.

Smart decisions. Decisions that wouldn't—

A knock sounded at her door.

Maybe that was the doctor with her X-ray results. Maybe she wouldn't have to stay after all.

The person who opened that door was definitely not that doctor.

She swallowed hard. It was Dex.

This couldn't be happening.

Why? Why now?

Did he want to grind home the fact that there was no hope? That what was once over and done was still over and done?

Well, there was no need. He'd gotten that across loud and clear. "I thought you'd left for the night."

"I did. I just got off the phone with my mom, actually. We had a long overdue talk about moving on and living life." His face was deadly serious. "And then I heard you'd been in an accident. I came back."

He came back because she crashed.

Only because she'd crashed.

Her heart crumbled into ashes. That was almost as bad as when she'd toyed with telling him about the pregnancy and how afraid she'd been that he would only want to be with her because of the baby.

Her voice came out a little harsher than she meant it to. "As you can see, I'm just fine. There was no need to change whatever plans you'd had for tonight. Especially not on Christmas. You should go see your mom."

"You misunderstood. I didn't change my plans because of the accident. I changed them because of you. I was actually headed to your house when the call came through."

"You were? Why? I thought you said you'd just gotten off the phone with your mother."

"I did. I called her. Because I can't get that man's words out of my head. It's why I was coming over to see you, next."

She had no idea what he was talking about. "What man?"

"The caller at the hoedown. He said, 'That's what we all want, isn't it? The chance to be happy.'"

She remembered him saying that. But she didn't see how it changed anything. "Sometimes it just doesn't work that way. As much as we might want to be happy, it just isn't in the cards. Let go of the bull and fall, remember?"

"But what if I don't want to fall this time? What if I want to hold on tight until the very end of the ride?"

The pain pills must be impairing her cognitive skills. "I don't understand."

"I sat down over the last two days and played back everything that was said when you came to my house.

And although the words were different than the ones that ended our relationship fifteen years ago, the underlying issue was still there—fear. I threw it all away because I was afraid. Because I didn't think I deserved to be happy. My mom and my heart finally told me otherwise."

He took her uninjured hand in his, and her eyes prickled in dangerous ways. "I don't want to make the same mistake, Maura. This time, I want to hold on."

"And if you change your mind and break my heart all over again…?" Her words scraped past a rough patch in her throat and she ended in a whisper. "Please don't."

A muscle worked in his jaw. "Hell, Maura, I am so sorry. Sorry for what I put you through back then. And sorry for what I did at the house. I have no right to ask you for another chance…" He gave a visible swallow. "But here I am."

"You want a second chance? For what?"

"For us. Because I realized two nights ago that I was still in love with you, and it scared me shitless. Tonight, I finally worked through my fears and decided I could either let all the what-ifs destroy any chance for happiness. Or I could change them and force those same what-ifs to look toward good things."

"Good things?"

He nodded. "Like what if I kick my fear in the teeth and ask you to marry me. Like what if I ask you to have those babies you talked about having earlier. Only they'd be *my* babies."

She stared at him. "I really do have a concussion."

"What?"

"If I'm imagining all this and wake up tomorrow

alone in this bed, I am going to come and find you. And you won't like it when I do."

He kissed her hand. "You're not imagining it. And I probably deserve whatever bad things you want to do to me, because I've wanted to do them to myself for years. But I hope you'll believe me when I say I love you. I want to spend the rest of my life with you."

He took a shuddery breath. "When I heard you'd slid on some ice and hit a light pole, I was frantic. They were bringing you in and wouldn't tell me how you were. You can't imagine where my thoughts were."

"I think I can."

"The whole drive back to the hospital, my brain fixated on all the time I'd wasted worrying about what could happen. I'd rather be with you for whatever time we both have on this earth than do nothing and wake up wishing I'd done things differently. So what do you say?"

She tilted her head, only to have the world roll to one side. "Whoa, remind me not to do that again. And if you're serious about asking me to marry you, the answer to that is yes. I love you, too, Dex. And I want to spend whatever time I have left on this earth with you as well. And with those babies we're going to make. Six? Seven?"

When his eyes widened, she laughed. "I'm kidding. I'm fine with one or two."

"How do you know I didn't consider six or seven a lowball number?"

"Um, yeah…no."

"Okay, one or two it is."

She pulled her hand from his and reached up to touch his face. "I need you to do something for me."

"Okay, what is it?"

"I need you to find out where they took my car."

He smiled. "I'm pretty sure I'm going to call your parents first, so they know what happened to you."

"I'm serious." For some reason, it was suddenly very important that he find her car.

"Did you leave something in it?"

"No, I left something *on* it, and I really, really need it. Especially now."

He looked at her like she was crazy, and maybe she was.

"What is it?"

"It's my Christmas tree. The guy I bought it from at the store was shivering from the cold, and yet he still wrapped that tree for me and helped me strap it on top of the car." The tears that came to her eyes this time were ones of gratitude. "I drove really slowly because of that tree. The EMT says it probably saved my life."

"Thank God." He leaned down and pressed his cheek against hers. "I'll find the car, honey. And when I do, I'm taking that tree to my house and giving it the treatment it deserves. The treatment you deserve."

Her voice was shaky as she tried to find something humorous to say. Something that wouldn't turn her into a wet dishrag. "You're stealing my tree?"

"Not exactly. But when they finally spring you from this place, you're coming home with me. I'm not spending one more night without you by my side."

"It's for real, this time, isn't it?"

He didn't ask her what she was talking about. They both knew.

"Yes, Maura. It's for real." He kissed her softly on the mouth. "And this time, you'd better hold on. Because it's forever."

"Forever." The word came out as a sigh.

"All anyone wants is to be happy," he murmured against her mouth. "And that includes you. And me."

EPILOGUE

One year later

CHRISTMAS MUSIC FLOATED through the house as Dex threw more tinsel on the tree until the box was almost empty. "A little more on the left."

"If I put any more weight on that side of the tree it's going to topple over."

She threw him a fake glare. "Is that a euphemism for my belly?"

He left what he was doing and came over to her, kissing her forehead. "Your belly is gorgeous, Maura. Just like the rest of you."

"Good answer." She groaned. "But if little Noah doesn't come soon, I'm going to have to go through Lamaze classes all over again. It's been ages." The baby was a week overdue and seemed to be in no hurry to put in an appearance.

"The doctor said there's no reason to worry. Not yet."

She glanced out the window and saw the first flakes of snow. She tensed, glancing at her husband.

"I know. And I'm fine."

They'd talked through all his baggage regarding the

snow and what had happened to his family. He had told her he now realized there was good and bad in everything. What had happened had been awful, no doubt about it. But it had also brought them together in the end. That slip on a patch of ice had knocked some sense into both of them.

He tossed the empty tinsel package into the kitchen garbage and then came over and sat beside her. He'd started a fire in the fireplace a few hours earlier and the sounds of crackling wood was heavenly.

She couldn't be happier. She had the man of her dreams, and soon they'd have a little one to share their lives with.

Sliding her fingers into those of her husband, she leaned her head against him with a sigh. "I love you so much, Dex."

"Right there with you, babe."

A twinge in her abdomen made her jump. "Speaking of babes…"

Dex glanced down. "Kicking again?"

"I'm not sure. I think… Oh!"

Her hand went to her stomach, rubbing in little circles.

This time his voice held a little more concern. "What is it?"

"Well, I didn't plan it this way. But I think we might just be getting a baby for Christmas."

Dex was up in a flash. "Are you serious? I need to get the go bag. Wait here."

She watched him rush from place to place getting what they needed for the next day or so and putting out the fire. A huge lump of emotion clogged her throat.

"This is our first baby—I think we have plenty of..."
She stopped midsentence when another wave of tension
squeezed her belly. Okay, so that was a little closer than
she expected it to be.

"Okay, don't panic, but we might want to get a move
on. A Christmas baby is one thing. A Christmas baby
born in the car is something else entirely."

Even as she said it, she went over to him and stopped
his frantic movements, laying her head on his chest, her
belly pressed tight against him. "God, Dex. It's so perfect. So very perfect."

"What is?"

"Life," she said. Then she stretched up to receive his kiss.

* * * * *

THE SINGLE DAD'S
HOLIDAY WISH

SUSAN CARLISLE

MILLS & BOON

To Ryan.
Thanks for joining our family.

CHAPTER ONE

Dr. Liz Poole stood in the corner of the large room watching the other event attendees. *I have no business being here. A social butterfly, I'm not.* She wasn't any better now in interpersonal situations than she had been as a girl. Times like this she missed her sister, Louisa, the most. She'd been the one everyone wanted around, the life of the party. Yet Louisa wouldn't have come with Liz. This event she'd have considered dull.

Against Liz's better judgment and after the insistence of Melissa, her head nurse, Liz had decided to join the Christmas get-together. Melissa stayed on Liz about needing to go out more, be more social, meet someone. Often Melissa had teased her about turning into a hermit and becoming one of those cat ladies. Liz didn't even own a cat. To get Melissa off her back for a little while, Liz had forced herself to make an appearance at the party being held at the Riverside Country Club in Decatur, Alabama. Surely she would know a few people from working with them during one of the citywide events?

Liz took a sip of her sparkling pink drink so she'd have something to do. *At least it was good.* She scanned the small room. The group drinking cocktails appeared festively dressed in mostly red and green right down to the man with the plaid bowtie.

This party had been organized as a thank-you for the volunteers who had helped at festivals throughout the last year. One of the local businesses hosted it. Liz volunteered in the medical tent as often as her schedule would allow. Truly she wasn't as pitiful as Melissa and her mother believed.

Outside of her volunteer work, she had her chess and book clubs. She got out.

Dinner should be served in a few minutes. As soon as it was over, she'd slip out. Already fretting over having to make small talk during dinner, she searched for someone she knew to sit with. She could only hope her table companions would have partners on either side of them who would keep them occupied so she could just eat her meal.

She returned to her original thought of why she'd let Melissa talk her into coming. *Because it's advantageous for your job, your position in the community. You need to get out more*, Melissa's words singsonged through her head. No doubt her head nurse was correct but that didn't mean Liz found that a comfort.

Just the other day, her mother had once again lectured her on taking chances. Being her mother's only family and sole focus wasn't fun. Maybe by attending this event she would make her mother happy. Something Liz often found difficult to do.

The chairman of the city council's volunteer program tapped his glass, getting the crowd's attention. "I'd like to thank everybody for being here tonight." He looked directly at Liz.

No doubt he was surprised to see her since she'd been adamant she wouldn't be attending when he'd called the day before. He had invited her to a number of these events over the last few years and she'd declined them all.

"I hope everyone's looking forward to the holidays. We'd like to thank you for your service to the community during the past year and hope you consider helping us again." He twisted up his face and shrugged. "I also want to remind everyone that we have the Festival of Trees on the River event happening in a little less than two weeks. Those planning to help, please stay for a few minutes afterward. On that note, let's go in for dinner. It's buffet style, so feel free to fill your plates more than once."

Liz sighed. *There went her chance at a quick getaway.* She'd signed up to help in the medical tent during the festival's flotilla. Walking toward the double doors leading to the next room, she joined the line forming. She soon found herself sandwiched between two men. One was an older gentleman with a large belly and a red-tipped nose. She gave him a slight smile. Glancing at the tall man behind her, she found him busy talking to another man. He had a nice voice. Smooth, warm and inviting.

Her attention turned to the round dining tables. They had been covered in red cloths with greenery surrounding a candle. She needed to start her Christmas decorating soon. After the loss of her sister a little over a year ago and her father four years earlier, the holidays weren't as fun as they had been in the past. This year she planned to have more Christmas spirit than the last. The first holiday without a loved one was the most difficult.

A bump to her back made her lurch forward. She took a quick step to keep from falling as a firm hand grabbed her arm, steadying her. A zing of responsiveness ran through her.

"I'm so sorry. Are you all right?" The deep voice she'd admired a few moments earlier said close to her ear.

Liz shivered as the heat of his hand seeped through the material of her blouse. "Yes, yes, I'm fine."

"Are you sure?" His intense green eyes studied her. "I didn't mean to almost knock you down."

"I'm okay. Really." He looked as if he were about her age. He towered over her. As an above-average woman in height, she appreciated his. For once in her life, she stood beside someone who fit her. She'd heard all the tall jokes in school, even knew she'd been rejected for dates because of her height. Add that to being "brainy" and high school had been painful. Louisa had saved her back then, but now she was gone.

"I'm glad. I apparently can't walk and talk at the same time. Or maybe it's that I don't look where I'm going." He offered her a charming smile.

Liz had no doubt he could use the same one to get out of a speeding ticket from a policewoman and succeed. It didn't hurt he was handsome with blond wavy hair trimmed tighter on the sides and longer on the top. He had the type of locks that invited a woman to run her fingers through them.

Oh, my goodness, she really had lost her mind.

Over a white shirt, he wore a burgundy cable sweater. Tan slacks hugged trim hips and dark brown suede shoes finished his outfit. All in all, he was the complete package of a fine-looking male.

He indicated with his hand. "We'd better move ahead or the line will start going around us."

"Oh," she gasped. She'd been staring. A gap had grown between her and the man ahead. Liz hurriedly closed the space.

The man with the plaid bowtie walked past them with his plate full.

"Not everyone can carry one of those off," the man behind her whispered, as he stepped up beside her.

Liz giggled and nodded. "I agree."

"By the way, I'm Carter Jacobs." He offered his hand.

A large comfortable hand surrounded hers as she took it. "Liz Poole."

"Nice to bump into you. I mean uh…meet you." He grinned.

"You too." He certainly could charm. She stepped forward, making sure a break didn't form again. When she stopped, she glanced back.

Carter's gaze returned to her. "So, do you come to these sorts of things often?"

That question made Liz grin. He could only be sincere because that come-on line must be the oldest of them all. "Truthfully, this is the first one I've been to."

"It's my first, as well. I'm sort of new to town."

This time she suppressed a laugh. Was he for real or was his entire vocabulary nothing but pickup lines? "Welcome to Decatur. I hope you're happy here." Liz groaned to herself. She had started to sound as lame as him.

"My grandparents used to live here so I'm familiar with the area."

She nodded. "I was born and raised here."

"Then I guess you know all the in+s and outs of living here." He looked directly at her.

Her cheeks grew warm. Was he flirting with her? If he was, she liked it. "I don't know about that."

He glanced around the room. "Do you volunteer often?"

"Three or four times a year. Usually at large events where a doctor's needed."

"You're a doctor?" A note of surprise hung in his voice.

"I am an otolaryngologist."

"An ENT. My son spends his fair share of time with one of those despite his father being an internist."

"You're a doctor, as well. Small world." Now she was the one amazed. In the medical world, she felt confident. "Sometimes the most you can do is put in tubes. Infections can be hard to cure otherwise."

"So I've learned. But like most parents, I don't want to go there even if my training says differently. Why haven't I met you before? I've worked a few events."

"I've been on call the last two so that might be why." Was he coming on to her? Even if he wasn't, it was still nice to have a man pay her some attention. That alone made the awkwardness of coming tonight worth it.

Liz arrived at the stack of plates at the end of the buffet table. Taking one, she started down the long table, filling her plate with food. Carter followed the line to the other side. Liz finished well before he did. She looked back to find him. Not wanting to appear presumptuous that he might want to sit with her, she went looking for a place without waiting on him. A woman she knew called her over to her table. Liz took the last open seat. She noticed Carter looking her way before he moved to another area of the room.

Carter exited the building, zipping up his jacket against the cool December weather. A breeze rolling in off the nearby Tennessee River always made it feel colder. He ran his hand into his trouser pocket, searching for his keys.

The parking lot was almost empty. His SUV and a small compact car were all that remained on this side of the building. As he walked, he saw the woman he had brushed against in the dinner line, the one with the pretty smile, sitting in the driver's seat. She appeared perplexed.

A grinding noise came from her car. Carter approached a little slower. The sound came again. Walking wide around the car, he circled toward the front so that she could see him. He raised a hand in an effort not to frighten her.

Her eyes widened. He went to her window and tapped, making a circular motion with his hand for her to roll it down. She hesitated, then did as he requested. "I didn't want to scare you. Can I help?"

"I don't know what's wrong. It just won't start." Frustration rang loud and clear in her voice. "Everything was fine when I got here."

"Try it one more time." Carter kept his voice calm while hoping he could actually help.

The same grinding noise reverberated around the car. Liz gave him a look of expectation as if he'd have the answer. Carter wished he could give her more encouraging news. He shook his head. "It's not the battery because it wants to turn over. I wish I could tell you more. I'm a much better doctor than I am a mechanic."

She huffed, hers lips thinning. "I appreciate your help. I'll call the auto service and have them come."

"It's too cold for you to wait out here."

"I'll go back inside." She gathered her purse.

"I saw them locking up on my way out. Even the caterers are gone. I can't leave you here by yourself."

"I'll be fine. It shouldn't take the tow truck too long to come."

Was she afraid of him? Outside of their short conversation, they really were strangers. "You might be surprised. Why don't you give them a call while I wait?" He stepped away, giving her some privacy.

She picked up the phone. Shoving his hands into his pockets, he rocked back on his heels while she talked.

"Really? It's going to take that long?" Liz said into the phone. Soon she hung up.

He winced. "That didn't sound good."

She dropped her phone into her purse and gave him a disgusted look. "It wasn't. It's going to be over an hour before they can get here." She looked past him, then at the dark building, her attractive face drawing up with concern.

"You don't need to stay here by yourself. It's already dark." His lips tightened. "My teenage babysitter has to be home soon since it's a school night. I know we don't know each other well but I wish you'd let me take you home. I just need to stop by my house for a sec."

She shook her head. "That's not necessary. I'll just stay here and lock the doors."

"And freeze to death." He couldn't be that scary. "Come on, it's too cold for you to do that." He stomped his feet to warm them, emphasizing his point. "I promise I'm a good guy. You at least know me better than you do the wrecker driver."

She bit her bottom lip, looking unsure. "I don't know."

"So you do know the wrecker driver?"

She gave him a quizzical look, then a slight smile. "No, I don't know him."

"See, you do know me better. Do you have someone you can call to come pick you up who can be here in a few minutes?" Carter checked his watch. He should be going.

"Not really. My mother's out this evening and my nurse lives thirty minutes away." Her pitiful look tugged at him.

"Come on then. You've no choice. I'll need to take you home. If it'll make you feel better, you can call someone and tell them who I am, where we're going and what's going on. Leave the phone on the whole time."

Liz exhaled, looking over her shoulder at the building again. "I'll call my nurse."

Carter listened as she explained her predicament.

"Melissa wants to know your home address."

He gave it to her. Glancing at him, she lowered her eyelids and said into the phone. "Yes."

If the light hadn't been so dim, he could have confirmed his suspicion that she'd blushed. What had her nurse asked her?

"I'll call you the minute I get home. Promise." She hung up, then gathered her purse and stepped out of the car, locking it. "On our way I'll call the tow truck and tell them where to take the car. I don't live far. About twenty minutes from here."

"My house is a little farther but I'll make it as short a trip as possible." He started toward his SUV.

She hesitated. "I'm still not sure about this."

"It's either go with me or I'll call the police and have them come." He hated having to blackmail her but his conscience wouldn't let him leave her, and he had Ryan to see about, as well. His son had been abandoned by his mother one too many times and Carter refused to let Ryan worry his father might do the same. Keeping his word to his son was of supreme importance.

Liz's shoulders lowered in defeat. "That's not necessary. I'll come. I just hate having to put you out."

"It's not a problem." They continued toward his SUV. "We'll get it all worked out." Carter unlocked the car, held the front passenger door open until she climbed in and closed it behind her.

Minutes later they headed down the highway. She called the motor service, then an unsure silence settled over them. Carter glanced over to find her sitting rigid with her hands clasped in her lap as if she were ready to spring out at a moment's notice.

Went he first met her, he'd been struck by her height. She had super long legs. The kind that could wrap around a man. Ho, that wasn't a thought he should be having about a woman he didn't really know. Had he been without sex for so long he'd started to lose his mind? That aside, he liked that he didn't have to bend down to talk to her. Even though she wore a sedate black pants suit, he could tell she had some nice mature curves. Beneath the jacket, she had on a red shirt that she filled out nicely with full breasts.

She'd appeared insecure when they first met. He'd actually been surprised she spoke to him. He liked the way she giggled. All girlie-like. It rippled around him, urging him to join in her humor. He'd not shared laughter with a woman in too long. "By the way, where do you live?"

"In Ridgewood. In this direction but you turn right just down here." She pointed north at a major intersection.

"We're not that far apart. I live in Mooresville."

"I've heard of it, but I've never been there."

He sensed her looking at him. "If you blink, you'd miss it. It's just across the river and a little way off the main highway. It won't take long to get there. I'll have you home soon. Promise."

Liz fell quiet again. Something about her made him believe she'd never gone off with a man she didn't know. She didn't strike him as someone who picked up men in bars. In fact, he'd call her wary of others. As if she might have been hurt one too many times by people.

He'd also noticed she had rich brown hair and wide dark expressive eyes. He couldn't think of any reason why a man wouldn't want to pick her up. Even him, if he were looking for someone, which he wasn't. His ex-wife had seen to that. Peace and security were what he wanted. He and Ryan had found that between just the two of them. But would it be so bad to have someone to spend time with who could talk about more than the latest cartoons?

He shot glances at her as they crossed over the river bridge. He should focus on the road. "So, where's your office located?"

"It's downtown close to the hospital. It's in one of the older brick medical buildings that has been renovated."

"I know the ones. Mine's in the medical park about a mile away. I can't believe we haven't met before now."

"It happens." She went quiet once again.

"We're almost there." He turned off the main highway.

Making a right, he drove about a mile and came to the historical marker that read Mooresville. He glanced at Liz to find her leaning forward, looking out the windshield with interest. "You can't see much because we don't have streetlights. You need to come back when it's daylight. It's really a great place."

"I'll have to do that. Why did you decide to buy here when you came to town?"

"I bought my grandparents' house when they decided to move to Florida. I wanted to bring my son up in a place where the neighbors knew each other." He chuckled. "I might've gotten carried away. This place is tiny, but it has a big caring vibe for sure."

"It looks like a safe and secure place for a family. What's your wife going to think when you show up with a strange woman?"

"I'm divorced. Four years." That had become easier to say with each year.

"I'm sorry."

Carter nodded. He wasn't. Outside of having Ryan, his marriage had been toxic at best. A mistake not to repeat. Making a left around the large township square, he then turned again to the right and made an immediate left into his pebbled parking area behind his house.

"What a great house." Liz cocked her neck upward to see his two-story home out the side window.

He grinned. "I'm pretty crazy about it. Even if it can be drafty this time of year and it needs some work in a couple of areas. As my grandparents got older, it became more difficult for them to do upkeep. I've been slowly getting things back in order." He opened the door. "I won't be but a few moments. Would you like to come in or wait here?"

"I'll just wait here."

"Okay, I'll be right back." Carter shut the door behind him.

Liz watched Carter lope to the back steps. Only desperation could have made her go off with a stranger. Or almost stranger. Carter couldn't be all bad if he lived in this community.

She looked at the house again, a clapboard building painted white. She guessed it must be around a hundred years old. She'd glimpsed a front porch before he had made the turn onto the second street that led to the back of his house. The windows were tall and light shone out of those along the back, giving her a view of a brick patio surrounded by a wooden trellis. A firepit sat in the middle with chairs around it, including a child-sized one.

Good as his word, Carter soon headed her way. He had a young boy wrapped in a blanket in his arms and a teenage girl following him out the door. Liz turned and watched Carter set the child in a booster seat behind the driver's seat. The boy, who already showed signs of looking like his father, now studied her.

Carter must have sensed his son's curiosity because he glanced at her. "Ryan, this is Dr. Poole. She's a new friend. Her car wouldn't start so we're going to take her home."

"Hello, Ryan. It's nice to meet you." Liz gave him her best reassuring patient smile.

"Hi," the boy said after a pause.

"Buckle up, Ryan." Carter closed the door.

Ryan buckled in as Carter climbed behind the steering wheel.

The girl took the seat behind Liz. "Liz, this is my sitter, Betsy."

Liz twisted to see the girl. "Hello."

The girl offered her a slight smile.

She reminded Liz of herself at that age. Painful.

"Okay, everyone in. Betsy, I'll drop you off first and Liz, you'll be next. Then it's back to bed for you, Ryan."

Liz shoulders sank. "You had to get him out of bed. I'm sorry. I should've just stayed with my car."

"Don't worry about it." He reached over and patted her shoulder but quickly removed his hand. Still, a tingle ran through her. "He wasn't asleep, and he thinks this is a great adventure."

"Daddy, can we get an ice cream on the way back?" the boy asked.

Carter chuckled. She liked the sound. It reminded her of the ripples of an echo, smooth and easy.

"I think it's a little too late for ice cream. How about some hot chocolate before you go to bed again?"

There was a pause. Liz glanced back. The boy appeared to give the idea some thought. "Okay, but I like ice cream better."

Carter chuckled again and turned into a subdivision. "I do too." At the second drive, he pulled in and stopped. "Betsy, thanks for tonight. I'll call you about watching Ryan while school is out."

The girl said softly, "Okay."

"Also, be sure to tell your parents they're welcome to come to our community Christmas event Saturday evening. See you later."

"Bye, Betsy," Ryan said.

"Bye." Betsy climbed out of the SUV.

Carter waited until the girl went inside, then backed out.

Liz said, "I appreciate you being a taxi driver for me."

"I would've had to bring Betsy home anyway. You're the one being patient about getting home."

"I didn't have much of a choice." She hesitated. What made her say something that ill-mannered? "I'm sorry. That didn't sound very grateful."

He looked at her. "I know what you mean." His attention returned to the rearview mirror. "How were things tonight, Ryan?"

"We watched TV and ate pizza. Do you like pizza?"

"You know I do," Carter replied.

"No, I mean her."

Liz turned to see him pointing a finger in her direction. "I do very much."

"What kind?" the boy asked.

"Almost any kind, but I especially like a meat lover's. What's your favorite?"

"Cheese."

She smiled at the boy's enthusiastic answer.

"I hate to interrupt this conversation, but I need to know where you live." Humor filled his voice as he drove toward town again.

"At the third light, turn right," Liz told him.

Ten minutes later they were at the gated entrance to her townhouse complex. She told Carter the code and he punched it in. Somehow the place she lived seemed sterile compared to his house. As if she were marking time instead of living. "Mine's the third one on the right."

He pulled to the curb in front of it and turned off the SUV. "Let me walk you to the door."

"That's not necessary. You shouldn't leave Ryan." Liz located her keys in her purse. "Thank you again for bringing me home. What do I owe you for your trouble?"

He leaned back as if she had hit him. "Nothing."

"I need to do something to say thank-you. Would you and Ryan like to go out for pizza on Saturday? My treat."

"I do!" came from the back seat.

Carter shook his head. "That sounds nice, but we can't."

Disappointment washed over her. *That figured.* For once she'd put herself out there and what happened? She'd been turned down. It shouldn't hurt but it did.

"We've a community event and we both have to be there. Hey, why don't you join us? Ryan and I'd like you to be our guest."

She couldn't do that. Go to a neighborhood party with Carter. What would people think? Would people assume she and Carter were in a relationship? "I'm supposed to be doing something nice for you."

"It's a community Christmas Stroll. We have a pot-luck/grill-out meal just for the neighbors beforehand, then the public's welcome to tour a couple of open houses and the Brick Church. There's caroling. I think you'd enjoy it."

At least that sounded better than what she'd imagined. Carter made it sound interesting, and she'd like to see Mooresville in the daylight. "I don't know. I don't want to be in the way."

Carter turned to her with an eager look on his face. "I promise you won't be. There'll be plenty of people around who don't live in Mooresville. Come join us. You'll be glad you did."

"Should I bring something?" Was she really thinking of attending?

"If it'll make you feel better, then bring something. If you decide to come, make it around three. We eat early so we can have everything cleaned up before the program."

"I'll think about it. I may have to work. I really appreciate the ride." She climbed out of the SUV. "Bye."

As she went inside Carter pulled away from the curb. This evening hadn't turned out at all as she had expected. To her surprise that rather excited her.

CHAPTER TWO

THE NEXT MORNING Liz still puzzled over having asked Carter and Ryan out for pizza. It wasn't like her to invite strangers to dine with her. However, she'd wanted to say thank-you to Carter in some way after he'd gone to so much trouble to help her. The impulsive pizza invitation was out of her mouth before she'd thought.

More mystifying was that she was actually considering going to the community event. She did want to see Mooresville. And Carter. It had been a long time since she'd been around a man that interested her.

Melissa, sporting a pink streak in her hair and wearing purple scrubs, started quizzing Liz about the night when Liz opened the door to get into Melissa's car.

"So, did you find yourself a knight in shining armor?" Melissa laughed as Liz shook her head and closed the door. "I told you going to the party would be good for you, Liz. Tell me the details, girl. Details. You said he was good-looking. How good-looking is he?"

"He's tall—"

"Aw, come on. You can do better than that. Does he have dreamy eyes? A sweet butt?" Melissa looked over, wiggling her brows. "Big hands?"

Liz laughed.

"Well?"

Heat surged up her neck. "Okay, he has all of that."

"Oh, wow. The full package. You go, girl," Melissa crowed.

Liz huffed. "It wasn't like that."

"Who says it can't be?"

"He just gave me a ride home, that's all. He did invite me to a community get-together on Saturday, but I don't know if I'll go."

Thankfully they were at a light as Melissa glared at her. "Are you crazy? You go Saturday to that community thing and he'll find out how wonderful you are and the next thing you know, you're in love." Melissa's excitement could easily turn contagious.

Liz looked back at her. "You need to give up reading those romance novels during lunch."

"And you need to start believing there's someone out there who can give you a happily-ever-after. Show your mother you're as special as your sister was."

Too pragmatic for such nonsense, Liz remembered vividly the reality of being invisible when Louisa was around. Her sister had always been the center of attention. If Louisa wasn't, she made sure she was. Liz had been okay with that because Louisa had pulled her along into the crowd. With Louisa gone, life had changed in that aspect. It was much harder to join in when Liz had to do it on her own. If Liz went on Saturday, she'd have to do it all on her own. The idea disturbed her.

Just before the lunchbreak the receptionist told Liz she had a call on hold from a Dr. Jacobs.

Carter. With hands shaking, Liz picked up the phone. "This is Dr. Poole."

"It's Carter. I just wanted to make sure you made it to work with no trouble."

She cleared her throat. It was really sweet of him to check on her. "Thanks, that's nice of you. I did. My nurse picked me up this morning."

"Great. And your car made it to the shop, as well?"

"It did." She wasn't used to receiving this type of attention. Nice, but unnerving at the same time. Maybe being new in town, Carter needed a friend and had latched on to her. "My mom's coming to pick me up this afternoon so I can go get a rental for a few days."

"Good. I'm glad you have someone you can depend on."

Had someone disappointed him?

"I also wanted to invite you again to come on Saturday. It'd be a great way to learn about Mooresville."

Why did he care so much if she attended? They had just met. He made it sound important that she come. "I'll try."

"Good. The community committee could use a fresh opinion on what we're trying to do."

There it was. His interest lay in her ideas. Hadn't he been just as enthusiastic about Betsy's parents coming? She wasn't sure if that made her feel better or worse. She'd like him to ask her to join him because he wanted to see her. What an interesting notion.

"I'll see you Saturday then."

He made it difficult for her not to go. After all the trouble he had gone through for her the night before, she did feel obligated to do something nice for him. As of right now, unless something came up, she'd attend. "I'll try, unless I have to be on call at the last minute. I'm sorry. I've got to go. I've patients waiting."

"Same here. Hope to see you Saturday. Bye."

Liz hung up and sat there for a moment. She'd spent most of her life in her sister's shadow, unnoticed by others unless Louisa pointed Liz out. She'd gotten used to making little effort because she didn't have to. She'd found out early on that people found her intelligence off-putting. So why did Carter *see* her? Whatever the reason, it felt good. And unnerving. Did he want something she didn't know about? Could he just be a nice guy? Or maybe he *was* a nice guy. Whatever the reason, she'd take it while it lasted.

She mentioned the call to Melissa, who jumped around. "You have to go. I've never understood why you hold yourself back when you're one of the most attractive and accomplished women I know. You need to work on believing that too."

Unsure how to respond, Liz looked at her. Had she really been hiding away? Liz had been living as she always had. Only now Louisa wasn't there to pull her along. Had it become easier just to not make an effort to get to know anyone new?

Melissa continued on, unaware of the turmoil her words generated in Liz. "I know what we'll do to help make it happen. Friday, since we're closed in the afternoon, we're going to go get haircuts and have our nails done. Then we'll see about buying you a new top to go with your jeans."

"I have paperwork to do." To prove it Liz looked down at her electronic device.

"Paperwork can wait. You need a little confidence builder. When was the last time you went out with a man?"

Liz hesitated to confess. "A couple of years ago."

"Wow. You need to make this one count. You like him, don't you?"

She did. More than she believed she would or wanted to. Liz nodded.

"Then make an effort. Do something for yourself for a change. You help people here every day, volunteer your weekends away, play chess with the elderly and jump when your mother says to. For once, think about yourself." Melissa sounded pleading and annoyed at the same time.

She pulled Liz to a nearby mirror. Her hands remained on Liz's shoulders as she looked over one. "Stop a minute and look at yourself. Would it hurt for you to try a little harder? Come on, Liz. Take a chance. Be fearless for once. You can do it." She grinned. "Think about how nice you told me his smile is."

Now Melissa teased her. Liz hesitated a moment before she sighed. "Okay. For you."

Melissa's eyes met hers in the mirror. "No. For you."

"Okay. For me too." Liz stepped back.

"You've got to start thinking about yourself. Get out more. Let people know the real you. Get your mother out of your head. Start taking some chances. Live a little."

Had Liz really become so unresponsive to men that she acted like a troll hiding away? That hadn't been her intent. She'd try. Really try.

Liz spent the rest of the week working up the nerve to take Carter up on his invitation.

Saturday afternoon Liz reminded herself again to pay close attention to her driving instead of the thumping of her heart as she neared Mooresville. It wouldn't do for her to cause an accident. *She was doing this.*

Just as Carter had said, Mooresville did look different in the daylight. She turned off the main road and faced a large grassy square where a huge redbrick building set. Making the turns she remembered, she traveled toward Carter's house. She pulled into the parking area behind it. Louisa would have found nothing about Mooresville exciting. Her interests had been in the new and exciting. Liz loved everything about the old buildings. Louisa would've hated them. She turned off her engine.

After knocking and finding no one at home, Liz gathered her pie plate and walked to the front of the house. She stopped to look at it closer. The porch looked comfortable and inviting. A place where a family could sit on a sunny afternoon and visit with friends. Nothing about this place could be called cold or cookie-cutter like the place she lived.

A Christmas wreath sporting a big red bow hung on the front door. Smaller, matching wreaths hung in the center of the windows on each side of the door. Two pots filled with greenery and large pine cones set on either side of the door. Pillows covered in a red-and-green holly print were stationed in the wicker chairs on one side of the porch, while on the other they were propped in the corner of a swing. Carter had been busy decorating. Interesting personality trait in a single father. One she hadn't expected.

She started across the central square toward a brown clapboard building. There people mingled around while others were busy setting up a food table covered by a green cloth. She passed a group of kids playing tag. Ryan ran among them. He stopped to study her for a moment. Liz smiled and waved, then concentrated on making steps toward the group of adults in spite of her apprehension.

If she turned around now, Carter would never know she had been there. Except Ryan would tell him. She'd handled medical emergencies that hadn't generated this amount of trepidation. Liz squared her shoulders with determination and continued.

"Liz, you made it." Carter came to meet her. His bright smile suggested he was both excited and somewhat surprised to see her. A large apron with a picture of a grill on fire covered his green fleece pullover making his eyes more brilliant. She blinked. Her heart raced. Below that he wore jeans and sports shoes on his feet. Carter looked happy, healthy and all male. Everything about him tempted her to dream of what-if.

"I did." She looked around at the people who watched them. They all had smiles on their faces. Liz returned them.

One middle-aged woman stepped forward. "Let me take that."

Liz released the pie plate with a smile of appreciation.

"You look nice. Have you had your hair cut since I saw you?" Carter asked.

"I did." She was glad now that she'd spent that time on her nails and hair. Carter noticing gave her a boost of confidence.

He watched her carefully. "You look nice."

"Hey, Carter. You better get back over here before these sausages burn," a man behind one of the two grills called.

"Come over here and talk to me while I *man* the grill." Carter turned with a grin.

Liz followed, unsure what she'd talk to him about.

He picked up tongs and moved to stand in front of a grill. "Hey, everyone, this is Liz Poole. I invited her to join us today."

A few people called hello. She nodded, making eye contact as much as she could.

"I'm really glad you decided to come." Carter moved around a couple of sausages he'd added to those already over the fire. "What kind of pie did you bring?"

"Apple."

"Aw, my favorite. Put some ice cream on it and I've found heaven." He made a sound of pleasure that pulled low in her body.

"Everything leads back to ice cream for a man," Liz said before thinking. She hoped he wouldn't take it as criticism. "My father loved it."

"If it doesn't, it should," Carter quipped and returned his attention back to his cooking.

"This is an interesting building." Liz studied the long narrow wooden structure with doors trimmed in red on each end. The screen doors wore greenery wreaths with plaid bows. Beside one door, an American flag hung from a pole attached to the building. In front of it was a small brick area with two benches facing each other.

"It's the post office. One of the four original buildings from 1818." A proud note rung in his voice.

"Carter, do we have another pan for the hot dogs?" the man at the other grill asked.

With Carter's attention diverted, Liz studied the area with its road around the huge square. She could now see that the township had been laid out in a grid. There were two main center squares. Off those were two streets on either side. Not as many houses were on Carter's side of the square. On the opposite were a number of buildings with picket fences, but there were still open lots. Undoubtedly those structures had gone with time. Charming was the only word she could find to describe the historic town.

"Ow," came a male yelp of pain.

Liz turned to see a man doubled over in front of a large pot. Hot oil streamed around him. She hurried to him, her focus on nothing but the man. Sweat broke out in the center of her back. "Are you all right?"

Others circled them. The man yanked at his sweatshirt, trying to remove it.

"Let me help." Carter started pulling on his shirt. Beneath it was another long sleeve knit shirt. The injured man pushed at it.

"Don't do that!" Liz cautioned. "Does anyone have a pocketknife?" Someone handed her one and Liz gave it to Carter. "Cut it back."

He nodded and turned to the man. "John, I'm going to cut your shirt. Karen'll have to get over it."

As Carter went to work on the shirt, Liz held it away from John's skin.

"Liz, pull it open and away as I cut," Carter instructed.

She did as he told her, being careful not to touch the man's burned skin.

John hissed and immediately jerked when air hit the burn.

"Please be still. I need to see it. I'm a doctor too," she informed him.

The man stilled. His other hand moved to touch.

"Don't touch. We don't want the skin to come off. It's your protective covering. It helps prevent infection."

Carter removed the fabric of his shirt. The middle-aged man winced. An angry burn extending the length of his forearm came into view.

She grimaced. "We need to get some ice on this."

A woman volunteered, "I'll fetch an ice bag."

"This must be cleaned and bandaged." She looked at Carter. "We're going to need soap and water. Bandages."

"We'll go to my house." Carter turned. "Stan, see to the grill, please."

The woman returned with a bag of ice large enough to cover the burn.

Liz placed the bag over the burn area. "Keep that on it. I know it'll be uncomfortable but it's important."

The man stoically nodded and brought his arm to his chest.

"Okay, John, let's go get you fixed up." Carter looked around. "Where's Karen?"

"She's at the house, putting together some last-minute food." John's words were tight from pain.

The lady who had gotten the ice called, "I'll let her know what happened and where you are."

Liz and Carter walked on each side of John toward Carter's house.

"Ryan," Carter called. "Find Mrs. Wilson if I'm not back by the time dinner's ready."

The boy gave them a curious look. "Yes, sir."

They entered Carter's home through the unlocked front door. Liz would never dream of leaving her place open to anyone at any time. Inside, they continued down a narrow hall to the back of the house. Liz dodged a waist-high table sitting against a wall as she hurried across gleaming wood floors. The three of them stopped in front of a white country sink.

"We need some dish detergent to cut the grease and a towel." Liz turned on the water, making sure it was as cool as possible.

"John, this is Dr. Liz Poole." Carter opened the cabinet beside the sink and pulled out a plastic bottle of blue liquid. He sat it on the counter within her reach.

"Hi, John. I know you're in pain. You've a bad burn here. Carter and I are going to get it cleaned and bandaged up. Soon you should feel better. Carter, we're going to need a first aid kit too. Do you have one?"

"I do. Can't have a seven-year-old child without one." He left the room.

"John, I'm going to need to get the oil off your arm. This is probably going to hurt but I'll be as gentle as possible. I'll also be as quick as I can. I've got to be extra careful or I'll open up that blister. I don't want to do that. The main thing with burns is to protect you from infection. I can't stress that enough."

She scooped water on the man's arm, then lightly dribbled the dish liquid. Using her palm, she carefully applied light pressure to the red skin with a blister over it. As gently as possible, she worked to remove the oil without damaging the skin. Carter returned with the first aid kit and stood on the other side of John.

The man groaned.

"I'm sorry. I know this isn't any fun but it's necessary." Liz worked as quickly as she could.

"I shouldn't be such a baby," the older man said.

She smiled at him. "No babies here. Burns are painful and yours is a big bad one."

Slow and easy, she focused on removing the oil, continually adding water and liquid soap until satisfied the area was as clean as she could make it.

Carter reached across the counter, pulled out a drawer, grabbed a dry towel and handed it to her. She blotted it dry enough that it would quickly finish air-drying. By the time she finished, Carter had the first aid kit open.

He squeezed some antibiotic cream out of a tub on to a four-by-four square and placed that over a section of the arm and repeated the action until all the injured area had been covered. "The cream should keep the gauze from sticking when the bandage is changed."

Carter then pulled out a roll of gauze, opened it and started wrapping it around John's arm until all the damaged area had been covered.

At a sharp knock on the front door, Carter called, "Come in."

Rapid footsteps soon followed. A small white-haired woman with bright red cheeks rushed into the kitchen. "John, what have you done?"

"Karen, he's fine. He just has a grease burn on his forearm," Carter assured her. "We have it all protected now but he needs to keep ice on it until the pain goes away."

"Mary said you need clothes. I brought you another shirt and jacket." Karen studied her husband as if making sure he had no other injuries.

"Good. Why don't you help him dress? Liz and I'll get things cleaned up here." Carter looked over at the older couple and smiled. "Just be careful not to touch his arm any more than necessary."

John and Karen moved over to the wooden dining table near a rear window.

"They both need a few moments together," Carter whispered to Liz. "They've been married forty-five years. Are completely devoted to each other."

"I understand." What would it be like to have that type of relationship, commitment? Liz would like to have that. So far that hadn't been in the stars for her. After glancing at Carter, she picked up the bag of ice in the bottom of the sink and then dropped the dripping mess. "We're going to need another ice pack."

"I've just the thing." Carter went to the freezer compartment of the refrigerator and pulled out a bag of peas. "At least they'll be going to a good cause since Ryan won't eat them."

"I'm not a big fan of peas either. Wrap it in a dish towel and it'll be perfect."

Carter pulled out the drawer again and removed another towel. "Why don't you prepare this while I clean up our mess?"

His hand touched hers as he handed them to her. That current she'd felt before went through her. She managed to get out, "Okay."

Soon John and Karen joined them.

Liz said, "John, you need to keep some ice on that arm. It'll help with the pain and keep down swelling." She placed the improvised ice pack over the burned area. "Also, I'd suggest you have Carter do the changing of your bandage tomorrow. After that, I'm sure Karen can handle it. And no more cooking for you for a while." Liz smiled at him.

"Those doctor's orders sound like good ones. I have some pain medicine for you." Carter handed the man two white pills. "Take these now." He offered the man a glass of water. "I suggest you also take something before going to bed. It'll help you sleep. If you have any concerns, you call and I'll come running."

"My goodness, it's nice to have such good doctors looking after John." The concern on Karen's face had eased.

"I'm glad I could help," Liz said.

"Same goes for me." Carter patted Karen on the shoulder. "Now, why don't you take John to get something to eat and let him play mayor?"

"I *am* the mayor," John insisted with a huff, regaining some of his spirit.

Carter grinned. "Then I suggest you make the most of it and order people around for the rest of the day."

"I'll see he takes it easy." Karen took him by his good

arm. "Carter, just throw his shirt in the trash. I believe it's beyond repair."

"Will do. Sorry about that." Carter picked up the discarded clothing and stuffed it in the garbage can.

"I understand." She and John headed down the hallway and out the front door.

Carter leaned his hip against the counter, crossed his arms over his chest and studied Liz. "Well, you were certainly something, Dr. Poole."

Liz's heart thumped hard under his appraisal. She busied herself with emptying the old ice pack. Was that a compliment or a complaint? Sometimes her social cues could be off.

"I now understand why you're such a valuable member of the medical team at community events."

She looked at him. "Thank you. Who've you been talking to?"

He shrugged. "I asked around about you."

Liz wasn't sure how she felt about that bit of information. "You asked about me?"

"I did."

"Why?" Heat climbed up her neck.

"Because I wanted to know about you. What kind of person you are."

She looked away unable to meet his intense gaze any longer. "Why?"

"Because I like you and I don't trust my judgment where people, women in particular, are concerned, especially after my ex."

"Oh." Her heart jumped into overdrive. That was a forthright answer. One she wasn't prepared for. "It was bad?"

"Yeah. The worst. I can't have someone around Ryan that I can't trust." He took her elbow. "Come on. We'd better get back. All the food'll be gone or cold. Ryan'll be wondering where we are, as well."

Carter hoped he hadn't said anything wrong. Liz had looked both terrified and shocked at his blunt admission. She fascinated him. Tall, sleek and poised, he found her outwardly attractive but even more he liked her willingness to help others. The way she rushed to aid John, reassuring him. Carter hadn't seen a moment of hesitation. Liz knew her medicine and it was obviously the area where she felt comfortable. She had a great bedside manner, as well. Refreshing after his ex-wife's concern only for herself and her needs.

He was glad Liz had decided to come today.

They walked across the green toward the tables where many of his neighbors were already seated, eating.

"This is really an interesting place," Liz said, looking around.

"I didn't have to think twice about buying my grandparents' house when they offered it to me. Ryan and I moved here to lead a peaceful life. Mooresville has given us that. And friends."

"I'm glad you both are happy."

He glanced at her as they continued to walk. Was she happy? Something in her voice made him wonder.

As they reach the group, they received a standing ovation. He grinned and waved everyone down. Liz smiled shyly as if she didn't like the attention.

Carter took her elbow. "Come this way and we'll get some food."

A bright red spot rested on each of her cheeks. She'd been embarrassed by the response. "See, I'm not the only one who thought you did good."

"I was doing what I've been trained to do. No big deal."

"Maybe so, but you were great with John."

As they filled their plates at the long tables covered with food, more than one person said thank-you to them. They moved away from the food tables and Carter said, "Ryan should be sitting with the Wilsons. I saw them down this way."

He noticed her looking at his plate piled high with food. "I don't eat like this every day."

Liz gave him a knowing grin. "If you say so."

Was she teasing him? "You sound like you don't believe me."

Her grin grew to a smile. "I didn't say that."

"Are you concerned as a citizen or as a doctor?" He flirted with her and she was returning it.

Giving him a noncommittal lift of her chin, she said, "Just making an observation."

"That I might need to watch my weight?" He pushed for the back-and-forth to continue.

"Hey, I didn't say that. You know you don't. You look great." Liz's eyes widened before she shook her head and looked away.

Unable to contain it, he barked a laugh. "Why thank you for the compliment, Liz." When she looked at him, he added, "I'm teasing, you know?"

She looked perplexed. "People don't usually tease me."

"I'm glad. That makes me special. I get to see what few do—your beautiful blush."

"Now you're just trying to get me to blush more."

"There's Ryan." Carter continued to the end of a table and put his plate down in front of the chair beside his son's. "Liz, this one's yours." He indicated the place on the other side of him. "I'll go get us something to drink. Is iced tea fine with you or would you like something else?"

"Tea is good."

"Ryan, introduce Liz to Mr. and Mrs. Wilson while I'm gone, will you?"

Carter stepped away for a couple of minutes and returned with two plastic disposable cups. He placed one at his plate and another at hers. As he sat, he said, "Mrs. Wilson, I hope this is your mac and cheese."

His leg brushed along Liz's as he settled into his seat. Heat rushed up and down his leg. He stumbled over the words, but he got them out. "She makes the best."

Liz gave him a concerned look. "She does? I'm glad I got some."

Carter watched as Liz forked into the cheesy noodles. She closed her eyes and savored the taste. The expression on her face made his groin tighten. He forced himself to swallow. What would it be like to have her react to him with such obvious pleasure?

Where had that notion come from? He'd left a horrible relationship. He wasn't looking for anything but friendship. Liz didn't strike him as being someone who'd only be looking for a fling. That's the best he could offer. He and Ryan had finally settled into a good steady life. Rocking what they had wasn't his plan. Yet, the thought of touching, kissing Liz had its appeal. Pulled at him.

A few moments later, Liz said, "Mrs. Wilson, the mac and cheese truly is wonderful. Best I've ever eaten."

"Thank you. And you were impressive in your quick action to help John. I'm sure the burn would've been worse if not for you."

"I just did what needed to be done." Liz made it sound like it was no big deal to her.

"Dad, I can't cut this sausage," Ryan whined, drawing Carter's attention away from Liz.

Carter turned to him. "Let me help."

In the small space, his hip shifted into Liz's thigh. She stiffened against him. Apparently, she felt some of what he did. His body went into sensory overload. Soon he returned to his original position, but the awareness of their closeness didn't disappear.

Over the next few minutes, he made conversation with the Wilsons, all the while too conscious of Liz beside him. Occasionally she joined in with a thoughtful remark.

"Ryan, we're going to need to finish up here," Carter announced.

Liz moved to get up. "I guess I should be going."

Carter turned to her, putting his hand over hers. Hers was cold and he wanted to pull her to him and warm her up. That crazy thought made him pause. Liz had him thinking things he hadn't in a long time. He'd been out with a number of women since his divorce but none that affected him the way Liz did.

"Please don't go. We're just getting started with the

festivities. Ryan and I have a surprise for you. We just
need to change clothes. We won't be long."

An unsure looked entered her eyes but she nodded.

"Carter didn't tell you?" Mrs. Wilson's look went
from him to her. "He's playing the founder of Mooresville, Robert Moore, tonight. Ryan's playing his young
son."

"He is?" Liz's attention focused on Carter.

He straightened his shoulders. "You had no idea how
important of a man I was, did you?"

Liz's eyes twinkled as she looked at him. "I did not."

"Come on, Ryan. We need to go get dressed." He
stood and started cleaning up the plates.

Liz waved his hands away. "Leave those. I'll take
care of them since you're such an important person."

Carter grinned. "Thank you. We won't be gone long.
I'm sure Mrs. Wilson will keep you company. See you
in a few."

CHAPTER THREE

LIZ STOOD AND started gathering the leftover disposable plates and utensils.

"Leave those for a few minutes and let's get to know each other without the men interrupting us," Mrs. Wilson suggested.

Mr. Wilson had left them just before Carter and Ryan had walked away.

What was the older woman after? Liz met her look to find warmth and curiosity in her eyes. Liz's anxiety eased. She lowered herself into the chair.

"I don't know if Carter told you, but Leroy, Mr. Wilson, and I are Carter's grandparents' best friends and Carter's our closest neighbor."

"No, he didn't." Liz wasn't sure where this was going. She feared Mrs. Wilson thought there might be more between Liz and Carter than there was. Or was the older woman going to try to warn Liz off? Which Liz found laughable. She certainly wouldn't consider herself a threat.

"We still stay in touch. So, tell me, how did you and Carter meet?" Mrs. Wilson asked.

"At the community thank-you banquet earlier in the week. He helped me when I had car trouble."

The older woman grinned. "A cute meet. Damsel in distress. Just like in the romances."

Liz stopped a groaned from escaping. She'd not thought of it like that.

"He's a really good father." Mrs. Wilson looked in the direction Carter went. "Devoted to Ryan. Sometimes too much so if you ask me."

Liz turned to watch the man and his son walking tall and proud toward their home.

"Carter's trying hard to be both mother and father to the boy. We've heard horror stories about Ryan's mother."

"Now, Mary, that's enough." Mr. Wilson came up behind his wife and patted her on the shoulder. "Carter might not want you to be telling tales."

Liz cleared her throat and stood, uncomfortable with talking about Carter when he wasn't there. "Carter just invited me here to give him an opinion on the program, whatever that is. We're just friends."

"Those looks he's been giving you say otherwise," Mrs. Wilson murmured.

"I'd better get this cleaned up." Liz placed a used disposable plate on top of another.

With plates in hand, she took them to the nearest large garbage bag. A number of people spoke to her on her way to and from it. She returned to Mr. and Mrs. Wilson. She offered to take their trash and made another trip to the garbage can. On her return, she saw Carter and Ryan coming her way.

Her breath caught. She couldn't help but grin. Maybe

there was something to what Mrs. Wilson had implied existed between them. Carter looked so male. He wore a white shirt, long gray vest and navy coat that fit snugly over his wide shoulders. Dark gray flannel pants cuffed just below his knees and white hose molded to his calves with buckled shoes on his feet finished his costume. Carter looked the part of a country gentleman of the 1800s to perfection.

Ryan could have been his twin with the exception he wore no coat. Instead he had a leather vest that tied at his chest. The pair were impressive. Especially the father.

Mrs. Wilson said, "Look how handsome you two are."

Liz lowered her gaze, not wanting Carter to see how much she agreed.

"I'm having problems with this neck cloth." Carter pulled at it. "I can't seem to get it wrapped around my neck right."

"Liz, why don't you help him with that?" Mrs. Wilson suggested.

Was the older woman matchmaking? Unable to gracefully say no, Liz stepped toward Carter.

"I promise not to bite," he whispered.

Her gaze met his. "I'm not afraid."

"Could have fooled me. You've the look of a rabbit ready to jump." Carter's breath flowed across her temple.

Liz shivered. Her hands shook as she took the ends of the neck cloth. "This needs to go around one more time."

Carter stood still as she reached around his neck.

He smelled of smoke and something citrusy. His hair brushed the top of her hand. The texture fine and soft. Glad to have her fingers busy, Liz didn't act on her need to caress it just for the pleasure.

She returned to the front of Carter's neck with the material. His look locked with hers. Awareness flickered there. Her center reacted with a jolt. They stood there, looking at each other until the sound of someone clearing their throat caught her attention. Liz refocused on the simple knot she formed. Not soon enough to stop her hands from shaking did she pull the ends out, leaving them to stand straight across his neck. "Mmm... there you go."

"Thank you." Her eyes lifted. They sparkled. "You're ready to dazzle." She turned to Ryan who she felt much more comfortable talking to and bowed slightly. "You look very handsome, young squire."

He turned up his nose and pulled at his clothing. "I don't like this shirt."

Carter put his hand on Ryan's shoulder. "You don't have to wear it forever."

"I hope the other boys don't make fun of me," Ryan whined.

Liz went down on a knee so that she came to his eye level. "I'll tell you a secret." The boy stepped forward, obviously interested. "If they do, it's only because they're jealous that they don't have a part like you do."

"You really think so?" The boy looked at her eagerly.

"I do. People used to make fun of me. It took me a long time, but I learned they were just jealous of what I could do that they couldn't."

"Really?"

"Really."

With a smile, he looked up at Carter. "Okay, Dad. I'm ready."

Over the boy's head Carter mouthed, *Thank you*.

A woman hurried up to them. "Carter, Pam can't be Mrs. Moore. She's stuck in traffic on the bridge. There's been an accident."

Carter groaned. "I guess we'll just have to do it without her."

"Can't someone else be her? Is her dress at her house?" Mrs. Wilson asked.

"It should be. Richard's over there." The woman who had run up pointed.

"Then why can't Liz do it? She and Pam are about the same size. The dress may be a few inches too short but that won't matter." Mrs. Wilson gave her an expectant look.

Liz's eyes went wide as her chest tightened, and she shook her head. Her world was the background. Never up front. "I don't think—"

"You'd be prefect." Carter obviously liked the plan. "Will you do it?"

"I don't know what to do."

"All you have to do is stand beside me. Will you do it?"

How could she turn him down? "Okay."

Carter gave her a quick hug. "Great."

Liz wished it could last longer.

Carter raised an arm and waved. "Richard, come here a sec."

A man with dark hair hurried to them. "Liz has agreed to play Pam's part. Can we get her outfit from you?"

"Sure."

"Ryan," Carter said, "you stay with Mrs. Wilson. We'll be right back."

She and Carter followed the man to a house on the other side of the square. Fifteen minutes later, Liz found herself dressed in a ticking striped dress and wearing a shawl and bonnet. When she stepped into the room where Carter waited, his eyes lit up.

"You look perfect. You'll make an excellent Mrs. Moore."

Liz shook her head. "I don't know about that. I'm not use to being in front of people." That had always been Louisa's role.

"You'll be great." Carter grinned and took her hand. "Then come on, Mrs. Moore. Our audience awaits."

"I could have done without you saying that."

Carter chuckled. "You aren't as big a ham as I am."

Liz walked with him across the square. Maybe she'd just never had a chance to find that out.

When they joined the others, everyone told her she looked great.

Carter studied her and Ryan. "Ready?"

She and Ryan nodded.

Mrs. Wilson smiled. "I, for one, am ready to hear all about Mooresville's history from the lovely Moore family. Y'all look good together."

Mrs. Wilson didn't help her nerves with her implication.

Mr. Wilson spoke to his wife with a warning tone, "Jeanie."

"We'd better get started before the sun sets." Carter winked at Liz, sending a shiver of heat up her spine before he took her hand and they walked over to stand in front of the post office.

"Hello, everyone. Welcome to Mooresville's Christmas Stroll and Caroling." Carter's voice filled the air and drew people's attention.

Liz took her position beside him, trying not to look terrified or shake so much it showed. The crowd circled them.

"I'm Robert Moore and this is my wife, Martha, and our young son, Eli. My brother, William, and I settled here near the Tennessee River in the early 1800s. We were cotton farmers and we found this area perfect for the crop. I hope you're ready to go back in time."

Liz looked around the crowd that had grown from just those who had shared the meal to a much larger group. Carter had been right. More people had come for the evening. He had them all enthralled in his story. He played the part perfectly. Even she forgot her fear as she got caught up in his words and voice.

As Carter spoke, a couple of photographers' cameras flashed. That didn't seem to faze him. They were as different as winter from summer. Where Carter didn't mind the limelight, she'd have been happy being in the crowd.

Carter continued, "As the years went by, Mooresville grew."

Two women and three men dressed in period costumes joined the three of them.

"Along with homes, we built the post office." Carter pointed toward it. "The Stagecoach Inn for travelers passing through." He took her hand, which was warm and reassuring, and led them through the crowd. Ryan and the other members of the party followed.

He stopped in front of the one-story wooden building with a porch and picket fence around the yard. A wreath of greenery and apples hung on the gate, another on the door. That opened and out stepped a man and woman dressed in period outfits. They joined Carter. He turned and faced the people and post office again.

"From here you can see the sign above the door of the post office indicating that Mooresville became an official town in 1818. It's the oldest town in Alabama. My brother and I along with the other families living here partitioned to become an incorporated township while Alabama was still just a territory. On November sixteenth, 1818, we became official. Today our entire town is on the National Register of Historic Places.

"Now if you'll follow me." His little band of enactors along with Liz firmly in hand and the crowd went with him.

Carter was completely in his element. She, along with the others, remained enthralled with his telling of the story of Mooresville.

They strolled to the end of the next square to where a white clapboard church with a tall steeple stood. Carter stopped in front of it and everyone else did, as well. She noticed that the crowd had grown.

Ryan came to stand in front of them. He started to fidget and she took his hand. The boy settled. Carter gave her a slight smile and went back to what he had been saying.

"By the time we became a township, we were large enough to have two churches. This is the Church of

Christ." Carter paused for effect. "Here President James A. Garfield once preached."

Another couple with a teenage girl who were dressed up joined the group.

"We've one more stop." Carter looked at her and grinned.

A warmth filled Liz from the inside out.

"The place where Mrs. Moore and I were married."

Heat washed over her. Liz was grateful for the waning light so that her blush didn't show.

The group continued up the opposite side of the square. As they passed a house, the Wilsons came out the front door dressed in their 1800s clothes and blended in with their neighbors. From there, Carter started across the square toward the large redbrick building with two white columns. The lights were burning and the doors stood open.

Others, including John and Karen stood on the portico waiting. They too were in costume. John still held the peas on his arm.

Carter left her and Ryan in the grass in front of the church. He stepped under the porch in the center of the doors. He turned to face the group. The light glowed behind him, making him more impressive. "This is the Brick Church and the last of the four original buildings in Mooresville. The historic buildings are maintained by those of us who live here in order to preserve the history of our town. Mooresville is often called Alabama's Williamsburg.

"We invite you to join us in singing Christmas carols and having wassail afterward. I speak for all of us who live in Mooresville. We wish you all the best of holiday seasons. Thank you for joining us tonight."

Everyone clapped.

Carter reached his hands out to her and Ryan. They each placed theirs in his. His fingers clasped her cool ones, blanketing them in warmth. Together they entered the church. He led them down the center to a front row. There they sat. To her astonishment, Carter continued to hold her hand and even more surprisingly, she allowed it.

Only when Mrs. Wilson handed them a booklet filled with Christmas carols did he release her hand. She missed his touch deeply. The song "O Holy Night" was announced and Carter turned the pages until he found it. He had a beautiful voice. She'd always loved to sing, but her mother had told her long ago her voice wasn't as nice as Louisa's, so Liz didn't sing much in public.

Carter leaned over and whispered, "You can do better than that."

On the next song, she sang more freely. By the time they were done, she no longer cared who heard her. She'd enjoyed the music. In the high-ceilinged sanctuary, the sound of joined voices without accompaniment had been magical. They ended with "We Wish You a Merry Christmas." It was a Christmas experience she'd always treasure.

Afterward Carter asked her, "Would you like to have something to drink?"

"I probably should be going."

"Daddy, I want to change clothes." Ryan circled his father.

"Okay. You were extra good tonight." Carter mussed his hair. "Thanks for playing your part so well." His eyes met hers. "You were wonderful, as well. Thanks for helping out."

"Not a problem." To Ryan she said, "I agree with your dad. You were great." She looked at Carter. "You were, as well. That was a wonderful presentation. I was impressed."

Carter straightened his shoulders, puffed out his chest and looked down his nose at her. "You sound like you hadn't expected I had theatrics in me."

"I never implied that." He was teasing her again. "I also loved the way people dressed up and kept joining the group."

"Thanks. We in Mooresville take our history seriously."

She smiled. "I can see that. I liked being a part of it." To her surprise, she had. She'd certainly stepped out of her comfort zone today. In more ways than one.

"I'm glad you did." Carter pulled on his neck cloth. "Come on. I think we've had enough of the past for today."

The sun had set while they were inside. Carter walked with confidence across the yard toward his house. On unfamiliar ground, Liz stumbled. Carter's hand came to her waist to steady her. He took her hand and placed it around his arm.

"Hold on. I know where to step and not to. I don't want you falling headfirst."

Liz lightly touched his arm, then the ground dipped again, and she gripped it until they reached the pavement.

"Don't let go here either. Some of this road is pretty old." Carter's smooth voice reassured her in the darkness.

Ryan ran ahead of them, just visible in the moonlight.

"Straight to the house," Carter called to him. He said to her, "I'm glad we blocked off the street from the main road. I don't have to worry about him getting hit."

"I need to get my clothes and change. Return this dress." Liz pulled away.

Carter tugged her back. "I asked Richard to put them in a bag and leave them on my porch. You can change at my place. I'll return the dress."

By now the lights of homes and buildings were coming on. The homes had single candles in the windows. It was like being back in a slower, easier time. "This place truly is wonderful."

"I thought you might enjoy tonight." His voice came through the dark, deep and rich, soothing.

"Why did you think that?"

"Because you looked around when you came to my house the other night like a kid does when they get a gift they've been wanting."

How could he read her so well? They hardly knew each other.

"I do like old buildings and history. Thanks for inviting me to eat also. Oh, man, I forgot my pie plate." She moved to let go of his arm.

His hand came over hers, stopping her. "Don't worry about it. Someone will take it home, clean it and it'll turn up on my doorstep. I'll see you get it back. Dang, I didn't get a piece of your pie. I hate that." He gave her a pleading look. "Is there any way I might get some another day?"

She liked the tingle that went through her at the idea of Carter wanting to see her again. "You don't even know if it was any good."

"I figure that if you brought it, then you thought it was your best."

It was her go-to recipe. "Do you enjoy always knowing what I'm thinking?"

He felt more than saw him shrug. "I didn't know I did. Interesting. I might be able to use that to my advantage."

Wednesday morning Carter looked at his watch. He was actually ahead of schedule seeing patients. That almost never happened. On an impulse he picked up his phone. He'd use the extra time to have lunch with Liz. If she'd agree.

He'd thought about her far too often over the last few days. She'd been welcome company at the Christmas event. He'd been impressed she'd joined in as Pam's replacement. One thing he'd learned in the short amount of time he'd known Liz was that she liked to help out others. She'd been quick to care for John, then willing to help with the Stroll and had even put Ryan at ease when he'd been afraid of being made fun of. Something about how she'd told that anecdote made him wonder about her childhood.

Whatever had happened then apparently was no longer an issue because she fit in well with his friends. Almost too much so. Mrs. Wilson obviously liked Liz. She'd told him the other day when he'd been out in the yard he should start dating. She'd even offered to babysit Ryan. Carter liked being around Liz, found her stimulating. Yet he didn't know if he could trust his instincts where women were concerned. His ex-wife had certainly proved his inability to do so. He couldn't afford to make a mistake again.

After his marriage he'd sworn not to take any more chances no matter how much he liked the woman. He had Ryan's welfare to consider. Carter couldn't let him down. Trust was difficult for him to give, especially after it had been thrown back in his face. Carter shook his head. All that was overthinking. He intended just to ask Liz out to a friendly lunch. He was *not* offering marriage.

Liz's receptionist answered the phone. While he waited for Liz to come on the line, he drummed a finger against his desk. Why did it matter to him so much whether she agreed to meet him or not? If she said no, it wouldn't be a big deal. Yet he really wanted to see her.

"This is Dr. Poole."

"This is Dr. Jacobs." He mimicked her tone.

"Hi, Carter."

He smiled. Her words were low and shy-sounding. Was she as unsure about him as he was of her? "I'm calling to see if you'd like to meet me for lunch at a café on Sixth. That's about halfway between our offices."

"If I do, I have to be back to see patients by one thirty."

He used his most encouraging tone. "They're fast at the café. I promise to have you home by curfew time."

"Funny. Very funny."

Carter chuckled.

"I usually just eat here, but I'll make an exception this time. I think I'd like to get out today."

She made it sound as if he were a good excuse to do something she wanted to do anyway. Carter wasn't sure he liked that. All of a sudden he really hoped she wanted to see *him*. "Good."

"I can meet you in thirty minutes."

Why did his heart beat faster? It was just lunch. "Great. I'll see you at Café Decatur. Do you know the place?"

"I do."

"See you in a few, Liz." With a grin on his face, he hung up.

Carter stood just outside the café door while he watched Liz step out of her car. She had great legs. Today she wore a dress with a coat over it and tall black boots. Those legs of hers made him think thoughts that had nothing to do with friendship.

Shaking his head to clear those erotic ideas, he smiled and waved. "Hey."

"Hi." She gave him a timid smile.

Carter held the door for her to enter. "There's an open table over here." He led her to it. It sat next to the wall but where they could see out a window.

Before they could say more, the waitress joined them. "Hello, Dr. Jacobs. How're you today?"

He grinned at the girl who regularly waited on him. "Fine, Lucy. You?"

She cocked a hip and give him a come-on smile. He'd seen it so often he didn't take it seriously. "Doing great. What can I get you? Your usual?"

Carter glanced at Liz, who watched their exchange with interest. "Yes, but first see what Dr. Poole would like."

Liz picked up the menu that had been stuck between the napkin dispenser and the salt and pepper shakers. "Uh…how about the…green salad with chicken and an iced tea."

The girl wrote it down. "Will do."

As soon as she'd left, Liz met his gaze with brows raised. "Come here often?"

He shrugged. "A couple of times a week. I like to get out of the office. I usually walk over so I can get the free exercise and some fresh air."

"And apparently you've got a regular waitress." She fiddled with the saltshaker.

"Well, maybe I do tend to sit at the same table." He grinned at her.

Her eyes narrowed. "Your usual would be?"

Carter didn't hesitate. "Ham and cheese on rye, potato chips and an iced tea."

"Sounds good."

He liked that she had relaxed some. Crossing his arms on the table, he leaned toward her. "So, how have you been?"

"Fine."

"I'm glad you came Saturday. Must've been a bit overwhelming. Especially when you were pulled into the program. I hadn't intended to do that to you."

"I have to admit, I'm not used to being in front of people, but I did enjoy the program."

She'd said the same thing Saturday as she'd left, but

his ex-wife had lied to him so often he wasn't sure if he could recognize the truth anymore.

"How's John doing?"

"The burn is healing. I changed the bandage."

She nodded and placed her hands in her lap as if she'd realized she'd been abusing the shaker. "Good."

He grinned. "It seems like every time we're together there's some kind of excitement."

Liz looked over her shoulder toward the kitchen. "Should we say something to the people back there about being extra careful?"

A bang of pans falling filled the air. Their looks met a few seconds before they broke out in laughter. They couldn't stop. Carter glanced around to see other customers staring at them. Still he continued to chuckle.

Liz mesmerized him in her mirth. It changed her appearance from attractive to beautiful. If he hadn't found her interesting before, he certainly did now.

"We have to stop," she gasped. "People are looking at us."

Carter chuckled. "I can't if you keep laughing."

"Okay, on three we stop. One, two, three." She gulped for air on the last word.

Carter had to look away not to start laughing again. Thankfully their waitress brought their drinks and they sobered up.

Liz leaned toward him, still smiling. "If we aren't careful, we're going to be asked to leave."

"It'd be worth it. I needed a good laugh. I don't do that often enough. I've had a few lean years where laughter is concerned."

"Come to think of it, laughter is supposed to be the best medicine." Liz grinned.

He pointed a finger at her. "Don't you get us started again."

"That's funny." She quickly closed her mouth and looked away.

He took a swallow of his tea. "What's that look for?"

"I was thinking how ironic it is that I've been told I act like a wallflower and now you're accusing me of creating a scene."

"I didn't exactly say that." He grinned. Had she always stood in the background? Why?

Her eyelids flickered up, then down. "That's what I heard."

"Let's examine the evidence. I've seen you three times and you've had car trouble, taken care of a burned arm and pots have fallen. There's nothing quiet and unassuming about any of that. I don't know who's been lying to you or if you've been hiding all that talent on purpose but I've had more excitement in my life in the last few days than I've had in months because of you."

Liz lifted her head, her eyes bright. "Really?"

"Yeah, really."

"Me, exciting." She spoke more to herself than to him, amazement in her voice. A grin slowly formed on her lips.

He smiled as their food arrived.

"You're working the flotilla during the Festival of Trees on the River this weekend, aren't you?" Carter asked before taking a bite of his sandwich.

"I am."

"I'm surprised you're an ENT when you're so good

with emergency work." He watched her as she pushed around a cucumber.

Her gaze flickered up to his. "My sister wanted us to be ENTs. She wasn't wild about blood."

He huffed. "But she's a doctor? So, you're partners with your sister? Interesting."

Liz put down her fork and placed her hands in her lap. "Not any more. She died, August a year ago."

This he hadn't expected. He shook his head. "I'm so sorry to hear that."

"She was my twin sister."

Carter felt a stabbing pain in his chest for what Liz had suffered. To lose a sister was bad enough, but a twin sister made it worse. "Liz, I…"

"I know. I usually don't tell anyone because they have the same reaction. I not only lost my sister but my best friend and medical partner."

"I'd like to know about her if you want to talk about her?"

"Louisa and I weren't identical twins. We had some similarities in looks but just those of average sisters. Our personalities were our biggest difference. She was far more outgoing than me. Everyone loved her." Liz let the words trail off. "Do you have any brothers or sisters?"

Liz obviously didn't want to talk about her sister anymore. "I have a brother. He and his wife live overseas. He's in the military."

"So you don't get to see them often."

"I don't but when I do, it's like slipping back to where we were. We have a great time together."

She gave him a weak smile. "That's nice. Do your mother and father live close?"

"They live about three hours away." He took a bite of his sandwich.

"It's nice they don't live too far away. Ryan can see them often."

But that wasn't the case. Carter made excuses for them not to visit. When they were around, it just reminded him of how poorly his marriage had gone. What a disappointment to them and himself he'd been. His parents had the perfect marriage. They'd been married for thirty-eight years and he couldn't even make one last three years. They reminded him every time he saw them of his failure. His mistake.

"We don't see them as much as they or Ryan would like."

"Not you?"

"Me too. Of course," he quickly added.

She studied him a moment longer than made him comfortable. She wiped her mouth with her napkin. "I really should be getting back. I've a full list of patients this afternoon."

"Hold on a sec. I'll walk you out." Carter took one more swallow of his drink and picked up the check the waitress had left.

Liz led the way to the cash register. "I'll get mine." She reached for the check.

"I'll take care of it. You can get it next time if you want."

Liz waited near the door while he paid. She acted eager to leave. Their light lunch had turned heavier than he'd planned. Talking about her sister had rattled them both. He thought he knew hurt but his couldn't have been anywhere near hers.

"Hey—" he took her hand before she ran to the car "—I enjoyed seeing you again. Let's do it again sometime."

She finally looked at him. "Okay."

"In fact, why don't we do it Friday night?"

Liz gave him a wry smile. "That's not lunchtime and I already have plans. I'm working the Festival of Trees, remember?"

He slapped his thigh. "That's right, I forgot. We'll try another time. I'll call you. Bye, Liz." He kissed her cheek. As he watched her walk away, he grinned as her hand came to rest over the spot where his lips had been.

CHAPTER FOUR

LIZ LOOKED OUT of the medical tent at the crowd lining the river in front of her. The sun had almost set, and the Festival of Trees on the River had drawn a large mob this year with the weather having turned clear and crisp. Perfect for bundling up, hot chocolate and floating boats.

She and her EMT help, Ricky, had cared for a few patients in the last hour: a young boy with a nosebleed; after him came a girl who had fallen and needed her hands cleaned and bandaged; a woman who had been hit in the head when a boy threw a rock. The list, thankfully only filled with small problems, kept growing.

On her way to retrieve additional gauze from the supply box, she glanced up to see Carter and Ryan standing close by.

"Hi." Carter smiled. "We came by to say hello. How're things going?"

"Steady, nothing major. Hey there, Ryan. Are you ready for the parade?"

The boy nodded. "I've never seen a boat parade."

"I promise you'll like this one. My sister and I used to beg to come every year." Why had she said that? She hadn't thought of those days in a long time. To her surprise, remembering felt good. It seemed easier to say now that Carter knew about Louisa. Their lunch had had some difficult emotional moments for her but after she'd talked about Louisa she felt better. She needed to do that more often.

In the distance Christmas music began to fill the air.

"Come on, Dad." Ryan pulled on Carter's hand. "It's starting. We've got to go. My friend Mike's already down there."

"Better go. Come join us if you get a chance," Carter said over his shoulder, as Ryan pulled him away.

"Thanks. I'll see." Liz returned his smile, although she doubted she'd make it. Being responsible, she couldn't leave the tent. Disappointment filled her as she watched Carter and Ryan. She moved to the front of the tent but could no longer see them. She liked Carter. He had quickly become a friend. The fact he was a handsome eligible male didn't hurt. It had been a long time since she'd felt about a man the way she did about Carter.

Liz's attention became diverted by a man coming up with his hand wrapped in a bloody rag. He'd been using a pocketknife and it had slipped. The result ended up being an ugly gash in his palm. She and Ricky were just finishing up with him when a teenager came running toward them from the direction of the river.

"Help! Help! We need some help."

Liz rushed out to meet him. "What's wrong?"

The guy pointed back behind him. "A man on a boat got his arm caught."

"Listen! Go tell them not to move him until I get

there! Tell them not to move him," Liz repeated. "I'm on my way."

She turned and Ricky handed her the go-bag. "Stay on the radio. I'll call if I need you."

"Ten-four."

Slinging her bag over her shoulder, Liz took off running. She soon caught up with the teen. The crowd parted.

A low-in-the-water fishing boat was parked parallel to the bank and held there by two men with ropes. The craft had been decorated with bright Christmas lights and had a tree standing in the middle with more lights strung from the top of the tree to the corners of the boat. There were more bulbs lining the edge. Children dressed as angels sat and stood in the boat.

As she reached the river's edge, her breath caught and her heart pounded. What caught her attention could only be the worst sight she'd ever seen. A man lay half on and half off the back of the boat. A woman supported his head and had it turned to the side so his face remained out of the water. His right arm appeared pinned under the motor.

Two men started to raise the motor.

"Stop! Don't do that!" she yelled.

The men turned with obvious surprise.

She stepped over the side of the boat, careful not to make it rock. "I'm Dr. Poole. We don't want him to bleed out in case the radial artery has been severed. The pressure of the motor may keep him from losing his life or his arm."

Slowly she moved closer to the back of the boat. When it sank deeper in the water, she stopped.

"We're going to need to get some ballast to the front," a voice Liz recognized came from behind her. She glanced over her shoulder to see Carter standing toward the front. He didn't wait on her agreement before he said, "I'm Dr. Jacobs. I need all the children to get off the boat."

He pointed to two women. "You and you—help them off and stay with them until their parents get here. Everyone else, move to the front as far as you can." He pointed. "Including you two gentlemen in the back. Dr. Poole and I'll call you back when we're ready for you to lift the motor."

Liz wasted no time moving to the patient as the weight shifted, bringing the back of the boat farther out of the water. She went down on her knees beside the man and took over the lady's job of keeping his head out of the water. Liz gently cupped his cheek so that she could turn his face toward her. In the dim light, she could easily see the man's skin color had turned white. His eyes were wide and pupils large. He was going into shock. Liz feared he might pass out.

A strong light blinked on. She glanced back to see Carter, with his legs wide to steady himself on the floor of the boat, pointing a large flashlight in her direction.

She took a second look at the man's arm. It lay between the bottom of the large outboard motor and the top of the transom of the boat. She winced. He'd have a tough time keeping his arm. It looked crushed.

"Carter, I need some blankets or coats. He's going into shock."

He nodded and stepped to the front and spoke to the people.

"Can you move your fingers?" she asked the injured man, keeping her voice even despite the pace of her heart.

"Yes," he grunted.

"Good." That at least was encouraging. "We're going to get this motor off you and you to the hospital as soon as we can. Carter," she spoke over her shoulder, "I'm going to need you back here with me. We'll need those men now."

"Give me a sec to do some more counterbalancing. Both of us needing to be in the same corner of the boat is going to be problematic."

The light disappeared but soon returned. She looked back to find a man turned around on his knees in the driver's seat, holding the flashlight high. Liz returned her attention to the injured man while Carter went about trying to make them as safe as possible. "Can you tell me what happened?"

"Something got caught in the motor," her patient replied through clenched teeth. "I pulled to the bank and raised the motor. I reached under it, but the hydraulic lift gave out. The motor came down on my arm before I could pull it out." As he spoke, his voice became more labored.

She looked away from him to see Carter directing men to the other side of the boat while guiding two more to stand near the motor. He lay a blanket, then a couple of heavy coats over the man's body.

"I've disengaged the gear. We're ready when you are," Carter said.

"I'm going to need you down here with me. In my bag you'll find a splint and a package of eight-by-eight absorbent squares. Open a couple of those and have more on standby."

Carter worked quickly, soon coming to stand beside her. The back corner of the boat dipped low in the water. A trickle of liquid wet her side. Half the man's face lay in the freezing water.

Carter spoke to the two men, "As soon as you have the motor up and secure, I want you to move toward the front of the boat."

Both nodded.

Liz did her best to keep her teeth from chattering. "Carter, I'm going to need to support the arm and you to apply pressure as soon as you can. I'll pull him back and keep his head out of the water. We all go on three. One, two, three."

With low grunts, the men lifted the motor. Liz scooted and pulled the hurt man back against her body with one arm across his torso, holding up his head the best she could. She realized the moment the man passed out because he went limp and his head became heavier. Pulling hard, she held his back against her chest to keep him from drowning.

Over the injured man's shoulder, she watched as Carter positioned the splint and applied the large pads to the blood pouring from the wound on the top of his forearm. Liz put two fingers to his neck and located his carotid artery. "His pulse is low."

"I'm not surprised. He's lost a lot of blood. Would've lost more if they had lifted the motor. You were smart to stop them. Good work."

His praised warmed her despite the cold water running down her back.

"I'll get you out from under him just as soon as I get this arm secured," Carter promised. He called, "I need someone light in weight to help me with a bandage."

A woman joined him, going through the bag and finding a roll of elastic bandage.

"Start above his elbow and wrap but not too tightly," Carter instructed.

The woman started to work.

"You okay down there, Liz?" Carter asked.

"Yeah." Despite the fact she had a heavy man lying over her and her cheek and neck were smashed against the boat. There would be a mark for a while, but her discomfort came nowhere to matching her patient's. She shivered as more water rolled down her back. Truthfully she'd be more than happy to get up. "We need an ambulance."

"Already on the way. I radioed Ricky before we pulled the motor up." Carter's attention remained focused on the woman's work. "That's good. You're doing a great job."

His tone offered the obviously nervous woman encouragement. Liz liked Carter's ability to anticipate needs during an emergency and to make people feel at ease. That talent was a special one.

He gave the woman a reassuring smile. "There should be a Velcro end on that. All you have to do is press it down."

She did as Carter instructed.

He smiled at her. "Perfect. You can be my assistant anytime."

The woman returned the smile, indicating Carter

had clearly charmed her. He announced, "Liz, now we need to get this man off you."

The boat shifted.

Carter called over his shoulder. "Hey, I need everyone to stay put until we have this man off the boat. Please stand still." His tone allowed for no argument. "All right, Liz, I'm going to roll him toward me. I want you to shift out from under him. Can you do that?"

"Yeah." It wouldn't be easy, but she'd do it. "Protect his arm."

"Ten-four. Here we go." Carter slowly rolled the man toward him onto his good shoulder.

Liz pushed against the man's back being careful not to apply any pressure to his bad shoulder. Slowly she shifted out from under him, inhaling in her first full breath in a while. Staying on her knees, she helped Carter lower the man back down to the floor of the boat and adjust the blanket.

Soon the sound of the ambulance arriving filled the air.

Preoccupied, Liz said, "If you'll hand me the bag, I'll get some vitals. Also, that life preserver. Put it under his feet to help with the shock."

Carter handed her the bag, then the life preserver. "If you are okay here, I'll meet the EMTs."

She nodded, then started checking the man's heart rate, blood pressure, for further injuries, then made sure the bandage didn't restrict more blood flow than necessary. All the while she remained aware of Carter working behind her.

A few minutes later, a woman said in a shaky voice, "That man told me to bring this to you."

Liz took a blanket from her. "Thanks."

"Thank you. This is my husband."

Liz stopped long enough to place her hand on the woman's arm. "He's going to be fine. Hang in there. Will you help me put this blanket over him?"

Together they got it into place.

Carter returned with the EMTs who carried a board. She tried to stand but stumbled because her legs were stiff. Carter's hand took her elbow, steadying her, and remained there as they stepped back so the EMTs could work on the rocking boat. He let go only to help the EMTs carry the patient to the ambulance.

Once the patient was inside, she gave a report and soon the ambulance pulled away with its lights on. Liz rolled her shoulders and her teeth chattered.

A blanket came around her shoulders and large hands adjusted it. "You have to be freezing. Your back is soaked. Let's get you back to the tent. See if we can find you something dry and warm."

"Sounds good. I need to check on Ricky." She looked around. "By the way, where's Ryan?"

"With some friends. We were standing with them when I saw you running toward the boat. I figured you might need some help."

"I did. Much appreciated help. I hate that you missed watching the parade with Ryan."

He shrugged. "There's next year."

"You're a nice guy, Carter Jacobs."

He grinned. "Thanks, but it's more like I have a soft spot for you."

Heat washed through her that had nothing to do with

the blanket or the blood once again flowing freely in her limbs. "You shouldn't say things like that to me."

"Why not? It's true. Why do you think I wouldn't be interested in you?"

She had a difficult time looking at him. "I guess because through the years most guys have either found me too smart to be fun or weird. My last boyfriend stopped dating me because he said I was dull."

Carter put a hand on her arm and took a step closer, giving her an earnest look. "I assure you, you're not dull. Case in point, the last hour I spent with you. Please don't hide who you are from me. Ever."

What had Liz's ex-boyfriend been thinking to tell her something so untrue? In Carter's experience, she couldn't have been further from being dull. Her intelligence made her interesting. It made their conversations thought-provoking. What he found more fascinating was his reaction to her.

After his ugly marriage and divorce, he'd kept his distance from women. He'd dated occasionally but with little enthusiasm. Something about Liz pulled at him. At first, she'd seemed more like a damsel in need of his help only to morph into super medical woman when she was needed. It made him wonder what facet of her personality he'd discover next. His curiosity had been piqued.

Being around Liz made him question what might happen next. Excitement he'd not known in a long time made him look forward to the next day and the possibility of seeing her. She added an anticipation to his life that Ryan and work alone didn't fill.

"Hey," she said to Ricky, as she entered the tent and dropped her go-bag on the table.

"How did things go?" Ricky asked.

"Patient's gone. I sure hope he gets to keep his arm." Liz picked up a bottle of water and handed it to Carter before she took one for herself.

Ricky nodded. "Why don't you take a few minutes to regroup? I've got things under control here. The parade isn't over yet. Go catch the last of it."

Liz huffed. "I can't leave you. Who knows what'll happen?"

"You could go straight down from here." Ricky pointed the way out of the tent. "You'd be close enough to come right back. I can text you if I need you."

She grimaced but indecision still rooted her there. "I'd like to see some of the parade." She sounded wistful.

"Then come on." Carter took her hand.

"I need to put on a dry shirt first. Get rid of this blanket."

"Do it, then we'll go." Carter gave her a nudge on her back.

"You'll wait?"

Carter nodded. "I'll wait."

Liz smiled and hurried to a nearby car and grabbed a bag, then scrambled into the side door of the medical van. She soon returned with a heavy sweater on. "Okay. I'm ready." She pointed her finger at Rick. "But you call me if I'm needed."

Carter escorted her to the riverbank and they joined the crowd. She appeared surprised and happy they'd found Ryan and the family he was with. Carter quickly introduced her, but the boats were going by and they had no time to talk. Ryan came to stand between them.

"Hi there, Ryan," Liz said enthusiastically.

"Hey, Miss Liz."

"Have you been having a good time?" Liz's attention remained on his son.

"Uh-huh," Ryan answered.

"I'm glad. This is one of my favorite events. The boat owners are always so creative with their decorations."

Before she could say more "Here Comes Santa Claus" could be heard playing. "Hey, buddy," Carter said to Ryan, "let me put you on my shoulders so you can see."

With his son securely on his shoulders, the crowd pressed in, shifting Carter closer to Liz. His free hand brushed hers. He sought her touch again, intertwining their fingers. Carter glanced at her. "I don't want to lose you."

In an odd way, he meant that on a higher level. That shook him. He didn't even know if he could trust himself to feel that way.

Her gaze met his for a moment before she blinked and once again focused on the boats. Glad she hadn't pulled away, he tightened his grip. She adjusted her hand, applying the same pressure.

Smiling, he returned his attention to the flotilla. A glance at Liz revealed she watched the boats with great interest and with a large smile on her face. Liz didn't need to look for excitement elsewhere like his ex-wife had. She really did enjoy simple pleasures.

When Santa had passed, the crowd dispersed and Carter grinned at her. "That was really neat." He lifted

Ryan down. "We're gonna make this an annual event, aren't we, buddy?"

His son eagerly nodded.

Carter casually remarked, "Liz, I should hang out with you more often. There's always something exciting happening."

She grinned and freed her fingers. "I think you might be giving me more credit than you should. I've got to go back to the med tent and help pack it away. I'm glad you came tonight. And thanks for your help. I really appreciated it." Liz turned to go.

Carter grabbed her wrist, stopping her. "Ryan and I are going for pizza. You want to join us?"

She looked back toward the tent. "I don't know how long it'll take me to pack up."

"I'll tell you what, I'll text you what pizza place we're at when we decide. You can join us if you want. I hope you will."

And he did, very much. He wanted to spend more time with Liz. Have the chance to touch her again. Maybe more.

The entire time Liz hurried to pack away items in the medical tent excitement built in her at the idea of spending more time with Carter. He and Ryan were waiting on her. *Her.* Having a man attracted to her was stimulating. To have it be a handsome, intelligent and fun man like Carter made it even more thrilling. She liked him, too much. She had no doubt hurt lay ahead, but for now she would make the most of the time while it lasted.

Her phone dinged with a text. Carter and Ryan were at Pizza Joe's. It was her favorite pizza place in town.

"Go on. I've got this. I owe you anyway," Ricky said.

"Are you sure?" She had never thought of leaving a colleague like this before.

"I'm sure. Go on." He waved her away.

Liz picked up her purse. "Okay, but call me if you've a problem and I'll come right back."

"I'm good." Ricky returned to packing away a box. "We're almost done here anyway."

With a smile on her face and her blood humming, she climbed into her car and headed to the restaurant. Twenty minutes later she walked in the door of the darkened pizza joint located in a strip mall.

As if she were a heat-seeking missile and Carter the target, she found him immediately. He smiled, motioning her over to his and Ryan's booth. He sat on one side and Ryan on the other bench. Carter slid out and stood, waiting on her.

"Hi, gentlemen. I heard that I could get a good pizza here." What was she doing? That sounded too much like flirting. She didn't flirt. Didn't even know how to.

A quizzical expression came over Ryan's face. "It's a pizza restaurant so they have pizza."

She and Carter laughed. "You're right, and it's the best. My favorite place."

"Ryan said he was a big boy and wanted to sit by himself." Carter indicated with a hand for her to slide in. "So, you'll need to join me."

Liz gave him a speculative look. Had Carter put Ryan up to not sharing his bench so that she had to sit next to him? "Okay." She settled on the bench, placing her purse between her and Carter, making sure they wouldn't touch.

"Why don't you put that over there with Ryan where it'll be out of the way?" Carter suggested.

Unable to think of a good reason to disagree, she handed the purse to Carter and he placed it on the other bench. So much for her having a line of defense. The second her purse was removed her and Carter's legs met from hip to knee. Warmth simmered along her thigh.

He smiled. "That's better, isn't it?"

She couldn't say it wasn't, so she said nothing. Thankfully moments later the waiter arrived to take their drink order.

Liz grinned at Ryan. "I guess you're going to have cheese pizza."

Ryan bobbed his head.

"I'm having meat lover's," she announced.

Soon the waiter returned with their drinks.

Carter placed their order. As the waiter left, he shifted on the bench and gave her a head-to-toe appraisal. "I don't know where you put all that meat. It certainly doesn't show that I can see."

Liz's face heated. She leaned over the table and spoke to Ryan, "Do you think we should share ours with your dad?"

The boy acted as if he gave it serious thought. "Maybe one piece if we have enough."

"Ryan!" Carter sounded indignant but mirth filled his voice.

Liz put her hand out. "Agreed." She and Ryan shook hands.

Carter huffed and glared at them. "Hey, I didn't plan to be ganged up on when I suggested we go for pizza."

"You're not being ganged up on. We're just greedy where our pizza is concerned. Isn't that right, Ryan?"

He nodded with a grin on his face.

"So, what's the plan? For me to watch you two eat until you're full?" Disbelief circled Carter's words but he grinned.

"Maybe," Liz answered as seriously as possible. She like the banter. There wasn't enough of this type of interaction in her life.

"I think I'd better order my own after all." He raised a hand.

Liz placed hers on his forearm. "We're just kidding you."

"Yeah, Dad," Ryan said. "I'll give you a piece."

"And I will too." Liz added a sweet note to her voice. "We wouldn't want you to go away hungry."

Carter looked into her eyes. His holding a blaze. He said softly, "Maybe I should satisfy my hunger in another way."

Liz's eyes widened. She swallowed hard. Was Carter implying what she thought he was? Just as quickly his attention returned to his son. "Ryan, did you like the parade?"

He nodded.

Liz watched the child closely as she clutched her shaking hands in her lap. "Which was your favorite?"

"Santa Claus." The boy didn't hesitate.

She chuckled and so did Carter.

"Stepped into that one, didn't you?" Carter nudged her with his shoulder.

She glanced at him and smiled before returning her attention to Ryan. "What was your next favorite?"

"The one with the big blue tree and all the blue lights. The big fish was funny."

Liz nodded. "I know the one you're talking about. It was the one decorated like the catfish was swallowing the tree."

Ryan nodded, grinning.

"That figures." Carter asked her, "What was your favorite?"

"I like them all, but my favorite is always the pink frilly one with water ballerinas."

"Ooh, that's a girl float," Ryan complained.

Liz sat straighter. "If you haven't noticed, I'm a girl."

"I've noticed," Carter said in a tone that caused heat to whip through Liz again as his leg pressed against hers. Her hand trembled as she reached for her water glass, hoping to calm her nerves.

Carter picked up the discussion about the floating parade with Ryan. Liz enjoyed listening to the father–son conversation. Carter was a great parent. Especially so since he did it all on his own. What had happened to ruin his marriage? She couldn't imagine a woman not wanting either one of these males.

"My cheese pizza," Ryan announced, squirming in anticipation as the waiter approached their table, holding large pans.

Liz inhaled the wonderful smell of tomato sauce and meat. Carter handed out the plates that had been left for them. A feeling of rightness fell over her. When was the last time she'd been this carefree or had so much fun? For once she didn't feel like she'd been invited because it was the polite thing to do. Louisa had always asked if Liz could come too. This time she didn't feel like an afterthought.

"What're you asking Santa Claus for this Christmas?" Liz watched Ryan stuff pizza into his mouth.

Ryan said, "I want a puppy,"

Carter laughed. "Ryan's been trying to talk me into a dog for months."

"And how's that going?" she asked Carter.

Before Carter could answer, Ryan said in a bemoaned tone, "He says we've got to wait to make sure that I'm big enough to take care of a dog."

Liz thought for a moment before saying, "They're a big responsibility. I used to have one. They can be a lot of work but give a lot of love." She and Louisa had shared a poodle as children. It had always wanted to sleep on Liz's bed. Her sister hadn't liked that. Louisa had wanted to be his favorite. Liz hadn't realized that until this moment.

"Hey, are you all right?" Carter asked.

She looked at him and blinked. "Uh, yeah. I'm fine."

"You disappeared for a few moments there."

Liz forced a smile. "I was just thinking how much I've missed having a dog."

"See, Dad? Even Miss Liz thinks I need to get a dog."

Holding up a hand, she said, "Whoa, whoa! Don't put me in the middle of that argument."

Carter chuckled, obviously enjoying the exchange. "Welcome to the world of parenthood. Any slip of the tongue will be used against you."

"You two need to keep me out of it. I think I'll be quiet now." She took a big bite of her pizza.

Carter laughed. "You know I've not had this much fun in a long time."

Come to think of it, neither had she. Liz blinked. This was what happiness felt like.

"Daddy, when're we going to put up the Christmas tree?"

"I guess we better do that this weekend. I'm on call the next." He ate some of his pizza.

"Can it have the big lights with the different colors?" Ryan asked.

Carter wiped his mouth. "I don't know. We don't have any of those. We'd have to buy some."

"I bought some extra last year that I'm not going to use. You're welcome to them." Liz's heart expanded at the excitement on Ryan's face. She looked at Carter. "I can drop them off at your office."

Carter shook his head. "We can't take your lights. You might need them."

"Sure you can. I'm not going to use them," she assured him.

"I know." Ryan pressed his chest against the edge of the table. "You can come help us decorate."

"Hey, buddy, Liz may have other plans. We can't expect her to give us her lights and make her string them too."

Liz spoke before she thought. "Decorating the tree is my favorite thing to do at Christmas." Shocked at her outburst, she turned to Carter to gauge his reaction. The last thing she wanted to do was push herself on him.

Carter leaned back and looked at her. "How about this? You come join us for the decorating and stay for dinner, then we'll use your lights."

"You don't have to feed me to get the lights."

"Maybe Ryan and I like the idea of having a woman as a guest for a change."

Liz blinked. She'd have thought a man as charming as Carter would have a woman around all the time.

"How about we plan for Sunday at four?" He glanced at Ryan. "That'll give us time to get the perfect tree."

Liz wanted to join them. More than anything. She couldn't turn down the chance even if it had originally been Ryan's idea.

The boy yawned widely. Carter placed his napkin on the table. "I'd better get this guy home to bed."

A few minutes later, they stood outside the restaurant. Carter looked hesitant and touched her arm. "Are you sure you can get home safely? I'll be glad to follow you."

When was the last time someone had worried about her safety? A little over a week ago when Carter had taken her home. He'd done it twice more than any man had in too long. More than capable of taking care of herself, still it was nice to have someone concerned about her. "Thank you, but I'll be fine."

"We'll see you Sunday afternoon?" He looked at her for confirmation.

"I'll be there." She smiled, already looking forward to it.

"Don't forget the lights," Ryan added.

She went down to his level. "I won't. I promise." Once again standing, she looked at Carter.

"I'm glad you joined us tonight. See you Sunday." With a backward wave, he walked away.

"Me too." As she went to her car, she murmured, "Too much."

CHAPTER FIVE

CARTER DIDN'T KNOW what was happening to him. A simple Good Samaritan act in the country club parking lot had turned into meals and time spent with Liz. At first he'd seen them both as two people out of place at a party and now he found he truly liked Liz. His problem had turned into him liking her too much.

The fact Liz had such a good rapport with Ryan made her more appealing. Carter shouldn't have been surprised. From the interactions he'd seen her have, especially with patients, she had a real talent for putting people at ease, understanding and listening to them. Ryan responded to that.

Yet Carter had spent years protecting Ryan from hurt by not bringing women he dated around. He didn't want his son to become attached when he had no intention of making them a permanent fixture in their lives. Somehow Liz had slid under that fence. Even so, he had to keep her at arm's length despite being so enticed by her.

He'd found Liz intriguing to begin with, if a bit standoffish. When he'd invited her to the community meal, it had started out as being friendly, and he'd been looking for an unbiased opinion about the program.

After spending a few hours in Liz's company, he'd been impressed with her. His interest had continued to grow the more he was around her. Learning of her sister made his heart go out to her. Something about Liz made him suspect she hid a deep hurt. For some reason that occasional sadness he saw in her eyes touched him. He wanted to make it go away.

Working with her could be exhilarating, as well. As mild-mannered as Liz acted in normal circumstances, she naturally took control in an emergency. As far as he could tell, she could handle any injury with authority and skill.

She'd been more open at the pizza restaurant than he'd ever seen her. Her rapport with Ryan was amazing. Liz seemed to genuinely like his son, be interested in him. Carter liked that about her, as well. It didn't make it easier to keep his distance.

Determined the connection with Liz wouldn't go any further than friendship, he reminded himself that he still didn't know if he could trust her. Could he ever have faith in a woman again? Yet that sexual pull between them had him in its grip. Friendship had become the last thing on his mind. Her dewy pink lips took up more space in his thoughts than they should.

Bringing Liz, or any other woman, into the well-ordered life he'd established with his son wasn't what either of them needed right now. Carter didn't want to tip the fragile scale in the wrong direction. No matter how much he lusted after Liz.

But he couldn't stop himself where Liz was concerned. He might not want to admit it, but he looked forward to every opportunity to see her. Her soft ways and quiet presence eased his fears, made him think of possibilities again. Yes, he didn't want them to become too invested in each other's lives. Liz's background told him she searched for something he couldn't give.

Sunday afternoon Liz pulled into his driveway and he met her in the parking area. She looked unsure until she saw him, and a bright smile came over her face. One that sucker punched him. That reaction he hadn't expected. He'd been looking forward to seeing her much more than he'd realized or found comfortable.

Ryan came running out of the house without a coat or sweater on, or even shoes. Eagerness filled his face, his eyes optimistic. "Did you bring the lights?"

"You need to be dressed for the weather before you come outside," Carter reprimanded.

"I just want to see if she has the lights." Ryan eagerly looked into a window of Liz's car.

"I've got them. They're in the back seat," Liz assured him.

"Great. The tree's up." Ryan hopped around Liz. "Can I see the lights?"

"Go inside," Carter commanded, giving Ryan a nudge. "We'll be right there."

Watching to see if his son did as he ordered, Carter turned back to Liz who had gone to the back-seat door and opened it. She handed him a round plastic top container.

"What's this?" Carter turned the container back and forth, studying it.

"I made another apple pie. I thought the least I could do was bring dessert." She leaned inside the car again and pulled out a sack holding a gallon of ice cream and held it up.

"Okay. I'm officially in love."

A shocked moment hung between them.

A zing of awareness whipped through Carter that ended in embarrassment. "I'm sorry, that was just a figure of speech."

Liz quickly reassured him. "Oh, I know, I know."

"Hand me the ice cream. You get the lights and let's get in out of the cold." He waited on her and they walked to the house. "By the way, I've your other pie plate all clean and ready to go."

"I'd forgotten about it until I started looking for it to bring this one over." She pushed the back door to the house open and he followed her into the kitchen. "I didn't tell you the other day," she said as she set things down on the kitchen counter, "how much I like your kitchen. Your house is amazing. You've done a beautiful job with it."

"Granny and Pops restored it and updated a couple of rooms before I moved in. Since Ryan and I've been here, we've done more work, but there's only so much you can do with an active boy around. In fact, I have a few small projects outside I've got to get on right away, but I can't depend on Ryan to hold the ladder."

"I could help you with those after we decorate the tree, if you want." Her eyes went wide as if she'd surprised herself by offering.

Carter gave the idea a moment of thought. "That'd be great. I just need somebody there to call 911 if I fall."

She narrowed her eyes.

"Let's hope it doesn't come to that."

"Dad, come on," Ryan called in an urgent, impatient voice from down the hall.

"On our way, buddy." Carter pushed the pie back from the edge of the counter and grinned. "Wouldn't want that to fall." He turned to the refrigerator, placing the ice cream in the freezer compartment.

Ryan ran in, then jumped up and down. "Can I see the lights? Can I see the lights?"

Liz handed him the box. He dashed out of the room.

"You wait until Liz and I get there before you start putting them on the tree."

She laughed and the sound rippled through him. The pure notes reminded him of bells on a crisp cold day. Heaven forbid he waxed poetic over a laugh. *Wow, this is getting out of hand.* He had to get a handle on himself *now.* "We better get in there before he has the lights in a mess."

Liz headed up the hall and he followed. He could hear Ryan shuffling around and volunteered, "Ryan's been up since seven waiting on you to get here with those lights. I guess I'll have to buy some for next year."

"Just keep these. I'm not going to ever use them. I've a small tree and they're too large for it."

"Thanks. Obviously, they'll be treasured for years to come."

Over the next hour, they worked to get the lights on the tree and put what decorations he had on it.

Carter picked up one of the ornaments. "Look at this one, Ryan. It's the one you made last year in school." His son beamed at him, face aglow in the tree lights as Carter handed it to Ryan to hang.

Carter stood back and studied the tree. "We're a little low on decorations. It looks like we need to do a little shopping."

He hadn't bothered with holiday decorations during his divorce. The custody battle had been his focus. He'd bought a few ornaments over the years afterward, but it wasn't until this year that Ryan had really shown an interest in putting up the tree. What he had to hang on the tree wasn't near enough for its size.

"We can always make some," Liz suggested. "The homemade ones are the best anyway." An odd look came over Liz's face as if she'd said something she shouldn't have.

"Ryan, why don't you put your shoes on and take these empty boxes to the shed?"

"Aw, Dad."

"Go on."

Ryan went to work and soon left.

Carter stepped closer to Liz. "Are you all right? Something happened just a second ago. You want to talk about it? I'm a good listener."

She shrugged. "It's no big deal. I was just remembering something that happened one Christmas."

He waited.

She took a deep breath. "We always trimmed the tree as a family, had a big dinner, then sang carols afterward. I liked it almost better than Christmas Day. Each year Louisa and I'd make a handmade ornament. The same one. When we were about twelve, my mom suggested we should make our own individual one and surprise everyone on decorating night. She was trying to foster our individuality, I think." Liz looked at him with her lips pursed. "See, I was pretty dependent on Louisa.

Anyway, we did. I spent a lot of time on mine. Louisa didn't give hers much thought. Mother and Daddy went on and on about how nice mine was. That night before I went to bed, I went to look at it hanging on the tree. It was gone."

"What happened to it?"

"I found Louisa standing over the kitchen garbage can, tearing it up. She didn't see me and I never said anything about it. Until now."

Carter wrapped an arm around her shoulders and gave her a gentle hug.

"I don't know why she did that. She was the one everyone noticed. Except that one time."

Carter knew why. Her sister had been jealous.

Ryan came back into the room and Carter stepped away from Liz.

"Can we make some ornaments like you used to?" Ryan asked, looking from Liz to Carter and back again.

"Ryan, I don't think we need to do that today."

"I'm game, if you are." Liz gave Carter a wry smile.

"You sure?" He didn't want to make this hard on her.

She nodded. "I want to."

Carter gave her a reassuring smile. "Okay. What do we need? I'm about as good at crafts as I am cars."

A grin formed on Liz's lips. To his relief, it reached her eyes. Liz was strong. He'd give her that. She'd already pushed her sadness away.

She looked at Ryan. "That means it's up to us."

Carter put an indigent note in his voice, "Hey, at least I admit my shortcomings."

"And you make up for your shortfalls by being an excellent Good Samaritan."

Carter raised his shoulders and pushed out his chest. "That's more like it."

Liz turned to Ryan. "Do you have construction paper, markers, scissors and glue?"

"I can get the paper and the markers. Daddy has to get the scissors and the glue."

She nodded. "Okay. You go get those and meet me at the kitchen table."

The boy hurried off.

"You're sure you're good with this?"

Her gaze met his. "I'm sure. I didn't mean to bring a good time down a few minutes ago."

"Not a problem. You're a nice person, Liz Poole." In an impulsive move, he placed a soft kiss on her lips. She looked as shocked as he felt. And yet, along with other emotions, he wanted to do it again. Deeper and longer. A little taste wasn't enough. Doing so became overridden by the fear he might have scared her off, but she didn't move.

"Uh, thank you," Liz finally uttered.

He wasn't sure which she'd thanked him for, the compliment or the kiss. It didn't matter.

Liz's body heated as if it were a summer day and the sun beat down from the touch of Carter's lips. She started to speak but stopped when the words wobbled. She cleared her throat and started out of the room. Glancing back, she found Carter watching her.

What had made her think of that awful December day today, of all days? And to tell Carter. He must think her a nut case. For so long she'd chosen not to remember

it. Carter had been concerned about her making ornaments again, but she wouldn't disappoint Ryan.

She had just made it to the kitchen when Ryan entered. He put the materials on the table. Liz quickly
pushed the salt and pepper shakers and a couple of place
mats off to the side. "We're also going to need the scissors."

Carter entered and pulled a drawer out. "Right here."

Ryan scrambled up onto a chair as his dad placed
the scissors on the table.

She looked at Carter. "We'll need some glue too."

"I'll get it." He strolled out of the room.

Her attention returned to Ryan who played with the
scissors.

"What're we making?" Ryan snapped the scissors
closed.

Liz took them out of his hand and set them out of
his reach. "We're going to start with something simple
like stars."

"How do you make them?"

"I'm going to show you. First, I need to draw a pattern. Then we'll trace around it and cut it out. We can
leave it single or add another and make it 3D." Ryan's
enthusiasm made her sad memory start to disappear. It
would be replaced by a happy one.

"3D?" Ryan wrinkled up his nose.

Liz tapped the end of it with her index finger. "That's
when it stands out. Don't worry, I'll show you."

Carter took the chair on the other side of her and
placed the glue on the table. His eyes twinkled as he
looked between her and his son.

"Hand me a sheet of paper, Ryan." The boy quickly

passed one to her. Using a marker, she drew a freehand five-pointed star.

"Wow." Ryan set up on his knees in the chair and looked at her, amazed.

"You are good," Carter agreed.

Liz chuckled. They sure knew how to build her ego. She reached for the scissors. Soon she had the star cut out. "Now, this is our pattern. Hand me another piece of paper." Ryan did so. "Now we trace around this." She placed the star on the paper and asked Ryan, "Will you help me?"

He nodded with comical eagerness, bobbing his head up and down.

"Put your finger right here in the middle." She showed him how she wanted it.

Ryan followed her instructions. She used the marker to draw around the star. "We need to fill up the entire paper, then cut them out. Do you want to trace or cut?"

"I'll draw." Ryan took the marker from her.

"You trace a few, then I can start cutting," Carter offered.

After Ryan had a couple of wavy-lined stars traced, she said, "You're doing a great job."

"You think so?" Ryan looked unsure.

"I know so. Let me cut those that you've done so far, so your father can get started." She cut the paper down the middle. She handed the unused half to Ryan.

Liz pushed the other toward Carter. Their gazes caught. Warmth burned in his eyes. What was he thinking? His hand touched hers as he took it. That electric spark shot up her arm again.

Carter started cutting. "When was the last time you made Christmas ornaments?"

Her gaze met his again. "When I was twelve."

Realization filled his eyes.

"This will be a nice memory to replace the old."

He nodded, compassion in his eyes now. "I'm glad."

"Done," Ryan announced, having filled the rest of the page.

"Then start on another," Liz told Ryan. "It takes twice as many if we make 3D ones."

A few minutes later, they had a small pile of stars.

"We make a pretty good production line," Carter commented.

"What's a production line?" Ryan looked at him.

"It's where one person does one thing, then hands it off to another and so on." Carter returned to his cutting.

"Does Santa use a…a…?"

"Production line," Carter patiently supplied.

"A production line to make toys?" Ryan looked from one of them to the other.

Liz looked at Carter, who had a grin on his face. "Yes, he has a big production line."

Ryan searched his father's face. "The elves help, don't they?"

Carter nodded. "They do."

"Are we Liz's elves?" Ryan's voice had turned thoughtful.

Carter smiled and looked at her. "I believe we are."

Liz laughed and he joined her. She looked around the table. This moment would be the memory she would remember when she thought of making ornaments. The love and warmth between a father and a son, and the feeling of being included in their warmth. They were *her* elves. At this moment she felt special and needed, her world was right.

"We've enough stars. Now I'll show you how to make 3D ones." She picked up two stars. "All you have to do is make a slit halfway on one, then slip it in between two points." She did so. With two fingers, she held it up and twirled it around. "See?"

"Ooh, wow." Ryan looked at her in amazement. "You're smart."

"Thank you, but I can't take the credit. My mom taught my sister and me how to make them."

Carter placed his hand over hers. The prick of pain eased. She gave him a thin smile.

"Look." Ryan held up a 3D star. It was lopsided but he glowed with pleasure.

"That looks wonderful." Liz clapped.

"We can also do circles, if you want to." She took a sheet of paper, drew two circles and quickly cut them out. "You can leave it like this or make it 3D." She split one halfway and inserted another circle. "What do you think?"

"I want to make those too." Ryan reached for a sheet of paper.

"I thought you might." Carter winked at her.

A sweet warmth rippled through her. Liz looked around the table. This was what she had always dreamed of but feared she might not ever find.

She raised a hand. "Not so fast. I've one more to show you." She took a piece of paper and told Carter, "Put your hand out here. Spread your fingers."

He placed his hand on her paper. She gave Ryan the

marker. "Now trace around your dad's hand." When he had finished, she pushed the paper to Carter. "Now your part of the production line is to cut it out."

Carter screwed up his face. "It didn't take long to let your job title of Head of Elves go to your head, did it?"

Liz giggled. Something she seemed to do a lot these days.

"Can I do my hand?" Ryan asked eagerly.

Liz picked up the marker. "Sure. I'll trace it."

"Now we need to do yours," Ryan announced, speaking to Liz.

She shook her head. "I don't think you need my hand on your tree."

"Yes, we do. Don't we, Dad?" Ryan gave his father a questioning look.

Carter's look met hers. "Yes, we do."

She blinked, savoring the happiness that washed over her. "Okay, if you want." She placed her hand on the paper and let Ryan trace it.

Carter placed the cut out of Ryan's hand on the table. "What do we do with these after I *painfully* cut them out?"

Liz narrowed her eyes at him. "Yeah, my elves don't complain about their jobs. We'll write our names on them and the year, then they'll be ready to go on the tree." Liz looked at Ryan. "Each year you can add new ones.

"I got one more thing I can show you. How to make a paper chain." Liz placed a star in a pile, picked up a piece of paper and cut off a couple of strips. "Can you pass me the glue, Carter?"

He did so. This time his finger ran along hers as

she took the bottle from him. The man was killing her slowly with his touches. "All you have to do is make a loop." She made it. "Place a drop of glue on the ends. Then carefully slip another strip through the center and glue again." She looked at Ryan. "You keep going until you get it as long as you want it. Do you want to try?"

"Yeah."

Liz handed the chain to Ryan. "I'll cut you the strips."

"Remember not to overdo the glue." Carter continued to cut out the traces of their hands.

Ryan sat back in his chair and went to work.

She looked at Carter. He watched her with amazement and something else she couldn't name on his face. *Thank you*, he mouthed.

Unsure where things were heading with them, Liz still feared she was falling for him. While the thought should've scared her, instead it filled her with excitement.

The ringing coming from her phone in her purse ended the moment. She answered it. The voice on the other end of the line she recognized as one from the emergency room. "There's been an auto accident. We need you to consult before the patient goes to the OR."

Liz winced. "I can be there in twenty minutes. Have X-rays, anterior right and left ready for me to review. I'll also need to see all recent blood work." Liz hung up. She hated car accidents. They were the hardest for her to deal with.

"Apparently you're on call." Carter stood beside her.

She gave him a wry smile. "Yeah. You know how it is. When you don't have anything to do, they never call and then you agree to do something… There's been a car accident."

"You got to go?" Ryan asked while he remained busy gluing the chain together.

"I do." Liz went to him. "Why don't you finish up what we started and put them on the tree with your Dad's help? Then I can come back sometime and see how pretty it is."

"You'll come back tonight?"

She looked over his head to Carter, who nodded his agreement. She smiled and nodded to the boy, "I'll try to be back as soon as I can."

"Ryan, we need to let Liz go." Carter picked up her purse and handed it to her. "I'll walk you out."

She opened the door and Carter followed. "I'm sorry. I rarely, if ever, get called. I agreed to help out tonight, thinking it was no big deal. I'll try to get back before Ryan's bedtime. If not, I'll come tomorrow evening. I'm sorry about not holding the ladder for you, as well."

"Don't worry about all that. Just go do what you need to do safely. We'll be here waiting when you get back."

That sounded so perfect. *Waiting on her.*

"I'll save eating the pie until you return."

"You don't have to do that. I might be late. Or I might not get back."

"Then we'll share it for dinner tomorrow." He opened the driver's door for her. When she was in, he closed the door and gave her a little wave.

An hour and a half later, she'd taken care of her patient and was ready to leave the hospital. She waffled about returning to Carter's. Night had fallen, but it wasn't Ryan's bedtime yet. She texted Carter, I'm on my way. Is that okay?

Seconds later her phone dinged. We are waiting.

Liz couldn't help but smile. Soon she turned into the Mooresville community. The backdoor light burned brightly as she pulled to a stop next to Carter's SUV. Ryan ran toward her from the patio where flames flickered in the raised firepit. Carter wasn't far behind Ryan. She wished she came home to this type of welcome every night. She must be careful not to get too involved. Pain lived down that road. But loneliness wasn't much better.

"Liz, you need to come see the tree. It's so pretty." Ryan grabbed her hand. "Come see it from the front, outside. Then we'll go in."

"Hold up a minute, buddy." Carter put his hand on Ryan's shoulder. "Liz, have you had anything to eat?"

"No." She hadn't even thought about food.

"While you and Ryan are around front, I'll warm your plate."

"Can we go now, Dad?" Ryan took her hand again.

Carter nodded. "Yes. Go slow so Liz doesn't fall. It's dark."

She smiled at Carter as Ryan pulled on her hand again. They walked around the house, stopping on the walk facing the front door.

"Isn't it great?" Ryan asked with reverence, as they looked at the tree through the front window. The yellow, red, blue, green and orange lights shone brightly. A blinking star topped it off.

"It is, in fact, the best I've ever seen."

Ryan beamed up at her. She chuckled.

"Now you need to go in and see the decorations. Come on." With the energy only a little boy could have, he went along the walk, then clomped up the front steps and into the house.

Liz hurried after him. She came to stand beside him in the wide doorway of the living room. The tree had indeed been decorated with all the decorations they had made. A paper chain wrapped the tree. There among it all, right up front, was her handprint between Carter's and Ryan's. Her eyes watered. It was the most perfect tree.

"You're right. It's a beautiful tree. The prettiest I've ever seen."

Carter joined them, stepping up beside her, close enough that his heat warmed her. "Are you okay?"

She nodded. "Never been better."

"You sure?" he whispered close to her ear.

"Positive." Her voice becoming stronger.

"Your dinner's hot. I'm going to get Ryan started on his bath and put him to bed while you eat. Sorry I can't keep you company."

"Don't worry about it. I'll be fine. I probably shouldn't have come back. I'll just pack it up and take it home. I'll return your plate."

Carter placed his hands on her shoulders and gave them a gentle squeeze. "Stop, Liz. Ryan and I are glad you're here. Go eat your supper. I won't be long with Ryan." He kissed her temple and left.

Liz stood there a few more minutes, and then with a smile on her face, went to the kitchen.

Carter soon joined her.

"Thanks for this. It was great." Liz indicated the almost-clean plate.

He slid into the chair across from her. "I'm glad you like it."

Ryan entered. "Hey, Dad, can I watch some TV before bed?"

"As long as you don't argue when I tell you it's time to hit the hay. Liz and I are going outside to sit by the fire while we eat our pie."

"Can I—"

"No. You cannot have another piece of pie. Go watch your show and I'll come in and put you to bed in a little while."

Ryan hung his head and left.

Liz laughed.

"Now, about you." His attention didn't leave her. "You want your pie warmed? With or without ice cream?"

"Warm and with ice cream." Liz didn't hesitate to give her order.

"A woman after my own heart. Two pieces of warm pie à la mode."

Liz went to the sink and started washing her dish while he prepared their pie.

"How did things go at the hospital?" Carter pulled the ice cream out of the freezer.

"Not too bad. I just had to make sure a surgery was necessary. The man took a solid hit to the bridge of his nose. I also had to check for any trachea damage. It'll be an uncomfortable holiday season for him, but he won't have any obvious scars."

"Head injuries are never fun. I'm glad the case wasn't

too difficult, and you didn't have to stay long. Also I'm glad you got to come back to us." He placed a scoop of ice cream on the pie. "Let's pull on our jackets and have our pie by the fire."

With that done, Carter handed her a plate, picked up his, then opened the door. At the firepit, she took a chair and Carter pulled his up next to hers, but not too close. The clink of his fork against his plate reached her ears as she looked into the fire.

"This is the most amazing apple pie I've tasted. If you decide to give up medicine, you need to go into baking pies."

Carter's comment brought her out of her daze. "I think you're laying it on a little thick, Doctor."

He chuckled as he placed his empty plate on the ground beside the chair. "You're not eating your pie."

She glanced at the plate, then looked at him. "I had too much supper. Would you like to have it? I don't really need it."

"I won't let it go to waste."

She handed her plate over. Liz watched Carter's lips as he pulled a fork between them. He had a great mouth. Full and firm. That one little kiss had made her tingle so much she could only imagine what a real kiss would do to her.

"You really were great with Ryan today. You saved the day with the decorations. I know it had to have been difficult for you. I really appreciate it."

"It was a lot of fun. Good for me. Cathartic." It had been. She'd enjoyed every minute of it. "Ryan's a great kid. You're doing a wonderful job with him."

"Thanks for saying so. I don't always go to bed thinking that."

She looked at him. "He's seems pretty resilient to me."

"He's had to be with a mom like his." His jaw tightened as an expression of disappointment and anger came over his face.

Liz wasn't sure she should ask but her curiosity got the better of her. "Why?"

Carter looked at the fire instead of her. "Let's just say that she wasn't much of a mother. She was far more interested in herself and her afternoons in bed with her lover."

Liz chest squeezed in pain for what this nice caring man and his child must have endured. "I'm so sorry, Carter. You didn't deserve that."

He continued as if she weren't there. "The worst was I didn't realize she'd been neglecting Ryan until I came home early one day and found him alone in a playpen with a dirty diaper, screaming. I called for Diane and she wasn't anywhere to be found. Here I was with panic filling me that something had happened to her when she comes in the back door, buttoning her shirt with the guy next door behind her. They had obviously been having a quickie."

Liz gripped the chair arm, relieved she hadn't eaten the pie or she might have lost it when her stomach roiled. She placed a hand over his. Carter turned his so their fingers laced.

"I'm glad it's over and done with. She didn't even fight me for custody. She never wanted to be a mother." Disgust surrounded his words.

Feeling indigent on Carter's behalf, Liz sat straighter. "Doesn't sound like she was one anyway. It's her loss. Ryan's a fine boy. Fun to be around. You're a good father and he can feel it."

Carter squeezed her hand. "Thanks for that."

They sat in silence, processing what had been said for a few minutes.

Carter stirred. "I need to put Ryan to bed. Do you want to come in or stay out here?"

"I'll go in. I can say good-night. Then I'd better go." She stood.

"Please wait until I get Ryan to bed before you do." Carter picked up the plates.

"Okay."

Inside Carter put their plates in the sink, and she followed him into a small den area she hadn't seen before. One large wall had built-in shelves filled with books. There was a cushioned couch and two large stuffed chairs. A desk sat in front of a window. This could only be Carter's private study. Clearly it was here he and Ryan lived the most.

Curled in one of the chairs, Ryan lay sleeping. Carter scooped him up and brought him against his chest. Everything about the action screamed safe and secure.

Feelings she'd always dreamed of finding with a man. She must be careful not to expect more than Carter might be willing to give. Still, a girl could dream of being under Carter's umbrella of care. Finding that perfect place.

CHAPTER SIX

CARTER RETURNED DOWNSTAIRS to find Liz in the kitchen cleaning up the mess from making decorations that he and Ryan had left on the table. Their dessert plates were already in the dish drainer. Efficiency must be her middle name.

"You don't have to do that."

"I don't mind. I helped make the mess." She kept working, not looking at him. "I'll finish up and then go."

He went to the sink and filled a large glass with water. "I need to make sure the fire's out. I'll be right back."

"Okay."

When he returned, Liz was moving the place mats back into place.

"Leave that." He took her hand and led her to the living room where all the lights were off except for the tree. "Let's sit and enjoy the lights for a few minutes. I'd like to know what's going on in that head of yours."

"Nothing."

They settled on the couch but not too close and not touching. He didn't want to scare her off. He huffed. "I can't believe a woman as intelligent as you has nothing on her mind."

"I was just thinking how pretty the tree is. You guys did a great job."

Why he pushed her so, he didn't know. Something about Liz made him think she needed a friend, needed to feel needed, wanted someone to share her thoughts with. Why he believed he should be that person he had no idea, but he couldn't stop himself.

"It wasn't us that made it look great. We just followed your lead. By the way, I saw those tears you were holding back when you saw it. What was that about?"

"I think you need to have your sight checked."

Carter cupped her chin and turned her face toward him. "You aren't a good liar, Liz Poole."

She sighed. "I enjoyed making the ornaments with you and Ryan. It was special. For me, Christmas has already come. Today was a real gift." She nodded toward the tree. "To be included."

"Included?" What could she be talking about? She had been included all day.

"Y'all hung my hand along with yours."

"Sure, we did." Why did she think they wouldn't? "You showed us how to make them. We wouldn't leave you out."

Her gaze met his. "Thank you for that."

"You're welcome." He continued to hold her gaze. "You don't like feeling left out, do you?"

She looked down, picking at a fingernail. "Who does?"

He nodded thoughtfully. "That's true, but something tells me you feel it more acutely than most."

"I got over that a long time ago."

Carter knew that wasn't true. Her behavior at the community party and the expression on her face when she'd arrived at the Mooresville Christmas event said something different. "How's that?"

He feared that she might not answer by the look of apprehension on her face, but she said, "Let's just say I wasn't the party animal growing up. If it hadn't been for my sister seeing that I was invited, I might never have gone to anything."

"That was nice of her." Much more so than the ornament story. "Would you tell me what happened to her?" He really wanted to know, to understand Liz.

He sensed more than saw the tension in her body. Apparently she didn't like talking about her sister, yet she had mentioned her a number of times.

"She was killed in a car accident. She'd been to a party and was on her way home. She took a turn too fast, rolled over." Her words trailed off with all the pain Liz must have lived through at her sister's loss.

Carter took her hand. He didn't have words for what could only have been a horrendous experience. "I'm sorry. That must have been… I can't even imagine. And you had to go to an auto accident today. That can't be easy either."

"It isn't, but it must be done. Louisa's death completely changed my life." She looked at their hands as if studying them for details to complete a painting.

His heart went out to her. He thought a painful marriage breakup had been bad, but to lose a sibling… Somehow, he knew she needed to talk about it. "I bet it did, I can't imagine what I'd do if I lost my brother."

"Louisa was always the shining light in the room. If you had asked her to play the part the other night, she would've jumped at it and asked what she needed to say. I was the geeky one of us." She gave him a weak smile. "I wasn't very good at sports. You know, I was that person who was always the last to be picked. Totally socially awkward. Not Louisa."

Carter gave her hand a gentle squeeze.

Liz took a deep breath and slowly continued, "We were the exact opposite. Everyone loved her. She was the one people were drawn to. With her gone, I lost all of my social life, except for my book club, which she thought was a waste of time and the chess club, which she called *The Dull Club*. Without Louisa, it became clear that I didn't fit in."

Carter inhaled an audible breath but said nothing. He hurt for her. Her sister hadn't given her a chance to shine. The one time she had, Louisa had been jealous.

"Louisa was the one who wanted to be an ears, nose and throat doctor. I always liked the excitement of emergency medicine. She begged me to become an ENT too. That way we could start a practice together." Liz let out a dry chuckle. "Dr. Poole and Dr. Poole, your ears, nose and throat doctors and always glad to see you."

Carter couldn't help but chortle.

Her tone lightened. "We used to giggle over it all the time too."

"So, you became the doctor Louisa wanted to be, but you do the emergency work through volunteering because that's who you are." Carter winced at the note of disappointment he'd let slip into his voice.

She slumped. "I guess you could put it that way.

Louisa always gave me a hard time about using my off time *messing with blood and gore*. Even before she died, I'd thought about leaving the practice and doing emergency work but I couldn't disappoint her." She shrugged. "I'd probably have to do some refresher classes anyway. Now, somehow I feel I'd be disloyal if I closed the practice."

No, she wouldn't. He'd guess Louisa would like knowing she controlled Liz even from the grave. But he couldn't say that. "Life is short they say. I'd hate to know I wasn't doing what I loved."

"I know, but if I give up the practice, that means Louisa is truly gone. I just can't seem to do that."

Carter gathered her into his arms and kissed her on the top of her head. "You don't have to make any decisions tonight."

Liz looked at him. "I'm sorry I dropped all of that on you."

"Not a problem. What're friends for?"

"We're friends?" She pulled away and looked at him. Wonder filled her words.

"Of course we're friends."

"I like the sound of that." She wore a bright smile. "Tell me about your plans for Christmas, friend. Will your family be getting together?"

"You already know my brother is overseas. He'll be home in June on leave and we'll see each other then."

"What about your parents? You going there? They coming here?"

There it was. She'd asked a question he didn't want to answer. A side of him he didn't want to talk about. Was ashamed of. Especially since it was so irrational.

How could he not answer after Liz had shared her pain? She deserved an honest answer. "I don't see too much of my parents."

Her brow wrinkled. "Not even at Christmas?"

"No."

"Why?" she asked softly, as if she feared overstepping but her curiosity got the better of her.

Carter let out a deep breath. "I really disappointed my parents when my marriage failed. It's in their eyes whenever I see them. I still can't face them. They've had this perfect long marriage. They expected that of me. And Ryan. Their concern for Ryan hurts. They worry about his mother leaving him. The fact I'm a single parent. It's just easier to not do the—" he used air quotes "—happy family thing. I just can't deal with it."

"I'm sure they don't feel that way."

"Maybe not but it's the way I feel. I can't get past it."

She rested her hand on his thigh for a second. "Our feelings are our feelings. I should know. Will Ryan see his mother?"

"No. She hasn't made an effort in years." He was happy to have it that way.

"How sad. She has no idea what she's missing."

"She's made it clear she has no interest in being a mom or my wife." The bitterness still hung in his words.

"Did you know that before you married her?"

How like Liz to speak her mind. She might not say much but when she did, she came to the point. She didn't seem to have a deceiving bone in her body. That he could appreciate. "She told me she wanted children when what she really wanted was to be a doctor's wife. After Ryan arrived, I started to see differently but by then it was too late. The one good thing she did was give me Ryan."

"I'd never leave my child. Never."

"I can't imagine you would. Your compassion for others goes too deep. Your heart's too big."

"Thank you." She looked at the tree. "You know, this might be the prettiest tree I've ever seen." Liz's words had a soft sigh to them.

It was good not to hear sadness in her voice anymore. "All because of you."

Liz moved to the edge of the couch. "I didn't do much, but I enjoyed it. Every second. I'd better be going."

"I'll walk you out."

Carter stood and offered her a hand. She placed hers in his and he tugged her to her feet. His hands moved to rest on her waist. His gaze met hers before hers flickered away. "Liz?"

He waited until she refocused on him. "I want to kiss you."

She didn't say anything, and his mouth found hers. Her lips were lush and full and everything he dreamed they might be. She stepped closer and pressed against him. He gathered her closer. He took the kiss deeper, his tongue running along the seam of her mouth. She hesitated a moment before she opened for him. A thrill ran through him, making his manhood thicken. She tasted of sweetness and goodness and everything wonderful.

Wrapping his arms around her waist, he lifted her against him. She molded to him as if she'd been made just to fit him. Her hands crawled through his hair as she held his lips to hers.

Liz had fire in her. A fervor he wanted to explore, experience.

Just as quickly as she had kissed him, she backed away. "I can't do this."

"Why not? It seemed to me you were doing it pretty well."

Her look met his. "I don't think we're looking for the same thing."

"Maybe not, but I thought we were friends."

She licked her lips.

Carter suppressed a groan. Did Liz have any idea what she did to him? He doubted it.

"Friends don't usually kiss like that. I don't want to be hurt."

"I won't hurt you, Liz."

"You won't mean to, but it'll happen."

He watched her. "That's a very cynical way to look at a simple kiss."

"For me, no kiss is simple."

Before he could respond to that, she'd made it to the kitchen, picked up her purse and pie plate, and was headed out the door.

"Liz…"

"Bye, Carter."

Liz sat behind her desk on Friday afternoon filling out a form for a patient regarding their working abilities.

She hadn't heard from Carter all week. She wasn't surprised, friends or not. Why would he want to have anything to do with her after the way she had left things? He must think her emotionally stunted.

Rarely had she spoken of Louisa to anyone since she'd died. Not even her mother. It was too hard for both of them. In fact, she'd said Louisa's name more in the weeks since she had met Carter than she had in months. For some reason she wanted him to know about her. Through Carter, Liz had a window to her beloved sister. Louisa had been the other half of her. Part of who she was and would always be.

When she'd mentioned she chose to become an ENT and stayed one because that had been what Louisa had wanted and would want, there had been a note in Carter's voice that made her think he might have been saddened by her decision. Had she been right?

All that didn't matter now. She probably wouldn't ever see Carter again.

Melissa entered Liz's office and flopped down in the only other chair in the tiny room. "Well, have you heard from the hunky doctor again?"

"No." Liz didn't want to talk about it. She'd broken down and told Melissa about her and Carter's kiss. Melissa had squealed and hugged Liz, telling her how proud she was of her.

"I doubt I will after telling him my life history. Too much sharing, too soon. Once again, socially inept."

"Come on, Liz, don't you think you're being a little too hard on yourself?"

"Maybe. The kiss was good. Really good." Liz even heard the dreamy note in her voice. Carter had reached out and captured her heart like no other. She relived that kiss over and over during the day and in her dreams.

Melissa chuckled. "You should hear yourself. This guy has really gotten to you." She slapped her knee. "I'm glad to see it."

"Yet I've not heard from him since. It doesn't help that I told him I didn't want to be hurt. That's like saying I want to get married. Which I'm pretty sure, after his last marriage, he isn't planning to do for a long time. I'm sure he has run for the hills."

She'd had a special time making decorations with Carter and Ryan. For once she'd felt included, valued. Maybe she needed to chalk it up to a good time had while it lasted. The problem was she wanted more of them. For Carter to kiss her again. And again.

Melissa met Liz's look and grinned. "The weekend isn't here yet. Got to go. See you Monday. Hang in there and don't do anything I wouldn't do if he calls. And he will call."

Liz had already come to the conclusion she'd be back to spending quiet weekends at her condo. What bothered her the most was how she'd so easily become involved in Carter and Ryan's lives. Hers seemed gray in comparison. Returning to her solitary life wouldn't be easy this time.

An hour later when her phone rang and Carter's name showed up on the ID, her heart did a tap dance against her rib cage. Her hand shook as she picked up the phone.

"Hello." She forced her voice not to quiver.

"Hey there. How're you doing?" Carter sounded as if days hadn't passed between them or that kiss.

Liz wished she could be so cool. "I'm fine. You?"

"Great. I'm sorry I haven't had a chance to give you a

call this week. Ryan and I had a couple of things going on at his school."

Carter didn't have to make excuses, but she appreciated them. At least it hadn't been her oversharing that had kept him away.

"I was wondering if I offered you dinner tomorrow, would you consider holding the ladder for me? That's if you're not busy." Finally he sounded a little unsure. "I was gonna get someone around here to do it, but John still has the burned arm and the Wilsons have gone to their daughter's for the weekend since it's so close to Christmas. They're predicting rain and maybe snow, and I need to get this done."

He didn't have to sell her. She didn't care what excuses he had. She wanted to help. To see him again.

"What're friends for?"

"I promise to keep it that way." He sounded sincere.

A prick of disappointment stuck her. "I can be there tomorrow afternoon around three. Will that work?"

"Yeah, that'll work. I'll come up with something for us for dinner." He sounded uncertain as if he wasn't sure what that might be.

"Why don't you let me bring it? I'll pick up some fried chicken." Liz ran through a list of places she could stop on her way.

They settled on one.

"That sounds great." Happiness filled Carter's voice.

Maybe he hadn't been so sure about her. With her heart doing an extra tip-tap, she said, "I'll see you tomorrow afternoon then."

"All right. Hey, Liz…" Carter's voice dropped low.

"Yes?"

"I'm looking forward to seeing you again." Her heart fluttered. She ended the call with a smile and a sigh of happiness. He still wanted to see her, even if it was just to get her help. Still, she would take that. At least he thought there was more to her than the crazy person she'd been the other day. She valued his friendship and wanted to keep it.

The next afternoon, Liz arrived at Carter's as scheduled with a bucket of fried chicken and all the sides that went with it. Her body tingled with the anticipation of seeing him.

"I see you're dressed to go to work." Carter came down the back steps to greet her in the parking area.

She had pulled her hair back, wore a long sleeve shirt with a navy quilt zip-up vest and jeans along with sports shoes. "Didn't you say you were going to put me to work?"

He stepped to the car. "I did. I appreciate you being willing to help me out."

"Not a problem." She reached in the car and pulled the food out.

Carter took it from her as Ryan came bounding down the steps. "Hey, Liz."

Her smile broadened. He'd dropped the "Miss" to the more familiar first name. She liked that. "Hey there, Ryan."

The boy ran to her for a hug. She gave it. He then looked at Carter. "Daddy, I'm going to play in the square with the guys, okay?"

Liz watched as Carter's smile dropped and a shadow of reluctance formed in his eyes. He looked out at the square and then back at his son, disquiet obvious in his features. "Okay but stay where I can see you. Liz brought us dinner and it'll be time to eat soon."

"Yes, sir." Ryan ran off without a backward glance.

Carter watched him until he joined the boys. Liz followed his look. "That's hard for you, isn't it?"

"Yeah."

"You have given him a good safe place to run and play. So many kids stay inside and are on technology all the time."

His gaze finally returned to her. "It's one of the reasons I wanted to live here."

She studied him a moment. "It's hard to trust your judgment when you've been burnt."

"Yep." Carter made it sound easier than she knew it was for him. He took the bag from her. "Come in for a sec while I put this away, then we'll get to work."

Liz trailed him into the house. As he set the bulky large bag on the counter, she placed her purse in the seat of a chair.

Done with seeing about the food, he stepped toward her, his look penetrating. For a second she wondered if he might kiss her. Instead he blinked and the look disappeared.

"I think we'd better get to work before I change my mind about doing so." Carter opened the door.

Liz shook her head. She needed a moment to recover, refocus. She swallowed. "I'm ready."

His eyes twinkled as she passed him. "By the way, you look cute."

Cute? She couldn't remember anyone ever telling her she looked cute. Coming from Carter, she liked the compliment.

"I wasn't sure how to dress but I figured comfort should be the way to go."

"It is. I already have the ladder against the house. I just need you to steady it while I climb up. Before I get started, I'll just check on Ryan." He walked to the corner of the house and soon returned.

Carter pulled from a tool bag a hammer and a small bag of nails. He started up the ladder.

"Are you sure I'm the right person for this job?" Liz wasn't confident she'd be much help based on her size versus his. "Even though I used to help my father with stuff like this."

"I could've probably handled it on my own, but this type of work you shouldn't do alone. A doctor who does as much emergency work as you should know that."

"You're right about that. I see too many accidents from thoughtless mistakes." She put her foot on the bottom rung of the ladder and placed her hands firmly on the side rails as Carter climbed higher. She watched Carter's progress with an excellent view of his backside encased in worn jeans she could only describe as amazing. Yes, she had been given a good job.

"Hopefully this won't take very long. I'll have to move the ladder a couple more times, then that'll be it." He pulled the nails out of his pocket.

She watched him. "You be careful with that hammer. Don't drop it on my head."

"I promise not to. That would be an example of a thoughtless mistake."

"That it would, so don't do it," she told him in no uncertain terms.

Carter secured the board that had come loose with

a couple of nails and started down the ladder. "This wouldn't be such a big deal, but I'm afraid it's going to start raining soon and the next thing I know I'll have a problem with rot. You know how it is this time of the year in north Alabama, a lot of rain, freezing cold days and now the weatherman's predicting snow. I didn't want to wait any longer."

By the time Carter reached her, she'd again been treated to an up close and personal view of his behind. As he got to her, the ladder slipped a bit. She applied more pressure to the bottom rung, steadying it. Carter had to step through her arms.

His bottom brushed along her chest. Carter was all firm and delicious male. Her breathing picked up as blood whizzed through her veins. Not soon enough and too soon, he stood on the ground. She wasn't thinking friendly thoughts. Quickly she moved away.

Carter looked at her and grinned. "I'd no idea I'd enjoy this repair work so much."

Liz giggled like a silly girl. "Are you taking advantage of the situation?"

His gaze bored into hers. "If I were, I'd be kissing you right now out here in front of God and everyone but I keep my promises. We'll remain just friends until you decide differently."

Liz gulped. "Oh."

Carter handed her the hammer, then scooted the ladder along the side of the house a few feet. He found a level piece of ground and stopped. "I've this one and one more to do. Then there're a couple of little spots on the porch, but they don't require this long ladder."

Liz looked above the ladder to see a large board

sticking out that obviously needed securing. Taking the hammer from her, Carter once again climbed and proceeded to take care of the problem. He added more nails than before. Every time he swung, the ladder shook.

Tightening her grip, Liz applied additional body weight to keep it steady.

Carter returned to the ground safely only to do it all over again. He made another trip down. "That's the worst done. Now let's take care of the porch." Carter picked up his tool bag and started toward the front of the house. "Would you mind being the muscle while I hammer?"

"Sure." Liz fell into step with him. "I'm afraid I might not be much muscle."

Carter squeezed her upper arm. "I think you'll do."

He made that sound like he might be talking about more than just being handyman help.

On the porch, Carter let the bag drop to the floor. "If you'll just push right here." He placed his hand near the end of a board with a corner sticking out. "Just beside mine."

She did as he asked. It brought her body along beside his from shoulder to foot. Awareness shot like electricity through her. Carter acted as if the position was the most natural in the world as he put three nails in the board.

"There. That's great." He straightened.

Liz missed the firmness of him pressed against her.

"I'll need help with this next one, as well." They moved to another spot on the other side of the door. They assumed the same position.

Again, Liz's body hummed at his touch. She let

Carter get to her, and she shouldn't do that. Too soon, he finished. Disappointment washed over her.

"There's one more spot over here." Carter moved a chair out of the way. He placed his hand on the wall.

She assumed the position again. Looking over his arm, she studied the spot he should be working on. "I thought you said there were only a couple of spots. This doesn't look bad."

"You're right, there's nothing wrong with it. I just liked having your body up against mine."

Liz giggled and stepped away, giving him a light swat on the arm. "Here I was trying to help you and you're busy taking advantage of me. Friends don't treat each other that way."

Carter's eyes bored into hers. "If I plan to take advantage of you, I'll make it clear that's what I'm doing. Being around you makes it hard to just be friends."

Her mouth went dry. Molten heat ran through her.

He stood quickly and repositioned the chair before picking up his tool bag. "I need to put this up in the shed and hang the ladder up, then we'll have supper." He grinned at her as if nothing had just happened. "Hey, I really appreciate your help."

"You're welcome. I'm not really sure I was needed." Still it was nice to have him think she had been necessary.

"You're good help. Do you mind carrying my tool bag while I get the ladder?"

She picked up his bag and staggered for a second until she adjusted to the weight. "Do you have every tool known to man in here?"

He shrugged. "It never hurts to be prepared. I like

working on the house. It's a nice difference from practicing medicine."

"Apparently you're pretty good at it. It looks well cared for."

He seemed pleased with her statement. "I try, but it's an ongoing project. Today's an example." Carter glanced over his shoulder toward the square.

Liz looked as well, finding Ryan along with two more boys playing chase. "Does Ryan ever ask about his mother?"

"Not really. Not anymore." Carter's tone implied relief.

"I have a good mother, though she's not always great to deal with, but I wouldn't want her not to be around."

"He's better off without her." Bitterness hung in Carter's words. In that area he'd not moved on.

Maybe she should leave it alone, but she couldn't seem to. "What if he starts asking questions again?"

"I'll deal with that when it comes. Right now, he's my life's focus."

As in Carter didn't have room for anyone else in his life? "Ryan's a great kid. You've done a wonderful job with him."

"Thanks. Right now, I need to call him in to eat." Carter whistled, loud.

Ryan stopped and looked in their direction, then said something to the boys before heading their way.

Liz looked at Carter in wonder. "That's a neat trick."

"Yeah. I practiced an entire summer before I got it. It does come in handy. I usually stand out on the front porch and whistle. Ryan comes running."

"My dad whistled but not that loudly."

"You've not told me anything about your father really. Where's he?"

"He died almost five years ago from cancer. Between losing him and Louisa, it's been a tough few years. I miss him every day. He was my number one cheerleader." To her amazement, she continued, "Louisa might have been the apple of Mom's eye, but Dad made me feel special. I didn't, still don't, always measure up to my mom's expectations. Mom has a hard time accepting that."

Carter mouth pursed as he gave her a searching look. "Even after you became a doctor?"

"Yeah." Liz huffed. "Now her problem is that I'm not married with a family."

Carter faced her. "I think you're pretty amazing."

"You don't have to try to make me feel good. I accepted how things were a long time ago." She didn't want his pity or him saying nice things just because he thought he should.

"I can assure you, I mean it."

"You've given me more compliments in the last few days than I've had in years."

He started walking again. "More people should be complimenting you."

Liz smiled. With the firmness in Carter's tone, she might start to believe it.

CHAPTER SEVEN

CARTER STEPPED BEHIND the shed located adjacent to the parking area and hung the ladder on its hooks. Liz stood off to the side, watching him.

He glanced at her. A look of wonder covered her face. She held her palm up. "It's snowing."

Liz looked beautiful, angelic. A fat flake landed on her face and she brushed it away.

For a moment earlier, he had felt sorry for Liz, but he knew she didn't want that. It made him angry on her behalf that her mother couldn't see the amazing person she was. That her sister had taken advantage of her good nature. Now Liz looked so happy. He had to control his urge to pick her up and swing her around.

Instead he took the tool bag from her, opened the shed door and went inside. Liz waited outside. Placing the bag on the workbench, he headed out again. Liz backed away to give him room to exit. When she did, one of the pavers in front of the door tipped and she fell. Her hands flew up, but Carter wasn't able to catch her. Instead her body twisted and she went down on her backside.

"Liz!"

He went to one knee beside her. "Have you broken anything? Let me check."

"I'm fine."

Embarrassed, her eyes wouldn't meet his. "Don't move. Let me check for any broken bones."

She glared at him, all stubborn woman. He couldn't help but admire that. Liz stretched her hand out toward him. "I'll take a hand up."

Carter stood, then pulled her to her feet.

"Ow." Liz gripped his forearm as she held her right foot off the ground.

"You did hurt yourself." Carter didn't bother asking before scooping her into his arms.

"What're you doing?" she sputtered with indignation.

"I'm carrying you into the house," Carter said flatly.

Liz pushed against his shoulder. "I can walk."

He tightened his grip. "Yeah. I just saw you in action."

Ryan came running up. "What happened?"

"She fell. Go hold the door." The boy raced off. To Liz, Carter said, "You can stop struggling. I'm not putting you down until we get inside." He adjusted her against his chest. "It'll only make carrying you more difficult if you struggle."

Liz settled, putting an arm around his neck, making it easier to hold her. The slight floral aroma of what he guessed must be her soap found his nose. Underlying that, and much more tantalizing was the scent of Liz. He inhaled. That smell he'd forever associate with her.

She felt good against him—warm, all woman, right. Maybe too much so.

"I could've walked." That nervous sound in Liz's voice had returned.

"Maybe so, but I like this better." He took the first step to the back door. Why did he keep saying things like that to her? Because he meant it. He'd started to care beyond friendship.

She looked down. "Don't you drop me going up these stairs."

Carter took another step. "Oh, ye of little faith."

"I'll remind you of that when we're both at the bottom of the steps in a tangle."

"Mmm, that sounds nice. If you don't hush, I might trip on purpose." His lips brushed her ear. The shiver going through her pleased him. "Hold the door wide, Ryan."

Ryan did as he was told. Carter turned to the side so he and Liz could enter without too much of an issue. He set her on her uninjured foot while she held the other up. Jerking a chair over, he helped her to sit. Carter pulled another close before gently lifting her painful foot up to rest on the chair.

"Don't move until I've made sure you haven't broken anything."

"I can check." She leaned forward.

He placed a hand on her shoulder and nudged her back. "This time you're the patient. I'm the doctor."

Liz released a long-suffering sigh as he went to one knee and started to remove her shoe.

Ryan came up beside him. "What's wrong?"

"Hey, buddy, would you look under the sink in the hall bathroom and bring me the first aid kit. You know, the one we put up the other day after Mr. John got hurt."

"Yes, sir." He left like a rocket.

Carter carefully slipped off Liz's shoe and let it drop to the floor. He did the same with her sock. A blue spot had already formed on the left side of her ankle.

Ryan returned with the first aid kit as Carter examined Liz's foot by slowly running his fingers over her ankle area, applying pressure here and there. She winced only when he came near the discolored area.

"I believe you've a sprain here." Carter stood.

Liz sighed. "That's what I thought."

He reached for the box and pulled it to him. "I'm going to put on an elastic bandage. Then we'll ice it and keep it elevated."

"I'll go home and do that." She moved to raise.

Carter gave her a pointed look. "What's it they say about doctors making the worst patients?" He shook his head. "Don't be one of those. You can't drive and if you haven't noticed, it has started to snow heavily."

Liz swiveled in the chair toward the window. "So quickly?"

Carter shrugged. He opened the box and pulled out a thick roll.

Ryan stood nearby, watching wide-eyed as Carter wrapped Liz's ankle. "Now for an ice pack." Carter went to the freezer section of the refrigerator and pulled out another bag of peas, returned and placed them on her ankle.

"Ooh, I don't like those." Ryan wrinkled up his nose.

Carter and Liz laughed.

"That's what I've heard," Liz said.

He ruffled his son's hair. "It's a good thing you don't

because otherwise we wouldn't have any ice packs. They'll go to better use on Liz's foot than in your belly."

She smiled. "Glad I could help you out."

"Now you sit there while I get our supper on the table." Carter turned to the counter. "Ryan, you go wash your hands, then come back and set the table."

Ryan headed out of the kitchen without complaint.

"I hate it, but I need to do the same." Liz held up her hands.

"You sit right there. I'll get you a wet rag."

Carter turned to the sink, pulled a dishrag out of a drawer and wet it, then handed it to Liz.

Liz began cleaning her hands. "I'll give these peas about thirty minutes, then I'll head home before it gets worse outside."

Carter pointed with a thumb out the glass. "I think your window of opportunity has been lost. Even with this much snow, the road will be messy and the bridge icy. Especially the one between here and the highway. You're stuck with us for the night at least."

Liz reared in the chair. "I can't stay here!"

"Why not? I assure you that Ryan and I are gentlemen."

She moaned. "I know that but..."

"Complain all you want but I don't think it's a good idea to drive right now. I promise to make you comfortable. Now let's get this food on the table." Carter pulled the cartons out he'd placed in the refrigerator earlier. After opening them, he put them in the microwave to heat. He undid the bucket of chicken, then looked at Liz. "Do you like your chicken warm or at room temperature?"

"I'm happy with it right out of the box."

Ryan ran into the room and slid to a stop. "Dad, it's really snowing now."

"Yeah, buddy, it is. How about getting the table set?"

Ryan went to a drawer, grabbing a handful of forks.

"Bring those here and I'll help you." Liz reach out a hand to take the forks from Ryan. "I need to be useful."

Ryan gave them to her and scurried back to get napkins.

When the microwave beeped, Carter carefully took the hot items out and carried them to the table. "Sorry about the unfancy serving dishes."

"No problem. It makes cleaning up easier," Liz assured him.

"Dad, I need plates." Ryan waited near a cabinet.

"I'm on it." Carter pulled three plates from the shelf. He handed them to Ryan and watched as he slowly and carefully, with an air of importance, walked to the table.

Liz helped him place them. She fit in well in his house. Even when she was injured. Too well.

"Ryan, if you'll take this bucket of chicken over to the table, I'll get the drinks and we should be all set." Carter quickly filled two glasses with iced sweet tea and a smaller one with milk. He placed them on the table, taking a chair next to Liz. Ryan took the one at the end of the table since Liz had her foot on the other chair.

"Please let me serve since I've been little to no help with getting this meal on the table." Liz picked up a plate.

"Hey, you've a good reason." Carter handed her a serving spoon. His fingertips brushed over the back of her hand as she took it. At her soft hiss, he smiled.

* * *

Liz had enjoyed watching, helping where she could, as Carter and Ryan worked to get their dinner on the table. There was something pleasant about being in a warm kitchen with it snowing outside and seeing two males work together to get a meal together. Her home seemed sad and lonely compared to this one. Being around Carter and Ryan made her wish for a family more. It was everything she wanted in life. The type of thoughts she shouldn't have regarding Carter.

Her staying the night wasn't a good idea, but she couldn't in good conscience ask Carter to bundle Ryan up and drive around on slick roads for her. She couldn't drive with a messed up right foot. As anxious as she was about the arrangements, she couldn't come up with another plan.

As they ate, Ryan went on and on about getting to play in the snow the next day. "Dad, can we build a snowman?"

"Sure, we can," Carter answered between bites of food.

"Liz, have you ever built a snowman?" Ryan looked at her.

She wiped her mouth with a napkin. "I have, but a long time ago."

Carter's cell phone rang. He went to answer it and put it on speaker. "Hey, Carter, this is Joey's mother. Joey wants to know if Ryan would like to come spend the night with him and play in the snow in the morning?"

Ryan twisted in his chair. "Can I, Dad?"

Carter glanced at her. Liz wasn't sure if he was asking for her okay or not.

Ryan got to his feet and jumped around Carter. "Come on, Dad. I promise to use my manners."

Placing a hand on the boy's shoulder, Carter made him stand still. "Okay, I'll let you go but you must be on your best behavior." Carter said into the phone, "He'd like to come but he needs to help me clean up supper, bathe and pack. I'll have him there in about an hour. Will that work?" A few seconds later, Carter ended the phone conversation.

"May I be excused?" Ryan asked.

"Yes," Carter told him. "Go get a bath. I'll get your sleeping bag, then be up to help you get your warm clothes together."

Ryan dumped his plate in the sink with a rattle and hurried out of the room. Carter's concerned look landed on her. "I hope you don't think I planned this."

"That never occurred to me." She meant it. He'd made her a promise and she trusted him to keep it.

Carter wasn't surprised. Liz believed in the goodness of people. She wouldn't think he'd take advantage of her. She believed in him. He wouldn't let that go un-honored even if it killed him. "We need to take this ice off for a while. I'll get you settled by the TV and then go help Ryan"

"I'll see about myself. Don't worry about me. You take care of Ryan. I'm fine right here."

"Don't you get up and start cleaning the kitchen. You need to stay off that foot. How about I put you in there in front of the TV and you check the weather?"

"I'm fine, Carter. Go on." She waved him away. "It's just a little sprain."

"Yeah. One done while helping me."

Liz shifted in the chair. "I wasn't helping you at the time. It's my own stupidity for not watching what I was doing."

He smiled half-heartedly. "I don't think either one of us is gonna win this argument."

"Dad," Ryan called from above.

"I'm gonna go help Ryan. Retreat is the better part of valor."

Liz nodded. "Go. I'll be here when you get back."

Carter pointed a finger at her. "You'd better stay put."

"I think you're taking giving orders too seriously, Doctor."

Carter glared at her. Liz would do as she wished no matter the orders he gave. Stubborn woman.

She returned a serene smile.

Carter took the stairs two at a time. It was best just to see to Ryan and hope Liz didn't do any further damage to her ankle. Fifteen minutes later he returned to the kitchen with Ryan's bag over his shoulder and Ryan trailing behind him. To his great amazement, Liz still sat where he'd left her but his and her plates had been stacked and the food containers were consolidated, ready for the garbage.

"I see you've been busy."

She gave him the same serene smile as earlier. "Yep, but I still followed the doctor's orders."

Carter narrowed his eyes. "If I were to guess, you were tempted not to."

She raised both shoulders and let them fall.

"Let's go, Dad. Let's go." Ryan stood in the hallway.

"Give me a sec to get Liz settled in front of the TV.

Then we'll head out. Why don't you turn on the TV and put the remote near my chair?" he asked Ryan, as he stepped toward Liz and scooped her into his arms.

"I could walk." She sounded resigned instead of argumentative.

Her breath flowed over the skin of his neck, making his blood heat. "Maybe so, but I enjoyed last time so much I thought I'd do it again."

She clasped her arms around his neck. That brought her more securely against him. This might not have been such a good idea. Everywhere she touched him burned. His manhood needed a trip out into the cold weather sooner rather than later. He whispered, "You know, I could get used to this."

To his great pleasure, Liz turned a lovely shade of pink. She wasn't as unaffected as she wanted him to believe. She fought the attraction, as well. "You shouldn't."

"You can be hard on a man, Liz."

She looked into his eyes but said nothing.

When they reached the den, he settled her in his chair. Pulling the matching footstool close, he lifted her foot to it, adjusted the peas over her ankle, then handed her the TV remote. "I shouldn't be gone long. Don't get up and move around. I don't want you to fall and make matters worse."

"Let's go. Let's go," Ryan called from the doorway.

On impulse Carter kissed the top of Liz's head. "I'm coming, Ryan."

Liz watched Carter and Ryan leave. The tingle from Carter's unassuming kiss still lingered. She heard the click of the front door closing. The house turned quiet, yet she didn't feel alone. Something about being in Carter's space, the place where he relaxed, made her feel at home.

She settled deeper into the cushions. Her ankle shifted to the side, sending pain up her leg. A sharp reminder she sat here only because of an injury. She needed to keep that in mind. This was unchartered territory for her. She must be careful not to make more of it than it was.

Flipping channels, Liz found the weather channel. It apparently wasn't going to get any better during the night. Carter had been right. She shouldn't be driving. For the time being, she had to stay. The prediction said there'd be a warm up by midmorning. The roads should start clearing enough for her to get home then.

She'd just make the best of it and not be in the way any more than necessary. She imagined there were all types of women who wished they could take her place and here she was worried about spending the night at Carter's. She looked around. It really was a dream come true. Snowbound with a handsome man in a cozy home at night...

She jerked straight at the sound of the door opening. "Carter?"

"Yeah, it's just me." The sound of his voice flowing down the hallway wrapped around her heart. Would it be so wrong to relax and pretend for one night? Live out a dream.

The double thump on the floor must have been him removing his boots. A swoosh of fabric told her he'd taken off his coat. Seconds later he entered the room, looking gorgeous with his tousled hair and red cheeks.

Desire whipped through her. Yes, every woman's dream, especially hers.

"Hey." He sounded out of breath as if he'd hurried back.

"Hey yourself."

He dropped to the sofa, sitting at a right angle to her. "I hope you don't think I planned all of this."

"What? For it to snow?"

"Funny lady. But I don't control the weather. No, about Ryan not being here. I didn't set that up. I just couldn't say no because I've been working so hard for him to feel a part of this place. Joey's family, I trust. He couldn't just go to anyone's house."

Liz clasped her hands in her lap to keep from pushing the lock of hair off his forehead. "I understand. None of this you planned. Particularly me. I think we can handle this. I'm just sorry you have to nursemaid me."

"I don't mind. I hate that you got hurt." He leaned forward and put his elbows on his knees.

She tightened her grip on the arm of the chair. "I don't think it's going to be that bad. I'll probably be fine by tomorrow."

"We'll see. For now, how about a cup of coffee?" He stood.

She looked at him. "Any chance of a hot tea?"

Carter nodded. "I think I can find some. You stay put."

He strolled out of the room. Once more Liz listened to the sounds of his movements in the kitchen and those of the old house. It could be so quiet where she lived. Sometimes it echoed around her. Having someone else around felt nice. The fact it was Carter made it even nicer.

Soon he returned with a mug in each hand. He set the steaming cups on the table beside her. "Would you like some sugar or anything else?"

"No, just tea is fine. Thank you." She picked up the mug and took a careful sip.

Carter retook his place on the sofa. "How's your foot feeling?"

"The throbbing isn't as bad as it was earlier."

He brought his mug to his lips. "That's good to hear. Would you like to watch a TV show, play cards, chess or listen to some music?"

"You don't have to entertain me if you need to be doing something else."

Carter grinned. "I assure you, I've nothing better to do than spend time with you."

"If that's the case, then I do enjoy a good game of chess."

"Chess it is." He stood and went to a shelf. "I'll have to warn you, I'm pretty good at this."

"Then I'll ask you to take it easy on me."

Carter returned with a chessboard. He set it on the stool beside her foot as he moved the table farther out so that it was positioned within arms' reach of both of them. Placing the board on the table, he took a seat on the sofa again. "I promise I will."

"Thank you." She gave him a sly grin. Maybe it wasn't fair for her not to remind him she was a member of a chess club but his self-assured attitude he'd automatically win made her want to surprise him with her abilities. An hour later, she announced, "Check."

After studying the board for a good five minutes, Carter leaned back with a deep sigh. He glared at her. "I've been had. I'm the one who should've been asking you to be kind to me."

She giggled. "I did tell you I'm a member of the local chess club."

He groaned.

"I could've let you win but I thought you'd like that less than if we played an honest game."

"I've learned one more thing about you Liz—you can be sneaky." He grinned.

She returned it. Carter wasn't angry. She was glad. Other men might have been. "I can say you were a worthy opponent."

"Thank you for allowing me a little of my ego. You're good."

"I'm glad you're not mad."

Leaning close, he looked her in the eyes. "You do know that my ego isn't so fragile that I can't take losing to a woman."

Her smile grew and she said in her best southern belle voice, "Why, Carter, that never crossed my mind."

He glared at her. "You, Dr. Poole, are teasing me."

"And you, Dr. Jacobs, are right!"

"Another game?"

Liz yawned and shook her head. "Another time."

"You're tired. We need to put some ice on that ankle again before you go to sleep. How about we get you upstairs and I'll get your bed ready along with finding you something to sleep in?"

"The couch here'll be fine."

Carter stood and picked up the board, returning it to the shelf. "No, it isn't. I want you to be comfortable."

This part of the evening Liz had been questioning. She had no experience in how to act in these types of situations. "I'll be comfortable enough on the couch."

"*This* we won't argue about further." Carter's tone made the statement sound final. "For safety reasons I won't be carrying you up the stairs, but I'll help you. Are you ready to get started?"

She didn't seem to have a choice.

Carter moved the table back into place, then offered her his hand. She took it. He helped her to stand. She put as little pressure on her hurt foot as possible.

"Put your arm around me." His arm went around her waist, bringing her close to his side. "I'll support most of your weight. Okay, you ready to give this a try?"

Liz did as he said. Her fingers grasped the firm muscle beneath them. She liked the feel of him.

"Now hop along and I'll support you."

They made it out of the room and into the hall without a mishap except for her heart beating faster from being so close to Carter.

He flipped on the hall light switch. "The stairs will be a little trickier. I'll take most of your weight as we go up. This is the one time I hate that this old house doesn't have any bedrooms downstairs."

Liz leaned heavily on Carter as they slowly made their way up. Having his support assured her she wouldn't fall. At the landing she was both glad and sad they had made it. Happy because they hadn't had an accident and disappointed because Carter eased his hold.

"Down this way, second door on the right."

Liz knew the moment she saw the bedroom that it belonged to Carter. She jerked to a shocked stop. "This is your room."

"Yes, it is. It's the only one with a bath off it. I'm going to sleep in Ryan's room."

Staying in Carter's bedroom wasn't a good idea. The space was too personal. It made her nervous. Needy. Gave her ideas she shouldn't have. Carter was being considerate to give up his own well-being, but she'd gladly share.

"Come on in. I'll let you have some privacy in the bathroom. But first let me get clean sheets out of the cabinet in there." He led her to the bed. "Sit here while I get them."

He turned on a lamp beside the bed, then walked away.

Liz swallowed hard as she lowered to Carter's bed. "I'm… I'm sorry you're having to go to so much trouble for me."

"Not a problem." His voice carried from the bathroom.

She looked around. The space looked as orderly as the rest of Carter's home. The bed had a large sleigh headboard with big fluffy pillows positioned against it and what looked like a hand-quilted cover on it. She ran her hand over it. A window with a desk and chair sitting in front of it faced the backyard and a large tree beyond the shed. She grinned. The only evidence of disorder were books cluttering the desk. Beside it sat a cushioned chair that appeared far more comfortable than the other one. On another wall was the door to the bath, and beside it stood a tall chest of drawers. An oriental rug covered a great deal of the gleaming wide board floor. All in all, the decor suited the age of the house, and Carter. Every inch she loved.

Carter returned with a bundle of material in his arms and dropped it on the bed.

"Okay, your turn." He put his arm around her.

She limped to the bath.

"I'll find you something to wear. I left some supplies on the sink you're welcome to." Carter left her holding on to the door frame.

She entered the bath, holding on to whatever she could reach, being careful not to slip on the small black-and-white tile floor. Closing the door behind her, Liz looked at the space. It had been modernized but still maintained the flavor of the house with twin pedestal sinks, a large footed bathtub with a curtain to pull around for a shower and a pull-chain commode. It looked historical while being functional. Liz loved it. In fact, the idea of getting to soak in that tub sounded like heaven. With Carter would be nicer...

The knock at the door startled her. She jerked around.

"Hey, Liz, here's something you can sleep in." The door opened and Carter's long arm came through the crack. On the end of one of his fingers hung a navy T-shirt.

Liz took it, grateful he couldn't see the guilt on her face from her wandering thoughts. "Uh, thanks."

"Is something wrong?"

"No, uh, no, I'm fine." Heaven help her, she had to get control of herself. "I was just admiring your tub."

"Call me if you need help. Don't take any chances on falling."

Liz looked at the T-shirt. It'd be plenty big, but she wasn't sure about the length. She shrugged. It was that or sleep in jeans, which wasn't appealing. After taking care of her needs and washing her face, she removed all her clothes except her panties and neatly folded her clothing, placing the pile on a chest between the sinks. She pulled Carter's shirt over her head, taking in his scent. She shivered, then firmly adjusted the shirt to cover her.

Shuffling to the door, she pushed at her hair. She huffed. As if she knew about planning a seduction. The only reason she would be staying in Carter's bedroom was because she had hurt herself. He was just being nice. She'd been the one to establish the friendship rule. But she didn't want friendship tonight. She desired more. Squaring her shoulders she murmured, "Here goes nothing."

Carter straightened from where he'd been picking up a pillow off the floor. He looked at her. His eyes burned brightly before he blinked, and the flames were banked. He flipped the pillow to the bed and came toward her.

Liz had no idea what her reaction would be when he touched her. She might not have a lot of experience, but she could recognize when a man wanted her. Carter did. Excitement developed into a scorching need.

"I have to say without a doubt that T-shirt has never looked that good on me." He offered her his hand. "Let me help you to bed."

She chuckled.

Carter glanced at her. "What's up?"

"You've a way of using come-on lines without knowing it. You did it all the time when we first met."

"Huh?"

"Stuff like, *let me help you to bed*. It sounded like a come-on."

His forehead wrinkled. "I didn't mean for it to be a come-on." Carter paused. When his look returned to hers, his eyes had heated as before. "Unless you wanted it to be?"

She glanced at the bed and back to him.

Carter swung her up into his arms and carried her. He leaned down to place her on the sheet where he had turned back the spread.

Her breath caught.

Tension radiated through Carter as he studied her a moment before his arms relaxed and he moved to stand.

This might be her only chance and she planned to take it. Tomorrow she would deal with the fallout. She didn't want friendship; she wanted Carter. Her arms tightened around his neck, bringing him down to her. He supported himself on his hands over her.

"Liz?" He made her name sound like a word of pain and pleasure.

"Yes?" Her lips brushed his.

"Don't play with me," he growled.

She shifted her hips, getting more comfortable. "Who's playing?"

He nuzzled her neck. "I promised you I'd be a gentleman."

"A good host should make his houseguest happy." That was bold. She couldn't believe she'd said that.

Carter pursed his lips in thought and nodded. "That he should."

Liz's heart swelled as he lowered his body to hers. The heaviness felt right. His mouth took hers in a searing kiss.

Shed hotel lace and again from all his body from the
lift. He answered fall right. "It's getting that here you
answer You."

CHAPTER EIGHT

CARTER HADN'T SEEN this coming. Hoped. Imagined. But
the reality—no.

Liz tasted of mint toothpaste and all he could wish
for.

As he took the kiss deeper, he ran his hands along
Liz's side, following her curves. She wasn't a young
woman without dips and rises instead her body had a
maturity to it. All full, luscious and desirable. His manhood throbbed to experience all of her.

Hot didn't do her justice when she'd come out of
the bath wearing his T-shirt. Where the shirt would've
been to the knees on most women, it came high on
Liz's thighs. His mouth had gone dry and his length
had turned rock hard in seconds.

He shifted more strategically between her legs.

Liz yelped.

Her injured foot. Carter jerked back to sit on his
knees. He could kick himself. "I'm so sorry. I didn't
mean to hurt you."

Holding himself in check as Liz maneuvered her foot
outside his leg, his breathing caught as she opened her
center more to him. "I'm fine. Come back here."

It had been difficult spending the evening with Liz and not touching her. Still, he'd enjoyed their time together. It had been years since he'd had such a worthy opponent at chess. Yet visions of her sleeping in his bed, in his room, in his house kept disrupting rational thought. Only his determination to remain a gentleman had held him in check until now. After all, Liz was only staying the night because she was injured and couldn't drive home.

But she'd reached for him...

He'd not wanted to scare her, or worse, drive her away by pursuing her after he'd promised friendship. Yet now he couldn't stop himself from accepting the invitation. "Are you sure?"

She rested her hands on his forearms and gently nudged him to her. "I like the way you kiss me." Apparently, Liz wasn't timid about her bedroom demands. He appreciated her challenging him; he found it a stimulating surprise.

His gaze locked with hers. "I like kissing you."

She met his gaze. "Then why don't you do it?"

His lips found hers as he slid his arms beneath her, encircling her, bringing her tightly against him. She opened her mouth and her tongue tangled with his in an erotic dance that sent his body into a rage of need.

He hadn't been a monk since his divorce, but he had never been this needy for a woman this fast. He wanted Liz. Only Liz.

She removed her lips from his and nipped at his earlobe.

He shuddered. If he didn't slow them down, he'd

be a goner before they ever really started. "Aw, honey, you're killing me."

Her fingers fanned out in his hair as her lips trailed along his jaw.

Carter found the edge of the shirt she wore and pushed it up her thigh. His finger caressed small circles over the smooth skin of her inner thigh. Soon he planned to return to kiss the same spots.

Liz squirmed.

As he touched the edge of her panties, he traced it to the outside of her leg, then slowly returned to her heated center. He brushed his fingertips across the damp material. His jaw clenched as he worked to control his desire.

Liz tugged at his thermal shirt. Together they soon had it removed. He supported himself on his hands on either side of her head while she kissed his chest. His muscles rippled, his hunger escalated. Liz had such power over him. Her hands continued to roam, testing, teasing and tempting. Lowering himself beside her, his hand returned to her thigh.

Traveling up her leg over her hip and then along the smooth plane of her stomach, he reached beneath the shirt. He nudged it higher until a globe of a breast made an appearance. Her nipple strained upward for him. Using his index finger, he circled it. Liz hissed. Slowly he lowered his mouth to surround the erect flesh and tugged gently. Liz rewarded him with a flex of her hips brushing sweetly over his extended length.

Her fingertips gripped his shoulders.

Pushing the shirt to her shoulders, he took in the full view of her ample breasts. Cupping each in his hands, he appreciated their weight, the smoothness. The beauty. He kissed one, then the other before his gaze found Liz's. "You truly are beautiful."

Her hands captured his cheeks and she pulled him to her for a deep wet kiss that drove him mindless. He slid a hand over the curve of her waist, then along her hip, appreciating each dip and rise. When his finger found the elastic of her panties, he pushed beneath to brush her curls. She lurched, then moaned as his finger slipped slowly into her heated center.

His breathing matched her shallow pants.

Liz made sexy sounds of pleasure as he retreated and entered. His manhood pulsed in rhythm to his hand as he mimicked with his tongue his finger's movements. Liz pressed against his hand. Her fingers kneaded his shoulders, begging. She squirmed, shifted, then flexed her body. Her body tensed as her back bowed off the mattress. Her mouth left his. He watched as her head went back, eyes widened in wonder and her mouth formed an O. Her taut hips strained an inch higher. The dam broke on a moan of joy that rolled from her lips. She shook.

"I... I..."

Carter smiled before his mouth found hers again. He'd like to see that reaction to his lovemaking for the rest of his life. He rose from the bed, being careful not to hit her foot.

Liz made a small sound of complaint.

"I'll be right back."

A smile lingered on her lips.

Going to the bath, he found the protection he searched for and returned to the bedroom. He pulled the bedside drawer open, dropped the extra envelopes inside and slid it closed. With a quick movement, he removed the rest of his clothing.

Liz remained where he had left her with his shirt pushed up over her full and perfect breasts. A daze of wonder lingered in her eyes. Satisfaction filled his chest.

He didn't miss her eyes dropping to study his thick tall manhood as he stood at the edge of the bed. She didn't blush or titter. He could find nothing timid about Liz. Her bold appraisal heated his blood. She bit her lower lip, then the tip of her tongue moved over it. His length twitched, begging to have her. He feared he'd lose it even before he touched her.

Reaching for the shirt, he asked, "May I remove this?"

She nodded and lifted her arms over her head.

Carter tugged it off, then dropped it to the floor. As he did, Liz ran a finger down his swollen length. He watched as her hand encircled him. His breath stuck in his throat.

"So smooth, so strong." She gave him a gentle squeeze. Her gaze flickered to his.

He removed her hand. "And in far too much need of you to have you doing that."

She offered him a seductive grin.

Carter stepped out of her reach, not trusting her or himself. He tore open the package he'd gone after and rolled the protection on. As he placed a knee on the bed, Liz rose to him with open arms, bringing him against her bare heated flesh.

She gave him a wild kiss that had his muscles jumping in his efforts to control his desire. Fearing he might scare or hurt her, his muscles shook to hold himself in check. He moved between her legs. Liz raised her knees, opening wide in invitation. Settling himself in the cradle of her thighs, he shifted until his tip found her heated wet entrance and slid painfully slow into her.

He groaned when he filled her. Looking at Liz, he found her watching him with an earnest expression. Was she afraid of his reaction? "You feel so perfect."

That brought a smile to her lips. She flexed, taking him deeper.

He moved, pulling and pushing. Liz's hips joined him. The tempo increased, heated and became frenzied. As he plunged into her, her fingers cut into the skin of his hips. When he thought he could hold on no longer, Liz's hands dug in and held him to her. He thought he might lose his mind with the pleasure.

She pulled her mouth from his. "Oh, oh, oh," she whispered by his ear.

Liz's grip eased. Satisfaction, bottomless, rich and contagious filled his chest.

No longer able to control himself he thrust hard and deep, completely. Once, twice... He groaned as the force of his release took him to a place he'd never gone before.

His arms and knees weak, Carter lowered himself to her side and closed his eyes.

What had she done to him? He wanted more of this ecstatic rapture that only Liz could provide.

Very few times in Liz's life had she had to deal with the uncomfortable moments after lovemaking. During those occasions she'd not looked the man in the eye. But this time...

She sighed, closed her eyes and absorbed the warmth of Carter. So pleasingly relaxed she couldn't move, nor did she want to. Carter lay along her side, steady and heavy. His breathing had gradually returned to normal. She'd had no idea the languorous feeling she heard about could be real. Romance books touted it, but she'd never experienced it before. Now she understood the big deal other women had made of it. Maybe there was something to the "big hands" theory.

She almost giggled out loud. Melissa would so enjoy learning of this if Liz decided to tell her. Right now, she wanted to savor her time with Carter, share it with no one.

Carter kissed her shoulder, then reached for the covers and pulled them over them. His arm lay across her waist as he nuzzled her neck. "Liz, only an idiot would call you dull. You're amazing."

Something she could only term as love filled her, adding to the warmth Carter shared.

His breathing became even. Carter slept. She followed him.

A large palm skimming over her bare middle woke Liz. It felt so good, perfect. This is the way she always wanted to wake. A fingertip dipped into her belly button before the hand traveled to the curve of her waist and up. A thumb caressing the lower arc of her breast.

Liz absorbed the exhilarating feeling of Carter's hand, of his interest. Already her center pulsed with anticipation.

"I know you're awake." Carter's words tickled the

hair at her temple before his lips pressed against it. "I felt your heart rate pick up."

"Just my luck."

"How's that?" His voice rumbled low and sexy as he applied kisses along her jaw.

"To be in bed with such an observant doctor."

His hand traveled lower, brushing her curls. "I like observing you. In fact, I think I'll do more of it."

Liz giggled. Where she'd feared it would be uncomfortable after what they had shared, Liz discovered instead that it was easy, nice. Being with Carter anytime was that way.

Carter rolled to his back, bringing her with him.

"Hey." She opened her eyes and looked at him. The lamp remained on, but out the window it was cavern dark. She had no idea what time it was, and she didn't care. The covers had slipped down her back. "Cold."

"We can't have that." Carter reached around her and pulled the covers over her shoulders. "I rather like what the cold does to you." He lifted her upward. His mouth found one of her extended nipples, circling it, then sucking. He moved to the other breast. "Mmm."

Her womb tightened in the most pleasurable way. No longer cold, she tingled with the need Carter created in her. She ran her fingers through his hair, enjoying his attention. To have a man so fascinated with her body was a new and heady experience. She could get used to it.

Even her ex-boyfriend had spent a minimum amount of time with her in bed. He hadn't lingered, instead dressed and was gone with an excuse he had work to do or needed to get up early the next morning. She'd always wished for moments like this.

Carter's manhood stood tall and firm between them. He wanted her again. To know she created this type of desire in him, again and so soon, empowered her. She rubbed her center along him.

"You keep that up and it'll be all about me and I don't want that," Carter murmured between kisses. Setting her to the side, he twisted until he reached the bedside drawer and pulled out a package. He quickly opened it.

Bolder than she'd ever been before in her life, she took it from him. "Let me do that."

"Be easy with me. I hurt with wanting you."

After she sheathed him, Carter, with his hands on her waist, lifted her. Slowly and, oh, so sweetly she took him into her body. He closed his eyes and appreciated each of her movements. This time their mating remained deliberate. She rode him until she shuddered with delicious release and Carter soon followed. Gradually she came down to rest over him. Carter hugged her close. He had been everything she could want in a lover, willing, giving, caring and exhilarating. She had no idea this bliss existed. A sigh of contentment escaped.

Putting his arm around her, Carter tucked her head on his shoulder. She went to sleep, wishing she could have this forever. Carter, Ryan, they had been whom she'd been searching for.

Dappled light shone through the bedroom window when she woke again. She'd spent the night in Carter's bed, in his arms. She would've never dreamed it possible. Even with his kisses and compliments, she hadn't believed it could happen.

Liz shivered. It was cold. She burrowed further under

the blankets, looking for Carter's heat. He was gone. She ran her hand over the area where he had lain. Her heart raced. Panic grew. Had he left because he regretted their night together? Was he waiting on her to come downstairs? Was he thinking of a way to get her to leave?

Liz sat up. Carter's T-shirt lay on the floor and she pulled it over her head. She needed to get dressed, figure out a way to get home. Holding onto the bed, she tried to stand. A painful twinge in her ankle reminded her it had been hurt, but it wasn't more than she could manage. Going downstairs might be a whole other thing though. She carefully started toward the bathroom, applying most of her weight on her other foot.

She'd only been in the bath a few minutes when there came a knock on the door.

"Hey in there. Your breakfast is getting cold." Carter sounded good-humored.

Liz opened the door, still wearing Carter's shirt. Her intention had been to dress in her own clothes before he returned. They would've at least given her some sense of security.

"Mornin'." Carter held a tray loaded with food. He smiled, then headed across the bedroom in the direction of the desk. "Come on, I'm hungry."

He acted relaxed as if her presence in his bedroom happened every morning. Though he wore a T-shirt and sweatpants, he looked all sexy male. In contrast she had become a mass of jitters and nerves. Even in the cool room, he remained barefoot. He had nice feet. In fact, everything about Carter was nice.

Feeling she had no other choice, Liz hobbled after him.

"I see you're making it pretty good on that ankle."

He set the tray on the desk after pushing the books to the side.

She continued to move gingerly toward him. "Yeah, but I won't be running any races. I did make it to the bathroom without a mishap."

He returned to her, giving her a quick kiss on the temple, then guided her toward the cushioned chair. "Good to hear."

"I haven't looked out the window to see how much snow we've had." They kept their slow pace.

Carter helped her into the chair. "There's about four inches."

"Wow." She'd have to stay here a while longer. Maybe it would warm up quick. "As soon as it melts enough for me to get on the road, I'll be out of your hair."

Cupping her cheek, Carter said, "There's no hurry."

She hoped he didn't feel as if he were stuck with her, but she wasn't bold enough to ask him. In fact she wasn't sure she dare say much in front of him in the daylight. She had been last night but now... She shivered from the coolness and apprehension.

"Your nose is red. You must be cold. I'll get you something more to wear."

He hurried to the closet and stopped by the chest for socks. Returning to her, she stood and he helped her into a heavy housecoat. "Sit down and I'll put these socks on you. I forget how drafty this old house can be. It has so little insulation. Ryan and I've learned to wear layers."

Liz pulled the belt tight on the housecoat. Wrapped in warmth and the smell of Carter she felt better already.

"You know, that robe is far sexier on you than me."

Was he just trying to make her feel good? She gave him a weak smile and returned to her chair. "Thanks for this."

"You're welcome." Carter sat in the other chair and lifted her feet to rest on his thigh. He put the socks on her. "Let's have something to eat. I'm starving."

She was, as well. The activity of the night before had worked up her appetite.

"What would you like? I've got cheese, fruit, toast with jelly, of course."

Her stomach growled. "All the above."

Carter looked pleased with her choice. He picked up a small plate off the tray, loaded it with food and handed it to her. "I brought you hot tea but if you'd rather have something else, I'll be glad to go down and fix it."

"Don't do that. Tea's fine."

He placed a mug on the desk within her reach. They ate in silence for a few minutes.

"Liz, are you going to ever look at me?"

Hesitantly she met Carter's powerful gaze.

He smiled. "That's much better. Thank you for last night. It was very nice. Better than nice actually."

Some of her insecurity ebbed away. She returned his smile. "I think I'm the one who should be saying that to you."

"Now that we've settled that, how about we finish our breakfast, then let me have a look at your ankle."

Liz nodded and picked up her mug. Between the heat from Carter's look and the tea, her body warmed. Feeling more at ease, she allowed herself to relax some.

When they finished their meal, Carter took care in

unwrapping the bandage. The discoloration remained but it hadn't grown.

"I'm no orthopedic guy, but I think I can pronounce this pretty much on the mend." His hand ran up her calf, sending a tingle up her leg to pool at her center. "How about I watch you take a stroll across the floor?"

Liz limped toward the hall door. On her return, she winced. Carter quickly scooped her into his arms.

"You're gonna have to stop doing this. You'll hurt your back." Liz wiggled in an effort to get down.

Carter's hold tightened. "It's not my back that hurts when you're close. It's another part of my body."

She buried her face in his neck.

"I thought you might like to try out my tub. Have a good soak." He started toward the bath.

"Uh?"

"You know, sit in hot water, bubble bath. That kind of thing."

She raised her head to look at him. "I know what soaking in a bath is. I just hadn't planned to do it in yours."

"I thought since you admired it last night, you might like to try it." Carter put her down beside the bath.

He made it sound like it was no big deal for her to use his tub. He put in the stopper and turned on the water. Soon steam filled the air. He started pulling items out of the chest. "Here's bubble bath. A cloth. Soap is over there." He pointed to a narrow metal tray that spanned the width of the tub. "Can you handle getting in it by yourself?"

"I think I can do that." Liz would rather enjoy having Carter help her, but she wasn't going to admit it.

She'd no idea where this relationship might be headed, and she wouldn't take a chance on assuming more than she should.

With a hunger about to surface that he couldn't control, Carter left Liz. Thoughts of her luscious body in his tub was almost his undoing. Just carrying her had him throbbing with need.

Liz had the glow of being well loved when she'd come out of the bath earlier. Her hair mussed, cheeks rosy and still wearing his T-shirt. The only thing that stopped him from taking her to bed again right that moment had been the wariness clouding her eyes. That lack of self-confidence he'd seen when they had first met had returned. So instead of following his body's lead like he'd wanted, he listened to his heart and focused on their meal. When Liz had said she'd planned to put on her clothes, he'd known he'd made the right decision. She'd been planning to run.

At first he'd had no intention of offering her anything more than friendship. In the wake of his disastrous marriage, anything more hadn't appealed to him. He couldn't take chances with his and Ryan's life. Ryan and his welfare would be Carter's sole focus for years to come. Yet a problem persisted and grew the more he spent time with Liz. She'd become increasingly irresistible, important to his life.

He didn't like her being insecure after so much passion between them. Their lovemaking had been indescribably wonderful. He wasn't proud of it, but it had been a long time since a woman's fulfillment had superseded his own. He'd never experienced such desire, pleasure or satisfaction. Emotionally, as well as physically.

Could he be falling for her? He wasn't quite sure what that meant. He had Ryan to consider. He refused to let his son feel like second best. Ryan needed to know he was the most important thing in his father's life. Bringing another person into their world required careful thought. He'd never let his son feel abandoned. Not even for the best sex he'd ever had.

However, there were other things about Liz he found appealing. Her intelligence, the way she ran to help people without any thought of danger to herself, or the fact she'd gone into the medical field to honor her sister's dream, and the way she'd saved the day for Ryan with her creative tree decorations. More than those, he liked the way she had been so touched by something as simple as having a paper handprint hung on a tree.

Without a backward glance, he pulled the door closed. Instead of focusing on Liz, he tried to keep his thoughts on cleaning up their breakfast dishes. Liz continued to win. After stacking the tray, he carried it downstairs and put everything away.

Returning to the bedroom, he knocked on the bathroom door. "You okay in there?"

"Yes." She paused. "Carter... I need your help."

He opened the door. "What's wrong?"

Liz took his breath away. She stood in the center of the tub, holding a towel over her front as if she'd quickly grabbed it when he entered. A haze of steam hung around her heat-blushed skin. Her hair curled around her face.

"I can't get out of the tub. It's too slippery." She sounded perplexed and embarrassed.

Even with what they'd shared last night, she remained shy about her body. He wanted the bodacious woman who'd invited him into her body to return. The one that made his blood roar.

He walked toward her, his gaze locking with hers. He saw the moment hers widened in anticipation. His fingers trailed through the water. Carter stripped off his shirt. "I could help you out but I could use a soak too. Would you like to stay in just a little longer?"

"I…"

He stepped in front of her with only the side of the tub remaining between them. Starting low on her hips his hands ran up her slick skin to her waist as his lips found hers. Liz trembled. He pulled her closer. Even during his marriage, he'd not been this aggressive with his desire. Just standing near Liz had him hard. "You do know I want you."

"You do?"

Carter stepped back and met her look. "Why would you think I didn't?"

She swallowed. "Because I've always felt I was a disappointment to my partner. You're the first man who hasn't run out on me as fast as he could. I thought the only reason you hadn't was because this is your home and there's snow on the ground."

Carter looked at her for a moment in shock. He wanted to punch something on her behalf. "I'm sorry I failed you."

"How did you do that?" Liz tilted her head in question. He cupped her face in his hands. "By not making it clear how wonderful I think you are in and out of bed. But I especially enjoyed the bed." He kissed her tenderly.

Sometime later, after cleaning up the water sloshed on the floor, and them both well sated, he and Liz made it back to the bed. The sun had moved high in the sky by the time he opened his eyes. Liz remained nestled beside him.

Something had woken him.

The sound of the phone buzzing drew his attention. He leaned across her to the bedside table and picked it up. Liz moved beside him.

"Hello." He cleared his throat. "Hello."

"Carter?"

He knew the voice immediately. *His mother's.* "Hey, Mom."

"Hi. How're you and Ryan doing?"

"We're fine."

"Are ya'll ready for Christmas?" His mother sounded so cheerful.

"Yeah, we are."

"Good. The reason I'm calling is that your daddy and I would like to come see you and Ryan. Remember, we're flying over to see your brother for the holidays. We wanted to visit with y'all before we left. Celebrate Christmas, you know."

His jaw tightened. He couldn't get out of this. His parents didn't deserve the way he treated them. He just wished he felt more enthusiasm at the idea of seeing them. "Sure, Mom. When should I expect you?"

Liz shifted beside him. With her sensitivity, she had

no doubt caught on to the fact he wasn't excited about seeing his parents.

"We'll be there day after tomorrow. In the evening. We'll get a hotel room. We don't want to put you out. We look forward to seeing you and Ryan. We've missed you." The last few words trailed off on a wispy note.

"See you soon, Mom."

He pushed the disconnect button. Staring at a non-existent spot on the wall across the room, he worked to get his emotions under control. His attitude about his parents was irrational but still he felt it. He would just have to fortify himself for their visit.

Liz's hand touching his arm brought his attention to her. "That didn't sound like a phone call you wanted to take."

"No, it was my mother. My parents are coming for a visit. They want to see Ryan. Christmas and all."

"That sounds nice. I know Ryan will be happy they are coming."

"He will be. I just wish I felt the same. I just hate the way I feel about seeing them."

"Have you ever told them that? I imagine they have noticed something's wrong."

"What am I supposed to say? That they make me feel like a failure whenever I'm around them. They have such a great marriage and mine was such a disaster. That I let them down. I can't say any of that."

"Why not?"

He said nothing for a few moments. "Hey—" he rolled toward Liz "—I don't want to talk about this. I've got to go get Ryan in a little while and I'd rather

spend what time I have with you doing other things."
He nuzzled her neck and Liz took him into her arms
and into her warmth. Nothing but rightness filled him.

CHAPTER NINE

LIZ SAT AT the kitchen table, sipping hot tea while waiting on Carter to return with Ryan. She looked around the kitchen and sighed. A home like this and waiting on two people she loved to return was what she'd secretly dreamed of. Having her own family, a place where she was loved and accepted.

Love. She did love Carter. He was the best man she knew, smart, quick-witted, caring, a great father, the perfect lover. She could find little to complain about where he was concerned. He was everything she'd ever wanted in a man.

Ryan? He was the cherry on top of the sundae. Could Carter possibly feel the same about her?

Despite her insecurities that morning, it had turned out beautifully. Much like how she wished all of her mornings would begin, especially the bathtub experience. If she lived here all the time, it might become her favorite spot to spend time with Carter.

The midday sun streamed through the kitchen window. Melting quickly, the snow would soon be gone and she'd be headed home.

The sound of stomping boots on the front porch

brought a smile to her lips. The bang of the front door told her Carter and Ryan were in the house. Liz stood and hobbled into the hallway. The big man and his small replica pulled their coats off and hung them up. Both had rosy noses, pink cheeks and looked like the sweetest candy to her. She had it bad.

"Hey, Liz, you won't believe the snowman I built." Ryan came running and hugged her around the waist.

She returned it and looked at Carter over Ryan's head. Carter smiled that special one she now realized was for her alone. The one that involved a small flame of heat in his eyes. The look that said, *You're special.* Her attention returned to Ryan. "Tell me all about it."

"We even put a scarf around his neck. There's a carrot for his nose."

"That sounds so cool." She looked into Ryan's glowing face.

"I wish I could see it. Is it in the front yard?"

Ryan gave her a big nod. "Yes."

"Then I'll go by on my way home and give it a good look. How does that sound?"

That put a huge grin on Ryan's face.

Carter stepped forward and placed his hand on Ryan's shoulder. "Take your stuff up to your room and put it away. There's some hot chocolate waiting for you when you come down. I need to tell you something."

Ryan headed upstairs while she and Carter walked back to the kitchen. When they were in it, Carter grabbed her, giving her a deep kiss.

"I missed you," he whispered across her ear.

She giggled. "You weren't gone thirty minutes."

"Still, I missed you."

The clomp of Ryan's feet on the stairs notified them he would soon join them. They broke apart, both breathing heavier than normal.

Ryan came in the room.

"Have a seat at the table, buddy." Carter pulled out a chair.

"I'll get the hot chocolate," Liz offered, well aware Carter wasn't thrilled his parents were visiting. She moved across the floor with a minimum of pain. Her ankle felt much better.

She listened as Carter told Ryan about his grandparents' plans.

"We'll need to buy them presents," Ryan announced. "We can go to the mall."

"I don't think they're expecting any. They're just bringing you some."

Ryan's voice turned pleading. "It's Christmas. They need presents too."

Liz turned so she could see them.

Carter looked perplexed. "I have to work tomorrow, buddy."

Ryan's face dropped its happy demeanor.

Liz stepped to the table and put her hand on Carter's shoulder for a second. "I have a light afternoon tomorrow. I could take him."

Carter looked at her a moment, then at Ryan, then back at her. Indecision rode clearly on his face. Was Carter afraid to trust her with Ryan? Or was this about his parents?

"All right." He didn't sound completely on board with the idea, but he had agreed. "Why don't I meet you there for dinner?"

Ryan jumped around. "Goodie."

Carter pointed a finger at him. "You have to promise me that you'll do exactly as Liz says."

"I will. Promise."

"All right then, we've a plan." Carter smiled at her. "Thanks."

The next afternoon Liz picked up Ryan at Carter's house. Betsy, the babysitter who they had taken home the night she and Carter met, had stayed with Ryan during the day since he was out of school for the Christmas holidays. Carter had called Liz the night before, letting her know the arrangements. Liz agreed to drive the girl home.

Her and Carter's phone conversation should have only lasted a few minutes but it ended up being two hours long. She savored the call, never having had one like it before. When other girls had been chatting about their long phone calls with boys during high school, she'd been doing homework and reading. She'd enjoyed listening to Carter's deep soothing voice. She sighed at the memory.

She glanced back at Ryan, belted in place in the back seat. This was a first, as well. She'd never transported a child in her car. The fact that Carter trusted her enough to let Ryan go off with her hadn't escaped her. It was a heady and scary feeling at the same time.

As they walked into the mall, she took Ryan's hand. Everything about it felt right. She couldn't imagine having a child and giving it up. She'd fight for her child. Never would she sign away her rights.

"We'd better get busy. We're supposed to meet your

daddy at the food court in an hour. So, what do you think your grandparents might like?" She looked at Ryan.

"Maybe a remote control boat and a puzzle." Ryan grinned at her as if he'd given the correct answer.

Liz chuckled. "I think that's more like what you want. What do you think about a sweater for your grandfather and a scarf for your grandmother?"

"I guess so," Ryan agreed with less enthusiasm than when he'd offered his suggestions.

"There's a nice store right down here. I need to buy my mother something for Christmas too. Let's try it. I think we might find everything we need there."

"Could we get Dad's too?"

"Sure." She'd waffled back and forth about buying Carter a Christmas gift from her. Would they be exchanging presents? She shrugged. It was Christmas. She could give a gift if she wanted.

They started down the mall toward the store she had in mind. Liz quickly learned that Ryan was as full of opinions as his father. She had to make more than one suggestion on gifts until Ryan found what he liked. The gift Ryan found for Carter took the longest but, in the end, Liz believed Carter would like it. They bought a multi-colored sweater for Carter's father, a scarf for his mother and a leather wallet for Carter. Liz had picked out a housecoat and matching house shoes for her mother. Still, Liz left the store disappointed not to find Carter something from her.

It wasn't until they passed a kiosk in the middle of the walking area of the mall selling paintings by a local artist Liz saw what she wanted to get for Carter. It was an oil painting with an angle of the Mooresville's square showing the historical sign, the Brick Church and his home in the background. Perfect.

"Now, Ryan, this picture is our secret from your father. Okay?"

Ryan nodded. "I won't tell."

"Good. I'm going to count on it."

Pleased with her shopping skills, Liz gathered their bags and gave Ryan the smallest to carry. They then, hand in hand, strolled toward the food court. Her heart filled with happiness at the thought of seeing Carter and thinking about how pleased he'd be with the painting.

"There's Dad!" Ryan called. He pulled away and ran to Carter.

Liz's heart leaped. Her gaze met Carter's, who walked toward them with long sure strides and a smile on his face. What would it be like to have Carter look at her that way every day?

When Ryan reached him, Carter gave Ryan a brief hug by putting a hand on his back and pressing the boy against Carter's thigh. He never broke their gaze. As Ryan danced around him, Carter continued toward her.

"Hey." The word came out of her mouth breathy sounding.

"Hi." He pulled her close and kissed her temple. "I wish I could give you a proper hello."

Sweet heat ran through her.

Carter pulled back. "Who's hungry?"

"I am," Ryan announced.

"Me too," Liz said.

A flame blazed in Carter's eyes. "I am too." He took her hand, squeezed it and they headed down the mall.

Was it wrong to wish for forever?

They were almost to the food court when she noticed a middle-aged woman slumped on a bench with an anxious-looking man speaking earnestly to her. He searched the area, then said something more to the woman. Liz pulled her hand from Carter's.

"That woman needs help," she said and hurried ahead of Carter and Ryan.

She reached the couple. "I'm a doctor. Are you all right?"

"Elaine doesn't feel good," the man said, his face drawn in worry. "She's dizzy and sweaty. She was recently diagnosed with diabetes."

Liz went to eye level with the woman. "Do you have an emergency insulin pen with you?"

The woman shook her head. "I forgot it. It's at home."

"She needs sugar," Carter said from behind Liz. "I'll find some. Ryan, you stand between the end of the bench and the directory and don't move. Take Liz's bags."

Liz gave them to him.

Ryan glanced at the woman, then nodded.

Carter hurried off.

The man hovered nearby. "Sir, could you wait out of the way? She's going to be fine. I promise." Liz sat down beside the woman on the bench. Liz picked up the woman's arm and started taking her pulse.

"Here." Carter handed Liz a piece of hard candy wrapped in a clear cover.

"Thanks," Liz said over her shoulder, as she unwrapped it. She held it to the woman's lips. "Here, you need to put this in your mouth. Suck on it."

She took it.

Liz returned to checking the woman's heart rate. It was elevated. Ninety-six. Liz suspected her blood pressure was high, as well. At least she didn't seem to have a temperature. Liz touched the woman's arm. "Are you feeling any better?"

She nodded.

"Good. The sugar's working. You're still going to need to go to the hospital and be checked out."

The man stepped forward. "I'll drive her."

Carter said, "I've already called 911. The EMTs should be here in a few minutes. I'm a doctor too. We can't in good consciousness let you do that."

Liz looked to find Ryan still waiting where Carter had left him. She gave him a reassuring smile. "Your daddy and I'll only be here a few more minutes."

Soon the emergency personnel were climbing the nearby stairs. A crowd had started to grow around them. While the EMTs worked to get the woman on a gurney, Liz gave them a report.

As the EMTs took the woman away, Carter came to stand beside her. "I can't take you anywhere without you finding some excitement, can I?" Carter put his arm across her shoulders and pulled her against him. "You're amazing."

She smiled at him. "You weren't half bad yourself."

"We make a good team."

She beamed up at him. "The best."

Carter stepped back and looked around the area. "Where's Ryan?"

Liz's head swung to where Ryan had been standing just a few minutes before. Her chest hurt as if it had taken a hit. Ryan wasn't there! The bags still remained on the floor but there was no Ryan.

Fear rose in her throat. She rushed to the sign and looked behind it. *Ryan!* Her pulsed raced. She scanned the area but saw no little boy. All the loss she'd experienced before came flooding back. They had to find him! Her look locked with Carter's. The terror in his eyes matched what she felt. Panic became pain.

"Ryan," she called, circling the area. "Ryan!"

Carter ran to the food court area. His voice boomed around them. "Ryan?"

The area quieted as everyone's heads swiveled in Carter's direction.

"Dad. Hey, Dad. Here I am." Ryan ran up to him.

"Ryan!" Liz yelped, hurrying to them.

Carter scooped Ryan into his arms, hugging him tight. Tears rolled down her cheeks as Liz put her arms around them. Carter opened an arm and brought her in to the circle. They had become her family so quickly.

"I had to go to the bathroom. I couldn't wait any longer," Ryan cried. "I'm sorry."

"Honey, you should've told one of us," Liz said.

"I couldn't get to you."

A security officer joined them. "I was called. I see you have found him."

"Yes, thank you," Carter said.

"I'm glad you have your family together again. You've got a beautiful one. Take good care of them."

Carter nodded. "I will, sir. I promise."

"Merry Christmas then." The security guard walked off.

Carter looked at the food court full of people still

watching them, then at Liz. "Why don't we pick up something and go home to eat? I need to settle my nerves."

"Sounds like a good idea."

Carter and Ryan walked her to her car and left to find theirs.

Carter still shook with residual fear that had stayed with him all the way to the house. When he pulled into his parking place, Liz was already there. She stepped out of her car and joined him and Ryan with a drained look on her face.

"Let me have those." She reached into his SUV to take the two bags from a local hamburger joint. He carried the drink holder and went to the back door. As subdued as he and Liz were, she was thankful Ryan took no notice of it.

As they entered the house and ate their meal, Ryan happily talked about the gifts he and Liz had bought. After their meal, Carter sent Ryan up for his bath.

Liz helped clean away the dinner leftovers, then she walked over to Carter and put her arms around his waist, pulling him close. She lay her head against his chest. Carter wrapped his arms about her and squeezed. He let Liz's big heart and comfort flow into him and ease his anxiety.

"If I had lost him—"

"Shh. He's safe and upstairs." Her hand rubbed his back, soothing him.

"I didn't even check on him during that time."

"I did. He was there. He's a good boy. A very smart one. He knew where the restroom was, and he knew to hurry back. You're a good father. You've taught him well. He's safe, that's what you need to think about."

Carter squeezed her and kissed her temple. They stood like that for a long time.

Ryan called from upstairs. "Hey, Dad, can Liz come read me a story and say my prayers tonight?"

Carter looked at Liz. She smiled and nodded. "We're on our way up."

As he and Liz walked hand in hand to the stairs, another fear pushed the one over Ryan away. Were he and his son becoming too dependent on Liz?

Liz saw Ryan to sleep. Afterward Liz said she should go. She'd made an agreement with Ryan that she'd take the presents home, wrap them and get them to Carter so Ryan would have them to give his grandparents the next day.

Carter walked Liz to her car. They kissed but mostly they held each other.

During the night his fear of losing Ryan still lingered. Carter wished Liz had been there to hold him, to share his bed. He remembered that moment when he'd seen her and Ryan walking hand in hand with smiles of welcome on their faces toward him in the mall. Everything important in his life came down to them and that moment. His heart had swelled.

He and Ryan were becoming too dependent on Liz for their happiness. Liz wasn't supposed to become this ingrained in his family. He had to put a stop to it. Now, before any of them got hurt more.

Carter slept no more during the night. It wasn't a pleasant decision. His mind kept reliving all those sublime moments of Liz being in his arms, his bed, his bath. Those would be no more. Despite what he knew about her, he couldn't take chances with his heart or Ryan's. Or in hurting her further.

In the middle of the afternoon the next day, his receptionist called back to let him know a Dr. Poole wished to speak to him. Carter didn't want to see Liz today, but she had promised to bring the presents by. He was already too close to his emotional overrun level. "Hey, Liz."

"Hi. How're you doing today?" Sympathy surrounded her words.

"Better. I can at least breathe now."

"Good."

"I have the presents wrapped. I wanted to see if I could bring them by your office after work. Around five fifteen."

She really had gone the second mile. Carter hadn't invited her to meet his parents, not wanting to involve her in something that might turn uncomfortable. They hadn't even discussed doing so. Was she hurt by that? Carter didn't want to know. He didn't want to imply that there was more between them to his parents or to her.

Soon enough he'd be causing her pain for sure. He didn't like himself much for that, but it was necessary. "I'll wait on you."

"I'll see you then."

The office had emptied out by the time Liz arrived. He waited for her in the reception area. She smiled as she entered, carrying a number of large paper bags with a Christmas design on them. "Hi."

"Hello." He stepped toward her, taking a couple of bags from her. His hand brushed hers. That electricity that had always been between them flashed. He'd miss her with every bone in his body. "Thanks."

She looked hesitant for a second but soon recovered.

Had she expected him to take her in his arms? He wanted to but with what he had to say, he didn't need to lead her on further. "Come back to my office. It was very nice of you to drop these presents off. I appreciate you doing this."

She followed.

He entered his office and walked around his desk, putting it between them. She placed the bags she held in the chair in front of the desk.

"Liz."

Her eyes rose to meet his look. Concern filled them. "Carter, what's going on? Has something happened?"

He couldn't put this off. It wouldn't be fair to her. Taking a deep breath, he said, "I don't see any other way to say it, but this isn't going to work between us."

"I realize I'm the one who stepped over the line, but I thought it was mutual." Her gaze left his and went somewhere left of his head.

"It is, was, mutual. I care for you—"

"Yeah, I get it. I've heard it before," Liz responded, as if she had been expecting those words. She turned, about to leave. He couldn't let her think this was because she wasn't good enough.

"Liz."

She looked at him.

"It's not like that. I just think we've been moving

too fast. As much as I've enjoyed the time between us, I just don't see us going any further."

Liz's bottom lip quivered. She bit down on it and nodded.

If he'd been another man, he'd have punched himself. That wasn't what any woman wanted to hear from a man she'd spent the night with. He made himself finish. "I need to focus on Ryan. I had a bad marriage. I'm just not ready to get involved in another relationship right now. I can't afford any more mistakes."

She flinched as if he'd slapped her. He recognized the instant the Liz who handled emergencies with such determination and authority, the one who knew her own mind, emerged. Fury flashed in her eyes. "So now I'm a mistake. How very romantic of you, Carter. You sure know how to sweet talk a woman. No wonder your wife went elsewhere if that's the best you've got."

That was harsh but he deserved. It was Carter's turn to wince. He wasn't handling this well. Or he'd thought Liz would go off into the sunset without any argument. He held up a hand. "Liz—"

She took a step toward the desk. "Oh, no, you're not going to brush me off that easy. Just so you know, I get it. No mistakes allowed. I didn't measure up. Not the first time I've heard that."

Carter started to say something, but Liz went on, "I get that Ryan's mother abandoned him, that you feel you were inadequate in your marriage and that you've disappointed your parents, but I've not done that to you or Ryan. In fact, I've never hinted at doing it. I never would. I'm made of better stuff."

"What matters is I can't trust my thoughts and feelings where you're concerned. What I do, who I do it with directly affects Ryan."

"You can't be there all the time for him," she snapped. "You can't hover over him. I know that first-hand. My mother has been trying to tell me what to do my entire life. Trying to make me be someone I'm not. After Louisa died, even trying to turn me into her. You're going to have a lonely life if you don't believe in yourself and other people. Sometimes you just have to take a chance. Take my word for it, being alone isn't all it's cracked up to be."

"I'm not alone!"

She glared at him. "What're you going to do when Ryan grows up? Creates his own life, family?"

"You've no idea what you're talking about."

"I've made mistakes. Your parents have made mistakes. Your ex-wife made a colossal one. The difference between me and her is that I would never, *never* give up my child or hurt yours in any way. Or intentionally hurt you. Stop putting your past off on me!"

Carter gaped at her, but she didn't slow down.

"I bet if you think really hard, you might come up with a mistake or two you've made. The thing about mistakes is they have to be learned from, forgiven and not repeated. I don't know what I'd have done differently between us. I've been more of a real person with you than anyone I've ever known. I've held nothing back. In bed or outside of it." Liz threw up her hands. "I don't know why I'm still trying to explain myself to you. Your mind is made up. You closed it the day you caught you wife coming in the back door. You put me in the same basket as her because we are both female. I can tell for a fact that's all we have in common. That's a huge basket and you have a long life not to pick someone out of it. Either me or someone else. You need to deal with your issues!"

Carter had heard enough. Liz had given it to him with both barrels. It was time she heard a few home truths, as well. He widened his stance, placed his hands on the desktop and leaned toward her, ready to go to battle.

"Wait a minute. You sure have taken the high road when you've got your own demons. You want me to trust you with my kid, trust you with my life but you're the one who needs to learn to trust. To trust yourself. Instead of being who you are, you're who your sister wanted you to be. You live your life as an obligation to her. For example, your work. You're a good ENT doctor but you're a greater ER doctor. You're not really doing what you love. Louisa is still holding you back.

"Or you're conforming to who your mother wants you to be. You live in the shadows hoping no one notices you, unless an emergency happens, and then you come alive. You're so busy being what others want you to be, you don't know who you really are. You need to step out of the box and stand up for what you want. Be the woman you should be. You let your sister run your life when she was alive. Now you let her memory and your mother run your life."

His chest constricted at the sight of Liz's watery eyes. Her hands went to her ears, but she lowered them again and continued to glare at him.

"You need to decide who *you* are and what *you* want. Start standing up for yourself. There's no reason for you to stay in the shadows. Let your light shine, not Louisa's. You can choose. It's not too late to change."

Liz backed away, shaking her head. "It's just as well we're going our own ways. I was well aware of my issues before I met you. I didn't need you to point them out. Plenty of others already have. The question is, were you aware of yours?" She sucked in a breath. "Thanks for pointing mine out. I'll continue to work on them. Good luck doing the same with yours."

"Liz, you just don't—"

"Hey, I do. I recognize we both carry baggage. That's part of being human. You've had disappointments. I get that. You're just protecting yourself. I have a hard time with rejection. I get that. We don't owe each other anymore explanations. I think we see each other clearly. It was fun while it lasted. Let's leave it at that. I hope you have a good life, Carter. Please tell Ryan the truth about us. I don't want him to think I rejected or abandoned him."

With that, she left his office without looking back.

CHAPTER TEN

EVERYTHING ABOUT THE last few days had been miserable for Liz. She'd barely kept her practice going. Relieved was the only way she could describe her feelings when she closed the office doors the day before Christmas Eve for the holidays. Being merry wasn't in her.

If it hadn't been for her professionalism being so engrained in her, she would've canceled her appointments and closed sooner. The idea of crawling into bed, pulling the covers over her head and not coming out had appealed. There were a couple of problems with that—the largest being it'd give her more time to think about Carter. That she didn't need.

For years she'd had the same routine. Chess and book club, and dinner at her mother's on Thursdays. Today she had to face her mother even though it was so close to Christmas. There could be no deviations on her mother's part. Liz planned to work Christmas morning in the ER for someone with small children so they could be at home with them. Afterward she'd make an appearance for Christmas dinner at her mother's as was their annual tradition.

As the dutiful daughter, she was here on Thursday night, as well. Liz walked up toward the house her mother had kept the same since her father died. Liz pasted on a smile in an effort to show some semblance of happiness, regardless of how she really felt. She entered the front door, knowing her mother expected her, and continued to the kitchen.

Her mother stood at the stove, no doubt seeing to a chicken casserole, spaghetti casserole or pork chops and rice. It had been one of the three for years. They were her father's and Louisa's favorites.

She turned. "Liz… My goodness, Liz, you look awful. You aren't sick, are you?"

"I'm fine." She wasn't, but she wouldn't go into it with her mother.

She pulled a pan from the oven. *Pork chops and rice tonight.* "You know you really should have a more fashionable haircut."

Liz shook her head. She'd just had her hair done a couple of weeks ago. Carter had even commented he liked it.

"I bet you'd have more dates if you did. By the way, have you thought about going on a dating site?"

Liz held her tongue. Maybe she could eat fast and get out of here before she said something she might regret. That was the problem—she never told her mother how she really felt. "No, I haven't."

Her mother shook her head sadly. "You're not getting any younger."

Carter hadn't thought she was old. She bit her bottom lip. It didn't matter what he thought now.

"If Louisa were here, she'd say you should go out and do things." Her mother placed a bowl on the table.

Liz felt the need to defend herself surging. "I do things all the time."

"I mean where you really socialize with people. Louisa was so well liked."

Liz had stepped out of her comfort zone with Carter and look where it had gotten her. Hurt. Disappointed. In love and heartbroken. Her mother still compared her to Louisa. And found Liz lacking. "Mom, I love you, I do, but Louisa isn't here anymore and I am."

"I know that." Her tone turned sharp.

"I'm not the one you wish had been left behind, but I was. I can't be Louisa. I don't want to be her. You're going to have to accept that."

"I do accept that." Her mother's voice rose in defense.

"Apparently you don't, because you tell me I should be more like Louisa every time we're together."

Her mother let the pan she held slam to the counter.

Liz didn't slow down. What she needed to say was long overdue. "I've gone through my whole life trying to measure up to a sister who's no longer here. When she was alive, it was bad enough but now it's impossible. Louisa is gone. I miss her. I loved her but I can't be her." Liz pointed at her chest. "I have to be me. You're gonna have to take me as I am. Because I'm good enough as I am."

Her mother's mouth gaped. "Liz, I can't believe you're saying all of this. It's not like you."

Liz couldn't believe it either. What she did know was it felt good. Before she'd met Carter, she couldn't have expressed her feelings. He'd given her the confidence to do so. "Until you can take me as I am, we can't have an honest and open relationship. I need you to love me for me."

Her mother moved toward her. "Honey, I do love you. You're a wonderful doctor. A wonderful person. I just want you to be the best you."

Liz stepped back. "I realize that, Mama, but I've got to figure out what's best for me, not you."

"What's gotten into you?" Her mother looked at her with disbelief.

"Nothing. I just need to stand up for myself, be proud of who I am. Not who people think I should be. I can't, I won't, let you or anyone else make me feel bad about myself any longer."

Her mother's face turned worried. "I never meant to do that."

"I know, Mom." Liz softened her voice. "And I shouldn't have let you do it to me. I should've said something sooner."

Her mother stopped before touching her. "I'm only trying to help you. I just don't understand you."

"I don't think you ever have. I don't need you to understand me. I need you to love me. I may never marry and have a family. I've accepted that and you should too. Not harp on it every time we're together."

Her mother looked perplexed and hurt.

Over the last few days, Liz had had enough emotional upheaval to last her a lifetime. She needed to go home and regroup. "Mom, I think you're right. I don't feel good. I hate to leave you with all this food, but I need to go. Wrap it up and we can eat it on Christmas Day."

Liz couldn't leave the house quick enough. She

needed to breathe. What she'd said had been liberating but the pain in her mother's eyes still pulled at her. She climbed in her car and drove with no direction in mind.

That brightness she'd felt when she'd been with Carter had left. She'd been dumped and rejected before. She refused to let it define her this time. Or for her mother's view of her to do so, as well. Carter had been right about one thing, it was time she made some changes in her life, set her path toward what she wanted and not be defined by the loss of her sister. She'd start doing that tonight. It wouldn't be easy, but she would continue forward.

The next morning, Liz went to Louisa's grave. She often visited, usually when she felt down. She could talk things out here in the quiet without repercussions. Stepping carefully across the wet grass, she made it to the bench beside the well-tended graves. Her father rested next to her sister. Liz took a seat on the bench and looked at the tombstone that shared her birthday.

Louisa Joanne Poole. Beloved daughter and sister. Gone too soon.

"Hey, Louisa. I'm sorry I've not been by in the last few weeks. I met a man. A very special man. It didn't work out between us, but I fell in love. He made me realize I'm good enough. That I'm worth fighting for. That I have to stand up and be proud of who I am. He made me see I shouldn't worry about letting you down."

She pushed a tear off her cheek.

"After I lost you, there's been very little happiness in my life until I met Carter. I felt happiness in abundance with him, and his son, Ryan. I've lost it again and I'll learn to live with that but as who I want to be.

Not who you thought I should be or who mother wanted me to be."

She wrapped her arms around her waist and rocked back and forth on the bench.

"I've already told Mom everything except about Carter. I just didn't want to go into it with her. At first I was afraid it'd end before it began, then I wanted to keep it to myself because it might end, which it did, and I'd disappoint her once more. When it did end, I couldn't say anything. I hurt her yesterday, but I know we'll get beyond it because I know she loves me. I love her too."

She started to walk off, stopped and turned back to Louisa's grave.

"By the way I saw you tearing up my Christmas ornament. You shouldn't have done that. It hurt me. You were wrong. One more thing—I'm going to give up my practice. I never wanted to be an ENT. That was your dream. I don't mind blood. I'm going into emergency medicine full time. That's what I love and I'm really good at it.

"Wish me luck. I love you, Louisa."

Carter fortified himself against what the next couple of hours in his life would be like. After the scene with Liz, he couldn't imagine it being much worse, until he'd learned his parents had arrived earlier than he'd anticipated.

Betsy had called to let him know. He'd been coming across the river bridge when he received the call. Carter asked if she would ask her parents to pick her up. He didn't want to have to leave again to take her home. He pulled in to his parking area next to a late-model luxury car.

Carter inhaled a deep breath and released it slow and steady. He had to get it together if he planned to get through his parents' visit.

Betsy sat at the kitchen table. "Mom'll be here in a few minutes."

"Please tell her I appreciate her coming for you. I wasn't expecting my parents this early."

"It's not a problem. They're in the living room with Ryan."

Carter handed her some money. "Thanks for watching Ryan this week. You have a Merry Christmas."

"You too."

Life would have to improve significantly for that to happen. He headed toward the sound of voices and laughter. Carter found Ryan sitting between his mother and father on the couch. They were looking at the latest high-demand toy of the season. Ryan face beamed.

"Hello."

They all turned in his direction.

Ryan jumped up and ran to him with the toy in hand. "Daddy, look what Grandma and Grandpa gave me. Isn't it the best?"

"It's wonderful. Did you say thank-you?"

Ryan turned to his grandparents. "Thanks, Grandma and Grandpa."

They both stood and smiled.

Carter's mother said, "You're welcome." She stepped to Carter and opened her arms. "Hi, honey."

Carter hugged his mother.

His father offered his hand and pulled him into a quick man hug. "Hello, son."

"I'm sorry I wasn't here when you got here. I had to stay a few minutes extra at the office."

"No worries, we've been having a good visit with Ryan," his mother said.

Carter looked at his son. "Ryan, run out to the SUV and get the bags out of the back seat. Your presents are in them. You may need help. If Betsy is still here, get her to help you."

"Yay! Liz gave them to you." Ryan ran out of the room.

"Liz?" his mother asked.

"Just a friend." Not even that now, but Carter wasn't going into any of that with his mother and father. He refused to disappoint them more.

"How've you been, son?" his father asked, as he sat back on the couch.

"I've been doing fine." Not true either. "How've you both been?"

"Good. We just miss seeing you and Ryan," his mother said.

"Would y'all like something to drink?"

"I'm good for right now," his father said.

"I'm fine too," his mother said, joining his father on the sofa.

Carter took a seat in the chair near the fireplace.

"We were hoping that when we return, you and Ryan would come to see us for a long weekend? We could catch a couple of basketball games at Memphis State and check out the barbecue places."

"I don't know, Dad. School will be back in and I have work."

Disappointment showed clearly on his parents' faces.

Ryan hurried into the room, lugging the bags with him. He dropped them in the middle of the floor and started reading the tags. "Grandma, this one's for you." He proudly handed her a box wrapped to perfection, including a fancy bow. Liz had done an excellent job, having seen to all the details. Grabbing another, he gave it to Carter's father. "This is yours."

His parents opened the presents with enthusiasm.

His mother pulled the scarf from the box. "Oh, Ryan, I love it. Thank you." She opened her arms for a hug. Ryan went into them. Guilt larger than what Carter usually carried welled in him at the fact he'd kept Ryan from his parents. It wasn't fair to either one of them. Carter should've been better than that. The three of them obviously adored each other. Liz had been right. He needed to get his act together. It was time to clear the air between him and his parents.

His father held the sweater up to his chest. "Very nice. I'm going to take this on our trip. Thank you so much."

Ryan beamed. "Liz helped me pick them out."

Before his parents started asking questions, Carter said, "I thought we'd go out to dinner. Ryan, you need to go clean up and put on some of your nice clothes. Let me know if you need some help."

"Do I have to wear my nice clothes?" His eyes pleaded.

"Just change into some clean clothes that don't have your lunch on them."

"Okay." He headed out the door.

Carter took a deep breath and looked at his parents. Here went nothing. "I owe you an apology."

"For what?" his mother asked looking perplexed.

"I've been unfair to you both and Ryan because of how I feel."

"Feel?" Again, his mother spoke.

"I know you're disappointed in me and that my marriage ended. You guys make it look so easy and I couldn't hold mine together. Every time we're together, I feel ashamed. I'm sorry I've disappointed you. And sorrier that I've kept Ryan from you. He needs you. I've just recently had it pointed out to me that I have to trust others where he's concerned and that we all make mistakes. I made one by marrying Diane, but Ryan isn't one of those."

His mother was already moving to him. She put her arm around his shoulders. He stood and she enveloped him in a hug that almost stopped his breathing. "Oh, honey, we're proud of you. We know you were destroyed by what Diane did to you and Ryan. We had no idea why you kept pushing us away. We hoped time would make it better. We love you and always will."

His father joined them and hugged Carter, as well. "We've missed you and Ryan."

When his parents stepped back, his father said, "Let me assure you that your mother and our marriage has been far from perfect many times, but with the right person you just keep moving forward. You'll find that right person. I promise."

His mother, with a twinkle in her eyes, said, "If my

guess is right, you already have. Maybe that Liz Ryan keeps talking about?"

Anxiety filled Carter. "That's if I can make it right with her again. I may have messed that up too."

His father slapped him on the shoulder. "Humble pie I've found works wonders."

Ryan came back into the room. "I'm ready."

"We are too," his mother said with a bright smile on her face, as she wrapped her arm through Carter's.

A couple of hours later, they were saying their good-byes in the restaurant parking lot. "I wish you didn't have to leave so soon," Ryan whined.

Carter's mother came to Ryan and gave him a kiss on the cheek, then looked past him to Carter. "I think we'll be seeing more of each other from now on."

Carter smiled and nodded.

"We already have plans for you and your dad to come see us in a few weeks. Will you see that Liz comes with you?" his mother asked.

Ryan eagerly nodded. "I will."

"Now give me a big hug." His mother reached for Ryan. Then took Carter into her arms. "I love you, son."

His father came forward and rubbed Ryan on the head and gave Carter a tight hug.

He and Ryan waved as his parents drove away.

Carter felt lighter, as if he'd dropped a pile of trash he'd been carrying on the side of the road. The evening had turned out better than he would've ever imagined. The only thing that could've made it nicer would've been if Liz had been there with them. He and Ryan were incomplete without her.

* * *

Midmorning of Christmas Day, Liz sat in the office of
the Emergency Department doing chart updates on the
computer. She moved the small Santa out of the way.
Reaching, she picked up a piece of homemade candy
sitting on the paper plate she'd filled in the break room
earlier.

She glanced out the door to the unit desk with the
tinsel lining it and a small Christmas tree sitting on the
counter. The staff all wore Santa hats and had even presented her with one. She hadn't felt in the Christmas
spirit since she'd wrapped presents for Carter and Ryan.
At least helping people today had improved her outlook.

After a short and to the point phone call with her
mother, Liz still planned to go to her house for Christmas dinner when her shift ended.

The day had been going smoothly so far. Her cases
were much as she'd expected. The usual for holidays.
Burns, cuts, sprained ankles and the typical guy who
had a heart attack because he thought he was still young
enough to play football with his adult kids. Liz had
taken care of each one in her stride.

Liz smiled. This was where she belonged. She would
miss Melissa and her other office staff when she closed
the practice, but she'd see to it they had jobs elsewhere.
If she could, she'd convince Melissa to join her in the
ER.

She'd come to work with a newfound confidence
of knowing she'd be doing what *she* loved. Standing a
little taller and feeling a little stronger, she'd begun to
like herself.

One of the nurses came to the door and leaned inside. "We've got a case right up your alley."

Liz looked up. "How's that?"

"An acute ear infection."

With a grin, Liz scooted back in her chair. "Those I can handle. I'll be right there."

The nurse smiled. "I thought you would."

Liz took a bite of chocolate fudge and headed to the unit desk. There, she picked up a tablet and checked the pending charts. *Patient: Ryan Jacobs. Seven years old.*

Her heart hammered in her chest. It couldn't be. There must be more than one Ryan Jacobs in the Decatur area. With a foreboding that made her blood run faster, she walked to the exam room. She straightened her shoulders and slid the glass door open.

Ryan lay on the bed. "Liz! It hurts." He pointed to his ears; his face twisted in a grimace.

Carter stood beside him. "Liz." Her name came out as a surprised whisper.

She ignored Carter and focused on Ryan, moving to the opposite side of the bed from Carter. "Ryan, I'm sorry your ears hurt. I'm going to check you out, then I'll get you all fixed up and stop that pain." She looked directly at Carter. "If your father will let me?"

To her satisfaction, Carter flinched. "Of course, I will."

She watched him a second longer. This wasn't the time or the place to get into it with Carter. They'd said all they needed to anyway. She reached for the otoscope. "I need to look in your ears. This may hurt just a little."

She placed the tip of the instrument in Ryan's ear. He flinched. "I'm sorry. But I need to look in the other one too." She did so. "Yikes, you have a double infection. I'm going to give you something for the pain and a prescription for some medicine. You should be good in no time."

Liz turned her attention to Carter. It was so good to see his handsome face, but she couldn't think about how much she'd missed him. "You should consider having tubes put in after the holidays. His ears are badly infected. I'll refer you to a good ENT."

She patted Ryan's leg. "I hope your Christmas gets better."

Carter caught her arm as she stepped toward the door. "Couldn't we make an appointment with you?"

"No."

"I'm sorry about what I said, what I did. I was just scared. I overreacted. I let my past control my here and now. It wasn't fair to you."

"Thank you. I appreciate you saying that," she said politely. As much as she wanted to go to him, he'd hurt her deeply.

"Then you'll see Ryan?"

Liz shook her head. "I can't. I'm not taking any new patients. I'm closing my practice. I'm going into emergency medicine."

"You are?" Carter's voice rose in surprise while at the same time he looked proud of her.

"Yeah, somebody told me recently I needed to make some changes."

"Hey, Dad," Ryan said. "You need to tell Liz she's supposed to go to Grandma and Grandpa's with us."

"You're right, buddy." He turned back to Liz. "My parents would like to meet you." He offered her an unsure smile. "I'd like to introduce you to them too. We're going to see them for a long weekend after the holidays."

Hope filled her. "You talked to them?"

"I did. I cleared the air and they understood. Even better, they still love me. Someone very important to me said I should get my act together. I'm hoping she will forgive me now that I'm starting to." Carter's gaze met and held hers.

Joy she hardly dared to feel filled her.

"Can we talk when you get off? Please?" Carter's eyes begged.

She could make it hard on him, after all he'd hurt her, but he had been right. It was past time for her to take charge of her life. Be who she wanted to be. Apparently Carter had started to make some changes, as well. The biggest deciding factor was, did she love him? She did. Of that she had no doubt.

"I'm supposed to go to my mother's for dinner. But I bet she wouldn't mind you and Ryan joining us. There's always plenty of food."

He glanced at Ryan. "I don't know…"

"I'll tell you what—I'll call her and see if she'd mind packing it up and bringing it to your house."

Carter leaned back in his chair after finishing a full plate of food. "That was wonderful."

Liz's mother glowed.

He had no idea what Liz had told her about them, but her mother was all smiles when she arrived at his house. She'd taken over the kitchen and doted on Ryan during the meal.

He looked at Liz. Her smile reached her eyes. They still needed to talk, but for right now they were sharing their Christmas meal at his kitchen table. Ryan had said he felt good enough to sit at the table and try to eat. What Carter had at this moment was what he'd always wanted in his life, peace and happiness, and Liz brought that into his life.

She gave him a timid look. He loved those, but he equally appreciated those moments when her eyes heated as she took the lead in their lovemaking. Based on his one night with Liz, all of his other experiences with women could be described as bland. She was assertive and sensitive, and very sensual all at the same time. What made it even better was he loved her.

He winked at her. Her cheeks pinked.

He'd loved her when she'd told him how it was. She'd done that clearly at his office and had not backed down when she'd spoken to him at the hospital. He wouldn't be letting her out of his life if he could help it. He needed her, and Ryan needed a fierce mother, as well.

Liz had been there for Ryan more than once. She'd saved the day with decorating the Christmas tree. Again, when he needed someone to show interest in his snowman and as a caretaker when his ears hurt. Ryan should have a wonderful woman in his life, and Carter believed the right one was Liz.

"Ryan, I think it's time for you to get some rest." Carter pushed his chair back.

"If Ryan would let me get him in bed, I'd like to," Liz's mother offered.

Carter looked at him. Ryan nodded. He and Liz's mother were already forming a bond.

She stood and stretched out her hand. "Great. Can you show me your favorite book?"

"Okay."

Carter spoke to Liz's mother. "Ryan can also show you where everything is. A bath can wait until tomorrow."

"Yay." Ryan, with Liz's mom chatting to him, headed into the hall.

Liz rose and began cleaning away the dishes.

Carter stood as well, wrapping his fingers around her wrist. "Leave those. We need to talk."

She nodded. Carter led her into the living room where the only lighting came from the Christmas tree.

"I can't stand it any longer. I've missed you." He brought her into his arms and his lips found hers. To his relief and pleasure, Liz returned his kiss. A soft moan came from her, feeding his need, but that must wait. Banking his desire, he stepped back. "Come sit with me."

Liz took a seat on the sofa. Carter sat there as well but made sure space remained between them. He wanted them to see each other's faces. Continuing to hold Liz's hand, he faced her, waiting until her gaze locked with his. "I couldn't say everything I needed to say at the hospital. I'm sorry how I treated you. I hurt you and I never meant to. I've let my bad marriage, the enormous mistake of it, overshadow my thoughts and actions. I put that off on you and that was wrong. You're nothing like my ex-wife. You never will be. You didn't deserve how I treated you. I realize that. I was already planning to come to see you. You're the best thing that has ever happened to me. To Ryan." Carter looked deep into her eyes. "I love you. I always will. I'll honor you always. Please just say you'll forgive me."

Liz sucked in a breath. Her eyes widened. Finally she blinked. "Carter, I'm not the person you met a few weeks ago. I thank you for that. You've helped me learn to stand up for myself. To recognize I'm good enough. That I have my own light to shine in. That I don't need anyone else's approval."

Carter wasn't sure where this was going. He feared she might've realized she didn't need him. She'd said nothing about loving him. He didn't know how he'd survive if she didn't. His hand tightened on hers.

She cupped his cheek. "From now on, when you're scared, promise me you'll talk to me. I'll do the same. It hurts too much to have you reject me."

Carter cringed. His thumb rubbed across the top of her hand. "I can't change the past, but I can make the future different. It'd be easier for me to do that if you were beside me. Will you give me another chance?"

"Silly man." Her fingertips brushed his hair from his forehead as she smiled at him. "If I couldn't, then I wouldn't be here."

"Does that mean you love me?"

Her hands cupped his face. "I've loved you since you came to my rescue in the parking lot of the country club." She kissed him long and deep.

Carter pulled Liz into his lap and poured all his love into his kisses. He broke away long enough to ask, "You'll be mine and Ryan's forever?"

"I can't think of anything I want more."

EPILOGUE

Almost one year later

LIZ SAT ON the sofa in the living room, looking at the Christmas tree lights. She and Carter had spent a lot of time doing that together this year. Ryan had gotten to keep the large ones she'd bought him the year before. In fact, he'd gotten to keep her too.

She glanced at the painting over the mantel. It was the one she'd bought Carter a year earlier. He'd been excited to receive it, even a day late. It meant more to him, and her, now than it had to begin with. They'd been married in the spring in the Brick Church pictured.

Their wedding had been the most amazing one she'd attended and the one of her dreams. The sun shone bright, the trees were green with new growth and the dogwoods were filled with white blooms. All of Mooresville attended, along with family and friends.

Ryan had stood tall and important beside his father as best man. Carter's father had honored her by walking her down the aisle. Melissa had served as her maid of honor. She'd worn an I-told-you-so grin the entire ceremony. Her mother had sobbed like a baby. Liz wasn't sure if it had been from happiness, or relief Liz had found someone. Carter's mother hadn't been much better. What really made the day perfect had been Carter standing breathtakingly handsome at the altar, waiting for her. There had been no fear in his eyes, only love.

Ryan ran into the living room, bringing her back to the present. Behind her son was his year-old Labrador retriever, Rex. Liz worked in the ER with someone who had new puppies and Carter had agreed Ryan could have one as a late Christmas present. "Grand said to ask you if I could spend the night with her."

Her mother had come for dinner and had insisted on doing the cleanup. Liz had taken the chance to put her feet up. After a hard and fast day in the ER, Liz gladly accepted the offer. Her mother had embraced being a grandparent as if she'd been made for it, which she had.

Liz smiled. "As long as you promise to help Grand and not make a big mess for her to clean up. Remember, Grandma and Grandpa will be here tomorrow to spend Christmas with us so you'll need to be home early to see them."

"Okay. Thanks, Mom." Ryan shot toward the door.

Liz liked the sound of that. "Oh, one more thing. I need a hug."

Ryan stopped short, turned and came to wrap his arms around her neck. "I love you."

"No more than I love you." She kissed the top of his head.

As Ryan left, Carter entered. "I was wondering where you got off to. Hiding out from doing the dishes again." He sat down beside her, gathering her into his lap.

Liz snuggled against his chest. She'd found home. "I'm almost getting too big to do this."

"That's not going to happen." Carter's hand caressed her rounded middle. "You'll always be welcome in my lap." The baby kicked. "Apparently Mary Louisa agrees with me." He kissed Liz's temple.

"I think she's going to be as crazy about her daddy as her mom is. I love you, Carter Jacobs."

"And I love you, Liz Jacobs." His kiss proved it.

* * * * *

MILLS & BOON

Coming next month

MISTLETOE KISS WITH THE HEART DOCTOR
Marion Lennox

Oh, she wanted him. She ached for him. Her whole body felt as if it was surrendering.

She was being kissed and she was kissing. He didn't need to balance on his bad leg because she was holding him.

Maybe it could count as therapy, she thought, almost hysterically. Helping patient stand. Maybe this was a medical tool designed to make him feel better.

It was surely making her feel better. Every sense seemed to have come alive. Every nerve ending was tingling.

More. Every single part of her was screaming that she wanted this man, she needed this man, that she wouldn't mind in the least if they fell back on the bed and...

Um, not in a million years. Not!

Because this was a hospital ward and any minute the door could open as a nurse arrived for routine obs. This was a patient and she was a doctor and...

Shut up, Elsa, she told her inner self fiercely. Just let this moment be.

So she did. Her mind shut down and she let herself just kiss. And be kissed.

The kiss was deep and long and magical, and as it

finally ended it was as much as she could do not to weep. But Marc was still holding her. He had her at arm's length now, smiling into her eyes with such tenderness that...

No! She made a herculean effort to haul herself together. This was way past unprofessional. She could just about get herself struck off the medical register for this.

But right now she was having trouble thinking that it mattered, whether she was struck off or not. For Marc was smiling at her, and that seemed to be the only thing that mattered in the whole world.

But this was still well out of order. This man's life was in Sydney. It could only ever be a casual fling.

Oh, but his smile...

'About that date...' he ventured, and she needed to shake her head but all she could do was look up into his deep eyes and sense went right out the window.

But then reality suddenly slammed back with a vengeance. The hospital speaker system cracked into life and she heard Kim, one of the hospital's junior nurses. Even through the dodgy hospital intercom she heard the fear in Kim's tone.

'Code Blue. Nurses' station. Code Blue.'

Continue reading
MISTLETOE KISS WITH THE HEART DOCTOR
Marion Lennox

Available next month
www.millsandboon.co.uk

Copyright © 2020 Marion Lennox

COMING SOON!

We really hope you enjoyed reading this book.
If you're looking for more romance, be sure to
head to the shops when new books are
available on

Thursday 26th November

To see which titles are coming soon, please visit

millsandboon.co.uk/nextmonth

MILLS & BOON

WE'RE LOOKING FOR NEW AUTHORS FOR THE MILLS & BOON MEDICAL SERIES!

Whether you're a published author or an aspiring one, our editors would love to read your story.

You can submit the synopsis and first three chapters of your novel online, and find out more about the series, at **harlequin.submittable.com/submit**

We read all submissions and you do not need to have an agent to submit.

IF YOU'RE INTERESTED, WHY NOT HAVE A GO?

Submit your story at:
harlequin.submittable.com/submit

MILLS & BOON

LET'S TALK
Romance

For exclusive extracts, competitions
and special offers, find us online:

 facebook.com/millsandboon

🐦 @MillsandBoon

 @MillsandBoonUK

Get in touch on 01413 063232

For all the latest titles coming soon, visit
millsandboon.co.uk/nextmonth

WANT EVEN MORE
ROMANCE?
SUBSCRIBE AND SAVE TODAY!

'Mills & Boon books, the perfect way to escape for an hour or so.'

MISS W. DYER

'Excellent service, promptly delivered and very good subscription choices.'

MISS A. PEARSON

'You get fantastic special offers and the chance to get books before they hit the shops.'

MRS V. HALL

Visit millsandboon.co.uk/Subscribe
and save on brand new books.